GRACE IN THE WINGS

A GRACE MICHELLE MYSTERY

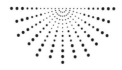

KARI BOVÉE

BOSQUE
PUBLISHING

For my dad,
I miss you every day.
Thank you for believing in me.

A NOTE FROM THE AUTHOR

The Ziegfeld Follies. What a fantastical experience it must have been to see one of Ziegfeld's over-the-top, elaborate, and entertaining shows!

It was so much fun to immerse myself in this colorful, sparkling world, while telling the story of a young, innocent girl who comes to realize that she has the strength and power to navigate life on her own terms.

Grace Michelle and Sophia Michelle are both fictional characters. Grace was inspired purely by my imagination, but Sophia was inspired by the tragic Ziegfeld actress, Olive Thomas, who was indeed married to Jack Pickford. I feel it is important to note that her ending was not considered death by foul play, or even death by suicide, but death by accident.

That said, I would like to invite readers to engage in a little suspension of disbelief as they read this book. While I have tried to maintain accuracy, it must be noted that I have taken a bit of creative license with some of the real-life characters and their situations in the telling of this tale for the sake of story—which to a writer of fiction, is the most important thing.

CHAPTER ONE

*a*PRIL 17, 1920 - NEW YORK HARBOR, NY

Grace Michelle braced herself for a possible spectacle as she threaded her way through the shimmering swarm of the wealthiest and most famous people of New York City. A wedding reception on a yacht would make anyone giddy, but Grace couldn't really appreciate the extravagance. Her sister Sophia's marriage to Jack Pickford promised nothing short of a disaster.

Grace drew in a sharp breath as she entered the glittering grand ballroom of the yacht Jack's sister, actress Mary Pickford, had let them use for the occasion. High ceilinged and skirted with rows of windows on each side, the *Extravaganza's* ballroom showcased a sparkling nighttime view of the skyline. Gas lamps from the city burned in the distance, their radiance reflecting on the rippling water of the bay. Candle chandeliers lit the parquet dance floor, making everything glow.

"Champagne?" A tuxedoed waiter approached her with a tray bearing crystal flutes filled with pink bubbly stuff. She raised her hand, declining the offer.

Grace sought a familiar face in the throng of elegant women, all wearing chiffon and satin gowns, accessorized with diamonds, pearls, and luxurious furs. She looked at the men wearing custom-made, long-tailed tuxedoes but saw no one she knew. Knitted together in groups, the guests sipped champagne or danced the Shimmy and the Charleston, laughing with abandon.

When the music paused between songs, the white-tied, tuxedoed master of ceremonies, the actor Eddie Cantor, tapped a table knife against his champagne glass, introducing the guests as they entered the room. His eyes shifted to Grace.

"I'd like to present the sister of the bride, Grace Michelle."

A hundred heads turned to look at her, sending a rush of heat to her cheeks. Grace nodded to people as she passed by, her heart in her throat. Her sister was the famous Ziegfeld star, not her; Grace preferred to stay in the background, assisting in the creation of the elaborate costumes for the Follies.

She pulled at the waist of her beaded, organza dress in an attempt to win a momentary reprieve from her tight corset. On any other occasion, Grace would have been honored to wear the garment designed and crafted by her idol and mentor, Lucile, Lady Duff Gordon, but tonight, wearing a gown made by "the designer of the decade" seemed to sanction, even glorify, the farce that was her sister's marriage. Grace felt little reason to celebrate.

Like her, her new brother-in-law walked in the shadow of his famous sister, who was very much in the spotlight. His union with Sophia seemed to be a desperate grasp at the limelight, and ever since they'd begun courting, Sophia had been increasingly lured into his dark web of alcohol, drugs, and gambling.

When Grace's eyes landed on her sister, she cringed to find Sophia dressed in a purple satin gown, her lips painted a garish shade of red that clashed with her auburn hair. She should have stayed in her wedding white—it enhanced her elfin beauty. She had once been voluptuous and striking, with a voice that rivaled the angels, but now Sophia's lithe, twenty-one-year-old body and usual liveliness appeared dimmed from too much alcohol. Where she'd once been Grace's strong, determined older sister—if only by a year—Sophia now seemed a ghost of her former self.

Jack, Sophia's lanky, too-tanned groom, stood with her near the bar, both of them likely readying themselves to give what Grace feared would be theatrical, overly dramatic speeches. Grace scanned the room, searching for colleagues and friends until, finally, her gaze settled on Florenz Ziegfeld Jr., the famous Broadway producer—and her savior. Flo had rescued Grace, aged twelve at the time, and Sophia, age thirteen, when he'd found them, homeless and huddled on the sidewalk near the theater. Captivated by Sophia's beauty, he wanted to make her a star. He took them in and gave them jobs.

Now, dressed in a dark tailcoat and trousers with a red waistcoat, stiff winged collar shirt, and white bow tie, he looked like a lion lording over his pride. Flo's face glimmered with amusement as he swirled a glass of brandy in one hand and lifted a fat cigar to his lips with the other. His expression seemed to convey that all was well and everything was going smoothly, but Grace recognized a slow burn rising to the surface.

He strongly objected to Sophia's marriage to Jack, but Grace surmised he couldn't resist attending the event. All his stars—past, present, and future—were there. With the magnetic showman in the room, no one would ever suspect that the bridegroom's famous movie star sister had paid for everything. Grace knew that Flo could—and would—take credit for "the social event of the year."

Grace cautiously approached him.

"Darling." Flo's eyes danced when he saw her. "You look divine."

"Thank you, Flo. I'm glad you're here."

"Well, much to my disappointment, I couldn't change

Sophia's mind." He took a drag from his cigar and let the smoke linger in his mouth before releasing it. "She was set on marrying the scoundrel. He's filled her mind with false promises of a film career, you know, and taking her off to California."

Grace and Sophia had not spoken much in the last few weeks. Like Flo, Grace found it hard to understand why Sophia would surrender her position as star of the Ziegfeld Follies and follow Jack clear across the country to an uncertain future.

"Might as well part on good terms, then, right?" Flo added.

Grace stood on her tiptoes and delicately kissed his cheek.

A tinkling sound filled the room, and all eyes turned to Sophia, who stood tapping a thin metal swizzle stick against her champagne glass.

"Attention, everyone," she said, standing beside the bar. Her tiny frame swayed against her groom. "I'd like to make an announcement, please."

The voices in the room quieted, all but the background noise of the waitstaff busying themselves with their duties.

"I would like to say a few things." Sophia patted at the damp curls on her forehead. A sheen of perspiration glowed on her skin, and traces of lipstick smeared her mouth. She looked pale, gaunt—not the picture of a blushing bride.

"First, I'd like to propose a toast to my wonderful husband." She raised her champagne flute and pressed it against Jack's face. He pushed the glass down a notch and planted a sloppy kiss on her cheek.

An approving murmur rippled through the crowd.

"Thank you for marrying me," she said, raising her glass again. "Thank you for saving me."

Grace drew in a deep breath, hoping Sophia's speech wouldn't last long. She didn't like the sallowness of Sophia's skin or the way she teetered unsteadily between Jack and the bar.

"And secondly, I would like to propose a toast to my beautiful sister."

All eyes turned to Grace again. Fire crawled up her neck, but she held her head high, determined to conquer the anxiety welling in her chest.

"As some of you know, Grace and I were orphaned at a young age."

Grace trained her eyes to the floor and tried to swallow the lump rising in her throat.

"Losing our parents in a train crash was horrible, of course, but Grace and I have always been there for one another. For a while, we lived in the streets, had nothing, and sometimes went hungry for days. Then Flo—the wonderful, magnetic, generous Flo Ziegfeld Jr.—found Gracie and me." Sophia lifted the champagne glass again, and this time it slipped from her fingers and shattered against the floor. A waiter swooped over, gathered the glass shards in his gloved hands, and hurriedly disappeared. Sophia reached for another full glass from the bar and gulped some down without missing a beat.

"As I was saying . . . Flo, the Great Ziegfeld, the most famous showman on Earth, discovered my sister and me on the streets and took us in by promising many things: *I'd become his newest sensation, become his star.*" Sophia held her arms aloft. "I would be adored, he said. Provided for. My baby sister would be cared for." She glowered at Flo. "And we were, we were . . . but all that generosity came at a price."

Grace's mouth felt suddenly dry. *Sophia, please, please, please don't insult Flo,* she thought. *Not here, not now.*

"I . . . I adored him, loved him, worshiped him." Sophia's voice faltered, and Jack pulled his bride closer and whispered something in her ear. When he looked up at the crowd again, his smile twitched in an odd, disconnected way.

"Flo said he would leave his wife for me," Sophia blurted.

Grace sucked in a breath and gasps echoed through the room. *What had she just said? He'd been like a father, to both of them, not a paramour.*

Grace looked over at Flo, who flinched, then composed himself in an instant. He raised his cigar to his lips, took a long drag, and then exhaled, expelling the smoke in a steady, linear stream. The guests' uncomfortable murmurs buzzed around them.

Sophia was drunk. That's why she'd said it, Grace thought. She'd just wanted to get back at Flo, angry that he had refused to give his blessing for her marriage. It couldn't be true.

When Sophia opened her mouth to say more, Jack removed the champagne glass from her hand.

"Now, darling." He slipped an arm around her waist, his voice rasping with exasperation. "*You've* had a bit too much champagne."

Sophia pressed her hands against his chest, pushed him away, and pointed her finger at Flo. "He *betrayed* me, broke all his promises, ruined me, and now he's turned Gracie against me."

Jack grabbed Sophia's hands and held them close to his torso, his jaw flexing. Sophia turned her tear-stained face to Grace.

"You'll see, Gracie," Sophia's voice dripped with sadness. "You'll regret turning against me. He'll use you, too."

Grace rushed to her sister, wrenched Sophia out of Jack's embrace, and shook her shoulders. "Stop it, Sophia! Don't say such things! How could you?"

Stars burst bright in Grace's eyes and her cheek was burning. Sophia had slapped her—hard.

A frantic tug on Grace's arm refocused her attention. Fanny Brice, Flo's most famous comedienne, slipped a firm arm around Grace's waist, and urged her toward the door. "C'mon, sweetheart. Let's get out of here. Sophia isn't herself. The only way to end this is to bring the curtain down."

Grace felt glued to the floor and watched as Sophia sank into Jack's arms and burrowed her head into his chest, sobbing.

Despite Sophia's unimaginable accusations, Grace wanted to hold her, to comfort her, but the tug on her arm persisted.

"Come along, honey," Fanny urged.

Grace finally surrendered and left the room, guided by Fanny's common sense.

CHAPTER TWO

*M*AY 1, 1920 - NEW YORK CITY, NY
Grace's body swayed back and forth with the
rhythm of the carriage as it wheeled its way down Broadway.
Through the window, she could see motorcars speeding by in the
whirling white snow of the early morning. Despite the roar of
traffic, trolley cars, and the bustling crowd, Grace focused on the
sound of the horses' hooves clopping on the street and the
squeaking of the carriage wheels.

Suited businessmen and ladies with parasols scurried about.
The city's majestic brick and stone buildings buffeted the late
spring winds that whipped through the streets. As they passed
the southwestern corner of Central Park, the shop windows lit up
and came alive with extravagant displays designed to lure rich
women into their impressive establishments. A horse-drawn trolley's bell dinged as Grace's carriage passed by.

Springtime in New York provided constant contradictions.
Even as the promise of sunshine and blooming flowers beckoned
around the corner, relentless cold often descended upon the
lively city. Two weeks earlier, at Sophia's wedding reception, the
night had been unseasonably warm, with a crisp breeze blowing

through the air, but this spring day a light snow whirled through the city.

But Grace didn't mind. The wintry blast mirrored the ache in her heart. Her last words with Sophia still haunted her. Grace squeezed her eyes shut to force the recollection away and placed her gloved hand on her cheek to soothe the sting that still burned in her memory. And since that night, Grace had not been able to look Flo in the eye. The thought of him and Sophia together, as a couple, still seemed unimaginable. Flo's affairs were legendary, but not with someone he had embraced as his own child.

Flo avoided her, too—proof of his guilt. He busied himself with finding a new headliner to replace Sophia. In fact, they had spent days without seeing each other at all, which made it easier for Grace, but she knew she'd have to face him sooner or later.

The pale sun rose into a gray sky, promising to warm the city, but the air left Grace feeling chilled. She pulled the luxurious ermine coat Flo had given her closer around her body. Grace chided herself for her lack of enthusiasm. She'd been asked by Lucile to design a few costumes for Sophia's replacement— whoever that would be. Grace knew she should be bursting with happiness at the honor, but given the circumstances, the opportunity held little thrill.

Grace reached into her clutch and pulled out the newspaper clipping the doorman at the Ansonia had given her a few days ago—an article from *Variety* about Sophia's wedding and reception. Missing her sister, she looked at it now and again. The publicity photo of Sophia they had used, one of Grace's favorites, brought tears to her eyes. In the photo, Sophia wore a whimsical, girlish expression, and her auburn hair hung in ringlets below a wide-brimmed hat. She looked so much like their mother. Grace clasped the clipping to her chest and stifled a sob. She hadn't heard from Sophia since she'd left.

The carriage pulled up to the towering white beaux arts columns of the New Amsterdam Theater. As Grace waited for the driver to open the door, she reached into her clutch again and grabbed a few coins. The driver helped her out, and she paid him.

She entered the gray marble building through the Forty-First Street side entrance and made her way down the narrow, low-ceilinged hallway to the costume room. Sounds of feet tapping in rhythm to the rich tones emanating from a piano echoed throughout the building.

Grace drew in a breath, readying herself for the day. Full dress rehearsal days meant hours of yelling, begging, arguing, cursing, and exhaustion because Flo demanded absolute flaw-lessness. He made it his solitary mission to perfect every single dance step, hemline, and musical score, managing all the details down to the props and lighting gels.

Grace entered the costume room, surprised to find it empty. Her gaze rested on the lavish headdresses she'd assembled, lined up in neat rows on one of the worktables. She removed her ermine coat and gloves, and made her way over to the bright pink plumed headwear. She gently laid a hand on one of the giant ostrich feathers and stroked upward, relishing the airy feeling of the plume tickling her fingertips. She then bent down to inspect the fine beadwork on the trim she'd completed the day before. Not a bead was out of place, everything secure, much to her satisfaction.

Just as she turned to hang up her coat, Charles, Lucile's assistant, strutted into the room. Always the peacock, he was wearing a maroon satin jacket with black lapels lined with rhinestones.

"Darling, how are you?" His large eyes widened with his question, and his full lips pursed under his too tightly twirled mustache.

"I'm fine, Charles. Could you please help me stack these headdresses on the trays? We need to take them to the girls."

"Heard from Sophia yet?"

Grace shook her head. "C'mon, help me here."

With a sigh, Charles walked over to the wall and picked up two large wooden trays. He and Grace gently set each of the elaborate headpieces on the trays in rows.

"You know, I always wondered how you and Sophia ended up here," he said. "Is it true? Did Flo rescue you from the streets?"

"Yes, true enough."

Charles rested a hand on his chest. "Oh, my dear. Living on the streets. How horrible that must have been for you. How did you stay alive?"

"I don't really like to talk about it. Or think about it."

"I'm sorry, darling. Didn't mean to pry."

Grace raised her eyes to his. "I made dolls' clothes. Sophia always managed to buy the fabric. We would sell them on the streets to mothers with little girls in tow."

"Where did she get the money?"

"I'm not sure. Many nights she would leave me alone for a few hours. She always made sure it was a safe place, hidden. And she always made sure I was warm. We found burlap sacks and flour sacks behind the restaurants and used those to wrap around ourselves. There was a man—"

"A man?"

Grace bit her lip and turned away from Charles. "I can't remember anymore."

"I'm sorry. I won't ask any more questions."

"We really should get these headdresses to the stage. Flo will be fuming if we're late."

Balancing the trays, they left the costume room and came to the main theater door. Charles leaned his shoulder against the door and pushed it open to reveal the beautiful, gaslit, 1800-seat, art nouveau auditorium. Circular box seats bordered with terra-cotta balustrades, adorned with carvings of grape leaves, apple blossoms, and pomegranates, jutted from the walls. Frescos of angels and demons, birds of prey, and other flora and fauna graced every flat and domed surface of the interior of the grand building.

"Ladies first." Charles motioned with his head for Grace to pass through.

Flo was pacing the stage, flinging his arms, his shirtsleeves hanging loose around his wrists. Usually, even in casual attire, Flo paid particular attention to his appearance. His lack of fastidiousness surprised Grace.

"One, two, three! One, two, three! Pick up your feet, girls!" Flo yelled at the chorus line. They scurried to match his rhythm. "Are those legs made of lead? C'mon now."

Grace's eyes settled on the stage just in time to see one of the enormous columns rise out of the stage floor, the buzz and hum of the electrical winch echoing throughout the theater. Once the music started, that noisy whir would be drowned out by the orchestra's expert harmonies.

Grace and Charles crossed the stage, approaching another group of girls who were idly waiting for their turn to fall short of Flo's stringent demands. They handed each one her headpiece. Charles supplied Grace with hair clips, Murray's Superior Hair Dressing Pomade, and other securing devices as she meticulously placed one of the three-foot-tall, plumed hats on each girl's head.

"Honey." Flo marched over to Grace, waving his hand. "Get some makeup artists out here. These girls look like ghosts." He took a drag on his cigar and then let it fall from his fingers before stomping it out on the stage. He turned and pointed to one of the backstage crewmen, a young boy who scurried out from the wings with broom and dustpan in hand.

When Flo turned his back, Charles leaned in closer to Grace. "I hate final dress rehearsals," he whispered. "Flo is worse than Attila the Hun."

"Take a breath," Grace said. "It won't last forever."

Grace then went backstage to find Blanche and Derek, the Follies' cosmetology wizards. She returned to a hushed theater, the rehearsal about to begin. Flo claimed one end of the piano bench while George Gershwin seated himself on the other end. Gershwin's exuberance at the piano always seemed to have a calming effect over Flo. The two often squeezed themselves onto the piano bench, George working diligently over the keys, a lock of wavy hair bouncing over his forehead, while Flo leaned his head back, savoring the music pouring out over the stage. Many times during the rehearsals Flo would snap out of his trance, jump up from the bench, dance a few steps, and then sit again, his foot tapping in time to the music.

Today, the tenseness pulling Flo's brow down over his long nose and stretching the skin taut at his jawline allowed no joy. For the first time, Grace noticed the slicked back hair at his temples had silvered, and his eyes, usually sparkling and mischievous, seemed to have dulled. Did he miss Sophia as much as she did?

The musicians settled in the pit, and a cacophony of sounds blurred into quiet conversation.

The usual observers sat in the first row: the composer, Irving Berlin; Flo's business manager, Jack Boyd; set designer Joe Urban; Lucile; and Charles. Gene Buck, another accomplished composer, stood to the side of the piano near Flo, smoke from his cigar billowing around their heads like a pale thundercloud.

The lights flickered and dimmed, summoning everyone to take their seats. Grace sat next to Charles. Despite her earlier mood, a rush of excitement bubbled up in her chest and the hairs rose on her arms. Seeing another one of Flo's brilliant creations brought to fruition always gave her goose bumps.

"Let the spectacle unfold," Charles whispered in her ear.

Grace smiled, her eyes locked onto the stage.

"To think, this genius of a man started as a vaudeville talent hawker." Charles leaned into her. "I remember 'The Amazing

Sandow, the Strongest Man in the World.'" He lowered his voice for dramatic effect.

"Yes. He's come quite far. From vaudeville, to nightclubs, to . . . this. . . ."

"Wasn't his father in show business?"

"He owned a music school and a nightclub. Anna once told me that it broke his father's heart that Flo didn't take over the family businesses."

"Anna Held." Charles turned in his seat to face her. "The Parisian beauty, God rest her soul. You knew her? Was it true that she took milk baths?"

She shrugged. "That's what Flo wanted everyone to think. He had gallons of the stuff delivered to the hotel. I don't know if she ever really bathed in it, though. By the time Sophia and I arrived, their relationship was nearly at an end. Anna wasn't around much, but I remember she was very sweet."

"So Flo just got tired of Anna and tossed her out? That must be when he started the affair with Lillian Lorraine."

Grace pulled at her bottom lip with her teeth. She didn't want to mention that the notorious femme fatale was still lurking in the wings and causing more trouble than most people knew about. Lillian had made it quite clear she didn't like Sophia and Grace around, but getting rid of Anna Held had proved far easier.

The orchestra buzzed with last-minute tunings. Grateful she didn't have to answer Charles's question, Grace refocused on the stage. With a stroke of the conductor's baton, all fell silent. An upstroke and the violins hummed. Gershwin's fingers brought the piano to life.

A dozen marble columns rose through the stage floor, each topped with a gem-studded girl. Each girl held a silver ball poised high above her head, her flesh-colored leotards splashed with crystals and rhinestones. From the wings, a stream of bubbles flowed onto the stage as ballerinas leaped and swirled in

the air. The column girls each released a pearly w
from her shimmering orb.

With an abrupt *thump*, one of the sixteen-fo
began to fall, and the girl on top of it struggled
footing. Thrown off-balance by her moveme
screamed in panic. Flo jumped to his feet
signaling others standing in the wings to f
technician to lower the columns. The music

Grace covered her eyes, bracing hersel
could fly into a rage at any moment. The
back into the floor and vanished, bringing
Nervous titters filled the theater.

"Quiet!" Flo yelled.

Everyone took a collective inhale,
inevitable tirade.

He lit another cigar. "People, take fifteen."

Onstage and off, they all exhaled again.

Flo strode toward the stage technician,
freckle-faced young man. A pang of sympathy
heart. She knew Flo would release a torrent
young man.

Sounds of stomping feet caused everyone—exce
was unmercifully chastising the stage technician—to
heads. A young boy in a Western Union uniform ran
aisle and onto the stage. He handed Flo an envelope. Fl
the pad and paid the boy without missing a beat in his rar
technician. Finally, Flo ripped open the telegram and read.

With all finally silent, Grace turned to leave, but s
screams made her turn back around. Flo had collapsed,
down, on the stage.

Grace ran up the stairs, and pushing the awestruck techi
aside, she knelt down at Flo's side. She gently grasped his
trembling shoulders and turned him over. His eyes

you all right? What is it? Are you hurt?"

iced the telegram clutched in his fist and pried his

read the yellow page. When her eyes settled on

reath lodged in her throat.

d.

CHAPTER THREE

*H*er thoughts in turmoil and numb from the news, Grace sat in the corner of Flo's office, not sure how she'd gotten there. She stared at the photos of Flo's starlets on the wall behind him. All their faces blurred into the same person—all but Sophia who stood out like a cosmic star, glimmering in a deep blue night.

Light and sound blurred, moving in slow motion. Grace remembered someone onstage snatching the telegram from her hand, people yelling, Flo unresponsive on the ground, and then hands wrapping around her biceps, pulling her up. She remembered the smell of Charles's cologne and realized he'd held her upright, had talked to her, even though she hadn't been able to decipher the words. When her knees had buckled beneath her, Charles had gripped her harder. Weight had pressed on her chest, but she hadn't been able to bring air into her lungs. And now she sat across from Flo in his office, his cheeks ashen, sweat dripping down his face.

Jack Boyd, his manager, sat next to him, his face etched with worry.

This couldn't be happening. Sophia couldn't be dead.

Matilda Golden, or Goldie as they called her, Flo's secretary, scurried around the office like a frantic hen trying to care for her ailing chicks. Although not a beautiful woman, Goldie was striking with her long face, green eyes, and silver hair always pulled tight in a knot at the back of her head. As Goldie stood at the bar pouring Flo a glass of whiskey, Grace could feel the woman's gaze on her. Whiskey in hand, Goldie rushed over to Flo and gave it to him. He sank deeper into his chair, closed his eyes, and sipped from the crystal tumbler.

Goldie approached Grace, her movements slow and fluid, like a flamingo gliding across a pond. Her eyes held Grace's carefully, as if Grace might break like a fragile glass figurine at any moment.

"My dear, what can I do for you? Would you like a drink? Something strong?"

Grace looked into Goldie's eyes, trying to formulate an answer. She didn't want a drink. She wanted Sophia back. "Why did she die, Goldie? How?"

Goldie leaned down and set her hands on Grace's shoulders, her sage eyes boring into Grace's. "They aren't sure, my dear. It seems to be a bit of a mystery."

Grace struggled to breathe. She closed her eyes to stop the tingling behind them, but giant tears rolled down her cheeks anyway.

TWO WEEKS LATER, Grace stood next to a framed, eleven-by-fourteen-inch photo of Sophia adorned with a black satin wreath. The memorial, held on the rooftop of the New Amsterdam—home of the Midnight Frolic, one of Flo's racier, bolder productions—was again nothing short of Ziegfeld extravagance. But Grace's heart felt like a heavy, black lump of coal. She gripped the telegram in her hand so tightly she could feel the blood pulsing in her fingers.

"How are you holding up, kid?" Fanny's voice broke the silence.

Grace turned to her. "Would it be easier if I knew *how* she died? *Why* she died?"

Fanny's dark, usually merry eyes filled with sympathy. Her talent shone, but sadly, good looks still eluded her. Small eyes set too close together made her nose look too big for her face, and her lips— her best feature—were full and rosy but wore the constant smirk of sarcasm. "I don't know," she said. "I don't think it's ever easy."

"From Jack." Grace held up a crumpled telegram. "Sending his condolences. So sorry he couldn't be here. So sorry he couldn't afford a decent funeral. His sister paid to have her buried at Forest Lawn Cemetery in Los Angeles. They didn't even wait to see if I could get there."

"I'm awfully sorry, dear, but look around you. This memorial Flo has put on is beautiful."

"Yes, as usual, a *monumental* affair, fraught with famous theater and film folk." She clutched the telegram harder. "Eddie Cantor and Will Rogers and W.C. Fields—it's just a show. Like everything Flo does." Grace closed her eyes and sighed, feeling awful for unloading on Fanny. "I'm sorry. I know I should be grateful. Flo's done so much for us. When our parents died, Sophia and I couldn't afford any sort of funeral. Afraid we'd be sent to the orphanage, we ran away with the little money we had, but it didn't last. We ended up on the streets."

"Oh, my dear. How old were you?"

"Twelve. Sophia was thirteen. Two years after our parents died, Flo found us wandering on Forty-Second Street, near the theater—bedraggled, thin, unwashed, and hungry. He seemed fascinated by us, by our predicament. He questioned us for a long time. Took us to a café to get some food. And then he offered to house us, train us, and give us jobs. In a moment, our lives changed." Grace surveyed the party. The rooftop glittered like a star-studded sky with gas lamps, elaborate and ornate bouquets, exquisite food, and dozens of society people.

"Come on," Fanny said. "Let's sit down."

Fanny led her to one of the tables, all of which displayed large, porcelain elephant vases, their trunks uplifted with white and purple orchids spilling from the rotund backs of the ceramic beasts.

"What's with the elephants? I've always wondered." Fanny fingered a purple petal of orchid.

"They're good luck," Grace said. "Flo's obsessed with them."

"*Eccentric* does not begin to describe the man." Fanny's face looked like she'd just sucked on a lemon.

Grace looked up to see W.C. Fields standing next to her at the table. He wore a fine Burberry London Sterling wool-and-mohair three-piece suit, his generous belly stretching the button-holes on his waistcoat beyond what seemed comfortable. He took off his boater and swept into a bow.

"My dear girl, your sister was a vision of loveliness, and she had one hell of a set of pipes. We will miss her around here."

"Thank you, Mr. Fields."

His pudgy face squished into a grin, amplifying his bulbous red nose. He winked at her, nodded to Fanny, and moved on. Before Grace could take another breath, Gene Buck approached the table.

"Your sister was a dream to write for. Perfect pitch, perfect pitch." He smoothed his hand over his receding hairline, and his bright blue eyes regarded her with kindness. He reached for her hand and brushed his lips against the back of it. "All my sympathies, Grace. You stay strong."

"Yes, yes, I must, mustn't I?" Grace said, a bit tongue-tied at his piercing stare.

"Oh, God," said Fanny.

"What is it?" Grace asked.

Fanny pointed to the other side of the rooftop. "*She's* here."

The slender, auburn-haired Lillian Lorraine had entered the room, resplendent in a black velvet gown, the neckline plunging inappropriately low for a memorial service. Her large brown eyes were downturned at the corners, and the cleft in her chin gave her face a strong, if not masculine, appearance. A wide-brimmed, black hat dipped seductively over one eye, with jet-black ostrich feathers set in a dazzling plume at the back of her head. She stopped to speak with Mr. Fields, who ogled her unabashedly.

"Do you think she'll come over here?" Grace asked, her hands starting to shake.

"Undoubtedly."

The velvet-clad woman let out a laugh so loud that the room went silent for a moment.

"Like a whore in church," Fanny said.

"Oh, Fanny. Don't embarrass me. Please. If she comes over here, be kind. I can't take a confrontation."

"Don't worry, kid." Fanny waved her hand in front of her face. "I won't drag her out of here by the hair."

Grace snorted and quickly put her hand to her face. She'd heard people talk about the time Fanny and Lillian had gotten in a fight backstage and Fanny had literally dragged Lillian by the hair across the stage to uproarious applause.

"I can't believe you did that. Onstage, no less! You should be ashamed."

"She took my man!" she explained. "Poor Freddy. They had the world's shortest marriage. Ten days. I should be over the louse by now. It was a long time ago, but. . . ."

"I think she just said something about Sophia." Grace strained to hear the conversation. She and Fanny both quieted to listen.

Lillian dramatically placed her cigarette holder between her lips and took a drag. She blew the stream of smoke over Mr. Fields's head.

"Yes, I know! Jack is quite the cad. Never was faithful to the poor girl. Left a string of harlots in his wake."

"Oh my goodness," Grace gasped.

"Don't tell me you're surprised, Grace. You know Jack's a scoundrel." Fanny leaned closer to Lillian and Mr. Fields's conversation.

"I think his sister, Mary, gave up trying to support him, so on to greener pastures," Lillian went on. "Too bad for Sophia, but better for me." She propped her elbow on her velvet-clad hipbone, her cigarette propped between slender fingers and nearly touching the brim of her enormous hat. Smoke drifted upward in an elegant line above her head.

Mr. Fields said something Grace couldn't hear. Then Lillian's voice raised an octave. "Flo? Oh no, he'd never come to a memorial, or a wake, or a funeral. The man is terrified of death. Didn't even go to poor Anna's funeral."

"That's because he was too busy with you, you tart!" Fanny said a little too loudly.

"Fanny, shh. I can't hear."

Lillian took another drag of her cigarette, Mr. Fields hanging on her every gesture, her every word. "Although, I must say, he did a fabulous job with this send-off. I'm not sure how much the girl deserved it. . . ."

Grace took in a sharp breath. "Fanny, it sounds as if Lillian *wanted* Sophia dead!"

"Don't listen to that garbage. Lillian was always jealous of Sophia."

Before Grace could let out her breath, Lillian approached their table. Her eyes narrowed at Fanny. "I'd like a word with Miss Michelle."

"Well, I'm not leaving, so you'll have to have your *word* with me sitting here," Fanny countered.

Lillian's mouth curled up in a smirk. "Very well, Brice." She focused her attention on Grace, her cherry lips protruding in a pout. "Condolences."

"Condolences?" repeated Fanny. "Bravo! You must add *sympathy* and *graciousness* to your acting repertoire. Award-winning stuff, darling."

Grace could see Lillian's jaw tense beneath her flawless porcelain skin. With a toss of her head, she turned toward a group of gentlemen, strolling away from Grace and Fanny like a sleek cat. The men's conversation came to a halt, and a lascivious smile crossed each and every one of their faces.

"Witch," Fanny said.

Grace felt as if she'd been punched in the stomach. "How could someone be so hateful?"

Fanny patted Grace's arm. "This is show business, darling."

CHAPTER FOUR

*C*het Riker sat ramrod straight in the red velvet booth across from famed mobster Joe Marciano and two of his men. One of them gave Chet a raise of his chin and a wink. Usually, he wouldn't see that as a threat, but considering that this particular man looked like a beer keg on legs, the gesture didn't indicate warm friendlies. The other man, equally burly, had hands so hairy Chet wondered if the guy had just escaped from the zoo. Their hats rested on a hat stand behind the table with silver toothpicks—Marciano's signature—tucked into the hatbands.

Sitting in Delmonico's, one of New York City's swankiest restaurants, with the known criminal and his thugs did nothing to help Chet's standing in the community, but since he owed Marciano money, declining the invitation had seemed foolish.

Around him, waiters in black coats and ties held silver trays of food high above their heads as they hurried to serve their waiting customers. In the booth next to them, a group of women wearing ornate hats and silk gloves chatted in whispers.

Chet bounced his heel up and down beneath the table. With his reputation as a private investigator teetering on marginal, he

hoped any past or potential clients—if present—didn't recognize
him.

The noises around him seemed to grow louder and more
extreme. Every clink of sterling that touched china and every ice
cube that clicked against a crystal goblet sounded like gunfire,
reminding him of the trenches in France with dirt walls and
death cascading down around him. Then, like now, he wanted to
get out and *fast*.

"Still working for Flo?" Marciano reached into his coat
pocket to pull out a silver cigarette case, his beefy, ring-clad
fingers dwarfing the delicate box.

"Here and there. Been awhile." Chet kept his voice casual,
trying to swallow the anxiety that threatened to strangle him.

The rotund mobster plucked a cigarette from the case, and
one of his henchmen lit it for him. Marciano, a formidable busi-
nessman who carried much social and fiscal weight in the city of
New York, dressed like a king, ate at the finest restaurants, ran
gambling houses, and killed anyone who crossed his path at the
wrong moment—or owed him money for any length of time.
Chet fell into the latter category, and the reality made him want
to vomit.

"Like being around all those girls?" Marciano grinned, his fat
lips curving into a repugnant smirk. He took a long drag on the
cigarette, so long that the tip immediately turned to a snake of
ash. Marciano blew the smoke out of his mouth in a violent
stream and then crushed the remainder of his cigarette in the
ashtray.

"Of course. Who wouldn't?" Chet gave a halfhearted smile.

*Money and power can buy tailored suits and elegant silk
shirts, but they certainly can't buy good looks,* Chet thought.
Marciano's face looked like it had been run through a cotton gin.
Pockmarked and red, his skin had an oily, white sheen, and his
jet-black hair hung in greasy strings over coal-black eyes. He
also ate like a pig: food stuck to his teeth as he shoveled it in,

openmouthed and grinning. Chet's stomach turned as he envisioned Marciano at a crude wooden trough, snout floundering in muck and rings on each cloven hoof.

Marciano stopped eating and eyed Chet's untouched plate. He snapped his fingers at a passing waiter. The waiter flinched to attention, like a soldier being summoned by a general.

"My guest, Mr. Riker, apparently finds his meal undesirable," he said to the waiter.

"The food's fine," Chet said.

It's the company that makes me want to retch.

The waiter turned again toward Marciano, awaiting approval to leave. He waved him away. "You're not eating."

"I'm not hungry."

Marciano laughed. "Not hungry." He looked from one of his thugs to the other. They both gave an obligatory chuckle. "Riker here's not hungry," Marciano repeated, leveling a malevolent stare at Chet. "I'm always hungry." He curled his lip. "Especially for what's mine."

Chet returned the glare, refusing to betray any sign of intimidation to this loathsome man. Marciano used a napkin to wipe the remnants of oily roast duck from his lips. The attempt failed; he only succeeded in smearing the bits around on his face. Apparently, money didn't buy manners, either.

"I understand you have a . . . proclivity for gambling," Marciano said.

"I've gambled in the past, yes."

"It seems that you are quite indebted at one of my establishments and have been for some time. Now, you have a couple of choices." Marciano threw the napkin down next to his plate. "You can either pay off your debt and you'll never see me again, or I can employ you on a little venture. Your investigative knowhow would be of great service. So what'll it be, Riker?"

Chet studied the thugs across from him and then bent forward. "I won't work for you, but I *will* pay off my debt."

Marciano leaned over the table and strained his neck toward Chet until his face loomed over Chet's plate. A piece of duck hung precariously from the corner of his mouth, threatening to drop.

"You don't wanna work for me? I'm gonna try not to take that personally, but let me tell you something, Riker. My boys are gonna be hounding you twenty-four hours a day, seven days a week, 'til you pay up. I'm giving you one month to come up with the cash, or you're gonna end up sorry. Do you understand me?"

Never taking his eyes away from Marciano's, Chet let out an exasperated rush of air, hoping the bits of duck wouldn't land on his plate. "Got it."

"Now," Marciano said, fiddling with the chunky rings on his fingers. "Are you gonna eat your meal, there?"

Chet pushed his plate away. He couldn't believe he was in this mess. All for his mother, a woman who'd given him away at birth, sent him to an orphanage where life was more than hard and less than pleasant, and drilled home the fact that love only caused pain.

After he had returned from the war still in one piece, he'd wanted to know the woman who'd given him life. When he finally found her, sick and wasting away, he learned she'd been diagnosed with cancer and needed an operation. She'd die if he didn't come up with the money. He couldn't be responsible for his own mother's death.

"Vito," Marciano said, taking the plate from Chet. "It's yours. Enjoy." He set the plate in front of the beer keg on legs. "Ciao, Riker."

Chet tossed his napkin on the table, grabbed his hat off the back of the booth, and got up to leave. The voluptuous woman in the neighboring booth gave him a dazzling smile, catching him off guard. He smiled back, and she gave him a wave of her fingers. He hadn't eaten, but his stomach wanted to come up anyway at the thought of ending up as fish food in the Hudson. He swallowed down the bile.

Outside, on the street, Chet pulled a cigar from his coat pocket. *One month.* He shook his head. Business had been slow —no missing persons, no cheating husbands, no wayward kids. Or at least not any thrown in his direction. Word had gotten out about his time at the tables, and it had hurt his reputation. Who wanted to hire a PI with a gambling habit? Hopefully, he could find *something* and find it quick.

He looked down the street and saw a brightly lit marquee. The theater business might need his services. It was time to make a visit to Florenz Ziegfeld Jr.

CHAPTER FIVE

*a*fter the memorial service, Grace returned home to her suite at the Ansonia Hotel, a place that she and Sophia once shared. Exhausted but too wound up to sleep, she lay on the bed and stared at the moiré taffeta-covered canopy, letting her eyes roam over the pink swirls and folds of the fabric that had been molded to form a giant rose petal above her head.

Several vases of flowers filled the room with a sweet fragrance—almost too sweet. Grace knew that this aroma would forever remind her of death, and she fought to not let her senses overwhelm her.

She didn't remember falling asleep, but a knock at the door the next morning woke her. With legs weighed down by exhaustion, she dragged herself from her bed and opened the door a crack, peeking through. Flo, wearing a velvet dressing gown over silk pajamas and holding a copy of *Variety* in one hand and a cigar in the other, stood at the door. Grace couldn't bear to look into his grave face.

"You need to see this." He held up the newspaper. "Put your robe on and come to my suite. Immediately."

He left her at the door and walked down the hall, tapping the paper lightly against his thigh.

Grace didn't like the scowl on his face. She didn't really like anything about Flo right now. For weeks she'd entertained the notion of leaving the theater, leaving Flo. It made her sick each time she thought of Flo and Sophia as lovers. But where would she go? Back to the streets? The very idea left her even more nauseated. What did he want?

Grace moved to the vanity to re-braid her hair. She spotted one of Sophia's dressing gowns hanging in the wardrobe and slipped into it, wrapping it tightly around her body, longing for the comfort of her sister. The scent of Sophia's favorite perfume still lingered in the Oriental silk. Grace breathed in the aroma and took solace in the good memories it produced. Memories of them laughing together and whispering in the dark, pillow fights and long conversations about what their lives would be when they were older.

Grace left her room and made her way toward the double doors of Flo's suite. She knocked. Flo's valet, Harold, a stocky, balding man who always bore a grim expression, opened it and showed her in.

Decorated in shades of deep brown, burgundy, and taupe, Flo's suite displayed masculine elegance. Flo's wife, Billie, didn't share these lodgings, and the lack of a feminine touch confirmed it. The double doors of the entry opened into a small, parquet floor hallway leading to the dining room. A long mahogany table with a set of stately armchairs dominated the space. Dark, metal candelabras hung over the table, giving the room an intimidating air.

Harold led her around the corner to the parlor. Grace peered in to see Flo sitting in a high-backed, silk-covered chair that resembled a throne. Harold motioned to a smaller replica of the chair, signaling for her to sit, and she obeyed. A knot of anxiety balled up in her chest. She'd never been nervous around Flo before, not like this, but things were different now. Would he expect her to replace Sophia as his mistress? The thought made her palms sweat.

Flo stared at the paper, seemingly unaware of her presence.

Harold brought them tea service and rested it on Flo's recently purchased, fashionable, mahogany coffee table in front of them. Seconds passed into minutes. Finally, Flo set the paper down and greeted Grace with a thin-lipped smile. He waved Harold away and poured each of them a cup of steaming tea.

Before reaching for his saucer, Flo handed Grace the newspaper. "There's no easy way to say this, so I'll just let you see for yourself."

Grace's gaze moved to the page. The headline read, ZIEGFELD ACTRESS SOPHIA MICHELLE'S MYSTERIOUS DEATH—SPANISH FLU, SUICIDE, OR FOUL PLAY? She lowered the paper to her lap, stunned at the last two words, their image burning into her mind.

Grace stared at the tea service, letting the information sink in. Despair rested so heavy on her heart she could scarcely breathe. She felt her head drain of blood, and her mouth went sticky, her tongue dry.

Flo leaned forward, his fingertips alighting on her knee. "Darling, I'm so sorry. For everything."

Grace offered a faint nod. She must collect herself, be strong.

"This has been a terrible shock, my dear." He took the paper from her lap and handed her a teacup and saucer. "I'm afraid I've neglected you during all this. Here, drink your tea."

Despite her shaking fingers, Grace raised the cup to her lips and sipped. She put the cup down on the saucer with a *click*.

"Sophia would never kill herself," she said. "The idea is preposterous. Could it have been Spanish flu?"

"It seemed a real possibility, but the pandemic was two years ago. Still, something is going around. People are dropping like flies. A few dancers have come down with it." Flo rubbed a hand over the stubble of his unshaven face. "But I don't think it's that simple." He paused a moment, staring at the ceiling. "I received a report from the Los Angeles Police Department. They say the circumstances of Sophia's death could have been consistent with poisoning. Either by her own hand or that of someone else."

Grace shook her head. "That can't be. It's not possible. I know she was drinking more than usual, but Sophia would never. . . ." She paused to draw in a breath. "What does Jack have to say about this? Have you spoken with him?"

"Hardly," Flo snorted. "Vermin. He's responsible for this, didn't know how to take care of her. Hell, he can barely take care of himself, the damned drunk. It wouldn't surprise me if he . . . well, never mind."

Grace blanched at his insinuation and swallowed hard. "Flo, I don't care for Jack any more than you do, but I certainly don't think he would—" Their eyes met for a brief moment. "No, he wouldn't hurt Sophia. If anything, he wanted to ride her coattails."

"Need I remind you that Jack's sister is Mary Pickford? Sophia was following *him* to a career in motion pictures." He pursed his lips and tapped his long, narrow nose. "I don't like the way this smells. No, I don't like any of it."

Grace slumped back into the chair, feeling lost, helpless. She remembered Lillian's words at the memorial and the way she had nearly gushed at the fact Sophia was gone, out of her way. Could she have been responsible in some way?

"Darling." Flo leaned forward. "We *will* get to the bottom of this, no matter how long it takes. We'll find out what happened."

Grace pulled her upper lip between her teeth, trying to wrap her head around this new information.

"Did you love her?" The words tumbled out of her mouth.

"You must think less of me after all this . . ."

"I don't know what to think."

"I did love Sophia."

"Did you make those promises? Did you tell her you'd marry her?"

"No, darling, I assure you I did not. She was too young. It would have ruined both of our careers." He paused, met her eyes. "Billie's not only my wife but one of my most important investors . . . I have to do whatever keeps her happy, so I broke it off with Sophia two years ago. That's when Sophia's drinking began in earnest."

"Yes, I did notice a change. Sophia used to tell me Billie hated her. Guess now I know why."

If Flo truly loved Sophia, someone who also made him a lot of money, would he really have let her go to California?

No wonder Billie traveled so much.

"Why didn't she tell me about you two?" Grace asked, thinking out loud. "I could have been there for her, comforted her when you broke it off."

How *could* her sister have hidden such a huge secret?

"Sophia felt responsible for you," Flo said. "She wanted to take care of you, not burden you as to how she would fulfill that responsibility."

"If you broke it off two years ago, why did you keep us around?"

"I care about you. I cared about her. And, I'd made an investment—in you both." Flo folded his hands in his lap. "Voice lessons, acting lessons, dance lessons. I received a return on that investment through Sophia. She made money for the theater."

Grace blinked. "You are admitting that you used her. Just like she said." She drew the words out slowly, trying to read his face.

"And did you both not profit from the arrangement? I fed you, clothed you—in grand style, I might add. Do you know how many girls are out there right now who would do anything to live the life you lead? I think it's been a fair trade, darling."

Flo *had* saved them from a horrible existence. Grace searched his eyes. "And what about me. Am I to be turned out?"

"Of course not, Grace. You'll continue to be provided for, your every need met. You have nothing to fear."

If only she could believe him.

"There is no need to fret, darling. I would never turn you out. I know I'll get a return on my investment in you, too."

"But, I—"

"Mr. Ziegfeld." Harold stood in the doorway, interrupting. "There is an urgent matter at the theater. Something about one of those contraptions on the stage floor."

"I must get dressed." Flo set down his teacup and leaned toward Grace. "Please stay and finish your tea. And please don't worry. I'll see you at the theater for the costume check, yes?"

Grace nodded. "I'll be there in an hour."

"Good."

Flo stood, pulling down the waist of his smoking jacket, and left the room, his shoulders thrust back, his posture perfect, his gait as elegant and relaxed as a lion's. Always the showman, always in control.

Grace sipped her tea alone in the opulent room, her heart crushed at the thought that someone would want to hurt Sophia, or that she would want to hurt herself. Which was it? Flo had said something about a police report. If only she could see it, maybe she could make sense of the unbelievable, senseless death of her only sister.

Her eyes scanned the room, and her gaze fell on Flo's large walnut desk strewn with papers. Could he have left the police report out? Or had he filed it away somewhere? A sinking feeling hit her stomach. Had there really been a police report, or did he just tell her he'd received one? Never, in all the years she'd known Flo, had she ever doubted his word, but now . . . .

She stood, teacup and saucer in hand, and meandered toward the desk, aware of the swish of her silken robe against her bare legs and the prickle shooting down her spine at her own audacity to snoop through Flo's things.

Pulling her robe tighter around her body, she walked over to the desk and set down the cup and saucer. She strained to hear if anyone was approaching. The only noise in the room came from the deep tonal ticking of the grandfather clock in the corner. Grace picked through some of the papers—bills, scripts, envelopes, drawings of sets, and scads of notes in Flo's erratic scrawl. Nothing that remotely resembled a police report.

The pungent, spicy odor of cigars drew her eyes to the crystal ashtray. It was filled with browned cigar butts adorned with teeth marks and squished completely lifeless. She slid open the drawer to her right, revealing neatly lined rows of files.

Files with girls names on the tabs.

Lots of files.

Grace sat in the chair and leaned over the drawer to read the names: *Billie Burke, Fanny Brice, Lillian Lorraine, Sophie Tucker, Felicity Jones,* and *Ann Pennington.* She fingered through more to one labeled *Liane Held Carrera.* She pulled out the folder and opened it up. Inside lay a photo of the voluptuous Anna Held, Flo's former common-law wife, in a shawl-collared wool coat and a jaunty cloche hat trimmed with a wide ribbon. She was holding the hand of a small child, who was dressed identically. The child looked to be about four years old. She must have been Anna's daughter with Maximo Carerra, wealthy play-boy, and her first husband. Grace flipped through the pages of the folder and saw something titled *Adoption.* She looked to the bottom of the last page and saw the printed names *Anna Held* and *Florenz Ziegfeld Jr.* with lines above for signatures. Anna had signed; Flo had not.

Grace set the folder in her lap, thinking. She'd never seen Liane before—not that she could remember, anyway. She straightened the papers and tucked the folder back into the drawer. She perused the other files and froze when her gaze landed on a folder labeled *Sophia Michelle.* The one behind it was labeled *Grace Michelle.*

Grace listened for any noise that might mean Harold or Flo would come in and catch her snooping. Satisfied at the silence, she pulled out Sophia's folder. She opened it to find a few publicity photos and some letters. Love letters. To Flo. Dozens of them.

Her stomach twisted as she skimmed over the words written in Sophia's hand. Grace swallowed as her mouth dried, leaving her tongue feeling thick and sticking to the roof of her mouth. Unable to read any more, she flipped past the letters until her eyes rested on a very official-looking document with the words *Metropolitan Life* scrolled across the top. She scanned the document and clamped her hand over her mouth, her stomach threatening to heave. Before her was a life insurance policy taken out on Sophia a year ago—in the amount of twenty thousand dollars.

CHAPTER SIX

*W*ith trembling fingers, Grace quickly opened the file folder with her name on it. It contained a photo of her and Sophia when they were young, probably when they first came to the theater; a doctor's bill and some correspondence with the doctor in regard to the time Grace had suffered from a cold; a picture of Sophia Grace had drawn for Flo some years ago; and some sketches of gowns she had made. She hadn't seen them in so long, she'd entirely forgotten about them. But there were no letters, no life insurance policy.

A loud knock at the door sent Grace's heart straight to her throat. She fumbled with the folders, jammed them back in the drawer, and then slammed the drawer shut with a loud bang. Jumping out of the chair, she grabbed for her teacup on the desk and accidentally knocked it to the ground. The porcelain cup landed on the Persian rug, the remnants of liquid seeping into the inky blackness of the bold pattern. She grabbed the saucer from the desk, scooped the cup off the floor and hurried over to the chair she'd previously occupied.

Someone knocked again. Louder.

"Harold?" Grace called out. "Flo?"

Setting the teacup and saucer down on the coffee table, she stood up. Was anyone going to answer the door?

More knocking. Urgent knocking.

With shaky legs, Grace made her way to the doorway and readjusted her robe. She opened the door. Lillian Lorraine, in a white fox stole stood staring at Grace, her red mouth slightly opened, her large brown eyes glittering with surprise.

"Miss . . . Lillian. . . ." Grace stammered.

"I see Flo is *entertaining*." Lillian's eyes raked over Grace, and her mouth took on a determined sneer.

"No, it's not like that." Grace pulled at the collar of her robe.

"Your sister's not dead two weeks, and here you are filling the void in that poor man's life. Good for you, dear."

Grace felt her face flush crimson. She couldn't look the woman in the eye, but she couldn't help staring at the tiny head of the dead fox wrapped around Lillian's neck, its beady black eyes boring into her. She couldn't speak; she couldn't gain the momentum to lash back at the absurdity of Lillian's comment.

"You don't understand," Grace finally choked out. "I was just here because Flo wanted to tell me. . . ."

"He's got plans for you?" Her red lips spread into a confident, eerie smile. "Don't doubt it, sweetie. You're in his clutches. We all are. Is he here?" Her eyes widened, and her lips pursed to a crimson heart, her face the epitome of innocence.

Graced grabbed the side of the door for support.

"I resent your insinuation, Miss Lorraine. There is nothing untoward going on here. Flo is like a father to me, and I a daughter to him."

She scoffed. "I've heard that one before."

Grace's fingers gripped the side of the door so hard they hurt.

Lillian folded her arms across her chest, forcing the fox's nose to burrow into her ample, partially exposed bosom. She sniffed. "Flo here?"

Grace swallowed down her rage and embarrassment. She wanted nothing more than to get out of the woman's presence.

"Yes, he's . . . he's getting dressed. Harold's helping him. I was just . . . I was just . . . going."

"Don't let me keep you." Lillian stepped a few inches away from the door and held her arm toward the hallway.

Clutching the robe tighter to her chest, Grace slipped through the small space between the woman and the slightly open doorway. Accidentally, Grace's shoulder slammed into Lillian's, knocking her backward a step.

"I'm—" Instinctively, Grace wanted to apologize. But the look of smug satisfaction on Lillian's face instead made Grace want to slap those bright red lips to a pulpy cherry mess.

THAT AFTERNOON, Grace busied herself repairing costumes. She pulled one of the pink, jeweled shifts from the hanger and inspected it for missing beads, torn seams, and bedraggled feather plumes.

The memory of her recent encounter with Lillian plucked at her nerves. As did the life insurance policy on Sophia she'd found. Did all theater companies take out life insurance on their employees? She wished she'd had more time to look through the other girls' folders. She couldn't think of whom to ask about it. It seemed like a rather personal question.

"Hello, gorgeous." Charles entered the room. "Why aren't you at dance class?"

"I'd rather be here."

"You know Flo gets apoplectic when you miss it."

"I have no plans to be an actress." She wrinkled her nose. "I don't like singing and dancing."

"Yes, I know. I'll take care of the headpieces while you finish with the dresses." He cocked his wrist under his chin. "So. . . ."

Grace pressed her lips together, knowing what would come next. Everyone must be talking about Sophia's death.

"How are you holding up?" He took a headpiece down from the shelf.

Grace shrugged.

Lucile entered the room, interrupting them. Fanny trailed a few feet behind her. Lucile, always elegant, always dressed in a suit of rich velvet or lustrous linen and adorned in pearls, sauntered into the room commanding the authority of a grand-dame. She was stern faced with an aquiline nose, square jaw, and thin lips, and only in the glimmer of her eyes could one see the complete warmth and benevolence this matronly woman possessed.

"Hallo, hallo, hallo!" sang Fanny. "Charles, you dream! How are ya, kid?" The bangles on Fanny's overly jeweled wrists clanked as she set her hands firmly on her hips.

"Just fine, Fanny. You?" Charles asked.

"Absooooolutely miserable. Hallo, Grace."

Grace smiled, thinking the whole atmosphere of a room changed for the better when Fanny entered. Dim lights glowed, dingy floors sparkled, heavy hearts were lifted, and the stage came alive.

"Love that dress you designed for me, kid," Fanny said, pointing a bright red fingernail at Grace. "It hides all those little lumps and bumps, you know what I mean?" She playfully jiggled her hips. "Lucile, you've got some talent on your hands with this one. And she's pretty too."

Grace looked at the floor, her cheeks blazing hot, unable to stifle a small, proud upturn of her lips.

"Yes, Grace has got quite a career in front of her," said Lucile. "But she's also got a lot of learning to do. Now, we've got to go fit those girls. If you'll excuse us, Fanny?"

"Don't mind me, kids. I'm just hanging around waiting for my check. This is the third time Flo's been late with my money.

Guess I'd better have a chat with him. Geez, I wish I had been born rich instead of beautiful."

Grace's throat went dry. No one talked about finances in the Follies, especially about Flo's state of affairs. The life insurance policy flashed into her mind again. Had Sophia's death been an incredible convenience?

Grace bit the inside of her cheek to keep from dwelling on such thoughts. Flo had been good to them, despite his inappropriate feelings for Sophia. But those thoughts aside, if Flo couldn't afford to keep Fanny Brice, then what would happen to her?

THE NEXT DAY Grace entered the theater, a featherlight chiffon gown she had made for Sophia in her arms and a lead weight in her chest. A new starlet had been found to audition for Sophia's role. It seemed a betrayal of sorts, to fit Sophia's gown to a new actress. Lucile had offered to do the fitting herself, but Grace needed to keep as busy as possible. Only the hours spent embellishing costumes brought her any peace these days.

Onstage, several girls worked with the choreographer learning new dance routines. Others sat around smoking cigarettes and talking, their voices echoing throughout the cavernous theater. Grace noticed a girl she had not seen before talking with the others. She wore only a slip and red high-heeled shoes.

Must be the girl auditioning.

When she saw Grace with the dress, she stubbed out her cigarette on the stage floor and sauntered over, her blond, bobbed head held high, a shroud of arrogance wrapping around her like an expensive cloak.

"I'm Helga. Is that my dress?" The girl's voice revealed a clipped, German accent, and her startling blue eyes raked over every inch of Grace.

"Um . . . yes." Grace held out the dress for Helga to step into. Once they secured it on Helga's shoulders, Grace ran her hands down the fabric, scrutinizing the hang of the silk against the girl's slight frame to see where the dress needed to be taken in.

"Really, this dress feels like a cotton sack," Helga complained.

Grace bristled but busied herself with a visual measurement of the dress's waist.

"And so big! I have a twenty-one-inch waistline, you realize."

Grace stepped back, coolly surveying the dress and the outspoken girl in it. The dress, only a smidgeon large in the waist and shoulders, looked fine. The girl, on the other hand, made her blood boil. Grace swallowed her anger and continued pinning. She knew Lucile and Flo would accept nothing less than a perfect fit. She pinned the loose fabric with deft, fast fingers.

"So this was your sister's dress, no?" Helga said, craning her neck to look at her backside in one of the mirrored columns on the stage.

Grace drew in a breath so deeply she nearly choked on it. "Yes."

"Tch, tch, tch. Such a pity. Such a waste of talent."

Grace's fingers froze. "A waste?"

"Hmm." Helga nodded, tossing her platinum, finger-curled bob.

"Just what are you implying?" Grace stabbed the padded pincushion at her wrist with the remaining pins.

"Oh, dear. Don't take offense. The paper said perhaps she was murdered, or she . . . I only meant that she was so young."

Grace fought an impulse to chastise the girl for her rudeness, but instead, she placed a couple of pins between her lips for easier access and continued with the fitting. The scandal of Sophia and Flo's affair stung enough; the thought that her sister had ended her own life because of it was too horrible to contemplate. And who could possibly have wanted Sophia dead?

A hush fell over the cast and crew as Lillian Lorraine, in her white fox fur and oversized, overly embellished hat, entered the theater through the gallery doors. Quickly, everyone went back to the business at hand.

"God, I am burning up. Hey!" Helga screamed at the light man. "Dim those damn lights!" Her voice echoed through the empty theater, and within moments, the bright glare diminished. "I don't know why we have to do this here. It's so much cooler backstage."

"Please hold still," Grace said. "We'll be finished in a minute. Flo wants to approve the costumes onstage. He has to see how they look under the lights."

Helga gave a theatrical sigh.

Please, Flo, don't hire this one.

Lillian Lorraine would be a welcome substitute compared to this girl. Maybe if Grace could somehow make the dress look awful? One of the pins slipped in her hands and stabbed Helga in the ribs.

"Ouch! Damn it!"

"I'm sorry," Grace lied.

"Do it again and I'll—"

"You'll what?" Grace asked through a mouthful of pins. "You need to show a little respect here, Helga." She removed the pins from her lips. "You can't even begin to fill the shoes of my sister. Furthermore, this dress was designed and made by a legend in the industry, and you have no business criticizing any part of it. Now, you be quiet and let me finish fitting this dress, or you won't be able to audition."

"Feisty." Helga placed her hands on her hips. "I sense I may have offended you. Please accept my apologies. Sometimes I appear a little too abrupt."

Appear?

Grace released the air in her lungs and managed a tight smile. A lump rose in her throat, and she tried to swallow it away as she placed a few pins between her lips again. Maybe she should have let Lucile take this one after all.

Lillian had made her way down the aisle, walked past the orchestra pit, and came up the stage stairs. She approached Grace and Helga.

"Who are you?" she asked the young German woman.

"I am Helga," the girl said raising her chin.

"This part should be mine." Lillian secured her hands on her hips and thrust out a small-heeled, Mary Jane-clad foot.

To Grace's relief, Lucile appeared from the wings of the stage. "What are you doing here, Lillian? I thought you were in California."

"I got bored. This part—this role—should be mine. Flo had the show written for me in the first place . . . Until that silly, no-talent vamp bewitched him. But she's not around anymore, is she?"

"Hey!" Grace stepped toward her.

Lucile reached out, grabbed Grace's arm, and pulled her back.

"Oh, nice to see you dressed," Lillian said to Grace, eyeing her from head to toe, her voice sticky sweet.

Flames of embarrassment and anger licked the sides of Grace's neck and face.

"I thought you were working for the Shuberts," Lucile said.

Lillian shrugged her shoulders and pushed out her lower lip in a pout. "I am, but this show was written for me."

"Well, things have changed, Lillian. If you want, you can go talk to Flo, but leave us out of it. We're just doing our jobs here; we don't want any trouble. Now, go on. Leave us to our work."

"Very well." Lillian let out a dramatic sigh and crossed her arms over her chest. "But you haven't seen the last of me, Lady Duff Gordon. I can assure you of that." With a parting sneer at

Grace, Lillian strutted off the stage, down the stairs, and out the side door of the theater.

Grace stood with fists clenched, watching her go, even more convinced that Lillian was reveling in the fact that Sophia had died.

"Are these diamonds?" Helga asked, looking down at the bodice of the dress.

"They're rhinestones," Lucile said, her eyes on the gown, inspecting the fit. "We had to cut back." A wave of sadness passed over her dignified face.

"Cut back? Is money a problem around here? I don't work for free," Helga said.

"You won't work at all with that attitude, young lady." Lucile's brows shot up. "Mind your tongue, and your business. Flo supports many people, and he hasn't failed any of us yet."

"Duly chastised by the great Lady Duff Gordon." The girl sighed. "So, what was it like? The *Titanic*?"

Grace's stomach twisted. An immediate glance at Lucile justified Grace's discomfort. The woman's face clouded over in annoyance. "Stunning," Lucile said through tight lips.

"Such a pity it sank." Helga sighed again and turned her backside to the mirror again.

"Yes." Lucile abruptly turned and walked across the stage.

"What are you doing?" Grace whispered. "Believe me, you don't want to annoy Lucile. It won't be good for your audition."

"What did I say? Did I offend again?"

"You didn't hear the stories?"

"Yes, yes, of course. But she and her baronet husband were exonerated, no? They did not bribe the young man to get them off the ship. I probably would have. Every man, or woman, for themselves, no?"

"You are beyond words, Helga."

Laughter from some of the girls at the opposite end of the stage drew Grace's attention. Fanny, up to her usual antics, was walking around in circles, mimicking an ape. The choreographer desperately tried to regain control of his chorus line, but the girls paid him no mind. He threw his hands in the air and then lit a cigarette in surrender.

Their laughter stopped as a tall, slender man with broad shoulders entered through the theater doors and walked down the aisle. When Grace noticed him, the remaining pins dropped from her mouth to the floor.

"Well, hel-lo, handsome," Fanny said.

The man's face opened into a devastating smile. He removed his fedora and held it between his hands.

"Hello, Fanny," he said, his voice deep and melodious. "It's been ages."

He smoothed his shiny black hair into place. Light gray eyes contrasted with the darkness of his hair, giving Grace no other option but to gape, her previous troubles forgotten.

"Ages, yes. But you don't look a day different. Gorgeous as ever." She circled around him and wolf-whistled. "Goodness, I love the way you wear a suit."

Clearly hoping to capture his attention, the girls donned their most impressive stage smiles. Helga stood a little straighter, her complaining and insulting questions squelched by the presence of this mysterious guest.

Lucile walked back to oversee Helga and the dress. She nudged Grace and gave her a frown. "Back to work."

Grace resumed the fitting but continued to peek and eavesdrop, unable to resist his intriguing face and lyrical voice.

"What are you doing here? Come to see me?" Fanny asked him.

"I need to see Flo."

"Oh." Fanny's mouth turned down into a pout. Then she grinned flirtatiously. "What kind of nefarious wretch are you looking for this time?"

He gave a chuckle. "You never change, Fanny."

"Not on your life. I don't know where Flo is. I'm waiting on him myself."

"All right. I'll come back in a few hours."

Grace peered at him through downturned eyelashes to see him give Fanny a peck on the cheek. When he stepped back and his eyes moved toward the stage and locked with hers, her heart slammed against her ribs, and a flush of heat washed over her. Quickly, she refocused on her task. When she looked up again, he was gone.

The choreographer, finally able to gather the girls' attention, clapped his hands and signaled them back to their positions. He started counting loudly, encouraging them to start, and in seconds, the musical sound of tap dancing filled the theater.

"Wow," said Helga. "Who was that delicious man?"

"That was Chet Riker," said Lucile. "He works for Flo on occasion."

"Is he one of Flo's gangster friends?" A mischievous twinkle sparked in Helga's eyes.

"Not exactly," said Lucile. "Former military police. Sent home from the war after surviving a mustard gas attack. Now he's a private investigator."

Grace concentrated on the dress again. A private investigator. Did his visit have something to do with Sophia's death? She shook her head. She didn't want to think about Sophia and what might have happened to her. She didn't want to think about the insults Helga and Lillian had just hurled at her. She didn't want to think about Flo's files. She wanted to work, to lose herself in something outside her terrifying thoughts.

The image of Chet Riker's squared jaw and pale gray eyes also unsettled her. She'd been around a fair number of men in the theater, many of them handsome and charming, but none of them had knocked the wind out of her by merely walking into the room.

Uncomfortable with the shaky feeling in her stomach, she

tried to dismiss him from her thoughts. After all, if he had worked for Flo, he'd probably been entertained by some of these beautiful girls. In fact, she could almost be sure of it. Chet Riker didn't look like the kind of man to notice the little costume girl who worked in the background. But then again, maybe he had.

CHAPTER SEVEN

*C*het paced outside the closed door to Flo's office. Goldie had said that "under no circumstances" could Chet interrupt him. Chet glanced at his watch and then again at Goldie, who was busying herself at the noisy typewriter. He watched as her fingers punched away on the round disks at the speed of a runaway train.

"Goldie, why the cold reception? C'mon. Let me see Flo." Chet flashed a smile, trying to soften her with his charm.

She stopped typing and looked up at him over her rhinestone-studded spectacles. "He's very busy, Chet."

"Then you talk to me. Tell me what you've been up to? How many gents are trying to woo you away from me?"

Goldie's stern face broke into a smile. "You get me every time, Mr. Riker. I'm sorry to be rude. It's just with Miss Michelle's . . . death and Flo trying to replace her—"

"You mean, there is a shortage of beautiful women around here? That can't be possible."

Goldie took off her spectacles and dangled them from her hand, her elbow resting on the desk. "Well, it has to be the *right* girl. You know Flo. He has a vision for what he wants, and he won't stop until he finds it."

"Do you mind if I wait for him? It's rather important."

"Suit yourself."

Chet continued pacing and could feel Goldie's eyes on him.

"Are you all right, Chet? Would you like a seat?"

"No. I'm fine standing."

"A drink?"

"No."

"Well, you're wearing down Mr. Ziegfeld's very expensive rug. Are you sure you're all right?"

"Yes."

"Working a case?"

Chet sighed. "Business is slow."

"Oh dear. What about this situation with Miss Michelle?"

"I'm not sure there's anything to investigate. From what I've read, no one is certain who, if anyone, is responsible. Besides, she died in California. They'll be investigating it there."

Goldie shrugged her shoulders, her eyes never leaving Chet as he walked back and forth across the "very expensive rug." He couldn't relax after the meeting with Marciano. He suspected that Goldie's motherly instincts clued her in to his anxiety. He snuck a glance at her and saw the concern in her eyes.

"You must see a lot of heartbreak in your line of work, Chet."

"Yes. Sometimes."

"Why do you do it?"

"Sometimes I wonder, but I'm good at it. People need help." Chet shrugged. "I made a promise."

"To whom?"

"John Steinbrenner." Chet started to pace again. "He was a PI, gave me my first job. I was thirteen, had left the orphanage, and was on my own. He let me sweep the floors in his office."

"From sweeping the floors to the military, to private investigator. Sounds like a story to me."

"I watched that man like a hawk." Chet stopped pacing and let out a chuckle. "When I was a bit older, he'd take me on stake-outs; he started grooming me to become an investigator. I worked for him until he died. He was murdered . . . died in my arms. Made me promise I would take over the agency. Then the war came, and I had to leave. Now I'm back, but I'm having a bit of trouble getting things going again."

"Who murdered him?"

"A man who'd embezzled thousands from John's family's business. John found the proof, and the guy murdered him."

"Is he in jail?"

He nodded. "I made sure of that."

"Bully for you." Goldie's sage green eyes crinkled in the corners.

Flo's office door opened, interrupting their conversation. Chet's jaw dropped when a vision of loveliness made her way through the doorway. He'd seen her before—in the theater just this morning, in fact—hidden behind the brassy-haired, European vixen. A slim wisp of a girl with delicate features and creamy pink skin, like the color of the inside of a seashell. With her thick, golden hair piled high on her head, she looked like one of the fashion dolls he'd seen in windows of FAO Schwartz. Her green eyes opened wide with astonishment to see him standing there, and in them, he saw the wisdom of a much older woman.

"Darling." Goldie rose from her typewriter and approached the girl. "Do you need anything?"

The young woman's emerald gaze shifted from him to Goldie. "No, thank you." Her voice, too, sounded mature, deep with a silky resonance.

When her eyes flitted back to him, her lips twitched upward in a shy smile.

Flo came through the door, breaking the spell. "Chet, hello. Sorry I'm running late. We've had a loss here at the theater."

Flo rested his hand on the girl's shoulder. Her gaze dropped to the floor, and she bit her perfectly plump lower lip.

"You can go, dear," Flo said, giving her shoulder a squeeze. "We'll talk later."

"Flo." Chet stepped forward. "You haven't introduced us." His skin prickled under his suit. The girl smiled again, smoothing the tension from his shoulders.

Flo's eyes shifted from him to the young woman, then back to him. "Oh." Flo rubbed his forehead impatiently. "This is Grace Michelle. She assists Lucile in costume design. Grace, this is Chet Riker."

Chet extended his hand, and she took it.

Grace Michelle. Any relation to the dead girl?

"How do you do, Mr. Riker," she said, blinking up at him.

Their gazes held for a few moments, and suddenly, the temperature in the room rose, making him want to pull his collar away from his neck. He usually had no trouble talking to women, pursuing women, even getting women, but now the air in his lungs seemed to freeze, rendering him speechless.

"A pleasure," he choked out. Although embarrassed, he couldn't release her hand.

Flo stepped forward, inserting himself between the two of them. "Sweetheart, go get some rest." He ushered her toward the door.

"I've had more rest than I need, Flo. I'm going to see if Lucile has more work for me. I need to use my hands."

"Whatever you want, dear." Flo pressed his lips to her forehead.

She glanced sideways at Chet through long, featherlike lashes, and then left the reception area.

Chet followed Flo into his office. "Where've you been hiding her? She's lovely."

"Forget it. The girl's like a daughter to me, and she's too young for you."

Chet raised his eyebrows. "How old is she?"

"Twenty."

"Is she related to . . . ?"

"Her sister. You leave her alone. She doesn't need to fall in love with the likes of you."

"You're right, but I never said anything about love. I just want to know more about the girl, Flo."

"You just forget about her and let's get down to business, shall we? I have rehearsal in fifteen minutes."

Chet conceded and sat in a pointy backed, Gothic-style chair opposite Flo's desk. Flo reached into one of his drawers and pulled out a cigar box. "Cuban?"

"No, thanks."

"What can I do for you?"

"I need a case. I'm tapped out."

"Well, my man—" Flo leaned back in his chair and put his feet on the desk "—it just so happens that I need some publicity. I've just lost my biggest star, and I don't have anyone else worth headlining right now. We need to focus public attention on something else, get this mess out of the limelight."

"Do you know what happened? You know, to the girl?"

"I can't talk about it." Flo's eyes shifted from Chet's face to the desktop.

"What about 'La-La' Lorraine? Can't she headline?"

"We're not on speaking terms at the moment."

"I see."

"I have an idea," Flo said. "You tell me if we can pull it off."

"Shoot."

"Billie is going to California to do a film. I don't want her to go, but hell, I can't stop these damn motion pictures, and quite frankly, we need the money. But I need to stay afloat. *The Follies* need to stay afloat." Flo paused, wiping a flake of tobacco off his lip and flicking it in the air. "Billie is traveling by train. I just bought her a private car and spent thousands decorating it. What if, on the way to California, there was a theft? A big one. Jewelry. She's got boxes full of it. Practically priceless stuff, and she hauls it around like it's paste."

Chet's stomach turned. He needed a job, not a scam. He'd been hoping for a domestic case of some kind—affair, embezzlement, something that may have been marginally smarmy, but at least legitimate.

"You want me to steal from your wife?"

"You're not stealing from her. I am. And as she's still my legal wife, the jewels are also my property. Plus, if I benefit financially, she benefits. Billie Burke and the Follies would be splashed all over the papers. Publicity keeps us alive in this business, good and bad."

"I don't know, Flo."

"I'll split half of what it's worth with you. I have a man who will buy the jewelry back for almost retail."

Chet sighed. He needed the money. He also knew some gents in the Bronx who owed him a favor. He'd buy them a train ticket. That way he'd have nothing to do with the robbery. Well, almost nothing.

"When does she leave?" Chet asked.

"Two weeks."

His stomach tightened again. He needed something sooner, but he had no choice. *Damn.*

"Fine," he said, giving in. "I'll arrange everything."

GRACE HELD OUT HER ARMS, bent at the elbows, palms up like a table as Charles laid each shimmery pink garment across them, one at a time. Her mind was still awhirl with her confrontation with Helga, and her last conversation with Flo about his getting "a return on his investment." He'd made it clear that she'd be indebted to him—indefinitely—but how? Working for him in what capacity? And then there was that man, Mr. Riker, she'd met outside Flo's office door. He was even more dashing up close. She couldn't seem to find any sort of emotional rest lately.

"Are you sure you can carry these all the way up to the office?" Charles's perfectly groomed eyebrows pressed down toward his nose. "I would do it, but Lucile is after me to tape the soles of all the girls' shoes. Don't want anyone to 'break a leg,'" he said with a snicker.

"Funny. I think I can manage. How many are there?"

"Twelve."

The costumes, made of chiffon, should be light as a feather, but voluminous beads and sequins weighted them down.

"Charles, you've known a lot of theater people in New York for a long time."

"Are you referring to my age, my dear?"

"No. I'm just wondering, did many people know of Sophia's affair with Flo?"

"I don't think so. It was certainly news to me. Why?"

"That *Variety* article . . . mentioning foul play."

Charles took hold of her hands, relieving the weight of the garments. "The papers sensationalize everything."

"But Billie knew?"

Charles let go of her hands and placed his in his pockets, rattling spare change and his keys. "Billie and Flo have an . . . understanding. She knows that Flo loves her above all others, but that he gets . . . distracted. Billie wouldn't hurt a fly."

"What about Lillian?"

"She and Flo have been off-and-on for years. She might have known about the affair."

"She's quite chilly with me. I overheard her talking about Sophia at the memorial—and not in the best of terms."

"You know these girls all have their cat fights. Sophia was no angel, let's not forget that."

Pain stabbed at Grace's heart. It hurt hearing those words

from Charles, even though she knew they were true. She'd never known him to say anything negative about Sophia.

"Everyone vies for Flo's attention."

"But do you think Lillian would be capable of . . . you know?"

"Grace, darling." Charles placed reassuring hands on her shoulders. "You must stop these questions. You'll drive yourself mad. If there was foul play, the police will take care of it. But honestly, I think you're just overwrought."

"Possibly . . . I'll get these costumes upstairs."

"Be careful with the beading."

"Charles, I'm the one who stitched every bead and sequin in place. Do you think I want to do it again?"

"Are you quite all right, dear?"

"I'm fine."

Grace pulled the garments closer to her body to relieve the ache in her arms. Her thoughts turned back to Flo and the weight of obligation she now felt crushing her—the same weight Sophia must have felt every day.

She maneuvered her way through the small doorway of the costume room and headed down the narrow hallway.

What would happen if *she* wanted to marry someday? Would Flo object to her marriage as he had Sophia's? Perhaps if Sophia had chosen someone other than Jack Pickford, a known philanderer, gambler, and general ne'er-do-well, Flo wouldn't have cared.

Doubtful.

How could she not have seen the depth of Sophia and Flo's relationship? Probably because she'd never had a romantic affiliation herself. Yes, there had been flirtations with boys who'd come and gone in the theater, and once, she'd shared a kiss with Stevie, the newspaper boy, but she'd never experienced a serious romance, the kind of relationship—Sophia's tortured face passed through her thoughts—that could break one's heart.

Suddenly winded, Grace stopped and leaned back against the wall. She shifted the garments more to her right arm, the stronger one, and stood for a moment, catching her breath.

A relationship with a man would be wonderful. Although, most of the women she knew had been made unhappy by their men, including her mother. She couldn't remember much about her father, only that he sometimes put her to bed at night and sometimes kissed her forehead.

That's all she'd remembered of a father figure until Flo had stepped into the role. She often wondered why Anna Held had agreed to Flo taking in two girls from the streets. Her own daughter, Liane, lived in Europe with her father, and perhaps Sophia and Grace had filled her need to mother someone. After Flo and Anna had split, Billie came on the scene, but by that time, Grace and Sophia had become permanent fixtures in Flo's world. Billie had tolerated them but soon moved to Los Angeles.

Grace took a breath and pushed herself off the wall with her backside. She made her way down the aisle to the back of the theater, toward the hidden staircase leading to the business offices. When she got to the door, she juggled the garments to free a hand. As she reached for the knob, the door swung open, knocking her off-balance. She fell to the floor with a thud, the garments landing on top of her. She looked up to see the perpetrator of the accident, and her heart skidded to a stop in her chest.

"I'm so sorry. Are you all right?" Chet Riker leaned down to give her a hand.

Grace stared, unable to move or speak, her heart pounding.

"Sorry, but I can barely see you. You're buried." He pulled a garment off her head, and a smile melted across his face. She could swear his eyes twinkled.

Her stomach was in knots at her embarrassing predicament and her body shaky from falling to the floor. Grace wrenched a hand free to smooth her bun. It felt as if whole sections of hair had come loose.

"Let me help you. Grace, is it?" Chet held out his hand for her.

"Yes." She took his warm, strong hand and allowed him to help her to her feet. She reluctantly pulled away. Straightening her skirt, she felt the pull of her corset hooks caught on the waistband. With a tight yank, she put it back in place, hoping he hadn't noticed. She picked up her feet one at a time, trying to gently free them from the tangled web of costumes at her ankles. She must look a clumsy sight.

"Thank you," she said, unable to divert her eyes from his persistent, smoky gaze. His light gray-blue eyes, rimmed with coal-black lashes, made her think of a storm—a storm that promised to devour her. She cast her eyes toward the costumes at her feet.

"Here." He scooped up the garments, one by one, his suit stretching taut across his broad shoulders and long arms. "Where are we taking these?"

"Up there." Grace pointed in the direction of the staircase to the offices. She followed him up the stairs, and when he abruptly stopped, pausing for her to open the door, she faltered, almost running into him. She tried to scoot past him but accidentally brushed up against him on the small landing, inhaling the scent of something like warm cinnamon.

Grace turned the knob and ushered him into the empty reception area. *Goldie must be gone for the day,* she thought. Flo was probably in the dance studio, drilling the girls.

"Over there." Grace pointed to the sofa. "Someone will come to pick them up for cleaning," she said, the explanation completely unnecessary.

After Chet deposited the clothes on the sofa, he smiled as if satisfied with the fine job he'd accomplished. "Anything else?"

"No, thank you." She led him back downstairs, her heart pounding in time to his footsteps behind her. When they reached the bottom of the stairs, she turned to him. "Thank you, Mr.—"

"Please call me Chet. And it was my pleasure . . . to see you again." His eyes roamed her face and Grace's cheeks burned under his gaze.

"Do you visit Flo often?" she asked in an attempt to regain her composure. "I've not seen you here before. Well, that is, until . . . you know, earlier, in the theater . . . with Miss Brice."

"It's been a while. I worked for him a few years ago. Um, listen . . . I am sorry for your loss."

Grace's stomach twisted. "Yes. Thank you."

"It must be a difficult time for you."

"Yes. Quite. So, I heard that you're a private investigator."

His smile deepened, revealing charming dimples that softened his square features. "How'd you know?"

"I overheard some of the others . . . um, Lucile said it, I think."

"Ah. I see."

His concentrated scrutiny of her made her want to lower her eyes, but somehow, she couldn't. She struggled with the desire to leave, to rid herself of the itchy anxiety his gaze produced and the paradoxical longing to make the moment last forever.

"How long have you known Miss Brice?" she asked.

"About three years. I've known her husband, Nicky, for a long time. I've done some work for him."

"Business with Nicky Arnstein can land you in jail."

Chet's mouth twitched. "Behind that pretty face you have quite a mind, Grace. Are you always so direct?"

Oh, God. Blood surged to her face.

"I'm sorry, I—" *How stupid and presumptuous of her.* "I need to get back to work."

"I understand. Sorry to have detained you so long."

Unable to resist, she looked up at him again for an awkward moment and then turned to leave.

"Grace?" He reached out and stopped her with his fingers on her sleeve. Her stomach flipped. "I hope to see you again."

"Yes. I'm sure you will . . . if you happen to be around."

She could feel his eyes on her back as she walked down the aisle. Finally, she reached the side door next to the stage, opened it, walked through, and then closed it behind her. She leaned against the smooth wood and exhaled, her shoulders sinking down. She hadn't realized she'd been holding her breath. And what had come out of her mouth? What a fool. She'd practically accused him of the crimes that had landed Arnstein in Sing Sing. She shook her hands, as if doing so could stop them from trembling.

What did it matter anyway? Chet couldn't possibly be interested in her. He probably had his pick of women. How could such a handsome man not have, especially working with Flo and Nicky, both of whom always surrounded themselves with beautiful, sophisticated starlets? Not a backstage costume girl. *Well, no matter,* she told herself, straightening her shoulders. She'd just avoid engaging in conversation with Chet alone . . . ever again.

CHAPTER EIGHT

*G*race headed back to the costume room in search of work to keep her hands and mind busy. "What can I do to help?" she asked Lucile.

"Fanny should be here any second. Her dress needs some alterations. She's lost weight again. But don't cut the fabric; she'll gain it back as soon as Nicky's out of prison."

Grace nodded and pressed her hands together, still shaking from the encounter with Chet Riker.

The familiar whine of Fanny's voice boomed down the hall and echoed throughout the room. "Girls, girls, girls! So many girls." Fanny, wearing a felt cap with a giant peach rose anchored to the side of it and a luxurious sable fur, pushed her way through the throng of dancers being fitted for their costumes. "There must have been a sale on legs at Macy's I didn't hear about. You all look fabulous." A twitter of giggles filled the room.

"Where's my dress?" She glanced at Grace with big eyes and raised eyebrows.

Grace marched over to the clothes rack, plucked the hanger from the rod, and held the garment up for Fanny to see.

"Ah yes. A treasure to behold. C'mon, kid, let's go to my private dressing room. These girls and their gams are too much for my eyes. So much beauty can blind a person."

The sound of the girls' laughter followed them out of the room.

An endless hallway, a flight of stairs, and another long corridor led them to Fanny's dressing room. Although often the life of the party, Fanny made it known that she treasured her privacy.

"Home sweet home. Close the door behind ya, kid."

Grace complied. Fanny slinked out of her fur coat and threw it on the love seat next to the door.

Nancy, Fanny's maid, stood beside the sofa, her hands folded quietly at her waist. Bone-thin with skin the color of mocha, Nancy wore her usual, meticulously pressed navy-blue uniform with white, starched apron and collar.

"Nancy, you are an angel in the midst."

"Hello, Miss Brice. I made your tea." Nancy turned her attention to Grace. "Would you like a cup, Miss?"

"That would be lovely, Nancy. Thank you."

Nancy poured tea from Fanny's opulent, sterling tea service into delicate, floral porcelain cups. Fanny placed a cigarette in a diamond-studded holder and held it aloft for Nancy to light, then inhaled the smoke, making the tip of the cigarette glow bright red. She held the smoke in her lungs for several seconds and then exhaled with a flourish, ever the entertainer.

"I just need a sec, kid," Fanny said to Grace. "I had one hell of a morning."

Fanny ripped the hat from her perfectly coiffed waves, plopped down on the sofa, leaned her head back, and closed her eyes. The hat fell to the floor, but Fanny didn't bother to retrieve it. Grace watched Fanny instantly shut out the rest of the world.

Unsure of what to do, or how long she would have to wait, Grace settled onto a wooden chair next to the vanity, sipped her tea, and scanned the room. Framed and unframed photographs, along with several show posters she recognized from the theater offices and backstage rooms, filled virtually every inch of wall space. Grace's gaze settled on a show poster she had never seen before. It depicted a beautiful black woman in a voluminous red dress, caught tightly in the embrace of a handsome, mustachioed gentleman. The title read, *The Ziegfeld Frolics, starring Felicity Jones.*

Grace could not stop looking at the enchanting woman on the poster. There was something so unusual about her face, the bright azure eyes. Grace had never seen a colored woman with blue eyes. Could the image have been accurate, or had the artist embellished?

"How you doin', kid?" Fanny asked, raising her head and opening her eyes, back from her mental hiatus. "I mean, with Sophia and all. How are you holding up?"

Grace shrugged. She had been trying so hard to focus on work and not think about Sophia. And she didn't want to go around crying, particularly in front of Fanny Brice, who'd been nothing but kind to her and who had her own problems.

"I'm sorry things ended on such a sour note between you two. Did you get to speak to her before she left for California?"

Grace shook her head. "I should have said goodbye." She raised the shaking teacup to her lips.

"Ah. Don't beat yourself up, kid."

"Fanny," Grace said, hesitating to sip her tea, "how well did you know Jack?"

"Not well at all. Just know what I've heard."

"What have you heard?"

She shook her head. "Nothin'. I shouldn't have said that."

"Fanny?"

The woman reached over to grab the small ashtray on the arm of the sofa. She put it in her lap and flicked the ash off her cigarette.

"This isn't gospel now, just a rumor, but I heard he had some trouble with the law—selling cocaine." She took a drag on her cigarette holder, her eyes avoiding Grace's.

"Gosh, how awful. I mean, that he sold drugs. Do you think Sophia partook . . . ?" A vision of Sophia's diminutive frame popped into Grace's mind. The frame that seemed to be shrinking by the day before she'd left for California. The look on Fanny's face answered Grace's question. Her own naiveté infuriated her. How could she have been so blind?

"Do you think Jack would ever *intentionally* hurt her?" Grace's voice came out in a whisper, the thought of it pressing down on her lungs like an anvil.

"Oh, honey. Sophia was a big girl. She made her own decisions. I may not have known Jack well, but I do know he loved her. You could see it in his face. I don't believe he would have hurt her." Fanny leaned her head back against the sofa and closed her eyes again, once more shutting out the world.

Grace's mind was reeling from this new information, and she went back to scanning the room, looking for a distraction. Her gaze moved across the walls from photograph to photograph. Almost every one of them contained the dashing figure of Nicky Arnstein.

Grace stood, balancing her teacup in her hands, and approached one of them. She peered closer, studying Nicky's face, wondering what fascination it held for Fanny. A heavy, dark brow balanced his chiseled jaw and encased dark, almost black, eyes. Grace pulled back and let her gaze fall on other photos: Nicky on his polo horse, Nicky leaning against a Model T Ford, Nicky waving bon voyage from an ocean liner, Nicky steering a speedboat, and in many of them, Nicky staring into the eyes of his beloved Fanny.

One photo in particular caught Grace's attention. It depicted a foursome sitting in a Rolls-Royce, smiling enthusiastically at the camera. Fanny and Nicky were in the front seat of the Rolls

Royce, and in the back was someone familiar. Grace leaned forward to get a better look. Gasping, she almost spilled her tea. Chet Riker, in a crisp, light-colored suit and devilish fedora, stared back at her. A lovely girl sat next to him, leaning intimately close.

Who was she? Had he loved her? Did he still love her? Were they married? The questions rattled around in her brain. She looked over at Fanny, who took another drag on her cigarette holder, eyes still closed.

Nancy broke the silence. "Is there anything else, Miss Brice?"

"No, dear, you can go."

The maid gave Grace a shy wave, retrieved her coat and hat from a stand in the corner, and left the room.

"All right." Fanny stood up wearily. "Let's get this beauty on." She turned her back to Grace, indicating that she wanted assistance unbuttoning the hooks on her dress. Grace helped her undress and slip into the new gown.

Fanny then stepped atop a footstool, and Grace set to work, plucking pins out of the pincushion fastened to her wrist and placing them into the pinched seams and hem of the dress. Despite her sad feelings over Sophia, she had to admit it was gratifying to see the first dress she had ever designed worn by Fanny Brice. Black, sequined, and elegant, the dress made Fanny look even taller than her five feet eight inches. The back of the dress cut low, hitting almost at the waistline, and the top fastened at the neck with a single button. Two slits came up from the floor-length hem to mid-thigh.

"You've lost some weight," Grace said, pinching the fabric together with her fingers.

"I smoke too much, worry too much." Fanny eyed herself in the mirror. "It shows in my face, also."

"You have a lovely face."

"And you, sweetheart, are a lovely liar."

They both laughed. Grace wanted to ask her about Chet but didn't know how to bring him up.

"Don't ever fall in love, kid," Fanny said as if reading Grace's thoughts. Still admiring herself in the mirror, Fanny tilted her head one way and then the other. It seemed as though she was trying to reconcile something to herself through the image of her body. "How'd you like the pictures? I saw you looking at them."

"There are so many."

"I know every inch of those photos." Fanny sighed and turned away from the mirror, absently pulling the hemline away from Grace's working fingers, which might have been irritating if Grace hadn't wanted the conversation to continue. She decided to come back to the hem later and focused on the waist of the dress.

"The one over there." Grace pointed. "Is that Mr. Riker?"

"Yes, I was wondering if you would ask. I saw the way you looked at him in the theater."

Blood rushed to Grace's face, and she bent her head closer to the garment to hide her embarrassment.

"Oh, honey. You weren't the only one. He's quite a dasher, Chet."

"Mr. Riker told me he and your husband had worked together." Grace wondered again if it was the type of work that had put Nicky Arnstein in Federal prison.

When she received no reply, Grace glanced up at Fanny in time to see a distant pain flit across her face. Grace knew in an instant that she'd brought up a tender subject. She knelt down and busied herself with the hem again.

"Chet was an apprentice to a private detective who owned a small agency," Fanny explained. "The guy treated him like a son. When the PI was killed, Chet took over the business. But he was young, and green . . . like you." Her eyes twinkled as she looked down at Grace. "Nicky hired him to dig up some information on a potential business partner. In the meantime, Nicky got himself in trouble and was sent to prison, leaving Chet out of work. Chet joined the army soon after, and it was probably the best decision he could have made. A young man shouldn't get mixed up with the likes of Nicky."

Grace's fingers froze. She was surprised that Fanny would speak of her beloved so. She allowed her gaze to trail up the dress and rest on Fanny's face, where a mysterious smile lingered.

"Hey, my Nicky is a wonderful man, but he's got some bad habits and he keeps company with the wrong kind. Chet wanted to be just like him." Fanny's voice caught, as if she was going to say something else and then decided not to. She cleared her throat and placed her hands on her hips, skewing the hemline. Grace had to stop again. "You like him, don't you?"

Grace accidentally stabbed herself with one of the pins, flinched, and brought the injured finger to her mouth. "Well, I don't really know him. I was just curious."

"Hmm. I see."

Grace stood back and surveyed the nipping and tucking she'd accomplished with the pins. "I think you're finished," she said, silently chastising herself. What did she care of Chet's activities, criminal or not? It really had nothing to do with her. And she had no right to ask Fanny anything that might upset her. Flo wouldn't be happy if Fanny started to complain about a fresh seamstress who'd only recently been promoted to junior designer.

"I feel like a pincushion." Fanny's smoke-riddled voice distracted Grace from her thoughts. "Get this thing off me, will ya, kid?"

Grace unhooked and unbuttoned the gown and then held the garment while Fanny slipped out of it.

Fanny wrapped herself in a satin dressing gown and walked over to the lavish vanity filled with rouge, lipsticks, and powders, and a massive collection of fancy perfume bottles. She sat down and fiddled with the shiny earrings hanging from her earlobes.

Grace gathered her sewing items into a pile, still thinking about Sophia and Jack, and Chet and his relationship with Nicky. Fanny's narrow-set, dark eyes were trained directly on Grace.

"Listen, kid," Fanny said. "You're a real beauty, but you've got brains and talent, too. Take it from a broad that's been around the block a few times: don't throw it all away on a handsome face. It ain't worth it."

Grace felt another flush of heat in her cheeks. Had she been so obvious about her attraction to Chet? She'd have to be far more careful. In fact, she had to stop thinking about him altogether.

Grace laid a hand on Fanny's shoulder. "Don't worry, Miss Brice, Chet Riker is way out of my reach."

CHAPTER NINE

MAY 20, 1920 - NEW YORK CITY, NY
Flo slammed the latest copy of *Variety* down on his desk so hard it made Chet flinch. Chet picked up the discarded paper as Flo paced back and forth behind the desk, the cigarette never leaving his mouth, his hands crammed into his pockets. He was like a moving stick of burning dynamite ready to blow.

Chet looked down at the paper and read:

TRAIN ROBBERY THWARTED, SUSPECTS STILL AT LARGE
Billie Burke, famed actress and wife of Broadway impresario Florenz Ziegfeld Jr. creator of the Ziegfeld Follies, was the target of an attempted robbery aboard the Atchison, Topeka, and Santa Fe Railway. On her way to California to star in a motion picture, Miss Burke was awakened in the night when two men attempted to break into her private railcar. Conductor Stan Bartholomew intercepted the would-be burglars and chased them through the train until the two men escaped by leaping off the moving train.

*By the time the engineer was alerted and the train stopped, the
men had vanished . . .*

CHET RAISED his eyes from the article to see Flo glaring at him,
cigarette still clenched in teeth, hands on hips. "What the hell,
Chet? How'd this get botched?"

"I don't know what to say." Chet's mind swirled with questions as to what could possibly have gone wrong.

"I have zero funds to start a new show. I *need* a show." Flo
pinched his cigarette between thumb and forefinger, and yanked
it from his lips, not even bothering to expel the swirling cloud of
smoke hovering around his mouth and flaring nostrils. "This new
girl, Helga, isn't working out. People don't like her. She's too
cold, too . . . German. They want Sophia. I need a new show and
I need a new *Sophia*, and that takes money." Flo bent over the
desk, braced himself with his arms, and peered hard into Chet's
eyes. "For heaven's sake, tell me what happened! How the hell
could you screw up such a simple heist?"

Chet shifted in the chair. "Look, Flo, I didn't feel comfortable doing the heist. I am *trying* to make it as a private investigator, not a thief. A couple of guys owed me a favor, so I put them
on it. This is all news to me. I gave them explicit instructions,
thought they could follow them—"

Flo leaned over the desk and stuck a finger in Chet's face.
"You're fired! I can't afford mistakes like this."

"It made the paper," Chet said, grasping at a bright spot in
the debacle.

"For one day, in a small clip on page seven that few will
read. I needed a story with legs, with heat, one that would stick
around for a while. Damn it, Chet, the whole idea was to keep
the Follies at the front of everyone's mind." Flo mashed his
cigarette out in a filigreed sterling silver ashtray on his desk. His
eyes settled on Chet's.

Chet knew if he looked away first, he would be admitting failure. But he couldn't help secretly feeling relieved that the boneheads had botched the heist. The idea had been foolhardy from the start. Known for his outrageous ideas, Flo had a talent for fabricating stories that created headlines—and an uncanny way of managing to keep his nose clean. For Chet, any connection to a jewelry theft could tank his credibility, and PIs who lacked credibility went under. Fast.

Chet inhaled deeply, a slow, comforting realization sneaking into his thoughts and quelling his anxiety. "You *can't* fire me."

"I think I just did."

"This attempted robbery won't be traced back to me. I have information on those two clowns that would bury them. Even if they get caught, they won't implicate me. But, it could get traced back to you."

Flo shrugged. "I don't know how."

Chet leveled a stare at Flo and could see his intimation sinking in. Chet had him. He hated to blackmail his way into keeping a job, but he didn't have a choice at the moment. He watched as Flo leaned back into his chair, his posture wilting, resigned to the truth.

"I'm sorry, Flo." A pang of regret stabbed at Chet. "Really, I am, but you give me no choice. I have my own problems. I need money, and I need it fast. I've got Marciano breathing down my neck."

"Joe Marciano?" Flo raised his eyebrows and fished around in his coat pocket for his cigarette case.

Chet snorted. "Is there any other? Look, my mother needed an operation. I gambled to make the money but lost miserably. I borrowed from the house and won enough for her operation, but not enough to get straight with the gambling hall. Marciano called me in and gave me a month to get square—and that month is nearly up. Marciano's not someone you string out, Flo. He'll kill me and not lose an hour's sleep over it."

"Aren't we a pair?" Flo ran his hands along the mahogany desk and exhaled loudly. He opened the sterling silver case, drew out a cigarette, and pointed it at Chet. "You know, Joe Marciano and I go way back." He lit a match and held it to the cigarette in his mouth.

"I did not know that."

"We have a mutual . . . well, one could say a mutually complicated relationship. Sometimes we hate each other, and sometimes we tolerate each other. Joe's mother worked as a maid at my father's music school. Sometimes Joe would come with her to work when she couldn't find anyone to watch him. His father had abandoned them years before." He took a long drag on his cigarette. "Many beautiful girls lived at the school, wanting to cultivate their vocal and musical talents. I guess that's where my *love* for them was born." He raised his eyebrows at Chet and a wry smile crossed his lips.

More like lust, Chet thought.

"The girls were merciless with poor Joe. Shy, awkward, not the best-looking fellow, the girls teased and taunted him, and I joined in whenever possible. Pathetic really, not very kind, but I was a kid and intent on impressing the girls. His mother became ill eventually and left the school. I didn't see him for a long while, but I later learned about him and his illustrious life of crime. It wasn't until Felicity Jones came along that I saw him again, though."

"Felicity Jones." Chet let out a puff of air. "I knew a Felicity Jones when I was a kid. Colored girl, blue eyes?"

Flo nodded. "One of my headliners. Stunning, talented, and boy, that woman could sing." His eyes drifted to a corner of the office, as if he'd gotten lost in a memory.

"What happened?"

"He stole her from me. Said it was to get back at me for laughing at him all those years ago."

"He took her?"

"In a manner of speaking. He *lured* her away. By that time, Marciano had made his riches and he used them to promise her the world. Never very comfortable on the stage, she took him up on his offer. Assumed she'd be on easy street from then on."

Chet stretched out his legs, feeling much more at ease now that the discomfort of their original confrontation had waned. "And since then?"

"Joe tries to lure away a lot of my girls. Sometimes he succeeds. I think he gets a kick out of taking them from me. It irritates me to no end, but what can I do? I offer the girls fame, riches, and a place in the Ziegfeld family. But sometimes they choose other things."

Flo stubbed out his cigarette and then steepled his hands under his chin. Chet waited. He could see something brewing behind Flo's aging, muddy-brown eyes. "You let me handle Joe." He pointed a finger at Chet. "I have an idea."

CHET ENTERED the theater through the main doors, trepidation building in his gut like a pile of sand being sifted into a quarry. Even thinking about the showman's past schemes made Chet's hands sweat. What kind of chicanery would ensue now?

He entered the main lobby at 1:00 p.m. sharp, as instructed by Flo. A barkeep served drinks to a few tuxedoed gentlemen and bejeweled ladies. Otherwise, the place was empty. Flo popped out from one of the side theater doors, also wearing a tuxedo.

Chet, in his only suit, felt underdressed. "What's going on?"

"Just a little party. I invited Marciano to watch the rehearsal for the show. He'll be here any minute."

"But why the bar? The elegant clothes?"

"It's all part of the fantasy, my man. I know how Joe thinks. He had nothing as a kid—the son of a maid, living hand-to-mouth. Now he's wealthy and powerful, and he likes to be reminded of what all that money and notoriety buys him. I'm simply feeding his ego, trying to soften him up."

"What are you going to propose?" Chet hated having to ask.

Before Flo could answer, two hefty men with muscles bulging out of their suits walked through the doors of the theater and then stopped to hold them open as wide as they could go. Joe Marciano entered, wearing a ridiculous black velvet smoking jacket and white silk ascot. The flash of gold and diamonds on Marciano's pudgy hands distracted the eye from his oily, misshapen face. Chet stifled a smirk.

"Joe." Flo walked up to shake the man's hand. "Welcome to my theater."

Marciano grunted, and his eyes shifted to Chet. With feet like lead, Chet walked over and offered his hand. He felt the metal of Marciano's rings press into his palm as the mobster squeezed harder than necessary.

"It's been awhile, Mr. Riker. The clock is ticking."

Chet's gut gripped with hatred, but he nodded, of course, and forced a tight-lipped smile.

Flo stepped between them and turned Marciano's piercing glare toward the stage. "Rehearsal has just begun." Flo ushered Marciano down the aisle, where several rows of chairs had been removed. In their place stood a table dressed with a white table-cloth bearing ice buckets filled with expensive champagne, the finest crystal glasses, and a large dish of caviar with crackers attractively presented.

"I hope you like Russian caviar and French champagne, Joe."

"It'll do."

Marciano's bodyguards took two of the theater seats close by. Chet, Flo, and Joe sat at the table, and a voluptuous redhead wearing bright red lipstick and a kelly-green satin gown joined them, promptly scooting her chair closer to Marciano. As his eyes traveled from her ample breasts to her full lips, she offered her hand, and he kissed it.

Suddenly, the charade made sense: a staged production to get in Joe Marciano's good graces—and his wallet. Flo obviously knew that Joe would be a sucker for expensive food and champagne, even if he didn't take a single bite or a single sip of it. Everyone knew Joe liked big breasts and women who made him feel like a big man.

Music came from the orchestra pit.

"This number is called 'The Trousseau,'" Flo said, waving his arm toward the stage. "Enter the singing lingerie salesman."

Chet knew of this popular number: A lingerie salesman displays his designs on an oversized pad of paper, and a girl comes onstage wearing the item. Each time he turns the page, the more revealing the garment becomes. When the salesman shows a drawing of a naked woman, the cowboy Will Rogers enters, bedecked in all his Western finery. It never failed to please and always garnered a hearty round of applause.

Marciano's eyes flicked from one girl to the next as they paraded across the stage. Chet could hear the man's breathing quicken and his lips smack as he licked them. During the finale, when Will Rogers stepped out onstage, everyone but Marciano clapped. Instead, he remained quiet, scowling. He was obviously disappointed he didn't get to see a naked girl.

Flo turned to Marciano. "What did you think, Joe?"

"I think you're up to something, Ziegfeld."

"Oh, Joe, come on now." Flo laughed, pulled a chair closer to Marciano, and sat. He lifted his chin toward the cast, signaling for them to exit the stage.

"What is it? What's up your sleeve?" Marciano's face looked like a thunderstorm brewing.

"I would like to offer you an opportunity to co-produce one of my shows." Flo beamed at Marciano. "A new show. A great show. A really high-class production with lots of beautiful showgirls in stunning costumes—something that will knock everyone's socks off."

Finally, Marciano's face split into a grin, the same menacing grin Chet had seen on the fat man's face in the restaurant three weeks ago.

"You would, would you? And why is this?"

"I'm not going to lie to you, Joe. I need money. Big money. I need someone like you to finance it. And I *personally* picked you because I know you like to be the talk of the town. This show, Joe," Flo sat up straight, raised both arms, as if to keep Marciano in his seat. "This show will be in all the newspapers across the country. Hell, we'll even put your name in lights."

Whoa, he's overselling, Chet thought, stifling a frown. Flo would never let Marciano's name appear on one of his marquees.

Marciano nodded and drained his champagne glass, a satisfied gleam in his eye. The redhead draped herself over his arm and shoulder. He glanced at her breasts pressing against him and then turned back to Flo.

"What's Riker got to do with this?" Marciano and Flo both looked at Chet.

"I'll pay off Chet's debt to you, if you agree to finance the show. I'll give you every penny from opening night and then fifty percent of the profit for the run of the show for the *entire* run. If it's as good as I know it will be, that will be a long time— months, perhaps a year."

"Why are you making good for this low-level goon?" Marciano tilted his head toward Chet.

"He's working for me. He's hit on some hard times—his mother got sick and he paid for her surgery, Joe. Unfortunately, he had a few gambling losses that put him in a bind with you. I'm willing to make it right—in exchange for your generosity."

Marciano's attention drifted to some of the scantily clad dancers who'd sauntered back onto the stage. They stretched their long limbs, practicing dance steps under the stage lights, accentuating their shapely figures and their see-through costumes. Marciano visibly drooled. The redhead took the opportune moment to run her hand over the back of his greasy head and caressed his cheek.

"You can watch every rehearsal." Flo swept one arm in a wide semicircle. "I'll introduce you to all these fine girls."

"I don't need your help to find women, Ziegfeld. The dolls come to me like bees to honey, begging to be my girl."

"How *is* Felicity?" Flo leaned back in his chair.

"Wouldn't you like to know?"

"I miss that dame. The Follies haven't been the same without her. Luring her away was a big blow; some might say you *owe* me."

Chet winced. It was risky for Flo to say that, but he sure knew how to stroke the fat man's ego and insult him at the same time.

"I didn't steal nothin'. She loved me." He pointed to his chest. "Me."

"Loved? Past tense?"

Marciano shoved his chair backward, threw his linen napkin onto the table, stood, and nodded to his henchmen, who quickly approached.

Flo stood, raised his hands in surrender. "Now, now, Joe, no need to get testy. I'll admit that was over the line."

One of the girls onstage squealed, and Joe snapped his head around to see why. She coquettishly placed her hand over her mouth, as if she was embarrassed at her outburst, and winked at Joe. His angry face softened to a hairline smile. He waved his boys off and sat down again. "Okay, so tell me: what's this classy show you got in mind?"

Flo's eyes lit up, and he squared his hands out in front of him, as if making a frame.

"It's about a girl, a beautiful, innocent girl who's a dish-washer but dreams of starring in the Ziegfeld Follies. So she makes a plan to pretend to be a socialite. She gets herself a few nice dresses and starts going to all the soirees and parties, risking complete humiliation if she is found out. By the time it's finally discovered that she's a sham, the public is endeared to her even more. Her dream comes true. Her deception becomes her truth. Beautifully ironic, isn't it?"

Chet snorted, he'd never heard of anything so silly. Both men turned their heads to him, looks of irritation etched on their faces.

"Sorry," he said. "I'm sure the public will eat it up. Everybody loves a story about someone who makes it big. Right, Joe?"

Marciano narrowed his eyes but said nothing. He stood and motioned for his monkeys to follow. "I'll think about it."

Just as Flo stood and offered his hand, Grace Michelle came bustling into the theater, looking flustered, which only added to her appeal.

"Excuse me. I'm sorry." She glanced briefly at Chet and then back at Flo. "I didn't mean to interrupt, but Lucile has an urgent question about the costumes for the 'Shining Star' number. She's all up in arms." Grace put her hand to her collarbone, unintentionally drawing their attention to her glowing skin and face.

Chet noticed Marciano's eyes alight on her.

Flo noticed, too, and put his hand on Grace's shoulder, spinning her back in the direction she had come.

"We're discussing something important now, darling. Please tell Lucile she'll have to wait."

Grace nodded and made a hasty exit.

"Who's she?" Marciano asked, watching her walk away, his eyes focused on her slim hips and long legs.

Chet watched Flo's thought process play across his face. Within milliseconds, his eyes brightened. "That lovely little lady is Grace Michelle, the star of the new show." He leaned closer to Joe. "*Our* show."

A flutter of something like fear bloomed in Chet's stomach.

"You say she's the star?" Marciano straightened his tie and smoothed the front of his suit.

Chet wanted to blurt out some kind of protest, but he kept his trap shut, for now.

"Yes. Yes, she is." The glimmer of opportunity flickered in Flo's eyes. "She's Sophia Michelle's little sister. Who better to replace our fallen star than a younger version?"

"Are you sure she's the right one? The right girl?" Chet asked, unable to keep quiet. Grace looked nothing like her sister had. It was none of Chet's business, *she* was none of his business, of course, but the thought of that innocent beauty in Marciano's clutches made his blood boil.

Flo glared at Chet in a silent demand that he shut up. Indebted to both these hyenas, he had no dog in this fight, which left his stomach churning.

"Good idea," Marciano said. "I like it. But I'd like to meet with her first. You know, see if she's the one. Maybe you can introduce us . . . as soon as possible?"

"Absolutely, Joe. Producers always get to meet the cast, and naturally, once you're officially the producer, you'd be seeing her and the other girls—a whole bevy of girls—often." Flo clapped a hand on the big man's shoulder. "But Grace is heading west for a while. Poor kid is still a bit shattered about losing her sister, so I'm sending her on a transcontinental rail tour to give her time to clear her head. And we're already booking stops to promote her and the show. No one knows anything about her, so I have to build her up, get the newspapers talking, make her the public sensation we know she's going to be. You understand, don't you, Joe? She'll be back in a month, and it will all pay off. I promise you won't regret it. Any of it."

Overselling again. *Hell, seems Flo would sell anyone down the road for a buck,* Chet thought, fuming. Something in the back of the theater caught his eye. A woman, wearing a white fur and oversized hat, sat in one of the seats in the back row.

Lillian Lorraine. How much had she heard?

"I want to be informed, Ziegfeld," Marciano said, pointing a finger at Flo. "We do this, you keep me informed. I'll give you the bucks, but I'll be watching you. You get me?"

Flo nodded and held out his hand. Marciano pulled a silver toothpick out of his breast pocket and picked between his crooked teeth.

"I'll have my man contact your man," he said, raking his gaze over both Chet and Flo in a silent threat before strutting out of the theater, his gorillas trailing behind him.

"You have company." Chet tapped Flo on the shoulder to distract him from his flirtation with the showgirl onstage.

Lillian sauntered down the aisle, her body moving like a cat searching for a warm place to sleep, but the expression on her face was like that same cat when intent on a kill.

"Lillian," Flo said, a chill in his voice.

She walked up to Flo and came so close that the head of her fox fur rubbed against Flo's pocket square.

"I'll just be going." Chet didn't want to be anywhere near this conversation.

"Stay." Flo raised a hand. "Miss Lorraine has nothing to say to me that she can't say to the public."

"You owe me this part, Flo." Lillian crossed her arms, her eyes intent on Flo, smoldering so intense they could start a fire.

"That's rubbish, and you know it."

Lillian opened her white clutch and took out a diamond studded, silver cigarette case. She removed a cigarette, placed it between her fingers, and looked at Chet with raised eyebrows. He fished in his coat pocket, produced a matchbox and lit her cigarette.

Flo exhaled, his irritation at Lillian's air of entitlement, her assumed importance to the theater and assumed importance to the world in general, quite apparent.

"This show was written for me and then you gave it to that tramp, your whore of the week. Now that she's dead, you need me."

"Now, hold on, Miss Lorraine." Chet stepped forward. "No need to be disrespectful."

"This is a private conversation." Lillian narrowed her eyes at Chet.

"Flo asked me to stay."

Lillian blew smoke in his face, and he tried not to wince at the burning in his eyes. It took every ounce of his self-control not to physically escort her from the theater. He imagined his hand squeezing her bicep and dragging her up the aisle and out the door.

"Settle down, Lillian," Flo said, physically moving her backward with his hands on her shoulders. "You have no claim on this show, this theater, or me. I thought I made that clear when you broke your contract to go work for the Shuberts. Go back to them. I'm done with you."

"Get your hands off me."

Flo raised his arms in the air in surrender. He may have gone too far, Chet thought. Lillian stepped forward again, her eyes blazing and her mouth twitching. Chet could see the cigarette shaking in her raised hand.

"And now, you're giving the part to that simp of a girl, that lackey to Lady Duff Gordon? She has no experience."

Flo grabbed her by the elbow and turned her away from him seconds before Chet did the same.

"This really is none of your business, Lillian. You work for the *Shuberts* now."

She shrugged him off. "You will go under without me."

Flo clasped his hands in front of him and rocked back and

forth on the balls of his feet, the expression on his face nothing less than amused and confident.

"Let's look at reality: you're a pretty face but not much more. You've been incredibly lucky in your career to have come so far with so little talent," Flo told her.

Lillian dropped her cigarette and let it smolder on the carpet. Her mouth twisted up in an enraged sneer and her eyes narrowed to slits. The muscles in her jaw flexed in a way that made Chet think of a vise closing on something hard and metallic.

Flo stepped forward and tamped the cigarette out with his black-toed Oxford shoe, remaining silent.

"I know you're in trouble, Flo," Lillian said. "Word travels. We've made lots of money together, you and me. You know we could do it again."

"I can't trust you, Lillian." Flo put his hands in his trouser pockets. "You ruined my first marriage, and I'm not taking any chances with this one. Besides, I have a new business partner now, and he wants Grace."

"So you're selling her off like that tramp sister of hers."

Chet clenched his fists, trying his best not to blurt out anything in defense of Grace.

"Get out of my theater," Flo said.

"This show will ruin you, Flo. You are making a huge mistake."

"I said, *Get out.*"

Lillian jammed her pocketbook under one arm, and with the other gloved hand, she reached for Flo's face and laid it gently on his cheek. Her face melted into a serenely seductive vision of pure confidence. "We'll meet again, my love . . . and you'll beg to have me back."

CHAPTER TEN

*T*hat evening Grace entered Flo's office and closed the door behind her, surprised to see Chet Riker sitting in a chair across from Flo's large walnut desk. He quickly stood and offered a mesmerizing, dimpled smile. He reminded her of the handsome soldier showing off his pearly whites in the S.S. White Tooth Paste ad.

"You wanted to see me, Flo?"

"Yes, dear. Please sit down. Have you met Mr. Riker?"

"Briefly. Hello." Heat rose to her cheeks. She hoped she didn't appear flustered, but she knew she did. Chet motioned for her to take the chair next to him.

"I've hired Chet to work on Sophia's case."

"Her case?"

"Well, it's not an official case. The police seem to think she —Ah, hell, Grace, I don't like the circumstances, and I can't have you moping around here forever not knowing what happened to your sister. That's the kind of thing that can eat away at someone. Chet is a private investigator who's done work for me in the past, so I thought I'd put him on it."

"So you believe she was murdered?" Grace asked.

"I don't know if it's murder, darling, but I promised you we'd get to the bottom of this, and I don't go back on my word. Besides, I think you should get away for a while. Have a change of scenery. You need some time."

"Go away? But why? I don't want to go away." She'd never gone anywhere without either Sophia or Flo.

"Please hear me out."

Grace diverted her eyes and snuck a glance at Chet, newly aware of his leather-and-spice aftershave. He gave her a tight-lipped smile.

Flo rubbed at the worry lines on his forehead. "I want you to go to California. Billie is filming a movie out there so you can stay with her."

"But I want to work here, with Lucile." Panic fluttered in Grace's chest. "She's been giving me drawing assignments for costumes. You won't regret it, Flo, I promise. I'll work hard for her, for you." She looked over at Chet, and he shifted uneasily in his chair.

"You will be working, darling. You see, I have bigger plans for you. I'd like for you to replace Sophia. This new actress, Helga, isn't panning out. I'm working on a new production, featuring you as the headliner."

Grace's heart stuttered in her chest. She clutched her hands together, squeezing her fingernails into her palms. "No, no, that's not a good idea, Flo. I don't—"

"You've impressed Mr. Marciano, and he's backing the show. I'm sorry, Grace, but I think I know what is best for the show, the theater, and for you. You'll be the perfect darling of New York— just like Sophia."

Grace's heart plummeted. She loved her sister, missed her sister, and wanted to find out what happened to her sister, but she was nothing *like* her sister.

"But, Flo, I'm not an actress."

"I've provided you with dance and vocal lessons for years."

"But—"

"You've got everything you need. You'll be just as good as Sophia, I am sure of it."

Desperate for an ally, Grace turned to Chet, but he wouldn't meet her eyes. He seemed focused on the collection of framed photos of showgirls on Flo's wall.

"That's why you're going to take a nice, long train trip." Flo said. "We'll provide additional training, and will groom you for the job. We'll teach you everything you need to know about working with publicity, being in the public eye. Our audiences miss Sophia, darling, and you're the next best thing. They'll love you."

"But I don't want—"

Flo leaned back in his chair and clasped his hands across his stomach. "I must be honest with you dear, the publicity surrounding Sophia's death is . . . not advantageous. With her drunken tongue-lashing on the yacht, her erratic behavior before and after the wedding, her reputation has been, well, tarnished. You can help rectify that, help the audiences love once again and make people remember *why* they loved *her*."

Grace could feel drops of perspiration forming on her upper lip.

"Would you like a glass of water, Miss Michelle?" Chet's fingers alighted on her sleeve. She nodded. Chet stood, opened the door, and summoned Goldie to fetch a glass of water.

Flo didn't move. He just sat there with that expression that Grace knew so well, the one that announced that this was not open for negotiation. She'd do what he wished, and that was that.

Goldie appeared with the water. "Are you all right, dear?" she asked, stroking Grace's hair.

Grace stiffened. *No! I am not all right.*

Chet pulled his chair closer to hers, so near she could feel the heat of his body. He took the water from Goldie and handed it to Grace.

"Thank you, Goldie," Flo said, waving her away. "You will take the Transcontinental Railroad to California, in Billie's private car, and there you will promote yourself and the new show. Chet will accompany you to investigate Sophia's murder. You want that, don't you, dear? To know what happened to your sister, find out who's to blame?"

"Well, yes, more than anything."

"Lucile will go along, too. She will organize your wardrobe for your appearances."

"But she's just signed the contract with Sears and Roebuck, and she can't leave her store!"

"I've worked out a deal with Lucile." Flo looked squarely into Grace's eyes. "It won't be a problem. You are not to worry about anything. Chet will be right there with you to protect you."

"Protect me? From what?"

The two men exchanged a glance. Flo tapped the desk with his fingers. "You're a beautiful young woman. There are a lot of scoundrels in Los Angeles, men who would take advantage of someone as innocent as you. You'll need protection. Though, it's only cautionary. Really, you have nothing to fear."

THE NEXT DAY, Flo insisted he take Grace to Bergdorf's for shoes.

"Are you pleased that Lucile will accompany you to California?" Flo asked as he turned the wheel of his Rolls-Royce Silver Ghost onto Fifth Avenue, headed north.

"I am, but it seems she's leaving a lot of unfinished business behind. Won't you need her for the Follies?"

Flo shook his head, puffed on a cigar, and then held it away from his body, the gesture uncharacteristically feminine for him. "We're throwing in some comedies for the time being. Nothing big until you come back," he said, winking. "Charles can handle anything that comes up. I've told him to hire an assistant if he needs one."

A wave of disappointment flooded her. She would have loved that assistant position.

"Lucile wants to showcase some of her designs on the West Coast. She's conquered Paris, London, and now New York. This will give her an opportunity to launch her line in Los Angeles. See? Everyone wins." He shoved the cigar back in his mouth and chewed on the end of it.

"Oh." Grace fiddled with her handbag, looking out the window. They drove in silence for a few more blocks, and then Flo turned the car onto Fifty-Second Street, headed toward the river, away from the shopping district.

"Aren't we going to Bergdorf's?" she asked.

"We're meeting Mr. Riker for breakfast first. He lives in Hell's Kitchen."

Grace pressed her lips together. Being around Chet reduced her to feeling twitchy and nervous, but she couldn't deny the pleasant flutter that also bloomed in her chest at the mention of his name.

As they neared Ninth Avenue, they saw a large group of women with children in tow, all heading eastward in a determined stream. Some of them held signs that read, *Food For Our Children!*

"What is this?" Grace asked.

"Bread riot." Flo swung the car up against a curb after they passed through Tenth Avenue. "They are headed to the mayor's office."

Several mounted policemen riding large Belgian draft horses trailed behind them.

"They have quite a distance to walk, don't they?"

He shrugged. "I suppose."

Grace watched as the women wearing tattered shawls and dresses with muddy hemlines marched down the street carrying infants and dragging older children behind them, their signs bobbing up and down above the sea of bodies. At that moment she felt ever more grateful. Even if Flo was asking her to pursue his dream rather than her own, if it weren't for Flo's ongoing support, she could be one of those women in the streets. Again.

Flo parked the car, got out, and then assisted her.

The crisp, cold air hit her face, and she reveled in the brisk refreshment after being cloistered in the smoke-filled car. Brown slush covered the streets—residue from the previous day's freezing rain. Grace aimed her buttoned boot for a clear spot amid the muck and stepped out. Once she was safely launched, Flo pulled his big, full-length fur tighter around him, pushed his hat down lower on his head, and led Grace across the street.

"Ho there," Chet called from behind them. His sparkling eyes looked at Grace as his fingertips grazed the brim of his hat. "Miss Michelle."

She nodded, diverting her eyes.

"There's a little café down here I'd like to try," he said, falling in step with Grace. "Nothing like the Plaza, but I've heard the food's wonderful."

Dodging a mass of people, all hurrying to get to their destinations, they rounded the corner and Grace noticed a black motorcar idling in the middle of the street. She thought it a strange place to park but continued to listen to Chet's story about the neighborhood.

The high-pitched squeal of the motor revving made her turn. The car pulled forward and accelerated—toward them. Pedestrians crossing the street dove out of the car's path. Seconds before the car was on them, hands grabbed her. She went sprawling onto the ground, the air forced out of her lungs.

When she opened her eyes, she found Chet's blue-gray gaze settled on her face. Feeling the need to gasp for breath, she inhaled deeply, and the cold air, once soothing, made her chest ache.

"Are you all right?" Chet held out his hand to help her to her feet.

"I think so." She winced, her elbow throbbing and her head pounding.

"My arm hurts." As she said the words, the world went white, her knees buckled, and Chet's arms went around her again.

GRACE LAY IN BED, drifting in and out of consciousness from the sedative the doctor had given her. She could hear murmuring voices just outside the door and could smell the welcoming scent of fresh roses next to her bed.

She again slipped into sleep and dreamed of walking alone in the streets, with Flo's big fur coat enveloping her. She walked at a fast clip, intent on getting somewhere in a hurry. She could hear the low, grating sound of a motor engine and the clip-clop, clip-clop of horses' hooves as they pulled the carriages in and around Central Park and through the streets. A loud screeching sound made her turn to see a car headed straight for her. A man gripped the wheel, his face sneering with malice. As the car sped closer and closer, his features became more defined. She knew him! She recognized the clump of bloody hair fringing his forehead, the lines of blood streaking downward between his eyes. The car was now inches from her. She opened her mouth to scream . . .

Grace bolted upright in the bed, her heart racing. She sank back onto the pillows and tried to close her eyes, but the bloody face wouldn't disappear. It couldn't be him. She and Sophia had left him for dead years ago. Dizziness consumed her until she slept again.

The next time she opened her eyes, Grace recognized Flo's

silhouette framed within the window. He stared out the paned glass, smoking a cigar.

"Is it morning?" she asked.

Flo spun around and smiled. "Yes, my dear. You've slept for over fourteen hours. How are you feeling?"

"Rested." Though Grace's head still throbbed, and her wrist felt stiff.

"I've been worried about you." Flo stubbed out his cigar in a crystal ashtray on the bureau and sank down onto the edge of the bed.

"About me or about your new star?"

Flo frowned, rubbed at the day-old scruff at his chin.

"I'm sorry, Flo. That was unkind."

"I was worried about *you*." He reached for her hand.

"I know. Thank you." She placed her other hand on top of his. His large brown eyes took on a dolefulness that startled her. "What's wrong, Flo?"

He inhaled, as if bracing himself for the words about to come out of his mouth. "I—we—don't think it was an accident. We think the driver intended to. . . do harm."

Grace's heart leaped to her throat. "Why?"

"He aimed directly at you, so we're guessing it has something to do with Sophia."

The bloody face from her dreams flashed in her mind. She tried to still the pounding in her chest. This couldn't be happening. He was *dead*. At least, she'd thought he was dead when she and Sophia left him lying in the alley, blood pooling around his head. And, that had been years ago.

"I don't want to alarm you, darling. It just means you're going to have to be extremely careful."

Should she tell him about the man—about how he had tried to hurt Sophia, and how Sophia had only tried to defend herself? Grace and Sophia had agreed to take the secret to their graves. But now, with Sophia gone, if Grace confessed, and she was mistaken about the man in the car, would Flo protect her or allow them to take her away? She closed her eyes and fought for calm.

"Why would someone want to kill Sophia? Or me for that matter?" She tried to disguise the waver in her voice. If he thought it was due to grief, she could hold on to the secret a little longer.

"I wish I could tell you more, darling, but I haven't sorted it all out. I did, however, relay my suspicions to the police—that someone may have murdered your sister—and they promised to dig deeper. However, the sooner we get you to California, the better."

"But will I be any safer there? That's where Sophia—" The realization suddenly hit her: It didn't matter where she went. She might never be safe.

CHAPTER ELEVEN

*M*AY 30, 1920 - NEW YORK CITY, NY
Flo told Grace that Billie's private train car had arrived in New York and that tomorrow, she and her entourage would embark on the railroad sojourn to Los Angeles, California. Once there, they would take motorcars to the beautiful, sleepy town of Beverly Hills.

After hearing the plan, Grace tried to rest, but she only ended up pacing the floor. Her nervousness increased when the bellboy delivered a telegram. Billie had wired it, expressing her condolences and her excitement at the opportunity to welcome "Flo's newest star" to her hotel suites in Beverly Hills.

Grace set the telegram on the table with dread in her heart.

Moments later, Lucile entered the room waving a copy of *Variety.* "Look at this," she said, tossing it onto the bed.

Grace grabbed the paper. *"Ziegfeld star nearly run down by Model T Ford,"* she read aloud and then continued in silence. She read of Sophia's suspicious death, her stomach churning, but the last few lines made her palms sweat and her knees grow weak: *Ziegfeld's newest protégé, the late star's younger sister, Grace Michelle, is under strict guard.*

She looked up at Lucile. "How did *Variety* find out about this?"

"Get used to it, darling. You now live in a fishbowl. Sometimes it's a hindrance, but often it can help."

"How can it help?" Grace asked, painfully aware of how it could hurt—especially if someone from her past came looking for her. Being in the newspapers would make her whereabouts easily known.

"Look at it this way, if you *are* in danger, the word is out that you're being protected." Lucile's voice projected calm, and her eyes crinkled in the corners, giving her face a motherly glow. Grace shifted her attention to the colorful pile of garments sprawled across her bed.

"I'm not sure what to pack." She had only placed a few simple sheath dresses in the teak trunk Flo had sent to her room. "The last time I traveled anywhere, all I had were the clothes on my back."

"And now you'll be all the rage in a new ensemble every day." Lucile shuffled through the clothes in Grace's wardrobe, choosing a few dresses for her to place in the trunk.

"Have you designed the new clothes yet?" Grace asked.

"Several, but not all of them."

"Lucile?" Grace bit her lip and looked down at her hands. "Do you think I could design some of the pieces? If I don't have something to do on that long train ride, I'll go mad."

"Oh, you won't be bored, I can assure you of that. You'll have speeches to prepare, events to attend—"

"Speeches?"

"Yes." Lucile placed hands on her ample hips. "As Flo's new sensation you'll be expected to make multiple appearances. I've been told that we'll make a few scheduled stops, beginning in Chicago. At each one, you'll be introduced to the public and paraded around to plug the Follies, especially the new show. They call it a whistle-stop tour, as most of your speeches will be offered from the caboose's deck. The public loves that kind of thing. It's a favorite of politicians."

Grace sank onto the bed. Speeches? Appearances? Sophia hadn't done those things. She simply walked onto the stage, sang a song or two, danced a little, and attended lots of soirees on Flo's arm. Why this big push? She'd never be a star of Sophia's caliber.

"I know you're feeling uncertain about it all, but Flo needs to redirect the publicity surrounding Sophia's death." Lucile's eyes shimmered with a sympathetic gleam. "He needs you to embrace the spotlight, use your good looks and intelligence to wow the reporters and get everyone focused on the new show."

Of course, Grace had to do whatever Flo wanted. She owed him that, and more.

"I'll go along, but I so wanted to become a designer and to have you teach me everything I needed to know. I love creating ideas, sketching them on paper, sewing. And frankly, it's the one area of my life that I can control. You do understand, don't you?"

When Lucile smiled, the corner of her blue eyes crinkled again. Not one to show much emotion, Lucile's pride in her craft showed in her expression. "I do. We'll just have to keep quiet about it."

Grace reached for her hand. "Thank you."

"Now, young lady, you need to finish packing and get dressed. I just came by to check on your wardrobe. We leave at six thirty tomorrow morning."

"Who else is coming?"

"Chet Riker and a publicist by the name of Donovan Green. Fanny will join us on the West Coast, in a week or two."

Grace smiled, hoping to disguise the apprehension that twisted her stomach into one giant knot.

∾

CHET LOOKED AROUND THE SMALL, grime-encrusted flat for anything he might need for the trip, thrilled he would soon be leaving this hovel. After California, his financial status would be secure, and he could finally be rid of this paint-peeled dump.

As he turned on the propane stove to heat dinner, he tried to piece together the hit-and-run. Flo thought it an attempt on Grace's life and one linked to Sophia's death, but Chet couldn't see it. The hugely famous Sophia and her somewhat notorious husband did associate with a loathsome lot, but even if someone had killed Sophia—and even he wasn't convinced of that yet— he couldn't see how Grace's death would accomplish anything. Unless Sophia had somehow blackmailed someone and they figured Grace also knew their dirty, little secret.

The thought of Grace in danger made his jaw clench, so he turned his attention back to cooking, pulled open the drawer beneath the oven, grabbed a pot, and filled it with water. He then opened a can of beans and set the can into the pot on the stove, waiting for it to heat. While it warmed, he opened a can of peaches, picked up a fork, and began to devour the sweet segments of flesh.

Marciano could have been responsible for the car. At least that was his first thought the minute he'd pulled Grace up from the slush-soaked pavement. Guilt wormed its way into his thoughts when he remembered his full weight falling on her. It surprised him how much he cared about this girl he hardly knew.

With the mob boss on his back, he could be a detriment to Grace. He shouldn't have taken the job as her bodyguard, but if he hadn't, who would have protected her? Flo? That man couldn't be trusted to take care of anyone. The sweet girl lived right under his nose and he didn't have a clue that she had no desire to become a star. Or if he did, he didn't care. Flo pushed her toward a destiny that favored *him*, not *her*.

Maybe Chet could find a way to protect her, at least from

Marciano and Flo. Protecting her from himself might prove much harder.

GRACE STEPPED onto the platform and steadied herself against the doorjamb to take in the beauty of Billie Burke's private railcar. The walls, paneled in deep, rich walnut, rose four feet to the wainscoting; deep-crimson fabric covered the remainder of the walls above that, all the way up to the rococo molding encircling the ceiling in swirling designs.

Oil paintings depicting lush landscapes, Louis XV–styled table and chairs, a white damask divan, and a mahogany writing desk adorned a sitting area. Grace caught a glimpse of herself in the gold gilt mirrors scattered among the paintings and was surprised at the look of panic in her face.

She moved through a narrow doorway framed with carved molding and made her way to the bedroom at the back of the railcar. A portrait of luxurious decadence, the bed took up one third of the room and the entire width of the car. Walnut panels framed the bed, creating a cozy "box," and swags of silk tied back with golden ropes hung down from the canopy ceiling at the foot of the bed, allowing for privacy, if wanted.

A vanity to her left displayed everything she could ever need for her toilette—a tray of cosmetics, brushes, powders, oils, scents, and creams. Another writing desk sat next to the vanity and another crystal chandelier lit the tiny bedroom, casting a fragmented rainbow off every surface.

"Getting settled?" Flo startled her as he entered through the narrow hallway into the bedroom.

"I don't know what to say. This is beautiful. It was so kind of Billie to—"

"You deserve it."

Grace shook her head. She didn't deserve any of this. She

hadn't done anything. She pushed the unease that had been plaguing her for days out of her thoughts.

"I'll have your trunks deposited in a few moments, but I want to speak with you first. I have a little something for you."

He handed her a small box.

"Oh, Flo, no. I—"

"Oh, don't be preposterous. Take it, darling."

Grace ran her fingers across the lid, hesitating to open it. Gifts from Flo came with a price. She thought of Sophia and fear crept up her spine.

"Open it," Flo urged, not moving his eyes from her face.

Grace cracked it open and discovered a sparkling diamond bracelet. A sinking feeling made her knees weak.

"I can't, Flo."

"But you must. You need to get used to this, my dear. Now that you're a star, men from all over the world will be showering you with gifts. I am but the first."

Blood drained from her head. Most women would be flattered by his comments, but they terrified her.

"Just smile and say, 'thank you.'"

Grace forced her lips into a smile. "Thank you."

"Wear it in health, my dear, and wear it every time you're in public. Flash it around a bit."

"But Flo—"

He put his hand up, clearly unwilling to hear further protests.

"I'll have your things brought in. Lucile, Chet, and the others will be boarding soon. Lucile will be traveling in a separate sleeper car. I think Chet should stay in your sitting room during the night. I want him as near to you as possible. That car episode shook me up." His gaze traveled to the floor. Grace knew his fear of death had no doubt become worse since the incident.

"That's fine, Flo. I'll be fine. Really, please don't worry."

"I miss her, you know." He looked into Grace's eyes with a

pain that startled her. "Things weren't good between us when she left, and—"

"Don't, Flo. Don't blame yourself." How well she understood his feelings of fear and regret. "It's going to be all right. We'll find out what happened to Sophia. We'll do right by her."

He nodded. "You take care, Grace."

"I will. Thank you. For everything."

"Knock 'em dead, honey." He gave her a gentle kiss on the forehead and squeezed her arms.

Grace smiled and watched him leave the train car. Her heart should have been filled with joy and excitement at her new, glamorous life, and she chastised herself for being so ungrateful. She would do this for Flo and she would do it for Sophia, but someday, she vowed, someday, she would have her own life. She just had to pay her dues to earn the privilege first.

CHAPTER TWELVE

a few hours later, iron groaned on iron as the train lurched into motion. Grace settled into the private car, alone, curled up on the damask sofa with Nathaniel Hawthorne's, *The Scarlet Letter*.

A loud rap on the door startled her.

"Who is it?" she called.

"Donovan Green, Miss Michelle. Flo sent me. I'm your publicist."

Grace slipped on her shoes, smoothed her hair, and opened the heavy door. A tall, reed-thin young man with a mane of blond hair and a hawk-like face stood there, hat in hand, smiling.

"Miss Michelle, you are more beautiful than I'd imagined." His deep-brown eyes twinkled when he spoke. He held out his hand.

Grace studied the halo of golden waves atop his head. The way the light shined on it gave him the appearance of saintliness.

She looked over her shoulder at the empty railcar, uneasy and a bit annoyed at Chet's absence. Lucile had told her to expect Donovan Green, but the impropriety of letting him into her private quarters without her "protector" didn't seem prudent.

"Come in, please," she said, hoping it was not the wrong decision.

Mr. Green entered, his face radiating a pleasantness that made it a bit easier to ignore her fears.

"What can I do for you, Mr. Green?"

"Please, call me Donovan." He smiled at her. "May we sit?"

"Certainly."

Donovan chose the sofa. Grace kept her distance and sat in one of the parlor chairs near the table.

He leaned his elbows on his knees and clasped his hands together. "First, my condolences."

"Thank you."

"Second, it is Mr. Ziegfeld's desire for me to create an image for you, Miss Michelle. You are unknown to the public, aside from the fact that you are Sophia Michelle's sister, but we want to give you a different image from hers."

"I am nothing like my sister, God rest her soul."

"You don't appear to be." He smiled at her with twinkling eyes. "Mr. Ziegfeld wants your image to be that of an intelligent, kind, and charitable benefactress. Stars, particularly Flo's stars, often have the reputation of being spoiled. So we'll create a plan that presents you as someone who gives back to her public, a star any woman and her daughters would look up to and admire. How does that sound?"

"Fine," she said. "I hope to be that kind of person."

"Good. Now, what are some of the things you'd—"

The door abruptly popped open, and Chet slid in the room.

"Oh. I didn't know you were expecting someone," the publicist said, irritation in his voice.

"This is Mr. Riker. He's a private investigator."

Chet walked in and threw his hat on the entry table. "Actually, I'm Miss Michelle's personal bodyguard. Anyone who wants to see her should go through me. And who are you?"

"I'm Donovan Green." He stood and held out his hand.

"Didn't Mr. Ziegfeld tell you? He's hired me to shape Miss Michelle's image."

Chet hesitated a moment and then shook his hand.

"We'll be finished in a few moments," Grace said.

"I'll be right outside the door." Chet aimed his words at Donovan.

Embarrassed at Chet's rude treatment of the publicist, Grace clenched her fists. She took a deep breath, released her fingers, and quietly waited for her publicist to speak.

"A bodyguard?"

"It's Flo's idea. It's just a precaution," she said. "You were saying? Before we were interrupted?"

"You have the most beautiful eyes I've ever seen." Donovan blinked and then looked at her with focused concentration, as if studying a piece of art, an object.

Heat rose to Grace's face, and her palms dampened again. She turned her back to him and wiped her hands on her dress, wishing he would hurry up and finish their conversation so she could go back to her book.

"I've embarrassed you. That wasn't my intent. Sometimes, when I am struck by things, the words just come out of my mouth. I hope you will accept my apology."

"Of course."

"Let's get back to the subject at hand, shall we? We were discussing some of the things Flo wants you to accomplish as a public figure. I would like to hear what you have in mind. Are there any particular causes or charities that interest you?"

"Orphans. I would like to help orphans."

Donovan nodded in approval. "You yourself are an orphan, correct?"

"Yes."

"It's a wonderful idea—very apropos and exciting. I'll book a tour of an orphanage somewhere along the way. Chicago's too close; there won't be time to get things in place, but maybe somewhere in the western states. Indian children, perhaps."

"Yes. Yes, that sounds splendid."

"Very well. I'll get started right away." Donovan hesitated a moment. "Miss Michelle, Grace, may I call you Grace?"

"Yes."

"Would you join me for dinner in the dining car tomorrow? We could discuss our plans further."

She tensed. The warm feeling vanished, replaced with dread. Dinner? With a man she barely knew? She bit the inside of her cheek and stalled for time. Several questions and ideas ran around in her brain. They *would* be discussing her new cause.

She nodded her assent.

"I'll come by at eight." Donovan took his hat and walked toward the door. Before he reached it, it opened once again, and Chet walked in.

Another twinge of irritation pricked at Grace. Had he been listening to their conversation?

She smiled at Donovan when he tipped his hat and departed.

Wringing her hands, she shifted her gaze to Chet, who stared and shook his head at her. She turned her back on him and picked up her book from the sofa.

"Sorry for the intrusion," he said.

"You could have knocked."

"I didn't realize the conversation was so private."

She turned around to face him. "That's not the point."

"Not very wise, you know, letting him in here like that when you were alone."

"You certainly weren't here. Isn't that why Flo pays you?"

He stiffened at her words. "I'm sorry. I was inspecting the train to be sure I wasn't—you weren't—being followed."

Grace frowned. She couldn't understand the tension between them. Not knowing what more to do or say, she took her book into the bedroom. Before she had a chance to close the door, she heard him curse and throw his hat on the table.

THE LOCK CLICKED on Grace's bedroom door, and satisfied at her immediate safety, Chet stepped out for some air. Her irritation at him both confused and disappointed him. He'd so hoped they would get along. On a purely professional level, of course. Now employed to take care of the woman, he couldn't let lust get in the way.

He looked back at the door, wondering if she too felt itchy and uncomfortable, as though any room they entered together suddenly grew too small. He let out a deep breath and secured his hat on his head. He stepped out of the car, took the key that Flo had given him—Grace had the other one—and locked her in. With Grace safely tucked away and his mind a jumble of thoughts, the moment called for a drink.

He made his way down the narrow hallway and through the sliding doors of several cars before he reached the bar car. Filled with smoke and hopping with passengers entertaining themselves before the nine o'clock dinner hour, the car felt as if it would burst at the seams. He worked his way through the press of elegantly dressed men and women, and searched for an open seat. He spotted one in the far corner.

He removed his hat and set it on the cocktail table, then sat down with his back to the corner, a habit he'd developed since the war. *Ears and eyes forward at all times.* He scanned the crowd but had difficulty seeing everyone because of the many passengers standing, their bodies swaying with the motion of the train.

A waiter appeared at the table.

"Scotch. Rocks," Chet said before the waiter even spoke.

A shift in the crowd presented a better view of the seated

clientele. His eyes were drawn to an extremely attractive woman with auburn hair and an oversized purple hat with white ostrich feathers streaming from behind. The two gentlemen sitting with her both leaned into the table, eagerly hanging on her every word, every giggle, every lick of her red lips. She looked familiar.

Recognition dawned. "What is she doing here?" he said under his breath. He thought she'd just signed a contract with the Shuberts for a new show. Why would Lillian Lorraine be traveling west? He took a closer look at her companions, and a sinking feeling hit his gut. One of the gentlemen had his hat resting on his knee—black, made of the finest beaver pelt, with two silver toothpicks nestled behind the leather hatband. Marciano's men.

So the mobster made true on his words. He'd be watching his investment. But what was Lillian doing with them?

Probably brownnosing to steal Grace's part in the new show.

"Your drink, sir." The waiter appeared at the table. Chet gave him a nod, took the tumbler, and sucked down a mouthful of the burning liquid.

Another man walked up to Lillian's table; The fellow looked like a goon with a scar streaking across his forehead and down his face. Not only the scar but the shabbiness of his brown coat and hat made him stand out like a guinea hen in a room full of peacocks.

With a pronounced frown on her face, Lillian abruptly stood up, gave the newcomer a scowl, and stormed out of the bar car. Chet swallowed down the rest of his drink, threw some coins on the table, and followed her.

Somehow, she had scooted through the throng much easier than he could. He kept the purple hat in view as he shouldered his way through the mass of people. The bar car doors hissed as Lillian made her way through them.

Chet followed her through the next car, and as she opened the doorway to the car after that, a family of four entered into the hallway, impeding Chet's progress. The boy, about four years of age, clung to his mother's skirt, whining that he wanted her to pick him up. The little girl, a few years older, pink and plump, stared at him with large blue eyes under a pink straw hat as she sucked on a lollipop.

She held the sticky thing out to him. "Want some?"

"Sally!" The mother's face flushed crimson.

The father stepped out of the compartment into the hallway and attempted to gather his family to scoot them past Chet. Chet strained to look through the glass windows of the hallway doors in search of the purple hat. The family headed in the opposite direction, so Chet let them squeeze by and then made his way to the door. He found Lillian out on the platform. She stood with her back to him, the wind making a mess of her ostrich plumes as she smoked a cigarette.

Chet took off his hat. "Miss Lorraine?" He raised his voice to be heard above the chugging of the train.

Lillian whirled around, surprise in her eyes.

"I'm sorry," he said. "I didn't mean to startle you."

Her eyes lit up with wide-eyed admiration, something Chet had seen many times when he approached women. "Oh, you didn't," she said with a seductive upturn of her lips.

"I'm sorry to bother you, but you seemed upset with those men in there. I just wanted to make sure you are all right."

"How sweet." She smiled, showing a row of perfectly white, straight teeth. "Yes, I'm absolutely fine. Fans. They can be so abrasive. Especially men. Present company excluded, of course. Do I know you?"

"I don't think so. Believe me, I would have remembered." Chet flashed his most dashing smile. "So where are you headed, Miss Lorraine?"

She batted her eyelashes at him. "I'm sorry, I didn't get your name."

"Charles Rockwell." His pride was a bit wounded she hadn't recognized him, although, on that day in the theater she'd had Flo in her sights.

She let out a laugh. "Sounds like a movie star. Is that where you're going? To California to be in pictures? I bet the camera loves that handsome face of yours."

Chet moved closer to her. "No. Unfortunately, my life isn't quite so glamorous." He knew her type well. There were some women who played hard to get, and some who didn't. She fell into the latter category. The type who basked in attention, like a cat in the sun.

"What do you do, Mr. Rockwell?"

"I sell insurance."

"Oh." A flicker of disappointment crossed her face.

"See? Nothing glamorous. But you, on the other hand, you must be going somewhere to light up the stage. Chicago? San Francisco?"

"Los Angeles." Lillian lowered her gaze and focused on her cigarette holder. "I've been offered a film."

Chet pressed his lips together. What about the contract with the Shuberts? Why would she lie about a film role?

"Sounds exciting. I'm sure you'll be perfect in the part, whatever it is."

"It's nice to meet such a gentlemanly fan." She looked up at him through impossibly long, black lashes, her brown-eyed gaze sinking into his. "Are you married, Mr. Rockwell?"

"Yes." Chet put his hands in his pockets and stepped back. "My daughter is a big admirer of yours. She's too young to see one of your shows, but she's seen photos of you in the magazines. I'm wondering if I could get your autograph for her."

A distinct wave of disappointment crossed Lillian's face. "Delighted," she said, her mouth tight.

"She'll be so pleased." Chet produced a small pad of paper and a fountain pen from his coat pocket.

Lillian didn't bother to ask the child's name and scrawled her autograph across the paper. She handed the pad and pen back to Chet, avoiding his eyes. "If you'll excuse me, I'm quite tired."

"Of course. Have a good evening. And thanks for the autograph."

She shouldered past him and left the platform.

Chet studied the handwriting and put the pad back in his pocket, satisfied his ruse had worked. Lillian's story of a film offer seemed flimsy. She had been none too happy about Grace getting the role she coveted. Was she accompanying them to California to cause trouble?

He sighed. He also had that twit Donovan Green to attend to. Something about the man annoyed Chet—something besides the way his eyes roamed over Grace like honey dripping over a honeycomb. Poor, naive thing had no idea the man had designs other than the publicity he was hired to create for Ziegfeld. Her attitude didn't help matters, either. She had been defiant, almost angry at Chet's intrusion of their conversation earlier.

He took his pocket watch from his vest. It was eight thirty. His stomach growled, and he wondered if Grace wanted to eat. He made his way back to the private car to find the parlor empty. He stared at the closed door of Grace's bedroom and contemplated whether or not to disturb her again. Taking a chance, he walked over to it and knocked.

"Yes," she clipped from within.

"Are you hungry? I'm going to the dining car."

"No." Anger reverberated through the door.

He sighed. This was going to be a long trip.

CHAPTER THIRTEEN

To Grace's delight, Lucile brought her drawing paper and pencils to the private railcar. The two had their breakfast and lunch brought in and spent most of the day laughing and working, which helped to distract Grace from her upcoming train-stop appearance in Chicago that evening. In the afternoon, when Lucile left, Grace stayed in her bedroom until it was time for her dinner date, not wanting to make conversation with Chet.

Once she was dressed and ready to go, she entered the parlor to find Chet sitting with his feet propped up on the coffee table.

"Going out?" He leaned back and laced his fingers behind his head.

"Yes. The dining car."

"Eating again? You must be very hungry."

"I haven't eaten since noon."

"Very well. I'll join you."

"Well, I don't know. We'll be discussing business." Grace fumbled with her handbag.

"We?"

"Yes. Mr. Green— I mean, Donovan and I."

"Sounds interesting." Chet swung his feet off the table. "Let's go."

Grace raised her eyebrows. Maybe she didn't want to go to dinner after all. She wouldn't be able to concentrate on helping orphans with Chet looming over them.

"Donovan is picking me up."

"Oh. I see." He flashed her a toothy grin.

She sighed. *When one has a bodyguard, I suppose there is no choice in the matter.*

Annoyed, she walked toward the sofa and took a seat, refusing to look at him. She focused on the walnut paneling, the window with the world going by, the silk drapes swinging around the window frame. Anything but Chet.

A few moments later, Donovan arrived. "Ah, Grace, don't you look lovely?"

She returned his smile, trying to ignore the weight of Chet's gaze.

"Your . . . bodyguard is joining us?"

"No," Chet said. "I'll leave you two alone—to discuss business."

Donovan took Grace's elbow and led her into the next passageway that led to the dining car. She glanced back and saw Chet following them, a scowl on his face.

Adorned with elegant furnishings, the dining car matched the rest of the luxury train. White tablecloths, six-piece sets of silver flatware, and the finest china and crystal goblets ornamented each table, which was lit by its own gas lamp. Set against the car's large windows, the tables provided privacy with brocaded curtains held back with silk ties. Gossamer sheers over the windows kept out the harshness of sunrise and sunset, but still offered a picturesque glow of the painted sky and fluffy clouds streaming by.

Donovan led her to a secluded table for two near the rear of the dining car. Chet took a table a few feet away and sat facing

Grace. She didn't know how she could possibly eat with Chet planted in front of her. He already made her so nervous she could barely swallow, and they hadn't even ordered yet. She sighed. Did he have to be so close? Couldn't he keep an eye on her from the other side of the car?

She would have to manage. The importance of the work Donovan had proposed finally made Grace feel good about her impending celebrity.

As Donovan ordered champagne, Grace glanced over at Chet, who seemed unconcerned looking out the window. Then he caught her eye. Embarrassed, she turned her attention to Donovan. "When do we start this project?"

"I found an orphanage in New Mexico in a village outside of Albuquerque. The orphanage is called St. Cecilia's. The train stops in Albuquerque in few days, so I've made arrangements for a short visit."

"What will I do? What will I say?"

"It would be nice to start out with the donation of a big, fat check." Donovan laughed and leaned in closer.

"Oh."

"I'll handle that part with Flo."

"But what can *I* do?"

"The money will be donated in your name, Grace. This is quite generous of Flo. You will take a tour, meet some of the children. We'll have someone take photos we can send to various newspapers."

She frowned. "That's it?"

"Yes. But don't think it's not important. You'll be giving these children clothing, furniture, further care, and a roof over their heads. You'll be giving them hope."

Grace wanted to do something more meaningful, work on a project with the children, read to them, and spend time with them. What he'd described sounded more like a purely promotional opportunity for the Follies.

"When we arrive in Chicago, we will mention it to the press." He sipped his champagne. "We should start writing your speech immediately. We'll be there in about an hour."

"An hour? But that's so soon." Her stomach flipped at the thought of speaking to a crowd of strangers.

"Yes, so we best get to work." He poured her another glass of champagne, then pulled out a notebook and pencil. Grace leaned in toward the table, her head mere inches from Donovan's, and became completely engrossed in the task of cowriting her speech.

CHET STIRRED his drink with the tiny paper straw, keeping his cool while observing the interplay between Grace and Donovan. He hadn't missed the man's physical overtures, nor, to his displeasure, Grace's acceptance of the man's affection. Occasionally, her eyes lit up or she laughed. She'd never been so animated in conversation with *him*, and her behavior rankled Chet. Didn't she see what lurked behind that man's greedy eyes?

After several glasses of champagne, their meal finally arrived, breaking up the couple's cozy little tête-à-tête. Grace glanced at Chet and held his gaze for a moment, but quickly turned her attention back to her meal, which gave him the opportunity to study her behavior further. But her blond hair, worn upswept and elegant and glistening in the candlelight, distracted him. He focused on a stray curl that had escaped the twist at the nape of her neck.

Grace took another sip of champagne. Chet could see the effects of the alcohol in her mannerisms—much like Sophia's, he imagined. Donovan Green, of course, took every opportunity to top off her glass. Grace couldn't appear before the Chicago crowd well into her cups.

Chet's dinner arrived, and he took a few bites but couldn't

enjoy it as he watched Grace sip more champagne and stop eating. Green put his notepad aside and concentrated only on his dinner partner.

Lecher.

Grace giggled too loudly, summoning the gazes of the other diners. Unable to watch any more, Chet threw a few bills onto the white tablecloth and walked over to their table.

"What are you doing?" Grace asked, raising glassy eyes to his.

"We arrive in Chicago in about fifteen minutes. Don't you need to freshen up before your appearance?"

"She shouldn't change a thing," Donovan piped up. "She's lovely the way she is."

Chet glared at him. "She's drunk."

"I've never been drunk in my life." Grace started to stand but collapsed back onto her chair.

"Mr. Riker, my dinner guest is fine. She's understandably nervous about her first public appearance. I thought the champagne would ease her tension."

"I do feel wonderful," Grace said.

Chet looked at her again. "You're drunk."

Grace narrowed her eyes at Chet and raised her glass. He took it out of her hands.

Her eyes opened wide in indignation. "Excuse me!"

"C'mon." He gently took her by the arm.

The publicist stood. "Pardon me, Mr. Riker, but we haven't finished our meal."

As Chet pulled Grace to her feet, she swayed against him. "If she can't make this appearance, you'll be finished," Chet snapped. "Isn't it your job to make her presentable? How could you let this happen?"

"She's fine," Donovan protested.

Grace wobbled on her heels as Chet ushered her away from

the table. When the train lurched, she held on to the back of chairs to steady herself and nearly fell on a fellow diner.

Once inside her private railcar, she plopped down onto the sofa. Chet pulled the chain for a porter. "You need coffee."

"I've got a headache." Grace slid down the back of the sofa and lay down.

"Don't do that." Chet hurried over and pulled her up. No stranger to the effects of the bubbly, he knew if she moved into a prone position, it would be all over. He propped her up and sat next to her to prevent her from sliding off the sofa.

Someone knocked on the door.

"Come in," he called.

The Pullman porter entered.

"We need a pot of coffee—fast," Chet said.

The man nodded and left.

Grace leaned her head against Chet's shoulder. Drops of perspiration glistened on her forehead and nose. Not good.

"Is it hot in here?" she asked, pulling forward. She tugged at the buttons on her jacket and loosened them. She tried to take the jacket off but struggled with the sleeves. Chet helped ease the fabric off her arms. She slumped back and rested her head on his shoulder again. She mopped her brow. "I don't feel well."

"Oh no." Chet yanked her up and guided her to the bathroom. He stood her over the water closet and held her steady while she wretched and moaned. He grabbed a washcloth, soaked it with cold water, and cleaned her face. When finished, he picked her up and started out of the bathroom to be greeted by the Pullman porter, Lucile, and Donovan Green.

"She's not going to make her appearance," Chet said, his eyes leveled on the errant publicist. He exited the bathroom, took her down the small hallway, and tucked her into bed.

❧

GRACE'S HEAD hammered when she tried to lift it. To her left, a small shaft of light streamed through the velvet curtains, and the bed rocked and swayed beneath her with the movement of the train, making her unbearably queasy. She felt the urge to go to the bathroom to relieve the queasiness, but it hurt too much to lift her head. She groaned. Her mouth felt as if it were filled with cotton, and her sudden need for water drove her upward, despite the pain and dizziness. She had to have water or she would die!

As she began to crawl out of bed, she noticed a full pitcher and a glass on the nightstand. With shaky hands, she poured herself some water and gulped it down in seconds. She drank until she could drink no more, and her head started to spin again. She flopped back down against the satin covers.

When things seemed a little steadier, she slowly sat up. She was wearing only her day shift and bloomers. When had she undressed? She didn't even remember going to bed. Sunlight invaded the room as she lifted the edge of the curtain. Daytime.

She rested her head in her hands. What had happened?

A noise at the door made her jerk her head up, which she immediately regretted. She closed her eyes for a moment, and when she opened them, Chet stood in the doorway, staring at her in her unmentionables. She hurriedly gathered the bedsheets around her.

"How dare you—"

"How do you think you got to bed last night?" Chet smiled and leaned against the doorframe, crossing his arms. The smirk on his face was infuriating.

Grace cringed at the obvious meaning of his words. Suddenly, everything came back to her: Donovan the publicist, the champagne, getting sick. She groaned and buried her face in the sheets.

Chet laughed, and she peered out of the covers as he walked over to the vanity. He grabbed the stool and sat down, resting his elbows on his knees. "It wasn't your fault, you know."

She glanced up at him.

"He shouldn't have plied you with champagne," he went on. "I'm just glad I got you out of there when I did."

The comment irked her. Did he always have to play the knight in shining armor? Then she remembered the speaking engagement. She'd missed her first public appearance because of drunkenness? Shame made her want to sink back under the covers and stay there forever. She had behaved like Sophia. She wanted to cry and would have save for the man who sat on her vanity stool staring at her in her underwear.

"What about my appearance?" Her voice cracked.

"I told the press and well-wishers you had experienced some motion sickness and deeply regretted not being able to make it. They were quite gracious. Some even sent flowers. They're in the parlor."

A plausible excuse. "Thank you."

"It's what I get paid for." His words came out clipped, making her bristle.

"I'd like to get dressed now."

"Good. I've ordered your breakfast."

The thought of food made the blood drain from her face, but she didn't say another word. Her humiliation couldn't get any worse. Thoughts of Sophia made her chest ache. Why did she have to die and leave her to carry this burden? Grace immediately shook away her selfish question. And how could she have thought such a terrible thing of her sister?

"You okay?" Chet's brow knitted with what appeared to be concern.

She nodded and forced back the tears that threatened to burst forth. She'd never been more miserable. After Chet walked out of the room, she buried her face in the bed sheets again, and sobbed.

When she emerged bathed and dressed an hour later, her breakfast awaited her on the table in the parlor, and Chet was gone. She looked around at a number of the bouquets decorating the room, and guilt bloomed anew like a thorny vine. She'd behaved horribly. She'd been so excited about the plans to visit the orphanage. New Mexico seemed such an exotic place. That, combined with the nervousness of the Chicago appearance had made her lose her head and drink too much.

She managed to swallow a piece of dry toast but couldn't handle the eggs or bacon. She placed her napkin over them and pushed them away. She tried to remember her schedule for the day but couldn't think. The smell of bacon and eggs became unbearable. She picked up the plate to deposit it in the hallway.

When she opened the door, Lucile and a beautiful girl with strawberry-blond hair stood before her. "Are you recovered, dear?" Lucile reached for the plate and placed it on the hallway floor.

"I'm feeling better, thank you."

"Grace, this is Nicole. She will be assisting me on the trip. An associate of mine in Chicago recommended her. I've been assured she's quite capable." Lucile smiled at the girl, who beamed at the compliment.

Grace's heart sank. The position that Grace so coveted had been handed to this girl whom Lucile didn't even know? A wave of disappointment left Grace feeling woozy. "It's nice to meet you, Nicole," she forced out as kindly as she could.

The girl quickly turned her eyes to Grace but didn't say a word.

Grace looked to Lucile for an explanation.

"She's French and has difficulty speaking English, but I think we'll get on just fine."

"It's nice to have you with us," Grace tried again.

Still nothing from the girl except another cursory glance and the flicker of a smile. Grace tried to ignore the irritation prickling under her skin.

"Shall we have lunch before setting to work?" Lucile asked. She gathered both girls by the arms.

More food? She'd just been served breakfast!

She didn't complain, though, and in the dining car, Grace picked at her food and tried to make conversation with Nicole. She didn't have any more luck than she'd had before, so she listened to the girl and Lucile chat in French.

Later, back in the private car, Grace tried on one of the gowns Lucile had just finished. Just as she emerged from the bedroom wearing it, Chet entered. A bloom of heat rushed up Grace's neck as she saw the look of admiration on his handsome face. She smiled in complete agreement. The dress was stunning, yet more revealing than anything she'd ever worn before. It plunged low in the front and almost to her hips in back. When she mischievously twirled and saw Chet's eyes widen, she was struck with warm satisfaction. Having received his appreciative stares before, she suddenly realized she had begun to look forward to them. Many people spoke of her beauty, but no one made her *feel* beautiful the way he did. She stepped onto the portable wooden platform, and Lucile and Nicole went to work while Chet settled in the corner of the room with a newspaper.

Grace gazed out the window as the two women pinned the hem of her gown. Nicole's fingers flew, deft and fluid with precision as she pierced the fabric. Somewhere deep inside, Grace hoped Nicole's seamstress skills would pale in comparison to hers. She glanced over at Chet, who at least pretended to be completely immersed in his paper. Suddenly, guilt festered and grew at her desire for the new girl's failure. She shouldn't wish that upon anyone.

"Nicole, how long have you been in America?" Grace asked.

"Three months." The girl didn't look at her but remained focused on her work.

"How do you like it?"

"Hmm." Her voice rose. "I think I like." Her eyes landed on

Chet. He must have felt the stare, as he glanced up from his newspaper and smiled at the girl.

Grace raised her chin, trying to relieve the tightening in her chest. So Chet's admiring glances weren't reserved exclusively for her. But why should they be? Why would he be different from any other man? Just like Flo, who thought nothing of seducing women and then leaving them to move on to another. To Chet, Grace remained little more than another pretty face—or worse, a job.

"Lucile, I'm very tired. Will we be finished soon?" She wanted to be alone. She'd almost been caught up in Chet's charms like a fool, and it made her angry at herself.

"A few more minutes," Lucile said with a mouthful of pins. Grace stood still while they completed the work. "There, you're done, darling. Go ahead and change your clothes. Nicole, will you please go to our car and set up my sewing equipment?"

"Yes, madam."

Grace watched as the girl prepared to leave, then watched Chet smile at her again. The girl waved her fingers at him. Grace's gaze shifted back to Chet, who responded with an amused grin. She glared at him, turned abruptly, stepped down from the dais, and headed into the bedroom, Lucile following after her.

When she came out again, alone, after Lucile had gone, Chet was still reviewing his paper in silence. She sighed, thinking this arrangement with him so close all the time would probably drive her mad. To divert her thoughts, she took up the art pad and pencils Lucile had brought and began to sketch. As the pencil scratched against the paper, she imagined her visit to the orphanage in New Mexico. Donovan had mentioned something about horseback riding. How would she manage that in the fine gowns Lucile was making for her? She needed something more practical, more . . .

Chet lowered his paper, interrupting her thoughts. She looked up, annoyed to be distracted from the idea that had just popped into her head.

"What do you think of Nicole?" he asked.

"What does it matter what I think?" She lifted her head and narrowed her eyes at him.

"She seems like a nice girl."

"Didn't you have to approve her working for Lucile? As my 'bodyguard,' I assume you had to interview her or find out about her before she boarded. Isn't that right?"

"Yes, yes, that's right."

"Well, you've obviously had more conversation with her than I have. She doesn't seem to be too interested in anything I have to say." Grace tried to keep her jealousy at bay. She hoped it wasn't too obvious.

Just then, there was a knock at the parlor door. Chet got up and answered it. The porter handed him a sealed note. "For Miss Michelle," he said. Chet took the note and then handed it to Grace. She opened it.

"We should go to the observation car. Get out of here for awhile." Chet said. "What do you say?"

Grace looked down at her drawing pad. "No, I have some work I'd like to do."

"Aw, c'mon. The car has nice big windows. The sunshine will do you good."

She held up the note. "I'm having dinner with Donovan in a few hours. We need to discuss the plans for my upcoming appearances."

His mouth hardened at her words.

Grace smiled, pleased she'd received the desired reaction.

CHAPTER FOURTEEN

*J*UNE 5, 1920 - KANSAS CITY, MO

The mighty steam engine chugged its way toward the bustling town of Kansas City. As they made their way across the landscape, Grace marveled at the azure-blue skies, miles of golden wheat fields, and open land. Gradually, the scenery transformed and reduced itself down to busy, carriage-laden streets and stoic brick buildings.

Grace and Lucile settled in around the table in the parlor of Grace's railcar—Lucile sewing intricate beads on one of Grace's gowns, Grace sketching. Chet appeared engrossed in his newspaper as usual, but Grace knew he was listening to every word of her conversation.

"Where is Nicole this afternoon?" Grace asked. "I thought she would be here with us." Grace lifted her eyes to Lucile's and then glanced at Chet. No reaction.

"Poor girl's not feeling well. Says she has a headache."

"Pity," Grace said, trying not to display her glee at the young woman's absence.

"Tell me, what does Donovan have planned for you in New Mexico?" Lucile asked.

Grace put down her pencil and leaned in toward Lucile. "There is to be a brunch gala in Flo's—well, *my*—honor, at the central railway stop. Some place called the Fred Harvey Hotel and Restaurant."

Lucile looked up at her with sparking eyes. "The Fred Harvey has a fine reputation. Some friends of mine stayed there while traveling from Los Angeles to Chicago. Wonderful food. And the waitresses' uniforms are nearly as famous as the hotel. Ankle-length black dresses with white aprons, pinafore style, and a large white bow at the back of their heads."

"Sounds charming. I'm nervous about the breakfast but excited about the orphanage visit."

"You'll be fine, dear." Lucile bent her head over the bead-work again, concentrating.

Grace knew Lucile had trouble seeing the fine detail— another reason she had hired Nicole—but Grace couldn't deny the joy she continued to feel at the girl's absence.

Chet coughed from behind the paper but didn't move the journal from his face. What was in that paper that could possibly be so engaging?

Grace picked up her pencil and doodled swirls and flour-ishes, hard lines and angles, waiting for inspiration to hit. Thinking about her visit to the orphanage, Grace tapped the eraser against her chin.

"Lucile," she said, looking up from her drawings, "I have an idea for my ensemble in New Mexico."

"Oh?"

"Look."

Grace finished sketching her idea on the pad and shifted it over to Lucile.

"A riding skirt?"

"Yes. Donovan said we might take a horseback ride to the orphanage."

"But wouldn't you prefer jodhpurs? Although, I'm not sure I

have the right fabric for jodhpurs." Lucile studied the drawing with her hand under her chin.

"The riding skirt would be so much easier to make," Grace said. "And faster. Besides, don't you think this has more of a western flair?" Grace fidgeted at the woman's silence, hungry for approval.

"I think it's brilliant, dear. I'll whip it up for you. I have the perfect gabardine. Do you think they should be lined? I think most definitely," Lucile said, answering her own question. "I'll get to work."

"Really?"

Lucile put a hand over Grace's. "You are quite talented, my dear."

Grace could feel her smile split her face until she remembered that she was traveling with the great Lucile, Lady Duff Gordon as Ziegfeld's new star—a pretty face, a passable voice, a marginal dancer—but not a designer.

With a robust booming of the engine's whistle, they pulled into the train station where a large crowd had gathered with balloons and streamers, painting a colorful rainbow among the throngs of faces.

"What are all these people doing here?" Grace asked, walking toward the sofa under the window. She pressed her knee into the cushions and leaned forward against the back of the sofa, resting her arms along the wooden top get a better look outside.

"They're here to see you," Chet said from behind his paper.

She turned from the window to glance at him but was greeted with only the black-and-white, finely pressed newspaper in front of his face.

"Oh . . . yes." She turned back to look at the crowds. "I keep forgetting."

Someone knocked at the door.

"Yes?" Grace rang out, leaving her post at the window.

"May I come in?" Donovan cracked the door and peeked in.

"Of course."

Chet kept the paper up to his face.

After a cursory glance at Chet, Donovan focused his attention on Grace. "We're only in Kansas City for a few hours. You'll make your introductory speech here, from the caboose's platform, and then we're being escorted to the Barstow School. It's an innovative, very avant-garde preparatory school, newly founded by two fine ladies from Wellesley College."

"Will I have to speak at the school?"

"No, we are only going on a tour, to see their creative teaching methods and smile at the children."

Grace pressed her hands together, feeling the moisture that had bloomed at the mere thought of giving her first speech, due in just a few minutes.

"Very well."

Donovan seemed to notice her distress and placed his hand on her arm. "This is a short speech, mainly highlighting our stops along the way to California and paying special attention to your upcoming visit to the orphanage in New Mexico." He handed his notes to Grace. She sat down, her eyes glued to the paper, trying to absorb every word.

"You don't have to memorize it verbatim," Donovan explained as he sat down next to her. When his knee bumped against hers, Grace reflexively jerked away, stealing a glance at Chet, the newspaper still shielding his face. Donovan didn't seem to notice. "Just get an idea of the highlights," he said cheerily. "You're going to be fine."

Grace tried a few lines out loud, her voice cracking and the paper shaking in her hands.

"See," Donovan said. "Perfect. Just like you."

Chet lowered the paper and gave her a disapproving frown. She half expected an eye roll. Instead, he folded the paper and plopped it down on the coffee table. "How soon 'til we need to be out on the platform?"

"In about twenty minutes," the publicist said. "But you can stay here with your paper. I have things completely in hand, my friend."

"Sure. Just like the *last* time she was scheduled to give a speech and you got her drunk on champagne. I will be accompanying both of you to the platform—and I'm not your friend."

Now Grace wanted to roll her eyes. The bickering between these two did not ease the nervous ache in her stomach. She'd rather Chet not be there on the platform to see her stumble over her words and blush crimson with embarrassment at all the attention focused on her. She'd much rather deal with him in a more controlled situation, with no danger of her making a complete fool of herself.

She glanced up from her notes and caught him observing her, his face set in hard lines with the hint of a smile tugging at his lips. She quickly looked back down at the paper, trying to concentrate on the words and not the fluttering of her heart.

GRACE STEPPED onto the platform and into the warm, humid air. A hundred faces looked up at her, their expressions expectant and awestruck. Grace's knees threatened to buckle, and she tried to breathe deeply as she stared out at the sea of people. The sounds of carts rolling and horse hooves clopping on the streets blended with the clamoring voices of the crowd, making her dizzy. She leaned against Donovan's arm for support, but the set of Chet's shoulders and the steely expression in his eyes as he scanned the crowd gave Grace the comfort she craved. He exuded a confidence that made her feel safe. She hoped she could find her voice to deliver her speech and focused on Chet's determined assuredness.

"May I read the speech?" she asked Donovan under her breath as she smiled and waved to the audience.

"Absolutely not," he said, squeezing her elbow. "Use the notes for reference, but eye contact is of the utmost importance. Look confident at all costs."

Grace cleared her throat, took another look at Chet. "Good people of Kansas City," she said, projecting as well as she knew how. The crowd erupted with applause and then quieted, waiting for more. Grace conjured up the image of Sophia addressing her fans and emulated her famous theatrical gestures and affected speech. Before she knew it, she'd finished, and the crowd rang out their approval.

Donovan led her back inside the caboose and took both of her hands in his. "Astounding, darling! Well done!"

Grace gulped in air as if it were her first breath in the last ten minutes.

"Yes, thank you. It wasn't . . . horrible."

"Of course not! You are a natural—born to do this. They especially loved when you talked about visiting the orphanage. I could see it in their faces."

"I could, too."

Donovan grabbed her around the waist and folded her in his arms.

Grace shoved him away, her hands on his chest. "*Mr. Green,* I hardly think an embrace is appropriate. You are my publicist, not my—"

Chet walked into the caboose, carrying a newspaper, the brim of his hat hiding his eyes. Grace pulled her hands away from Donovan's chest. Chet removed his hat, and his gaze settled on the two of them. An awkward stillness electrified the space in their triangle.

"Everything all right here?" Chet asked.

Grace stepped away from Donovan Green. "Yes, perfectly all right."

The three of them stood in silence, Chet and Donovan in a

stare down. To Grace's relief, a Pullman porter knocked and then stuck his head through the doorway of the car.

He thrust a note into her publicist's hand. "Telegram for you, sir."

Donovan took the note and pursed his lips in a disappointed frown. "The tour of the Barstow School has been canceled. They've had a water main break."

"Oh, how unfortunate," Grace said, hoping the utter relief in her voice didn't betray her. She'd had enough of crowds and appearances for one day. "Well, I think I will retire to Billie's —*my*—car. I'm rather tired."

"Yes," said Donovan. "We can hammer out the details for the rest of the trip, if you'd like."

"She said she's tired." Chet secured his hat back on his head.

"Yes," she reiterated. "I think I'll read."

"Very well," said Donovan. "Good day, then." He nodded to Grace. Chet held the door open for him. Grace was about to squeeze herself past Chet and head into her bedroom when he stopped her. He handed her the paper, a copy of *Variety*.

"I thought you should see this," he said.

She took the paper and perused the first page. She glanced up at him, confused.

"Page three," he said.

She flipped through until her eyes rested on the headline of page three: Ziegfeld Star's California Funeral. Her jaw clenched at the memory that they'd had the funeral without her. Her eyes lowered to the photograph of a swarm of people approaching the casket. Grace's breath caught in her throat. She surveyed the mourning faces: Jack, of course; his sister, Mary Pickford; and her husband, Douglas Fairbanks. And then she spotted a familiar face among the strangers. Grace squinted to get a better look at the woman underneath the large, dark hat.

Lillian Lorraine.

Grace turned down her brows in confusion. "Lillian? At my

sister's funeral? The woman couldn't stand Sophia." She looked up into Chet's face.

Chet shrugged. "She was in Los Angeles at the time. Probably wanted to be 'seen' paying her respects." He paused. "Funny thing, though . . . I just saw her on the train. She's headed back to Los Angeles. Says she has a picture. She must have gone to the funeral, come back to pester Flo about the part in his show, and is now headed back to California."

"I can't begin to understand that woman. It always seemed like she was following my sister around. And now, me."

"This running back and forth to Los Angeles is a bit strange, but I think she's harmless. Regardless, I'll keep an eye on her."

Confused, Grace continued to peruse the article and stopped when she read, *Liane Held, daughter of actress Anna Held and stepdaughter to Florenz Ziegfeld Jr., flew in from Europe to attend the funeral.*

Grace let her arms drop, banging the paper against her legs. "Liane Held, too? Why would she attend the funeral?"

"Perhaps she thought Flo would be there. Maybe she wanted to see him?"

"Why would Flo go and not take me? Flo didn't even attend Anna's funeral. Liane would know that he wouldn't go all the way to Los Angeles for Sophia's." Grace's mind was racing. "Sophia and I never even met Liane."

"Could be the same reason Lillian was there." Chet quickly took the paper from her and folded it up. "I've heard that Miss Held is attempting to follow in her mother's footsteps, to be an actress. Hollywood seems to be the place for that these days."

"But it just doesn't make sense."

Chet put his hands in his pockets and rocked back on his heels, his mouth tight. "I'm sure they have their reasons."

∾

THAT EVENING, Grace shared a meal with Lucile in the dining car. They sat in the center of the car in a curtained booth, the curtains spread wide at Grace's insistence. She wanted to see everything that transpired around her. Chet insisted he come, but Lucile waved him off and promised she wouldn't take her eyes off his charge.

"Seems you two need a little space," Lucile said to Grace as she raised a wineglass to her lips. "The tension between you two is pretty thick. Is that a good thing?"

"I've not lived in such close quarters with anyone but Sophia. And the fact that he's a man—" Grace stabbed at a piece of asparagus.

"A very attractive man."

"You aren't making it any easier."

Lucile reached over and patted Grace's hand. "This is a very businesslike arrangement. Mr. Riker seems a professional in every way. You've no need to worry."

Grace pressed on a smile and picked at her food as Lucile prattled on about one of her new stores. Unable to finish her dinner, Grace set down her fork.

"Lucile, do you mind if I return to my car? I feel a headache starting." Grace pressed her fingers to her temple in an attempt to stop the throbbing. The constant strain of feeling as if she was being followed was taking its toll. Luckily, Lucile was agreeable, stating she had much work to do for their upcoming arrival in New Mexico anyway.

"Just give me a moment. I will walk you back to your car," Lucile said.

"No, no, don't worry about me. Enjoy the rest of your meal."

"But what about Chet?"

"I'll tell him you walked me back." Grace smiled. "He's probably still reading his paper." Lucile looked uneasy. "Truly, I'll be fine." Grace smiled again and bid Lucile good night.

Grace exited the dining car just as a group of new passengers were snaking their way through the railcars. When a family of five with three small children attempted to pass, Grace pressed herself against the wall as they pushed and shuffled down the corridor, their bulging suitcases bumping against her legs. Exasperated, Grace tried to be patient as she was squeezed against the wall. She looked through the windows to the next car and saw Lillian Lorraine, in her signature large hat, exchanging heated words with a man.

The man leaned toward her, his finger pointing at her face. His brown suit looked worn, old, like he'd had it forever, and the sleeves were three to four inches short of his wrist. Lillian slapped the man's hand away and her usually placid and smug porcelain expression turned to carved stone. Grace could hear nothing of their conversation with the chugging of the train and the constant creaking of the cars rattling along the track. The man raked off his hat, pointed that in Lillian's face now, and seemed to be on the counterattack.

Grace's legs turned to water when she saw the large scar running across his forehead and down his temple. He stood only a hundred feet away from her. Her breath caught. Could it really be him? The man who'd tried to run her down with the car? The man she thought was dead?

And what was he doing arguing with Lillian, let alone about what? How did they know each other?

Grace's knees wobbled even more. Chet had just told her Lillian was on the train, but why hadn't Flo mentioned she would be going to California, too? Maybe he didn't know. Grace took in a deep breath, trying to swallow her rapidly rising paranoia. She closed her eyes to steady her mind. She told herself that the man in the brown suit merely resembled the man from her past, and Lillian, never satisfied with her current situation, was probably going to California just to taunt Flo. But that still didn't explain why they were together.

She now wished Chet had accompanied her and Lucile to

dinner. She should never have let him leave her side. *He* never should have let her leave *his* side.

Grace pulled the brim of her hat lower over her eyes, and she pressed her way through the crowd, doing her best to hide her face from the man and Lillian. Once she had passed the other passengers, she ran down the aisle, her body bouncing off the walls as the train bent with a curve in the tracks. When she reached her private car, she frantically dug through her handbag for the keys. Mumbling under her breath and furtively looking behind her like a crazy person, her hands shook, her eyes unable to focus on the lock and key.

Within seconds, just as she was sliding the key into the lock, Chet arrived behind her.

"Grace," he said, placing his hand over hers, steadying her. "Why are you alone? Where is Lady Duff Gordon?"

"Oh." Grace jumped at the sight of him and the feel of his hand on hers. "She just left."

Chet turned the key and barely got the door opened before Grace shot past him and into the parlor. She let out a huge sigh of relief, her back to him, and tried to still her shaking hands. She took off her hat, turned around to face Chet, and attempted to smile with confidence.

"Are you all right? What happened?" he asked.

Not sure if she could speak, Grace cleared her throat. Should she tell him she had seen a ghost? That she suspected a dead man and a jealous starlet were following her across the country? For what, she had no idea.

No, she had to be wrong. What she had just seen had to be a delusion, an odd coincidence. Lillian Lorraine was known for her dramatic altercations with others. Her collusion with the man in the brown suit had just been a figment of Grace's imagination. No need to set off any alarms or make her bodyguard feel even more protective.

"Grace?"

"I'm fine." She fanned a hand in front of her face. "The crush of all those passengers unnerved me . . . but I'm fine. I just needed some air."

"A week on a train does get a little claustrophobic. Perhaps I'll go have a drink. Be sure to lock the door behind me."

"No!" she shouted.

Chet gave her a quizzical look. "You don't want me to have a drink, or you don't want me to leave?"

"Could you have a drink here?" Grace clasped her hands to keep them from shaking again. "I'm a little nervous and don't want to be alone."

If she had seen the man she thought was dead very much alive, Chet would want to know for sure, which could possibly expose her to an accusation of attempted murder. Lillian Lorraine's presence probably meant nothing, just the whim of a spoiled actress going to ludicrous lengths to get her way. The man in the brown suit might have simply insulted Lillian; it happened often, at least to Lillian's perception. No, nothing good would come of Chet's involvement. Grace could handle it for the time being.

"I thought you wanted to be alone." Chet put his hands into his pockets, confusion written on his face.

"That was before. Now I don't want to be alone." She sounded ridiculous. What she wanted was to retreat into the bedroom and hide from everyone.

Chet, completely dumbfounded, shrugged his shoulders. "Okay, I'll order a drink to be brought here. Do you need anything? Champagne?"

Stiffly, she shook her head. "Just don't leave." She walked into the bedroom and closed the door, irritated that she'd shown her vulnerability and praying the ghost had not come back to life.

CHAPTER FIFTEEN

hat night, images of Sophia, Flo, Lillian, costumes, stages, trains, crowds, and the scarred man in the brown suit plagued Grace's dreams. The desert heat trapped in the railcar made sleep impossible, and Grace tossed and turned, her sheer cotton nightgown wrapping around her waist and legs. Tangled and frustrated, she got up to untwist the nightgown and opened one of the small windows a crack. Perhaps if she cooled her face with some water she'd be better able to sleep. She tiptoed away from the bed so she wouldn't wake Chet and made her way to the bathroom.

Holding her hands in front of her in the darkness, she walked toward the bedroom door. Fumbling with the knob, she turned it and stepped forward, opening it, and ran headlong into a wall of skin and muscle. She screamed, and a hand clamped down on her mouth. Grace blinked, her eyes adjusting to the darkness, and saw Chet standing bare chested in front of her. He released her mouth and placed his hands on her arms, the heat of his palms burning her skin through the thin nightgown.

"Sorry." He let go of her. "I didn't want you to wake the other passengers. Are you okay?"

He stood so close she could feel his breath on her cheek and his chin brushing against her hair. "I was just going— You scared me." Grace clutched at her stomach.

"I can see that. I'm sorry. Ladies first." He motioned toward the bathroom.

"Thank you."

She scurried into the bathroom, shut the door, and pulled the chain on the lamp. Grace stared at herself in the mirror and tried to steady the furious pounding of her heart. Leaning over the sink, she turned on the water, closed her eyes, and splashed her face, trying to cool her senses.

As frightened as she had been, Grace couldn't help wondering what it would be like to kiss Chet. He'd been so close. The smell of him still lingered—musk and cinnamon. She had felt the weight of his hands on her body, his warm, masculine breath on her face and hair. She shook her head. A kiss could not happen.

Easing the door open, she saw Chet standing in the parlor, now clothed. She trembled as his gaze moved down her face, to her breasts, hips, legs, and then back up again. His gaze might as well have been his hands exploring her for the sensation it had produced. She had left the bathroom light on behind her and suddenly realized that the sheerness of her white gown had illuminated everything beneath it. She crossed her arms over herself and moved out of the light toward the bedroom door. As she opened it, she looked back over her shoulder and saw his eyes still lingering on her. There was a hunger in them that frightened and thrilled her at the same time.

For the first time, Grace fully understood men and women's attraction for one another, the burning desire that consumed hearts and minds. For the first time, Grace was consumed by the desire to know a man.

∾

CHET wet his face with the coldest water he could get from the little trickle of the tap and tried to forget the feel of Grace's warm, soft body beneath her cotton shift. This cohabitation was agony. The smallness of her waist, the silkiness of her hair, and the realization that she hadn't pulled away from him stirred his desire even more. How he had wanted to draw her fragile body into his arms and cover her with his mouth—taste her, smell her, touch her.

And he'd felt her desire, too. Before, he had doubted her interest because of her aloof behavior, but now he knew for certain the interest existed; she just feared it. Perhaps the petite Miss Michelle had never experienced the power of longing before. He, on the other hand, knew all too well the allure of lust.

He turned off the water and toweled his face. By early morning they would be in Albuquerque. That publicist buffoon, taking his job a little too seriously, had arranged a jam-packed day for Grace tomorrow. The memory of Grace wrapped in Green's arms sent Chet's blood pressure soaring. He'd seen her pull away from the man's groping hands but hadn't wanted to distress her by making any kind of a scene. Had she pulled away out of embarrassment, or had she thwarted Green's advances? He hoped the latter. The greedy, womanizing bastard would simply use her and throw her away.

But Chet couldn't get involved in her emotional life. How could he do his job objectively if his mind and heart became enmeshed with hers? He wouldn't be able to see clearly, react quickly. His senses would be clouded by the distraction of her. He had to keep his wits about him at all times. For her safety, she would have to be off-limits. He'd have to forget any physical attraction or emotional connection, and keep things strictly business.

He ran a hand through his hair, remembering Marciano's whelps who he'd seen on the train. His association with

Marciano put Grace in even more danger, and he hated that fact. He had to make sure nothing happened to her.

Chet went back to the sofa, discarded his blankets, and attempted to sleep.

~

ALBUQUERQUE, NM

The next morning, Grace woke to a rapping at her door.

Seconds later, Lucile burst in. "What are you doing child? It's nearly nine o'clock. They're waiting for you."

"I couldn't sleep last night." Grace tried to shake the fog of sleep from her head.

"Well, you must get up. We've arrived at the depot in Albuquerque. The hotel is right across the street. Your honorary brunch starts in one hour." Lucile opened the wardrobe and rifled through it for Grace's new outfit.

"It's toward the far end," Grace said, her mind beginning to clear. "I didn't want it to get mussed."

Lucile pulled the ensemble from the wardrobe and meticulously laid it out on the bed. Grace tried to focus, blinked several times, then yawned.

"I'll fill the ewer with water so you can wash up," Lucile said. "Quickly now."

Lucile dashed for the ceramic basin and pitcher and fled to the bathroom. A few minutes later, she returned and set the items on the bureau. Grace climbed out of bed and began to wash. As the water refreshed her, she became more alert and alive, like a flower opening its petals. She reached for her chemise, took off her nightgown, and dressed while Lucile clucked around her like a mother hen.

"The outfit you envisioned is truly avant-garde," she said, beaming. "I can't remember the last time I wanted to stay up all night sewing. I felt young again. What a splendid idea! Once they see you in this, every woman will want to wear this very ensemble. It is so becoming on you."

Grace trilled with pleasure. She *could* be a designer—and a good one—if only Flo wouldn't push her into stardom.

"You are a genius, my girl, a genius!" Lucile stood back, admiring the garments. "Oh! Don't forget the jacket. And here, look what I found to complement the look." She scurried to a nearby trunk and pulled out a western-style hat and animal-print scarf. "Will Rogers loaned the hat to me for a fashion show once, and when I tried to return it, he told me to keep it. I thought it might come in handy, as we were heading to the west on this trip."

"The scarf will lend a touch of the wild. You'll be all the rage, darling."

That will please Flo, Grace thought, frowning. She and the clothing would be looked at as objects, commodities. No one would know she was actually wearing her art, something she designed.

With a sigh, she braided her hair and let it fall down her back. After tipping the hat slightly askew on her head, she wrapped the scarf around her neck. She tied the ends with a loose slip knot.

Grace and Lucile emerged from the bedroom to be confronted by a tense wall of silence. Donovan Green sat on the sofa, and Chet stood near the doorway, both feigning ignorance of each other.

Donovan sprang to his feet, like a cat about to eat a goldfish, his face fresh and pink and full of awed excitement. "You look marvelous, my dear. Just perfect. They are going to love you."

Grace glanced at Chet, whose face remained stony. The clandestine meeting last night in the hallway might as well have happened a hundred years ago. Grace stamped down the flutter in her stomach. She had to focus on what lay ahead of her today.

"Thank you, Mr. Green . . . Donovan. Shall we go?" She

gently wrapped her fingers around Donovan's arm, refusing to meet Chet's eyes as the smug publicist escorted her to the cheering crowd.

GRACE and her small troupe of people—Lucile, Nicole, Donovan, and Chet—entered the hotel to find it resplendent with the unusual decor and smells of the southwest. The dining room resembled an old Mexican cantina. The weathered, hand-laid brick floor, dotted with Navajo rugs woven to feature complicated angular designs, effused warmth. Electric lights fashioned into faux candles lit up the cowboy-rustic iron chandeliers, and the tables and chairs were made of tanned pigskin that was pulled tight over sinewy willow bark.

Waitresses bustled about in the famous white-on-black Harvey hotel uniforms. "Absolutely delightful," Lucile said as the maître d' led them to their table.

A portly man with a curved wax mustache and a monocle approached Grace. He held a cigar aloft in one hand. "Miss Michelle, so delighted you could join us. I'm Charles Wade, Mayor of Albuquerque."

"Mayor Wade," Donovan said, elbowing his way past Lucile and Chet. "The pleasure is ours."

Grace gave him a look of disdain, beginning to understand Chet's annoyance.

Mayor Wade nodded to Donovan but placed his hand at Grace's elbow. "Please, come have a seat." He led her to a chair and then motioned for the others to sit. Nicole deliberately chose a seat next to Chet, who pulled the chair out for her. Grace bit the inside of her cheek to stop herself from looking sullen, but she graciously accepted the mayor's assistance with her own chair.

Mayor Wade settled his bulk into the curve of his seat and leaned closer to her. He held the cigar in front of his face, inspecting it. "It's not very often we receive a celebrity in our little town."

Not sure what to say, Grace gave him a tight smile. Fortunately, four waitresses appeared at the table as if they'd been wished there by a magic wand. They held food-laden trays and began to serve the meal.

Mayor Wade held his arm out toward the food. "May I present Huevos Rancheros, refried beans, rice, and tortillas. Just some of the specialties of this part of the country."

"It looks divine," Lucile said, her eyes alight with eagerness. Grace glanced at Chet seated on the other side of Wade and then at Donovan at her elbow. Their animosity vibrated on either side of her, making her squirm.

"The cuisine is most unique." Lucile grabbed for her glass. Her eyes watered, and she stifled a cough.

"You've noticed the green chili," Donovan said. "The New Mexicans are quite liberal with the fruit. Most of it comes from the southern part of the state. The chilies are grown and cultivated with the greatest of care, and the spiciness of the chili is dependent upon the amount of rainfall per year. We've had a fairly good rainfall this year, so this chili is quite mild compared to the chili of other years. You are simply not used to it."

Chet gave a great sigh as he wiped his mouth with one of the colorfully printed napkins. When Graced looked up and caught Nicole boldly staring at him, she clenched her jaw. The girl's headaches apparently had abated.

"How is your meal?" Chet asked Nicole.

"Trés bon, merci. It's not like food from my home. It creates a, um, how do you say—sensation in the mouth?" She laughed. "Do I say correctly?" the girl asked Chet in her pretty accent, accentuating it with a pout and batting her eyelashes. Grace's stomach soured as Chet directed a gleaming smile back at Nicole.

A waiter brought a round of mimosas to the table. The

delectable combination of orange juice and champagne tickled Grace's nose, but unwilling to embarrass herself again, she pushed the drink away after two sips.

"Are you prepared for your speech?" Donovan whispered in her ear, laying a heavy hand on hers, its weight a bit too familiar for comfort.

In any other circumstance, she would have pulled away from his touch, but she decided to see if she could steer Chet from his isolated conversation with the French girl. She placed her other hand on top of Donovan's. "I think so. You've been wonderful."

His smile oozed over her like thick oil, making her feel like a Christmas goose.

Chet didn't seem to notice their interplay, though, and before she could test the situation further, the mayor rose from his chair, announced Grace as their guest of honor, and introduced her to the other patrons. Polite applause broke out when she stood.

"*Buenos dias!* To the wonderful, warm people of New Mexico," she said, raising her mimosa aloft.

After their meal, Mayor Wade led them outside to the dusty, bustling street. Another crowd awaited Grace there and cheered as she approached. A photographer and reporter stood nearby, as well. The loud pop of the camera flashes made her flinch, and her stomach fluttered as she looked out at the crowd that had gathered. A reporter, a small, skinny man who reminded her of a ferret, moved toward her.

"Miss Michelle, how do you do? I'm Spader, Sandy Spader." He spoke rapidly, neglecting to wait for her response. "How has the trip been so far? Made many appearances? Had many marriage proposals? Ha, ha, ha! Tell me, what is it like coming out to this vast wasteland? A little different than New York, yes?"

"Well, I . . . um. . . ."

A man with a weathered face, dressed in loose-fitting suede pants, a cotton navy shirt, and gauzy headband wrapped thickly about his head, waved the reporter away. Despite the earthy hues of his clothing, he wore an elaborate silver necklace with large chunks of turquoise fashioned and smoothed into a blooming floral design.

Grace leaned toward Lucile. "Look at that necklace. I've never seen anything like it."

"I understand that the Pueblo Indians are expert craftsmen and jewelers," Lucile said. "It's called a squash blossom."

The man motioned to one of the young boys who lurked near the mercantile. He came out holding the reins of a beautiful golden horse. Tall, lean, and well-muscled, the horse had a rich, custard-colored hide and flowing, flaxen mane that glowed in the sun.

Grace pressed her gloved hands to her lips. "She's magnificent."

The Indian man bowed low to her. "She is my gift to you for the day."

"I've never ridden a horse before." Grace grew suddenly apprehensive, but she knew it would be rude to refuse, and she'd created her beautiful outfit for the occasion. "But I'd love to try."

"She is a gentle mare." The Indian man approached her, handing her the reins. "You must trust that she will take care of you, and she will. Just make sure no one comes up behind her. She startles easily."

"Very well." A shiver of fear rose up Grace's spine, but the excitement was making her breathless. "What is her name?"

"Golden Ray of Light. I named her for her color; Palomino."

"It's perfect," Grace said, stroking the nose and head of the mare.

"We have horses for all in your party," the Indian said, addressing the rest of Grace's entourage. "All who wish to go to the orphanage, I will serve as your guide. My name is Frank Deerhunter, but you can call me Deerhunter."

The mayor and the guide motioned for the horses to be

brought out to the group, and several young boys emerged with the animals and waited for Deerhunter to tell them which horses went with which people. Lucile declined the invitation to ride, stating that she and Nicole had much work to finish.

Deerhunter returned his attention to Grace once again. "Another gift for the day," he said as a tall Indian youth walked toward them carrying a beautifully tooled Western saddle. "My other prized possession." He tossed a colorful blanket over the horse's back, and the youth placed the saddle on top of it. "Most of the young men still prefer to ride bareback, but my bones have grown too brittle. This saddle was made by a Mexican leather craftsman and silversmith—a friend of mine—and I use the saddle with pride." He tightened the cinch around the horse's girth.

Grace marveled at the ornate silver decorating the horn, stirrups, and the skirt of the saddle. "Thank you for the honor," she said, awestruck at the man's kindness.

"Are you ready?" Deerhunter asked.

Grace nodded, eager to climb astride, and accepted the man's help mounting the golden-dappled mare. He held onto the horse's reins and helped Grace place her foot into the silver decorated stirrup. Instinctively, she swung her other leg over the horse's back. When her foot found the stirrup, she instantly sensed the feeling of power beneath her.

"Remember. Trust," Deerhunter said.

Chet mounted a tall, dark brown horse with a jet-black mane and tail with ease. He looked natural in the saddle, as if he had been born to ride. She couldn't help but admire his handsome frame atop the majestic horse. The two looked like something out of a fancy picture book.

Deerhunter offered Donovan a beautiful chestnut mare with a coat that shimmered copper in the late-morning sun, but he put a hand up in hesitation.

"You're not going?" Grace asked.

He shook his head.

"Oh, come on, Donovan," Chet said, a devilish grin on his face. "It's good for publicity. Don't worry, you won't dirty your suit."

Donovan turned red in the face and then covered his obvious embarrassment with a chuckle. "So it is, my friend. And that's what I'm here for."

"You keep forgetting—" Chet's smile tightened "—I'm not your friend."

Grace wanted to chide Chet for his rudeness but was too excited about riding to care.

Deerhunter approached Donovan with the chestnut mare. The publicist's self-righteous smile faded, and his face clouded over like thunder before the rain.

The older man helped Donovan mount his horse. Once in the saddle, Donovan clutched the saddle horn. He looked stiff and tense, and ridiculously silly. Grace stifled a giggle as the horse pranced beneath him, draining Donovan's face of color.

"You must relax," Deerhunter said. "She senses your fear."

With a look of concentration on his face, Donovan loosened his grip on the saddle horn and accepted the reins the Indian offered him.

"Ah, nothing to it," Donovan said as if to assure himself.

The photographer and reporter loaded the camera into a small hitched wagon to follow behind.

Deerhunter mounted a regal, fiery, gray stallion and led the excited and anxious party down the dirt road and out into the colorful landscape of the New Mexican desert.

CHAPTER SIXTEEN

*J*t didn't take long for Grace to adjust to the rhythm of her mare's gait. The horse performed beautifully, and Grace had never been more thrilled in her life. Chet, too, looked comfortable astride his horse and experimented with different gaits. He'd trot the horse, then lope, then gallop, then come back to a brisk walk.

Deerhunter and Mayor Wade rode ahead, their mounts walking close together as they talked, probably about political matters and town concerns.

Grace glanced back at Donovan. His face had taken on the hue of day-old oatmeal, and he'd resumed gripping the saddle horn in terror. Grace, however, had quickly figured out that if she held on to the horn, she had less control of the horse. Constant but slight contact from the bit to her hands kept the horse in check. She hoped silently that Donovan's horse wouldn't do anything unpredictable to further embarrass the man. Though annoying, she didn't wish any harm to come to him. The wagon, pulled by two gray nags, ambled behind the party with the reporter and photographer on board.

Chet trotted his horse out ahead of Grace. Not wanting to be left behind, she lifted her body in the saddle and squeezed gently with her legs. The horse moved forward into a fast walk, almost as if the horse was jogging. Grace relaxed and moved with the horse's rhythmic cadence. Then she lifted her body again, squeezed her legs harder, and the horse moved into a trot. Finding the violent bouncing uncomfortable, Grace set her weight onto her right hip. Instantly, the horse's left leg jumped forward, and the mare's pace changed to a slow, rolling lope. It didn't take long for Grace to catch Chet and pass him.

"You ride well," Chet said as his horse matched her horse's stride.

"You too." Grace urged her horse a little faster. Chet kept up the pace and rode his horse ahead of her Palomino. Not to be outridden by him, Grace prodded her golden steed even faster and soon passed him again, offering him an I-dare-you smile. Chet took the bait and spurred his horse into a gallop. She followed suit, and the two horses sped through the desert. When they passed Deerhunter and the mayor, Grace beamed at the shocked expressions on their faces.

The longer the two horses remained neck and neck, the more Grace laughed with delight. The hot wind blew across her face and made her clothes flap in the wind, and her body hummed, her heart pounding as the exhilaration of freedom made her want to shout for joy. Out here, with the wind in her hair, she didn't have to be anyone except Grace Michelle.

From Chet's concentrated expression, it seemed he'd taken the challenge to heart, which made Grace laugh even louder and squeeze the horse's girth again. As she passed him, she saw his look of surprise and determination.

"Whoa, not so fast, Grace."

She squealed like a child outrunning the boogeyman and leaned down low over the horse's neck. She could feel the mare's legs pump and her rib cage expand and contract with rapid bursts of air. The mare snorted and huffed, foam dripping from the bit in her mouth.

Chet raced forward and maneuvered his way in front of Grace to slow her down. Her horse eased her stride, and soon they slowed to a quiet lope. Chet steered his mount close to Grace, took hold of her reins, and brought them to a halt.

"Poor sport." Grace gave him a pout. "You couldn't stand being bested by my trusty Golden Ray."

"Ha! We beat you hands down. I stopped you so we wouldn't get lost out here in the middle of nowhere. Look," he said pointing behind them. Deerhunter and Mayor Wade were mere specks on the horizon, and there was no sign of Donovan Green.

"Over there," Grace said, pointing to a cluster of white brick buildings to the northeast.

"That must be our destination."

Side by side, they walked the horses to let them catch their breath. Both horses had worked up a foamy sweat. Grace felt sorry for having run them so hard; they must have been thirsty in this searing, dry heat. She squinted into the sunlight.

"Here," Chet said, leaning over. He pulled her hat off her back, where it had been anchored by the leather strings coming from each side, and plopped it back on her head.

"Thanks. I didn't realize it had come off."

"I never pegged you for a competitive sort."

She shrugged. "Me neither."

Quiet, and now moving at an even slower pace, Grace surveyed the land around her. She never imagined she would see anything like this landscape. Pale green and violet hues painted the sandy, burnt sienna–colored desert floor with scrub brushes, silver-flecked granite boulders, and blue, majestic mountain ranges to the east and the south. The Rio Grande, like a ribbon of brown silk, shimmered in the distance in front of a thick forest of cottonwood trees the Mayor had called the 'bosque', which he said meant 'forest' in Spanish. If only Sophia could have seen this beautiful land with her, Grace thought, her heart aching with a longing she rarely allowed herself to feel. Her sister would have loved this.

They soon reached the buildings where there stood a large wooden sign with the words *St. Cecilia's Indian Orphanage* in large white letters, welcoming them.

As if they had been awaiting them, a mass of children and Franciscan nuns greeted them. The children surrounded the horses, their faces open, eager, and freshly scrubbed.

An elderly nun approached them. "I'm Sister Antoinette. You must be Miss Michelle."

"Yes," Grace said, dismounting. "And this is my . . . friend, Chet Riker."

The nun smiled, never once removing her hands from under her crisp, black-and-white habit. Chet tipped his hat and glanced at Grace. She diverted her eyes and focused on the children who were caressing her clothes and hair.

"I don't believe they have ever seen blond hair before," Sister Antoinette said. "We always keep our heads covered with our habits."

Grace looked down at the adoring brown faces, most of them with the wide cheekbones and proud foreheads of their Indian ancestors. Others looked characteristically Mexican and had large brown eyes.

"We expected more in your party." Sister Antoinette looked out into the desert.

"They are on their way," Chet assured her.

Two of the older boys hung back from the rest of the children. The slightly squinting eyes and the wary tilt of the older one's head exuded suspicion, or despair, Grace couldn't tell.

"Enrique, Manuel, water their horses, *por favor*," Sister Antoinette called to them.

The two boys obeyed, their eyes avoiding Grace's.

"You must excuse the children's behavior. Those two lost

their families to the Spanish flu. We've mostly been spared, but we did lose some, may they rest in peace."

"How terrible." Grace bit her lower lip. "I know what it's like to lose a family—" Her voice caught. "My heart aches for them."

Sister Antoinette lowered her head in an empathetic bow. When she raised it again, her serene eyes met Grace's. "Would you like to freshen up from the ride?"

Grace nodded to the nun and followed her toward a small building next to the massive one.

"Mr. Riker, there's lemonade inside and a fresh basin of water in back. Please, make yourself at home," the sister called back to him. "And children, leave the gentleman alone. Go play stickball or something."

The children ran to a wooden crate beside the door and retrieved leather gloves, homemade balls, and narrow sticks.

Inside the little brick building, a cool wave of humid but comforting air washed over Grace's face. Sister Antoinette led her to a small room with a long, skinny cot, a chipped but sturdy wardrobe, and, in the corner, a small kneeler adorned with rosaries. A fresh basin of water and a cloth towel rested on the vanity.

"I'm afraid we have no plumbing, but the water is fresh from the well."

Grace smiled and thanked her.

Once she had freshened up, Grace returned to the front of the building and leaned against one of the sturdy posts supporting the shaded overhang. Donovan, Deerhunter, and Mayor Wade stood at the water trough across the way, deep in discussion with Sister Antoinette, patiently waiting as their horses drank. The photographer busied himself setting up his equipment.

Soft, tinkling laughter distracted her. Three more nuns, their hands over their faces as they giggled, gathered at the far end of the building. Having seen her, they quickly stifled their amusement and approached her, offering warm greetings.

"We were laughing at the ball game over there." The nun with a small, button nose pointed to several of the boys and Chet. Atop the pitcher's mound, Chet had shed his coat and hat, and rolled up his shirtsleeves. He threw a slow, underhanded pitch to a skinny, knock-kneed girl of about six years old. She swung fiercely with her stick and missed. Several of the children giggled, and the more they laughed, the more the little girl's lower lip protruded.

Chet stopped the game, handed the ball to an older boy, and approached the girl. He knelt down in front of her and wiped her tears away until a grin appeared between her dimples. He motioned her to the plate again. This time, he stood behind her, his arms over hers, and helped her guide the stick to hit the pitched ball. Contact was made, and the ball soared over the pitcher's head and into the outfield.

When Grace witnessed the girl's face radiating with pride, a lump formed in her throat. Chet pushed the little one gently toward first base, and the girl ran, her skinny legs pumping fast. Grace's hands curled into fists as she silently urged the girl forward. She flew past first base and over second.

A boy in the outfield scooped up the ground ball and aimed for third base. He threw. The third baseman missed. The girl's feet skimmed over that base, too. Chet yelled, encouraging her to run faster. The ball arced toward home plate, but the outfielder overthrew, and the ball skipped past the catcher like a stone thrown flat on the water.

The girl ran over home plate and into Chet's arms. He lifted her high in the air and spun her in circles, her squeals of delight like the sound of a wind chime floating on the breeze. Chet raised her onto his broad shoulders, and she smiled wide. Her teammates surged forward, cheering and jumping around Chet and the little girl.

Grace's heart swelled. Chet's tenderness and encouragement of the girl created an ache she couldn't describe, an affection that made her head spin, her heart pound, and her limbs tingle. Was it respect, admiration, or something more?

Looking around to make sure no one saw her, she wiped the tears that had escaped from her lashes and tried to find some reason to harden her heart to the man who served as her bodyguard.

It didn't work.

~

THE TOUR of the orphanage began in the dormitory where beds with crisp white sheets had been stacked one on top of the other, three beds high. Between the crowded bunks sat small end tables. Grace's heart warmed over how thoughtful the compassionate nuns had been in designing and furnishing this small orphanage that housed too many children.

Now seemed as good a time as any to reward them. "I have something for you, Sister Antoinette," Grace said. When the nun turned to her with a questioning look, Grace presented her with the check. The pop of the photographer's flash made Grace jump once again. Would she ever get used to it?

"You are so kind, Miss Michelle." Sister Antoinette offered Grace a teary smile. "We will use the funds to expand the orphanage and build indoor plumbing."

"I will see about donating more later." Grace made a promise to herself to make it happen. Even if she had to come up with the money herself, she would help these children.

At 3:30 p.m., Mayor Wade announced that the party needed to head back to town. Two boys retrieved the horses, and the party mounted up, all except Donovan Green, who hung behind to speak with Sister Antoinette. Grace hoped it concerned another donation.

When Donovan completed his conversation, he approached her. "I'll arrange for Flo to send more money at the end of the month. He's going to love this."

Grace drew in an appreciative breath and nodded her approval. Donovan patted her knee and then walked around the back of her horse to get to his. Her horse immediately began bucking and kicking, thrusting Grace from her seat. She grasped the horse's mane and then reached both arms downward to encircle the mare's neck.

Though Grace managed to hold on like a bug clinging to a windswept vine, onlookers shouted and jumped away from the horse's flying hooves. Grace tried to speak to the mare in soothing tones, but the wild-eyed horse bucked again, propelling Grace forward. She grabbed the mare's mane and held fast as the horse bolted, taking off at a dead run. Grace tried her best to hang on while being jerked back and forth as Golden Ray raced into the desert. When several large boulders lay in their path, the horse zigzagged her way through them. The horse's quick athleticism jolted Grace from the saddle, but she managed to hang onto the horse's taut and pumping neck. Seconds later, she felt her grip loosen and the weight of one of the stirrups drag on her leg.

Golden Ray of Light cleared another rock bed and, likely agitated by Grace hanging on to her mane like a wild beast, ran even faster, her hooves thundering across the desert. Soon, Grace's arms tired and began to slide down the horse's mane. She gripped the hair as best she could, but her fingers, numb from holding so tightly, slipped free. Her upper body slid from the saddle, turning upside down, one foot still stuck in a stirrup. Her head and shoulders slammed into the ground, and her body jerked backward with the force of the horse's speed. She frantically struggled to release her foot from the stirrup. Grace's body bounced against the hard dirt and unforgiving brush like a limp doll. Then the world went black.

CHAPTER SEVENTEEN

*G*race opened her eyes to see Chet's face looming over her. Perspiration dotted his knitted brow and dripped from his temples. "Grace?"

She rolled her head back and forth, trying to make sense of her surroundings, the hard, spiky ground digging into her bones. "Where? What . . . ?"

"You were thrown from your horse. Don't move. Tell me where it hurts."

Grace swallowed, the dirt and grit in her throat feeling like a thousand straight pins. She squeezed her eyes shut against the pain. "Everywhere," she whispered.

"We have to get you back to town. Can you feel your legs?"

Grace moved them slightly and rolled her ankles in slow circles. "Yes. But I'm not sure I can stand." Pain seared her head, but she tried to focus on her arms and legs. She felt as if she'd been crushed in a rockslide.

Chet carefully placed his arms under her knees and the small of her back, lifting her effortlessly. "I hope this doesn't hurt too much," he said, adjusting her weight.

Grace winced at the movement. "Not any more than I already hurt."

She rested her head against his chest and closed her eyes. In a single sweep, he put his foot in the stirrup and mounted the bay, never releasing his hold on Grace. Once they were on the horse, she lost consciousness nestled in Chet's arms.

"WHAT IN THE hell did you think you were doing?" Chet shoved Donovan Green up against the wall of the railcar's parlor. "You could have killed her." He imagined ramming one of his fists down Donovan's throat but instead clenched his hands to stifle the urge.

"I don't have anything to say to you," Donovan said.

"Like hell you don't. Flo put Grace specifically in my care, and I'll be damned if I'm going to let anything happen to her. Now you tell me why you spooked that horse."

"I didn't."

Unable to control himself any longer, Chet grabbed Donovan by the collar, turned him around, and shoved him up against one of the antique mirrors. The mirror shattered into a million shiny fragments around Donovan's head. The terrified look on the publicist's face gave Chet satisfaction, and he wanted to see more.

"I saw you prod that horse in the flank, you pathetic liar. Deerhunter said not to go behind the horse. Now you tell me why you would want to hurt Grace."

"O-okay." Donovan's eyes brimmed wide with fear. "Just put me down. I'll tell you everything."

Chet released his grip, and Donovan fell to the floor, the remaining shards of mirror clattering down around him. Chet moved closer to him and stood over the trembling man.

"It was Flo." Donovan wiped his mouth with his sleeve and

ran his hands through his hair, releasing another shower of mirror fragments. "He wanted me to cause a commotion at the orphanage."

"What are you talking about, man?"

"Publicity. That's why the photographer and reporter were along."

Chet planted his foot on Donovan's chest and shoved his torso to the floor. "Why do something so stupid?"

"Sensationalism . . . Drama." The gasping man placed his hand around Chet's ankle, trying to relieve some of the pressure. "Flo ordered me to make sure Grace gets in the newspapers as often as possible. He needs her debut in the new show to make the Follies wildly popular, so the more press, the better. He's in a bind with Marciano and needs this show to be a big moneymaker."

"So you thought getting her thrown off a horse and dragged through the desert was a good idea?" Chet eased the pressure on Donovan's chest.

"I didn't think the horse would take off. I promise, I just thought it'd buck a little, long enough to snap a few photographs."

Chet gave his foot one last push and then turned away from the sniveling publicist. That ingrate Flo would do anything to keep his neck out of the ringer and his name in the papers—rob his own wife, even risk the life of his rising star, a girl he claimed to love like a daughter. Chet rubbed the stubble on his face and shook his head in disbelief. "What else? I know there's more."

"Nothing!" Donovan, rising to a sitting position against the wall, spit the word out, his lip curling with disdain.

"What about Lillian Lorraine? Why is she here? Did Flo send her to cause trouble, too?"

"I swear, I don't know." Donovan shook his head, his hair getting mussed against the wall.

Chet leaned down, grabbed Donovan's collar, and hoisted him to his feet. "What else?" He placed his wrist against Donovan's throat and applied pressure until the man's eyes bugged out and his face began to turn red. Only then did Chet let up, ever so slightly.

"Okay, okay. Get off me."

"Talk first."

Donovan squinted and struggled for breath. "The car. In the city."

Chet pulled his arm away from Donovan's throat but pinned him up against the wall with both hands on his shoulders. The defeated publicist let out a gasp of air and leaned his head against the wall.

"The car?"

"The one that almost hit Grace."

"Flo was responsible for that?"

Donovan nodded. "It was meant to be a scare tactic, not to harm her."

Chet wrapped his fingers around the man's neck. "Keep talking," he said through gritted teeth and squeezed a little harder.

"Flo wanted it to look like Sophia's supposed killer wanted Grace dead, too." Donovan's voice came out in a squeak.

Chet's fingers dug into Donovan's neck.

Donovan grimaced. Sweat trickled down his face and into his eyes. He blinked hard. "Are you going to let me go?" His eyes flicked across Chet's face.

Rage burned inside Chet. Flo had played them all, used this buffoon to stage an elaborate production to further himself. The smarmy, *I'm-untouchable-because-I-work-for-Flo* look on Donovan's face made Chet want to bash his head against the wall. Then Donovan's last statement rang back in his head.

"What did you mean by 'supposed' killer'? Was that a publicity stunt, too? Or was Flo so angry that Sophia left him, he had her killed himself?"

"No, no. . . ." Donovan's eyes widened again. "Flo would never go that far. We still don't know how Sophia died, but murder works better for Flo, so that's the story he's going to tell."

"Dammit." Chet released his grasp, letting the crumpled man drop to the floor again. "This whole investigation is just—"

A charade.

Flo had sent Chet to California to investigate a murder knowing full well he might find nothing. At least he'd be paid for this sham, but what about Grace? This whole farce Flo created had torn up the girl, physically and emotionally. Lying to her about her sister's death and then exploiting it? Manipulating her into an unwanted career? Putting her in harm's way? It was unforgivable.

Chet glanced over at Donovan. The sight of the pathetic puppet made Chet want to explode. "Get up," he ordered.

Cowering and using the wall for support, Donovan rose, inching away from Chet as he went.

Chet slapped both hands on Donovan's shoulders, grabbing the fabric of his coat in his fists. He dragged him to the center of the room and, with one hand, swept Donovan's hat up from the table. He shoved it onto the whimpering man's head so hard it covered his eyes, then Chet hauled him to the door and out onto the platform. Grabbing Donovan's collar and waistband, he hefted him up and shoved him over the railing of the speeding train car. He watched the mass of pinstriped suit roll and tumble onto the ground. After a few seconds, he saw the disgraced publicist get to his feet and run after the train. He'd never make it. Chet smiled, enjoying the rush of hot air slamming into his face and the dry, isolated New Mexico landscape speeding past. He brushed his hands together as if wiping off Donovan's stink and went back inside.

AFTER THE DOCTOR LEFT, Chet lay on the bed facing Grace, watching her fitful slumber. She rolled her head back and forth, mumbling whispered words, her face twisted in torment.

The doctor had diagnosed her with a concussion, many bumps and bruises, but no broken bones or permanent damage, thank God. That damn Donovan Green. And damn Chet's own inability to stop the horse from taking off.

He knew he'd catch hell for pitching Green off the train, and breaking the mirror, but the surge of rage he had felt at the man couldn't be stopped. Flo had manipulated Chet and Grace, exploited them, and Chet wanted nothing more than to get Grace off this publicity fiasco. Marciano's men were still on the train, however, which was an entirely different problem. He'd have to think it through, but for now, he'd make sure nothing dangerous happened to Grace again.

Her eyelids fluttered, and she moaned softly as she opened her eyes. The motion of the train gently rocked the bed, and the sounds of the wheels chugging gave the room a drowsy atmosphere. She rolled her head back and forth, as if working out a kink, and then stopped, looking directly at Chet. Her glassy, unfocused eyes blinked at him. Despite her injuries, she looked as radiant as a golden goddess. Her silky hair fanned out on the pillow like pure, thick honey.

"Am I dead?" she asked, her voice barely a whisper.

"Yes." He leaned closer to her. "And so am I, and we're in heaven. Or almost in heaven. We reach California in about fifteen hours."

Her eyes lingered on his face, as if studying its contours. "I really thought I was going to die."

She truly could have died, and the notion made his heart palpitate with regret that he hadn't been able to prevent the accident.

"The last I remember, there were hooves flying, dust choking me, and my foot was caught in the stirrup. I was struggling to break free, but she just kept dragging me and dragging me." She paused, looked directly into Chet's eyes. "I didn't think I was going to get out of that situation."

"But you did," he said, smiling.

"Yes." She lifted her head slightly and looked around the bed. "Wait, what are you doing *here*?" Her eyes clouded with sudden confusion.

Sensing her discomfort, he pushed himself upright and away from her.

"The doctor said you needed to be watched. I got tired. It's late, so I thought I would lie down." He started to get up, afraid he'd frightened her. In truth, he'd been unable to resist staying as close to her as possible. At least until he was sure she'd be all right. He hadn't wanted her to wake up disoriented and alone.

"No, don't go. Having you here makes me feel. . .safer." Her cheeks flushed the color of a soft pink rose. "You said it was late. What time is it?"

He pulled on the chain hanging from his pocket and produced a gold watch. "Eleven thirty."

"How long have I been here?"

"Nine hours."

Her eyes widened. "You've been here that whole time?"

He nodded.

"And Donovan?" she asked. "Where is he?"

"Gone."

When she squinted her lovely green eyes, he could see her mind working. Could she know, on some kind of subconscious level, what truly had happened?

"Where did he go? Why?"

"We can talk about it later."

Her eyes moved to the sparkling chandelier now dancing in rhythm with the train's incessant movement. Chet sat silently watching her long, sable lashes rise and fall with each blink.

"I've never come so close to death before." She looked into

his eyes. "I mean, when Sophia and I were on the streets, she always provided for us. And then, there was the car that almost hit me, but you reacted so quickly. You saved me. But when I was hanging from that stirrup, the world racing past, I felt it was the end. I was going to die."

Chet couldn't bear to watch her struggling with her feelings. He reached out and stroked her hair.

"You know what went through my mind?" she asked. "What I felt?"

Chet twirled a silky lock around his fingers, wishing he could grab a handful of her brilliant tresses.

"Sadness. Regret that I hadn't found out what happened to Sophia, that I'd never seen anything or lived anywhere beyond New York, that I'd never experienced . . . a man."

Chet raised his eyes to hers, and for once, she did not shy away from his gaze. She held it steady. Chet fought the impulse to smother her with kisses. He raised himself up on his elbow, his eyes never wavering from hers.

"It's not too late. You lived. And I will help you find out what happened to Sophia." He couldn't bear to tell her that Flo may well have intentionally exaggerated the mystery behind Sophia's death—or at least made use of it in a disrespectful and unforgivable manner. No need to tell her that just yet, though. "You can still experience all those things, and I'm confident you will."

Grace looked away and fingered the lace of the bedsheets. When she directed her emerald gaze back to him, Chet leaned toward her, his face hovering over hers. He placed his hand in her hair and slowly ran his fingers through it. She gazed at him, her eyes full of curiosity and wonder—and desire. He bent lower and brushed his lips lightly against hers, waiting for her to protest. Instead, she closed her eyes and pressed her hand against his face. He melted into the heaven of her soft lips for a few, brief seconds and then gently pulled away.

If he continued, he wouldn't be able to stop. He wanted to taste her, linger as long as possible, express the feelings that had been building inside him for days; but danger still loomed, and he needed his mind sharp, focused, unclouded. To fully protect Grace from whatever hell Flo had planned, and himself from Marciano's hoodlums, he needed to remain emotionally removed from her. Besides, he didn't like feeling overprotective, as if someone belonged to him. He had to get clear of Marciano before he could begin to get solidly back on his feet. This was no time to fall for a girl, no matter how beautiful and innocent.

Confusion swept her face.

"You need to rest," he whispered, reluctantly releasing her hair. He sat up and lifted himself off the bed. "I will be sitting in the parlor, right outside your door."

CHAPTER EIGHTEEN

*J*UNE 9, 1920 - LOS ANGELES, CA

When they arrived in Los Angeles at two o'clock the next afternoon, Lucile helped Grace dress and prepare for the motorcar trip to Beverly Hills.

"We're staying at the Pink Palace—the Beverly Hills Hotel," Lucile said, her voice raised in suppressed excitement. "Everyone who is anyone in show business has stayed there."

"How exciting." Grace tried to muster some enthusiasm, but her bones hurt too much.

Billie had dispatched two baby-blue—her signature color—Rolls-Royce limousines to meet them at the train station. One of the drivers, a stately older gentleman, was sent to drive the four travelers while the other would transport the luggage.

Rows of palm trees swayed lazily along the road. Balmy air and soothing warm sunshine created a languor Grace could almost taste. Her aching body calmed, and soon her muscles melted under the tender administrations of the caressing sunshine. No wonder Sophia had wanted to be here.

The moment she thought of her sister, a vise closed in on Grace's throat and she swallowed hard, sending a spasm of pain down her neck. She consoled herself with the thought that she was getting closer to finding out what—or more likely *who*—had caused Sophia's death. But now, to endure the journey, which had been made painful by her injuries, she focused on the beautiful Southern California scenery as they drove up Wilshire Boulevard toward the sweeping green hills.

Grace glanced over her shoulder at Lucile, Nicole, and Chet, all silently sitting in the back seat. Chet was gazing out of the window, his hat pressed low on his forehead, his square jaw flexing. She wondered what he was thinking about. Her? The kiss they had shared? He *had* kissed her, hadn't he? Yes, she was sure of it. She could still feel the gentle pressure of his lips and the way his kiss tasted. It surprised her how much she wished they would become lovers. But Chet's mysterious behavior left her feeling confused—desired one minute and dismissed the next. It didn't matter. It could never be. She wasn't free to love anyone; Flo would make sure of that.

Even now, as Chet's blue-gray gaze drifted out the car window, his expression aloof and distracted, memories of the kiss sent Grace reeling, making her forget the pain of the accident. She turned and faced the road again. Those few moments with Chet had taken her to a place she'd never been before. Her fingers and toes tingled at the thought.

When Chet said something Grace couldn't hear and Nicole giggled, a jolt of irritation pierced her armor. She sighed as misery edged out her blissful memory and seeped back into her bones like black bile.

At last, they finally arrived at the hotel, and the drivers swung the oversized automobiles into the circular drive, where the party was greeted by an assortment of valets and bellhops. A tall and gawky teenager escorted Grace to one of the more lavish bungalows—a split plan with two bedrooms separated by a large living area, bar, and dining room.

Mint-green walls, trimmed with gleaming white molding and

trim, decorated the interior of the bungalow, and the cool, serene hideaway smelled of citrus breezes. French doors from each bedroom extended out onto a private patio. Doors to another patio situated off the living area could be completely removed; thus bringing the outdoors in. The pleasant, spicy aroma of eucalyptus trees and the tang of lemon groves wafted into the room. As the dewy moisture of the air sank into Grace's skin and the warmth of the sunshine radiated through the windows, she began to forget the tumble of emotions Chet caused within her.

An ice bucket with champagne stood waiting on the coffee table in the living room. A greeting card lay next to it. Alone in the cottage now, Grace picked it up and read it:

To MY NEWEST and brightest star. May your success be monumental.

Love always, Flo

GRACE CURLED HER LIP, already tired of what little fame she'd experienced. She tossed the note on the sofa, flopped down, and propped her feet up on the coffee table.

A bellboy knocked on the frame of the open door. "Excuse me, Miss Michelle. I have a message from Miss Burke."

Grace rose from the sofa, took the note, tipped the boy, and thanked him. She turned the message over in her hand. Billie had invited her to a reception—a black-tie event—in her honor—in one hour. Images of past parties crowded her head. She knew this one would also involve too many people, too much liquor, hypocritical small talk, petty anecdotes, and leering men.

And how would she dress to hide the bruises on her arms? She wished she could wear the daring dress that had caught Chet's attention—the backless silver one with the plunging neckline.

Footsteps approached the suite. Grace glanced up as Chet came through the doorway, a bellhop struggling with her luggage behind him.

Grace stood there fiddling with the envelope in her hands. For the first time all day, Chet looked at her. She felt adrenaline pump as his blue-gray eyes met hers.

"Feeling okay?" he asked.

"Tired. But I want to talk to the police about Sophia, as soon as possible. Could you arrange that?"

"But the party. I need to be there with you."

She tilted her head. "How do you know about the party?"

"It's my business to know. Actually, I just saw Lucile. She was already fretting over what you should wear."

"Then first thing tomorrow. Please. Could you arrange a meeting?" she asked again. "My entire reason for coming on this trip is to find out what happened to Sophia. Everything else has been about what Flo wants. But me, I only came to make sure my sister's killer would be found."

"You're assuming she was murdered, and we don't have a lot to go on yet. It may not have been murder."

"If that is the case, then I will feel so much better."

Chet offered a brilliant smile, and she felt her reserve melt.

"Tomorrow," he said. "You know, if you're up to it. You might actually try to have some fun. You've been through a lot lately. Try to relax and enjoy yourself. We'll find out what happened to Sophia. I promise."

Grace raised her chin, trying not to let her emotions overwhelm her.

"Don't think of it as work," Chet added.

"But it is . . . and for you, too—the fearless bodyguard who has saved this lady more than once."

"It's what—" A look of disappointment clouded his eyes.

"You get paid for," she finished for him. "I know."

They stood in silence, looking at each other. His eyes, never blinking, bore into hers until her chest felt ready to cave in. She could scarcely breathe, nor could she move. Just as Chet seemed about to speak, Lucile burst into the room, Nicole trailing behind her. Grace inhaled sharply, relishing the rush of much-needed oxygen as it filled her lungs. Still, she rolled her eyes. Would she ever again have any privacy?

"We've got to get you ready for the party, darling," Lucile said. "I've brought body makeup for those bruises, poor dear. How are you feeling?"

"I'm quite tired. Lucile, I—" She wanted to ask if there was any way she could get out of going to the party.

"You won't look tired when I'm finished with you."

Grace wanted to groan out loud.

"Nicole, start her bath, would you, dear?" Lucile asked. "I'll get the gown ready. The silver one."

Grace suppressed a smile, glad she would get to wear the dress she knew Chet liked.

Nicole, who stood gazing longingly at Chet, managed to tear her eyes away from him and disappeared into Grace's bedroom.

Grace glanced at Chet to see if he had responded to Nicole in any particular way, but to Grace's delight, his eyes were locked on her.

"You've become friends?" Grace asked him, nodding toward her bedroom to indicate Nicole.

"Well, I wouldn't go that far," he said.

She raised her brows, pleased at his remark. "She won't say anything to me."

Chet sank his hands into his pockets and rocked back and forth on his feet. "You two don't have much in common, and . . . well, she works for you."

His words landed like a punch to the stomach.

"Like you." She knew she shouldn't have said it, but she wanted more than indifference from him. Even anger would be better than apathy.

He straightened his back and crossed his arms over his chest. "Yes."

There it was again. The indifference. It rankled her. She felt anger boiling up. "Speaking of people who work for me, what happened with Mr. Green? Why did you—or rather, what gave you the right to fire a member of my staff?"

Her staff. She cringed. She had no control over her emotions around this man.

"You're referring to the world's worst publicist?"

"Chet—"

"He put you in unnecessary danger."

Confusion wrinkled her brow. "How so? I don't see how visiting poor, motherless orphans is dangerous."

Chet's eyes narrowed and darkened. A small sense of triumph sparked within her at eliciting a reaction from him.

"He was responsible for your accident," Chet said through gritted teeth.

She raised an eyebrow. "Oh really? How?"

"He spooked your horse."

"He did not," she said on a sigh. The feud between the two men was truly becoming ridiculous.

But Chet's serious expression didn't change. "He went behind the mare and prodded her in the flank, Grace. I saw it."

His words stunned Grace into silence. She knew Donovan had stepped behind the horse foolishly, but surely he wouldn't have purposely agitated the mare. Donovan liked her. In fact, he more than liked her. He treated her like a woman, not a job.

She glanced up at Chet. "That's impossible. We were friends. He wouldn't have hurt me on purpose."

"Then you'd better choose your friends more carefully. I'm telling you, he intentionally spooked the horse after the guide clearly told us not to walk behind the mare. I even confronted him about it."

Losing ground, Grace placed her hands on her hips. "Why would Donovan want to spook my horse?"

Chet hesitated. "He . . . he was jealous."

"Jealous? Of what?"

"You and your ability to ride. He wanted to impress you, but you outrode him. It made him feel like a fool."

"Oh." She didn't expect that response. "He told you this?"

"In a manner of speaking." Chet coolly surveyed her, not giving an inch.

She lowered her brows, frowned, and looked away. She didn't think Donovan could possibly be so cruel, or so shallow. Her head began to pound, and when she reached a hand up to her temple and gently massaged it, she saw concern written on Chet's features but he said nothing.

She turned and walked out of the room. She needed to get ready for the party.

CHET SHOOK HIS HEAD. *Weak.* Donovan Green jealous of Grace's riding skill was a stretch, but he hadn't been able to think of anything else to say to her on the fly. He didn't have the heart to tell her the truth.

A knock at the door interrupted his thoughts. He opened it to find a bellman. "Mr. Riker, there is a telephone call for you in the lobby."

"Do you know who it is?"

"Mr. Florenz Ziegfeld Jr., sir."

Chet drew in a deep breath. "Very well. I'll be there in a minute."

He closed the door on the bellman, readying himself for the tongue-lashing he'd get in a few minutes. Hopefully Flo wouldn't fire him for throwing that bastard off the train. If so, he'd have no protection from Marciano or his goons, who seemed to be everywhere. It would also leave Grace unprotected. When he reached the lobby, he found the bellman standing next to a desk, guarding the phone. Chet took the phone from him and handed the kid a quarter.

"Hello?" he said into the receiver.

"Chet, old boy, how are you?" Flo sounded cheerful, bordering on giddy.

"Hello, Flo."

"I received a telegram from Mr. Green. Seems he made it back to civilization in one piece. You actually threw him off the train?" Flo chuckled. "Brilliant, my man, just brilliant."

Chet hesitated, letting the words sink in. "So you're not angry?"

"Well, he got results, but I never wanted Grace to be hurt. I care about the girl. Plus, hurting the Follies' newest star would be extremely counterproductive. Green proved reckless, and I would've chucked him off that train, too. The spin that you and Grace are lovers, however, is genius. As much as I tried to discourage you before, I think it adds spice to her story."

"Spin that Grace and I are lovers? What are you talking about?"

Chet heard the crinkling of paper on the other end of the line. "'Ziegfeld Star Survives Brush With Death,'" Flo's voice took on the monotone quality of reading aloud. "'War hero turned bodyguard, Chet Riker, swooped in to rescue Grace Michelle, sister of the late Sophia Michelle, after a bruising fall from a runaway horse. The lovers had just completed a promotional tour stop at the St. Cecilia's Orphanage outside of Albuquerque, New Mexico, when Miss Michelle's horse bolted, dragging her a long distance. Riker galloped after her and returned with Miss Michelle unconscious in his arms. No bones were broken, and the couple continued their trip to Hollywood, California, where the new star will be auditioning for a motion picture.' It's brilliant, I tell you!"

Chet took in a breath. *She's not auditioning for anything. And lovers? Hardly.* "Who blabbed to the paper?"

"You do remember the reporter and photographer who traveled with you to the orphanage." Flo said.

"I do," Chet's voice betrayed the fact that he was not at all amused. *Why the hell does Flo think this trash is good publicity? His latest stunt nearly got her killed.*

"Look, Chet. I know you are upset at this. But anything that draws attention is good for the show."

Chet flinched, not sure how he felt about Flo's last words. He decided to ignore them. "I saw some of Marciano's men on the train," he said instead. "Do you know anything about that?" Chet could hear Flo exhale, probably smoking one of his expensive Cuban cigars.

"Yes, well, I'm not surprised that he's on your tail. He's investing a lot of money in Grace, so he'll want to keep tabs on her. Don't let them rankle you, Chet. Stay the course."

"What about Lillian Lorraine? Are you aware she's on the train, too?"

The silence on the other end answered the question before Flo could speak. "No. Dammit. What's that woman up to? Must be sour grapes. I didn't give her the show so she's gone to California to lick her wounds. Probably trying to get a picture or—"

"Or what?" Chet pressed.

"She's picked up a bad habit—a drug habit. Cocaine. I think she's getting it from Joe, but she's always out of money."

"She told me she had an offer for a picture."

"Neither here nor there," Flo said. "Not my problem any longer."

"And what's this Donovan mentioned about you concocting a story of murder. Sophia's murder? Am I on a boondoggle here, Flo?"

He could hear Flo puffing on his cigar, then exhale.

"Until you, or the police, find out what really happened, it only seems reasonable to suspect it was murder."

Chet sniffed. So Flo stilled played the murder angle.

"You're a PI. Act like one. And, Chet," he said, his voice growing more insistent, "don't spill *anything* to Grace. Keep her in the dark until we sort this out. That's an order."

CHAPTER NINETEEN

*A*n hour later, Grace and Chet arrived at Billie's suite
dressed for the party. Chet seemed distracted and aloof,
and didn't offer any conversation. Grace didn't either. What
could she possibly say to lighten his dark mood? Feeling tired
already, Grace didn't have the energy to concern herself over
Chet's feelings. She had to dredge up enough of it just to get
through this party.

Billie greeted them at the door. "Darling! You look simply
marvelous."

Grace leaned close to her and made two air kisses on each
side of Billie's glittering face. Despite her melancholy mood,
Grace was relieved that Billie received her with such friendli-
ness, despite what she now knew about Flo and Sophia. Grace
couldn't help but smile at the pixyish woman, a beautiful elf with
red waves of curly hair. She now understood why few people
disliked her, aside from Sophia.

It was said around the theater that Billie had a special hold
on Flo, one that no other woman had been able to cultivate.
Sophia certainly hadn't. Grace remembered Charles's words
about Flo loving Billie above all others and Billie knowing it,

but what was it about Flo that made Billie put up with his affairs?

Billie slipped an arm around Grace's shoulder. "The papers have been filled with your ordeal. You look strikingly well considering what you've been through."

"Thank you," Grace said. "I'm doing much better. Your hospitality has been unsurpassed. Thank you for everything."

"You are a love. And here is your handsome Prince Charming we've been reading about! How are you, Chet darling?" She flashed a stunning smile at him. "You two are simply divine together—simply di-vine."

Grace felt a rush of blood rise in her cheeks and she noticed Chet flinch.

"And oh my." Billie placed her palm against her chest. "It's such a pity about Sophia. What you've been through, you dear girl." She clucked her tongue against her teeth, and Grace's skin prickled at the hint of condescension and distinct chilliness in Billie's voice.

"It's so brilliant of my Flo to see that you're protected," Billie went on. "He's simply wild about you, darling. You do know that, don't you?"

"I'm grateful for all he has done for me." Grace hoped her smile seemed sincere.

"Come. Let's join the party." Billie pulled Grace into the magnificent suite. High ceilings with thick crown molding lined the room. Lavish drapes in pastel moiré taffeta softened the room, looking very much like billowing gowns puddled on the parquet floor. The suite consisted of three bedrooms, a living area, bar, dining area, and kitchen. Additionally, a large, semi-circle balcony overlooked the lush valley.

Elegant ladies and distinguished men crowded the rooms. They sat or stood in small circles, smoking cigarettes, drinking, laughing, and talking. Grace and Billie entered, Chet behind them.

Billie stood close to Grace and then tapped her fingernails on her cocktail glass. "Ladies and gentlemen, please welcome the future star of the Follies, Miss Grace Michelle!"

Everyone turned toward Grace and greeted her with polite applause. She displayed her best smile and nodded at the guests, even as her stomach lurched. Although she was growing somewhat used to being the center of attention, she still didn't like it.

A waiter appeared with a tray of champagne glasses and offered one to Grace, then Chet. Grace accepted and toasted the crowd. They toasted back, the word *cheers* echoing around the room, and then everyone resumed their superficial conversations. Grace noticed only one woman who didn't raise her glass. Instead, she glared at Grace with a vehemence that made her stomach sink. Something familiar pricked at Grace's memory, but she couldn't place the woman.

To her right, an auburn-haired starlet engaged Chet in conversation. Suddenly alone, Grace took her drink and sought solace on the balcony. The warm, moist air caressed her skin, and she breathed in the fresh aroma of night-blooming jasmine. She let the beauty of her surroundings relax her. A full moon cast soft beams upon the citrus groves, making them almost luminescent, and the stars shone brilliantly, like silver slivers in the sky.

Feeling a presence behind her, Grace turned, presuming it was Chet. Instead, a tall, broad-shouldered man with unusually long, cinnamon-colored hair and a full, closely cropped beard smiled at her.

"It's a great pleasure to meet you, Miss Michelle. I'm Timothy O'Malley." His melodic voice revealed an Irish brogue. He took her hand and pressed it to his lips. His whiskers tickled and caused a tingle to course through her hand, up her arm, and into her chest. "May I join you out here?"

"Of course."

"I find these parties a challenge."

"As do I," she admitted.

"Too many people, too noisy."

"Yes." Grace nodded in agreement, relieved she wasn't alone in her discomfort.

As Timothy O'Malley sipped his champagne, his green eyes were confidently fixed on hers, leaving Grace feeling somewhat transfixed. The man oozed charm. He moved closer to her and focused his gaze on her hair, brazenly lifting a hand to caress the loose twist that Lucile had fashioned.

Although charming and handsome, his boldness made her feel twitchy. His closeness was too intimate. Instinctively, Grace stepped back, but he matched her steps. She turned her shoulders to the left and then the right, seeking an escape. He responded by pinning her against the stone railing, resting one of his arms next to her, and leaning his head close to her ear.

"You're exquisite," he murmured. Grace could smell the alcohol on his breath and feel the vapor hot and insistent in her hair. She inched to the left, delicately trying to sidle past him, but he moved with her again.

"I really should—" she started.

He placed his fingertips gently on her lips, and then trailed them from her mouth, to her chin, and down her neck. Panic fluttered in her chest like a frightened bird. When his hand approached her breast, Grace snatched it and held it fast.

A chuckle emerged deep and resonant from his throat. "Sorry, lass." He stepped back to a more comfortable distance. Grace felt the air seep out of her lungs in guarded relief, but she eyed him with caution. She stiffened as she leaned against the rail, trying to get even more distance from the man.

"A shy one," he said, draining his glass and blinking his attractive eyes. "I apologize for my manners. You're just so bloomin' breathtaking."

Grace raised her chin. "I'd appreciate it if that didn't happen again."

He stepped back another six inches. "I swear," he said, placing his hand over his heart, "on my dead mother's grave."

"Thank you."

He grinned at her like a satisfied cat who'd swallowed the canary. She wanted to scoot past him, but still, he blocked her way. She pressed her hand against his chest, and he stepped back, letting her through.

"You didn't come to the party just to see me, did you?" she asked, emboldened by her newfound self-respect.

O'Malley smiled and tucked his free hand in his jacket pocket. "No, I must admit, I did not. But it was a nice little perk to meet you."

"And why are you here?" Now that she'd established her boundaries with this Irish imp, Grace felt comfortable extending the conversation.

His smile turned to another deep, throaty chuckle. "Oh, I forgot, you are new to California, aren't you? You have no idea who I am. How delightful."

Grace squinted her eyes, trying to guess at what game he was playing.

"I'm the director of Billie's latest film," he told her.

Crimson crept up Grace's throat and face. Of course, *the* Timothy O'Malley. She'd read about him in *Variety* and had heard Flo talk about him many times. Not in the best of terms, either. Flo was jealous of the smooth-talking Irishman, and Grace could see why.

"Don't fret, lass. Actually, it's rather pleasant to meet someone who has no idea who I am. Again, I must apologize for my brash behavior a few minutes ago. I'm used to a bit different, well, reception from women."

"You mean you're used to women throwing themselves at your feet?"

Now it was O'Malley's turn to blush.

"I see you're not the average starlet."

"No. Not the average starlet."

"Aye, I've offended you again." O'Malley ran a hand through his auburn waves.

Grace pursed her lips, and the silence grew thicker. Thankfully, Chet stepped out onto the balcony. "Are you all right?"

"Yes," Grace said. "I was just saying goodbye to Mr. O'Malley. He's the director of Billie's latest film—very big in Hollywood, as he's been telling me." She turned her attention back to the brash O'Malley. "Goodbye, Mr. O'Malley. It was a . . . um, a pleasure to meet you."

"The pleasure was all mine," he said, bowing and clicking his heels together. "If you are ever in need of work, please give me a call." He reached into his jacket pocket, retrieved a calling card, and handed it to her.

Grace took the card and brushed past both him and Chet. She looked back to see Chet straighten his tie and follow her back in to the party. Where had he been when Timothy O'Malley had nearly accosted her? A wave of disappointment made her suddenly very tired.

Looking around the crowded room she could tell she had already been completely forgotten. Except by one woman—the woman who had refused to toast her. Grace shuddered at the ominous stare from across the room. Who was she?

Suddenly, Billie moved toward Grace. "Darling, you must be exhausted," she said, placing an arm around Grace's shoulders.

"I am. I'd like to go if you don't mind. It's a lovely party, but I'm still not feeling well."

"I completely understand. You go rest. We'll try to manage without you." Billie pulled her forward and smacked two air kisses, one on each side of Grace's head.

Once outside in the breezy night air, Grace inhaled deeply and felt the tension drain from her limbs. Chet appeared behind her.

"Thank God I'm out of there. I don't know how much longer I can endure this. I just want to go home to New York."

"It's going to be worse there." Chet moved next to her.

Maybe so, she thought, but at least in the theater, she could retreat into her own little world a bit easier, and no one there tried to stare her down at parties. Here, she had no escape.

"You're right, I suppose. How did I get into this mess? All I want to do is design and sew costumes."

Chet shoved his hands into his pockets and kicked at a pebble on the ground. "Is that really *all* you want?" His eyes met hers.

Grace blinked and swallowed, his meaning clear, but his words startled her. It would be no use denying her feelings; she knew full well that he'd sensed them.

"You know it's not," she said, barely audible.

"So any interest in that famous Irish director?" His tone hinted at sarcasm.

"Not my type."

"You really aren't interested in stardom at all, are you?"

"Glitz and glamor don't appeal to me. I want a simple life. Yet, here I am," she said, sighing. "This was my sister's dream." Grace's words trailed into silence. She closed her eyes, taking in the aroma of the jasmine-scented air. She struggled to compose herself and focus on the most important thing about this trip of theirs. "Speaking of, did you make any inquiries? Did you speak with anyone about Sophia?"

"Yes, that redhead I was talking to actually brought up the subject, but I fear she was simply repeating gossip. Still, it's worth looking into."

"Well, what did she say?"

Chet looked over his shoulder and behind Grace, seeming to be making sure no one could overhear. "She implied that Billie *hired* Jack Pickford to get Sophia out of New York and away from Flo."

Grace let out an exasperated rush of air. "So she may have seen Sophia as more of a threat than we thought."

"It's just gossip so far." He placed a warm hand on her shoulder. Grace tried to ignore the heat radiating from his touch.

"You don't think Billie would have done something more . . . sinister?" she asked, remembering the chill she'd gotten when Billie had mentioned Sophia earlier. "She had legitimate reasons to despise my sister—or at least to wish her gone forever."

Chet shrugged. "Jealousy is a common motive for murder. But we haven't any proof of anything. For now, it's idle gossip."

"I'm so tired of all of this. I'm going back to the bungalow." Without waiting for his response, she moved past him and began to walk away.

CHET INSTANTLY REGRETTED HIS WORDS. He wished he hadn't told Grace what the redhead said. It seemed to have made her sad, and he didn't want her going to bed sad. "Grace, are you up for a walk on the beach?" he asked.

She stopped and turned toward him. "Yes. That sounds nice."

The hotel provided them with a car and driver. They sat in silence together in the back seat, their hands so close they nearly touched. Grace rolled down the window and lifted her face to the wind streaming into the car. Chet couldn't pull his eyes away from her outstretched neck and her gossamer hair, pulling loose in the breeze.

When they reached the beach, Chet told the driver they'd be back in an hour. Grace ran down to the sand, quickly removed her shoes and then her stockings. Chet tried not to watch but couldn't help himself. Her skin glowed in the moonlight, and that backless dress was a stunner.

"There, much better," she said.

He fell in step next to her, his hands in his pockets. They

walked in silence, their bodies straining forward to push their feet through the thick sand. Chet could feel Grace fold into herself like a spring bloom retreating into the night. He turned to look at her. Tears glittered on her cheeks in the moonlight.

He stopped and reached out to touch her arm. "What is it, Grace, what's bothering you so?"

She wiped at her face with the back of her hand. "I miss Sophia. I should have spoken with her before she left."

"Look, Grace, I know it's hard, but sisters always fight. She left knowing how much you loved her. You have to trust that she knows it still."

Grace exhaled loudly and closed her eyes. She popped them open again. "Trust. I don't know who or what to trust anymore." Without waiting for Chet to respond, she resumed walking.

They strolled in silence for a while, alone on the beach; their only company the moon and stars. They listened to the sound of the waves roll in with a rush and then back out with a sucking sound as the foam rumbled pebbles back into the frothy water. Chet longed to comfort Grace, reach out to her, draw her into his arms. Instead, he took her hand and they walked on in silence.

The sound of the surf and the moonlight dancing on the ocean isolated them from the rest of the world. Chet could feel the beat of Grace's heart where her wrist pressed close to his. With each pulse, he almost felt as if he could read her every emotion, her every memory, and her every desire. She squeezed his hand tighter, as if she felt the same way, as if their thoughts and emotions were as intertwined as their fingers.

Grace turned to him and opened her mouth to speak, but Chet took her in his arms, his hands encircling her tiny waist, and his mouth found hers. Longing to envelope her body and soul, he crushed her against him and she did not resist. She simply leaned into him as if she could no longer stand on her own two feet.

∾

GRACE RETURNED Chet's urgent kisses, wrapping her arms around his neck and pressing her body against the lean hardness of his. His hand went to her hair and pulled out the comb that held what remained of the twist. Her golden curls tumbled down around her shoulders, sending a skittering chill up her spine. Chet plunged his hands into her hair and ran his fingers through its silken curls. When he pulled back and gazed into her eyes, she was startled by their glow.

"Grace, you are like no one I've ever met," he whispered, drawing her close. He kissed her again, causing waves of pleasure to course through her. She felt like putty, ready to be molded by his hands.

Suddenly afraid of his pull, Grace planted her hands on his chest and pushed him away. "Wait," she said, nearly breathless. "What about last night? You left me there, wanting you."

"You were hurt, Grace, and barely conscious. I didn't want to take advantage of your vulnerability." He paused and looked into her eyes. "It would be your first time, wouldn't it?"

"Of course it would! I am insulted that you'd think otherwise."

"But I didn't . . . think otherwise," Chet said, smiling. "I've been attracted to you from the first moment you walked out of Flo's office, looking like a naive but radiant goddess. But I am also—"

"Oh, please stop talking," Grace said, pulling him in for another kiss.

He let out a muffled groan and guided her down to the sand.

GRACE LAY with her head on his bare shoulder, the sand, saltwater, and grit tingling on her cheek. They lay on the beach, their bodies molded together on Chet's dinner jacket, their damp and mussed clothing, still partially covering their bodies. Her eyes roamed his chest and shoulders, and they were every bit as magnificent as she had imagined, with firm, rippled muscles and soft, olive-colored skin.

"How do you feel?" He lightly brushed his fingers down her cheek. "Did I hurt you?"

"No," she lied. It had hurt, but only for a moment. Once the pain had receded, a tremendous pleasure, unlike any she could scarcely have imagined, had enveloped her. Their bodies had entwined, impassioned, moving together in a harmonious rhythm, the most beautiful thing she'd ever experienced.

She stifled a grin when she remembered how it had felt when he'd touched her in all the right places and made her aware of others she hadn't known existed. His body had seemed to anticipate her every want and need. The experience had left her fulfilled, and yet, she craved more. She'd never felt such a hunger before.

"Although, I seem to have sand covering every inch of me," she said. "My dress, and your poor jacket—"

"Never mind that. C'mon," he said, sitting up.

"Where are we going?"

He pulled her to her feet and toward the water. "We're going swimming."

She laughed and began to run with him, the hem of her dress flapping against her bare ankles. They raced out into the water, jumping as waves washed over them.

When they were waist-deep, Chet pulled her to him and kissed her, fumbling with the fabric of her dress.

"What are you doing?" she asked, coming up for air.

"Okay, I'll go first." He undid the remaining buttons of his shirt and then took his trousers off with his shorts and let them float on the water.

Grace laughed at the exuberant expression on his face and

raised her arms in the air. He pulled the dress over her head and threw it toward the beach. She hoped it landed free of the water, but it was already ruined. What would she say to Lucile?

With the dress's plunging neckline and bare back, wearing undergarments had been impossible. At first, she felt self-conscious being naked in front of him, but when she saw his eyes and smile in the glint of moonlight, she let go and laughed again, throwing her arms around him. Electricity vibrated through her as his skin touched hers. They held each other for a long time, bobbing in the waves like a twin set of buoys, all the while talking and laughing.

Chet buried his head in the crook of her neck and kissed her shoulders and breasts. The feel of his mouth on her sent heat throughout her body, and that heat became so intense, she got lost in the sensation. She felt him grow hard against her and knew where they were headed once again. This time, she looked forward to the pleasure in earnest.

Suddenly, a large wave knocked them off their feet, washing away the moment. When they emerged, sputtering and choking on the stringent salt water, both burst out in laughter. Grace placed her hands on top of Chet's head and pushed him under. Instantly, he grabbed her by the feet and pulled her down with him. They both came up coughing. Grace felt wild and free and happier than she'd ever been.

The chill of the water gradually seeped into their playful bliss, and like two exhausted children, they let the waves push them back to the shore. Both shivering but still laughing, they looked for their clothes, which took a little longer than they'd expected. Luckily, Grace's dress had landed on the sand, but Chet's clothes had rolled in with the waves and were spread across the beach. Once they found them all, they both dressed in the wet, salty, sand-covered clothing. Grace grimaced at the cold silk and rough grit next to her skin, but she didn't care. She knew she'd soon be warm in the lush, pillowy bed of the hotel room, with Chet lying next to her. They walked back to the car, scrunched together against the marine chill.

CHAPTER TWENTY

Chet chewed on a toothpick while he sat in the reception room of the Los Angeles Police Department. His nostrils pricked with the smell of mold, and his feet stuck to the grime of the linoleum floor. Through the glass partition he could see the uniformed officers working at their desks or milling around the station with cups of coffee or paperwork in their hands.

He squeezed his eyes shut and pinched the bridge of his nose, the early hour making him groggy—that and the long night of lovemaking with Grace.

"Mr. Riker?" A skinny man, all elbows and knees in a poorly fitting suit, came out to greet Chet. "I'm Detective Barnett. I hear you're a private dick."

The hair on the back of Chet's neck bristled. "I prefer to call myself a Private Investigator, thank you."

"Uh-huh. You want some coffee?"

"I would, yes."

Detective Barnett waved Chet over to the door and ushered him to a beat-up, wooden desk. "Take a seat. I'll be back in a minute. Secretary called in sick today so I have all the domestic duties."

Chet took the chair angled next to the desk and settled into it, the smoke in the room burning his eyes and nose. Several of the police officers turned his direction, gave him the once-over, and then returned to their typewriters or conversations.

Detective Barnett came back carrying two steaming cups of coffee. His thin, pinched face, protruding nose, and thick lips gave him the appearance of a duck. He set one cup of coffee on the corner of the desk in front of Chet and then sat in his desk chair.

"I take mine black," he said, pushing his wire-rimmed spectacles farther up on the bridge of his nose. "I assumed the same for you."

"It's fine."

"So, how can I help you, Mr. Riker?"

"I'm here to look into the death of Sophia Michelle. I'm told that you are familiar with the case. She was the star of—"

"The Ziegfeld Follies. I know about her passing. Real shame, that one. She was quite the looker. How come *you're* looking into this?"

"I work for her boss, Florenz Ziegfeld Jr. He sent me here as a bodyguard to one of his stars, and also to investigate Miss Michelle's death."

"That death has already been investigated, son—by *real* detectives who do *real* police work. Nothing here for some private dick hired by the rich and famous to catch cheating spouses in the act."

Chet leaned back in his chair and crossed his legs, stalling to come up with something that would grab the guy's attention. He knew the police hated PI's on principal alone. He'd have to warm this guy up somehow.

"I understand your concern," he said.

"Oh, I'm not concerned," the detective said with a chuckle.

"There is no bad guy for you to catch so you can become a hero. Case was investigated and closed."

Chet drew in a deep breath and pressed his lips together, perusing the desk. His eyes lit on a lapel pin next to a pencil holder.

He pointed to the pin. "That yours?"

"'Tis." Barnett squinted his rheumy eyes beneath his spectacles.

"Thirtieth Infantry? Old Hickory, am I right?"

"You are." Barnett picked up the pin and placed it in his pocket.

"Battle of St. Quentin Canal?"

"Just what are you trying to get at, son?"

"Were you there?" Chet uncrossed his legs and leaned forward, resting his elbows on his knees.

"I was. I don't know what you are playing at here—"

"I was there, too. O'Ryan's Roughnecks. Twenty-Seventh Infantry."

Barnett's face relaxed. "Well, I'll be damned." He stared at Chet for a few seconds, and Chet sat quietly, letting the information sink in. Barnett took another sip of his coffee. "What was your question about that Ziegfeld star?"

Chet leaned back in his chair again, his shoulders resting comfortably against the wooden slats. "I've been led to believe she was murdered."

"Everyone was. Those damn reporters." Barnett folded his hands over his caved-in belly. "They were on that case like fleas on a rat. Said they'd been tipped off that it was murder. We found no evidence of murder."

"So the case is closed."

"Tight as a drum. But isn't it like these showbiz types to scare up a scandal?"

Chet nodded. "That sounds about right. Do you know what happened to her, then?"

Barnett picked up his cup and let the steam of the coffee swirl around his nose before taking another swig. "From what we could gather, she and her new husband attended a party at a Mr. John Barrymore's house, got back to the hotel in the wee hours, and she collapsed on the bathroom floor. There were no signs of violence, only an open vial of mercury bichloride in the bathroom. Seems her beloved had the clap."

Chet set down his coffee cup. "I don't understand."

"It's a medicine used to treat syphilis. Pretty nasty stuff. Mr. Pickford was using small doses of it for his condition. He said when they got to the hotel, the missus went into the bathroom, and he fell asleep. When he woke up alone, he went to the bathroom and found her on the floor. By the time the ambulance arrived, it was too late. The medics found the opened vial of mercury bichloride on the counter, and took it with them. The medical examiner determined she accidentally ingested it, and that's what killed her."

"So, not murder?"

"Her husband and his sister said she'd been feeling down of late." Barnett tilted his head, as if he wasn't quite sure about the question. "Could've been suicide, or an accident. But, not likely murder."

"How could you be sure?"

"Autopsy. When they opened her up postmortem, they found her kidneys damaged, which would be consistent with mercury poisoning. As you know, the husband is generally suspect number one, but there were no signs of a struggle, nor could we come up with a motive of why he, or anyone would want to kill her. Girl was a fallen star, and had nothing to her name. Based on interviews, Pickford adored her. Nothing added up to murder. Case closed."

Chet sipped his coffee, then rolled his tongue over his teeth, feeling the grit of the coffee grounds between them. He agreed that Jack probably wouldn't have killed her. Didn't have the smarts or the guts, but Flo would definitely benefit by a story of murder—a much more glamorous death than kidney failure or accidental poisoning. Suicide would prove far too scandalous, even for Flo. Could he have somehow had Sophia killed? Her leaving Flo and the show definitely had left him in the lurch, not to mention with a bruised ego. The whole idea stank like a bad hangover. Chet shook his head thinking about the lengths Flo might go to in order to create his own truth.

"What happened after the case closed?" he asked. "Did the local reporters walk away and just leave it alone?"

"Once the headlines lost their drama, they backed off. It comes up now and again, but mostly they've stopped writing about it. Guess that's the same nationwide?"

"Seems to be," Chet said, standing up. "Well, thanks for your time and the coffee. Do you have any idea where Sophia's husband may be? Did he stay in Los Angeles?"

"I have no idea. We had him stick around until we buttoned things up, in case we needed to question him again. He mentioned something about staying at his sister's house up in Beverly Hills. You know, Mary Pickford." He cocked his head and pursed his lips. "Another looker."

"Right."

Chet left the police station and stood outside on the sidewalk, pondering the information he'd received from Barnett. How could he bring himself to tell Grace that Sophia's case was closed? That Flo used the situation to garner more publicity. If Chet told her the truth, she might leave Flo and the Follies, and then she'd have Marciano after her. He had to keep the truth from her in order to protect her, at least for now.

GRACE AWOKE to a note on her bed stating that Chet had gone to see the police. He'd also told her to stick close to Billie. How fortunate, considering she'd received another invitation to yet another one of Billie's parties that day. Grace wasn't sure she could keep up with this excessive socializing.

Grace chose a linen dress that had come from one of her own drawings for a Follies beach number to wear to the party. Form-fitting with navy-and-cream stripes, it fell in a slim silhouette to her ankles. She pulled on navy ankle boots with a small, feminine heel that buttoned down the side of her foot. The pièce de résistance? A straw hat with a sleek navy ribbon and floppy brim dipping over one eye.

When she finally left the room and headed to the garden party, she ran into Chet in the lobby. He pulled her to him, lifting her off her feet, and kissed her tenderly.

"I missed you this morning," she whispered into his ear.

He set her back down and smoothed a piece of hair under her hat.

"What did you find out from the police?"

He was about to speak when a group of reporters descended upon them. "Miss Michelle, Miss Michelle!"

Chet slipped an arm around her shoulders and turned Grace toward the garden in an attempt to thwart the press.

"Miss Michelle, do you have any lingering injuries from the riding accident?" a voice rang out from the crowd. She turned to see who had asked the question but was confronted with a sea of faces.

A balding, heavyset man stepped forward. "Do you know who killed your sister?"

A photographer stepped forward and captured her surprise at the question with the blinding light of his flash. Before she could answer—if she dared to answer—more voices began shouting.

"Is your life still in danger?"

"Do you know who's trying to kill you?"

"I . . . Well, I, um. . . ." Grace raised a hand to her temple, her heart fluttering.

"Is there a wedding in your future?" The flashes from the cameras snapping photographs nearly blinded her.

Chet's hand tightened around her shoulders again, and he guided her away from the clamoring photographers and reporters. The voices diminished as they walked quickly toward the party. When they finally reached the garden, a tall, dark-haired woman wearing bright red lipstick approached her. The surrounding reporters stepped back like the parting of the Red Sea to let the woman through.

"It's Hedda Hopper," rippled through the crowd in whispers.

Hedda Hopper, the famed gossip columnist—known as a viper for mesmerizing her prey with sweet words until they confessed all, and then striking for the kill—stood before her. Grace took stock of the woman's overwhelming presence.

"Well, I finally get to meet the mysterious Grace Michelle." Without asking, Miss Hopper swung Grace around to face a camera on a wooden tripod. The photographer, a dashing, raven-haired gent who could have easily been mistaken for a film star, fumbled with the black silk hanging from the back of the camera. Holding the tray of gunpowder with one hand, he flipped the silk up with the other and buried his head behind the lens.

"It takes forever to get decent publicity photographs," Miss Hopper said through closed teeth as she tightly gripped Grace around the waist and preened for the camera. "Smile, Miss Michelle."

Grace forced a smile, her eyes blinded by the white light and her ears ringing with the pop of the flash. Miss Hopper's earlier words echoed in Grace's head. "Mysterious?" she repeated.

"Why, yes, the mysterious starlet playing the role of a damsel in distress. Everyone's talking about your convenient brushes with death and your handsome hero, Mr. Chet Riker, PI to the Stars." Her gaze pounced on Chet like a hyena ready to devour some leftover meat.

"You shouldn't believe everything you hear, Miss Hopper," Grace said. She felt the heat rise to her cheeks.

The columnist opened her mouth wide and laughed long and hard. The crowd followed suit.

"I've heard you're quite charming," Miss Hopper said. "I can see that now."

A woman approached them, the same woman who'd been staring at Grace at Billie's party the other day.

"Ah, Miss Held!" Miss Hopper rang out.

Grace's jaw dropped slightly as the photo Grace had seen of Liane Held at Sophia's funeral came back to her. This woman had the same long, pinched face—one that didn't seem to smile much. Short, brown, curly hair framed her face, and she towered over most of the women, as she had in the photo.

"You must be here for a film. When did you arrive from Europe? How are things between you and Flo? Tell me, darling, what's the news?" Hedda Hopper hovered over the woman, her notepad thrust into Liane's face.

"I, um . . . I . . . Yes, I'm here for a film," Liane said, her gaze never leaving Grace's face. "I arrived from Europe several weeks ago. Things with my stepfather are . . . strained. That's all I can say." She stood with her hands folded neatly at her waist.

"Well!" The reporter turned to the group. "I'd love to stay and chat, but unfortunately, I must run. I've an interview with Elmo in his bungalow across the way." Grace knew Miss Hopper had meant Elmo Lincoln, the star of the wildly popular film *Tarzan of the Apes*. At the mention of the much bigger name, reporters turned their attention—and their endless questions—to Miss Hopper, leaving Grace and Liane alone, an awkward silence filling the space between them.

"It's nice to finally meet you," Grace said in an attempt to be polite.

"Yes, I suppose." Liane's expression didn't soften or change in the least, as if it had been set in plaster.

"What film are you auditioning for?"

"I'm not here for a film."

Grace swallowed. "Oh?"

"Your sister had something that was mine—something very valuable. I had come to get it before— Well, before she died."

"Oh. . . ." Grace said quietly. Then more confidently, "What was it? Perhaps I can help."

"A ruby-and-sapphire-studded ermine cape—part of a costume, a genuine antique from the Renaissance period. Very rare. It was my inheritance from my mother, intended to support me for the rest of my life. *Your sister* stole it."

"What? Stole it? My sister would never steal anything."

"Of course you would say that." Liane's lips turned up into a smirk, the first hint of emotion Grace had seen in the woman yet. "I'm here to prove differently. Do you have it?" She shoved her small clutch under her arm.

Grace grappled with something to say. She'd never heard of this fur cape, let alone seen or touched it. "No, I don't. I didn't know it even existed." Her words came out clipped and desperate.

Liane raised an eyebrow. "We'll see," she said and stalked away from them, her stick-thin legs taking small, quick steps.

Grace's mouth hung open. "What was that about?" she said, turning to Chet, mouth still agape.

"Who knows? Liane's been out to get Flo since her mother died. She's just bitter and dramatic."

"But Sophia wouldn't steal, Chet. She just wouldn't."

"Flo probably gave Sophia the thing. I'm sure it's nothing to worry about."

"But why wouldn't I know about it, then?" Grace immediately thought about Jack and how he wouldn't think twice about selling something that valuable, whether it was stolen or not. A sinking feeling hit her stomach.

"It's become obvious Sophia didn't tell you everything," Chet said, concern in his eyes.

"Grace!" Billie called, approaching them at a brisk pace, her steps tiny and her hips swaying due to the pencil skirt plastered against her legs in its viselike grip. "Oh, you look marvelous. That Lucile is simply a wonder!"

Grace smiled politely but tensed inside, still disturbed by Liane's accusation.

"Chet, you are a sight for sore eyes, you handsome devil. Were you able to drive the car all right?" Billie asked.

"It was fine, thank you."

"Absolutely. No problem at all. Oh, and I also meant to tell you, don't let Flo make you feel too bad about the jewelry theft. These things happen."

Grace turned to Chet. "Jewelry theft?"

A flush washed over Chet's face. He cleared his throat and pulled at his collar. Grace faintly remembered a story about a robbery attempt on Billie's train car, but it seemed so long ago now and Chet had been in New York, not California.

"You must have been terrified, Billie," Grace said. "I'm so glad that they didn't get away with anything, and even more so that you weren't harmed."

Billie's face pinched and she looked at Grace as if she'd just fallen from the sky like an injured bird.

"Why, darling, the whole affair was a scam. Your friend here arranged it all. It didn't quite turn out as planned, but the publicity was marvelous. Producers were vying for my attention. I got two more motion picture contracts offered to me that very week."

Grace turned her eyes to Chet, who avoided her gaze. The sinking feeling in her belly was replaced with slow, crawling sludge.

"Shall I get us some drinks?" Chet asked, obviously seeking an escape.

Billie flashed her prettiest, pearly white smile. "That would be lovely, Chet."

Chet disappeared into the crowd, and seconds later, someone pulled Billie away into another conversation. Grace's stomach roiled. Could she trust Chet? Was she being played, as well?

Chet returned, a drink in each hand. "You're the most beautiful woman here." He slid closer to her, handing her one of the drinks. Now *she* avoided his cool gray eyes. He leaned in to whisper in her ear. "Let's go for a walk. I think the reporters are safely gone by now, or they've had enough Grace Michelle for one day."

But they hadn't. As they slipped away from the party and headed toward a breezeway, Grace noticed a few photographers moving their tripods to aim at her and Chet, who left arm-in-arm and only relaxed once they were safely free of prying reporters.

"You probably want to know what I found out from the police," Chet said the moment they were alone, standing in the shade of a grove of manicured olive trees.

"I do. Definitely." Grace turned to face him. "But first, tell me about the train robbery."

"It was a small job," he muttered. "Nothing worth talking about."

"Billie seemed quite impressed."

"She's easily impressed." He reached over to slip his arm around her shoulders. He kissed her on the temple.

Grace pulled back, shook his arm loose. "Don't think you can distract me, Chet. I want to know what the theft was all about."

Chet sighed. "It's really not important. You know Flo, always coming up with some scheme or another, solely designed to garner publicity for the Follies."

"But what did *you* have to do with it?"

He rubbed a hand across the darkening stubble on his chin and shoved the other hand in his pants pocket. He glanced around as if to make sure no one could hear their conversation. "Flo hired me to arrange the robbery."

Grace cringed and brought her hand to the crown of her hat as if it were going to pop off. "But how could you?" She couldn't believe what she'd just heard.

"I didn't have much of a choice. I'm in a bit of a financial bind."

Grace blinked up at him. "What kind of bind?"

"My mother needed help." He shoved his other hand into his other pants pocket. "I needed the money to help her."

"Is that why you agreed to protect me and find Sophia's murderer?"

"Yes, at first. But now the job has become more personal." Chet pulled his hands out of his pockets and ran them down the length of her arms. His face broke into a mesmerizing smile, causing his dimples to deepen. "I really care for you, Grace."

Not quite sure what to say, she leveled a stare at him. "So, what did the police say?"

"They're still investigating. Nothing conclusive." Chet held her gaze.

"Nothing?"

"They were reluctant to talk about it because it's still under investigation."

Grace let out a sigh, feeling as deflated as a worn tire. "I need to find out what happened to her, or this trip to California is worth nothing. It's the only reason I agreed to come."

Well, almost the only reason.

Chet raised his eyebrows at her.

"Well, you know I couldn't refuse Flo. But while we're here, we have to focus on solving Sophia's murder. *You* have to do more to solve her murder. You were hired to investigate her death."

"I was also hired to be your bodyguard, remember?" Chet removed Grace's wide-brimmed hat and kissed the top of her head. "I think I'm doing a pretty good job of that, wouldn't you say?" He smoothed several strands of hair that had been caught in the breeze off of her face and plunked her hat back on her head.

"You have done a marvelous job of that," she said, surrendering to her attraction. She ran her hands up his chest and over his shoulders, admiring the strong, taut muscles of his physique through his well-fitted suit. "But *my* primary mission is to find out what happened to Sophia, and I need your help. Promise me that you'll dig deeper?" she asked, putting on a pitiful pout.

Chet answered with a long, slow kiss.

CHAPTER TWENTY-ONE

*J*UNE 14, 1920 - BEVERLY HILLS, CA

Chet watched Grace sleep in the early-morning light. The dewy freshness of her fair, pink skin and the golden brilliance of her hair glowed against the pillow. Soft brown lashes swept down from her eyelids, casting feathery shadows on her perfectly structured cheekbones.

He should have told her the truth about Sophia's investigation, but at the time, he just couldn't bring himself to do it. He wanted to make sure she stayed the course, played along with Flo's little scheme until he could get out from under Flo, and Marciano. Then, she'd be safe.

And, the business with Liane was probably nothing, he tried to reason with himself. She had been known to make up stories about Flo, like the time she claimed Flo had made Anna get an abortion. Anna had gone along with the story, but only after Flo had flaunted his relationship with Lillian Lorraine in Anna's face. Both Anna and Liane were desperate to make Flo's life miserable. Unfortunately for Chet, Liane posed yet another threat to Grace. How far would she go to get back the cape that Grace obviously didn't have? If the damn thing even truly existed.

Chet sat up in the bed, still admiring Grace's face. How in the world had he come to care so much about this woman? He had promised himself he would never love another human being again, not after Sister Anne.

Sister Anne . . . He hadn't thought about her in years. She had been a sweet woman, who'd been kind to a lonely kid whose mother had dumped him in an orphanage. He could still hear Sister Maria's shrill voice in his head:

"Chet, why are you here?"

"Because my mother didn't want me."

"And why didn't she want you?"

"Because I'm no good."

"That's right, boy." Sister Maria circled the hard-backed *chair where he sat.*

"And why do you sit here today?"

"Because I picked a flower for Sister Anne."

Sister Maria's *large nostrils flared. "You violated the rules. The flower was not yours to take. Do you understand?"*

"Yes, Sister."

"You will do penance for this crime. One week in isolation."

"Will I see Sister Anne?"

"She's been sent to another orphanage. She'd grown too attached to you. We may not have favorites. Do you understand?"

Chet gently lifted himself off the bed, dressed, and then grabbed a pink rosebud from the vase of fresh flowers on the nightstand, along with a conch shell Grace had found on the beach, and lay them on his pillow. He took one last long gaze at her.

He had to extricate himself from this scam that Flo had orchestrated. He had to make some money, pay off his debt, and then he and Grace could be free of this charade forever.

∼

GRACE HELD the rosebud up to her nose, closed her eyes, and inhaled the lovely fragrance. She opened her eyes again to see the little white shell that lay next to the rose—a creation of perfection, with its pink underside and long white fingers. Its elegant form gave her inspiration. She could use it as a model for an exquisite gown, a white, formfitting sheath with plumes of delicate pink feathers extending from the shoulders. Perhaps ornately beaded to conjure the opalescence of the shell. She imagined the fine-boned Marion Davies wearing it for one of the Follies' numbers.

As Grace rose lazily from the bed and reached for her dressing gown, she wondered where Chet had run off to. She hoped he'd gone to further investigate Sophia's case.

Her stomach growled sending her in search of food. Just as she had expected, coffee and pastries awaited her in the living room.

A knock on the door was followed by one of the staff entering with a message: Fanny had arrived and requested that Grace join her in sunbathing by the pool.

A short while later, she joined Fanny under a large blue umbrella. Fanny was wearing the latest in swimwear: a scoop-necked wool tunic tied at the waist worn with leggings that reached to the middle of her thigh. Her stockings came only to her knee, exposing the delicate white flesh of her legs. Fanny blinked at Grace beneath a small-brimmed white hat that had been adorned with rhinestones.

"Morning, kid. How ya been?" she asked, then sipped a colorful drink.

"Fine. It's good to see you, Fanny. You certainly look relaxed."

Fanny took another swallow of her drink. "This is the life, kid. I should make California my permanent home. I'd never have a worry in the world."

Grace discarded her linen shrug, reveling in the soft, fragrant breeze.

"Hey, get out of the sun, honey. You'll get lines." Fanny sat up and moved her chair so Grace could place hers farther under the umbrella. "Lines are the death of a star, I'm telling you. My motto? Never let them see you age."

Grace laughed, glad to be in Fanny's company again. The woman used her sparkling wit and humor to take away the troubles of the world.

"So, I hear you've had a couple of tough breaks, kid." Fanny puffed on her cigarette holder and then blew a determined stream of smoke into the breeze.

"Yes. It's certainly been interesting."

"How are you handling the press? The reporters?"

"Okay, I guess. They've portrayed me as—"

"The damsel in distress? The victim?" Fanny guessed.

"Exactly."

"It's Flo. He's working the 'good girl' thing to counter Sophia's suicide."

Grace's stomach sank. "What?"

"You know, the poor, heartbroken, innocent little sister. The public loves it. He spoons it out, and they eat it up."

"So he's calling Sophia's death a suicide?"

"Oh, it's just another angle on what Flo sees as the ongoing story." Fanny sipped her drink, the ice cubes tinkling against the glass. "He'll go back and forth on theories—whatever works to keep reporters on the string. You know Flo: he always milks the melodrama."

Grace lowered her head, staring at her hands in her lap. *Not suicide.* How could Flo go back to a theory they'd both dismissed? Why would he let people think Sophia would kill herself? She drew in a breath, trying to resist showing how much Fanny's news had upset her.

"Oh, honey." Fanny's voice softened. "I'm sorry. Don't let it get you down. People don't believe everything they read. We all know drama sells papers and reporters will go for splashy headlines whenever they can."

"It's just . . . Flo sent Chet to investigate Sophia's *murder.*"

Fanny leaned her head back on her chair and sipped at her drink. "Could still be murder. No one knows yet. That's why there is so much speculation. You're her sister. What do you believe?"

"Not suicide. I know certain people had things to gain by my sister's death."

"Who?"

The life insurance policy flashed through her mind, but she dismissed it, the thought too horrid to bear.

"Jack, for one. Although he is beyond playing the grieving husband—the man is destroyed. I don't think it's him unless he's acting."

"He's not that good an actor."

True, Grace thought, *but then there's the ermine cape.*

"Fanny, did you ever see Sophia with a jewel-studded ermine cape?"

"No. No, I can't say I have. Why?"

Grace shrugged. "Something Liane said. Did you know both she and Lillian were here in California before Sophia died? They both attended her funeral."

Fanny put down her drink and leaned toward Grace. "Now that *is* odd."

"Yes."

"Doesn't mean they killed her." Fanny leaned back in her chair, shimmying her shoulders to get more comfortable.

"No, but their lives have been made easier by her death. Billie's too." Grace hated to say it out loud, but it was true. With Sophia out of the way, there was one less starlet for Billie to worry about.

"What does handsome Chet say?"

Her mind racing, Grace barely heard the question. "Um, I don't know. He left a note on the pillow—"

Fanny ripped the hat off her head, sat up straight, and put her drink down. "He put what, where?" Her eyes were the size of silver dollars.

Fanny's surprise startled Grace out of her brooding. "Oh." She hadn't realized what she'd said.

"You mean, you and Chet are . . . ?"

Grace put her hands to her mouth, stifling a smile. The expression on Fanny's face, with her eyes and mouth wide like three *O*'s, looked even more comical than her jokes, and made Grace want to laugh.

"Well, I'll be." Fanny's words rolled out of her mouth in a slow drawl. "So tell me."

"Tell you what?"

"You know—" Fanny rolled her hand on her wrist in a flourish "—spill the details, angel. I'm all ears."

"I'm not giving details." Grace blushed. "But it's the most incredible thing I've ever experienced in my life. He's gentle and kind and thoughtful."

"Of course he is, sugar. They all are in the beginning." Fanny relaxed back in her chair again.

"I think he's sincere, Fanny."

"Hey, I don't have anything against the man. From what I've seen, he's better than most. I'm just saying be careful, kid. Just because you fall for a handsome face and sleep with someone doesn't mean you know them."

Grace pushed a loose strand of hair behind her ear, thinking again of the train theft Chet had just confessed to organizing. She hadn't thought he'd do something like that. Could she trust him? Was he truly on her side? Was he really doing anything to investigate Sophia's murder? He could have lied about seeing the detective in charge of the police investigation.

"Oh, honey." Fanny's tone turned sympathetic. "I don't mean

to burst your bubble. I'm just speaking from practical experience. Me, I tend to like the louts." She reached over and placed her hand on Grace's wrist and gave it a little squeeze. "Look, if you were a sweet, little housewife from New Jersey and he were an accountant, I'd say hooray for you. But you're the innocent Grace Michelle, rising Follies' star, and he's Chet Riker, the suave sometimes PI. I don't think Chet's a rat, but you will encounter plenty of opportunists. Men love showgirls; they just don't marry them very often."

Grace looked off into the distance, annoyed at the very idea. Was Chet playing her for a fool?

She suddenly felt more alone than ever. If only she could see Chet right now, see his reassuring gray-blue eyes and his broad smile. Of all the emotions he'd generated in her, distrust and fear had not been among them—until now.

CHAPTER TWENTY-TWO

*N*ot long after Grace had returned to her suite, a persistent and peculiar nagging made her want to do a little more digging into her sister's death on her own. Flo's inconsistencies with the press, stating murder one day and suicide the next, sent her emotions reeling, and she wanted off the rollercoaster. She had to know more. Chet was still gone, and while she probably should wait for him, who knew how long he'd be? She could waste an entire day waiting for him, and she certainly didn't want to run the risk of having to attend another party.

She rummaged around in her handbag for the telegram Jack had sent. In it, he had given her his sister's phone number in case she needed to reach him for any reason, as he'd been staying with Mary since Sophia's death. Grace picked up the phone and called him, asking to see him right away. He'd been hesitant but finally agreed and gave her his sister's address. Next, Grace called Billie to tell her she needed to go see Jack, and Billie insisted that Grace use one of her cars and drivers.

The driver, Lloyd, was a robust man with red cheeks and a snowy, Santa Claus mustache and beard. He opened the car door for her, and she got in, pulling her skirt in behind her. When they reached the exit of the hotel grounds, a group of people crossed in front of the car, making them wait to pull out onto the main road.

Fidgeting with her handbag, Grace wondered what it would be like to see Jack again. Would he apologize for taking Sophia away? Would he take any responsibility at all for her death? Could he have *caused* Sophia's death?

Grace closed her eyes, drawing in and exhaling slow, deep breaths to calm her racing heart. When she opened her eyes again, she gasped to see the man with the scar in the tattered brown coat cross the street in front of the car. Grace raised her hand to her lips. Why did he keep showing up? She'd last seen him with Lillian, but where was *she?* Grace hadn't seen her since their arrival in California.

She leaned toward the center of the car to see around the driver's head, but the man was gone, lost in a group of people walking en masse. Grace sat back in the seat, gripping her hand-bag. She shouldn't have left without Chet. This man could be following her.

Maybe it isn't the same man, she told herself. She swallowed hard and tried to steady her breathing. It had to be her imagina-tion. Perhaps it was all the stress, not to mention the grief she still felt over her sister's death. She knew she hadn't mourned properly yet, and grief did strange things to people. She could be seeing things, imagining that people were after her.

Throughout the drive toward the lavish Pickfair, Mary Pick-ford and Douglas Fairbanks manor home, down sunny, palm tree–lined roads, Grace gathered her wits. The farther she got away from the hotel, the more she calmed.

When the car finally entered through the gates of the prop-erty, Grace gasped, awestruck. Magnificent acres of perfectly manicured grass rolled out in front of the car. Palm trees lined the drive that climbed up a hill, and giant eucalyptus trees served as a perimeter around the property. The mansion, set back against a grove of lemon trees, was a massive stone house with an arched portico and circular drive. Lush gardens featuring carved shrubs and flowers abloom in every color graced the manse's entrance.

When they stopped in front of the dark, wooden estate doors, Grace leaned forward. "I won't be long, Lloyd. Please wait for me here."

Lloyd nodded, but still, he got out of the car, opened the door for her, and accompanied her to the massive entrance. Grace rang the bell.

A stiff, sour-faced, thin man with bushy gray hair answered the door.

"I'm Grace Michelle, here to see Jack Pickford."

The butler gestured for her to enter and then led her toward a grand stone staircase. Their footsteps tapped along the foyer's terra-cotta floors, which were polished to a mirror gleam. Rainbows of reflected color from the sparkling crystal chandelier hanging from the alcove ceiling danced along the white walls that skirted the spiral staircase.

Once up the stairs, the butler led her down a great hall lined with classical paintings, portraits, and landscapes, all ensconced in thick, gold frames. When they reached a door at the end of the hallway, the butler knocked three times, turned the knob, and ushered her in.

Long, velvet curtains covered the windows, casting inky pockets of shadow in the dimly lit room. Daylight streamed through one window, highlighting strewn clothes, abandoned food trays, empty wine and liquor bottles, and used glasses. Grace squinted, her eyes adjusting to the darkness and saw someone slumped in a chair. The red, glowing end of a cigarette floated about his face.

"Jack?"

The cigarette glowed brighter, and then she heard a rush of air.

"Is that you, Grace?" the voice croaked into the darkness.

"Yes, it's me."

"Come, come in. Please. Excuse the mess. I haven't been well." He gestured with silk-robed arms for her to come closer and pointed to a chair perpendicular from his. "Please, sit."

Grace picked her way through the clothes and other objects littering the floor. Her stomach tightened. She'd never been comfortable with the man, and even now Grace tried to avoid looking directly at Jack. But she noticed his face had grown gaunt, highlighting the desperate angst in his eyes, the eyes of a man struggling with sanity.

"I . . . I'm so sorry about Sophia," he said as Grace settled into a nearby chair. "She was my life . . . my everything . . . you know." His words came out slurred and slow. "I am . . . *nothing* without her."

On the table next to him sat a large, half-empty bottle of whiskey and a glass. He reached over and poured some of the amber liquid into the glass, took a large gulp, and leaned his head against the back of the chair, eyes closed, silent, with the cigarette still burning between his fingers.

Grace cleared her throat. Had he fallen asleep? She waited a few moments, perspiration prickling the back of her neck. "Jack?"

He pulled his head forward and gave her a bleary-eyed stare. "Who are you?"

"It's me. Grace. You agreed to see me, remember? I have some more questions for you about Sophia."

A smile spread over his ghost-like, pallid face. He opened his mouth, still grinning. "Grace, Sophia's little sister. Grace and Sophia, Sophia and Grace . . . two lovelies."

Grace inhaled slowly, clenching her fists. "I can see you're drunk, and I'm sorry to barge in, but I need some answers. You owe me some answers, Jack. I need to know what happened. They say it was suicide, but I don't believe it. She would never—"

Suddenly light poured into the room, and Grace turned to see the silhouette of a woman framed in the doorway.

"Jack?" the woman said. "Jack, who's there?"

Grace stood and approached her. "I'm Grace, Sophia's sister. Jack invited me to come, but he's—"

As the woman opened the door wider, Grace immediately recognized her petite, curvy frame and pixie-ish face as that of the famous Mary Pickford.

"Dear, please, come with me. I'm sorry you had to see this. How did you—"

"I telephoned him, and he told me I could come over."

The woman placed her arm around Grace's shoulders and led her to another room—a bright, beautiful, immaculately decorated sitting room. They walked to a lush sofa positioned under an expansive, sunny window.

"Sit down, please. I'll ring for some refreshments. You look a little pale. Are you all right?"

"Yes."

"I suppose you know who I am."

Grace nodded, suddenly feeling very shy.

"I'm so sorry about your sister. It's so tragic for us all. Jack has been like this for weeks now." Mary looked down at the floor. "We were all fond of Sophia and welcomed her into our family. You should be very proud of her."

Grace bit her lip. Tears escaped her eyes and slowly rolled down her face.

Mary then took both her hands and held them in hers. "You must miss her so."

"I'm . . . so sorry," Grace said, her voice breaking.

"It's all right to cry." Mary reached over to smooth Grace's hair.

Grace drew in a deep, slow breath. "I need to know what happened to Sophia."

"Your sister was a fine person, but we, too, were unhappy about this union, at first. They weren't right for each other. But, then we accepted it. Accepted her."

Grace met her eyes.

"Oh, darling, I am not speaking ill of Sophia. It's Jack who wasn't—still is not—ready for marriage. I know I shouldn't criticize him, particularly to you. He's my brother and I love him, but he has insurmountable problems, which doomed them from the beginning. In a way, Sophia was spared a lot of pain."

Grace winced. Spared a lot of pain? Sophia had lost her *life*. "I don't believe it was suicide," she said in a rush. "I want to know the circumstances of her death. I want to know what Jack knows. I want a list of suspects, reasons, a thread to follow." She stopped and exhaled. She couldn't believe she could be so forward, but the anger just bubbled up.

"But who would want to kill her?" Mary's eyes registered confusion. "Who would have a reason to kill her?"

"Her husband perhaps?" Grace bit her lip, again shocked at her own boldness.

Mary's eyes widened. "I mean no offense, my dear, but your sister came into the marriage tainted."

Grace felt hairs stand up on her neck. *How dare she!* "Tainted? What do you mean *tainted*?"

"She confessed to Jack that she'd been Flo's lover and that she was running from another man. She was drunk when she told him this but confirmed it the next morning. She was miserably unhappy and took her own life, Grace."

"No one has proven that, and I still don't believe it . . . I'll never believe it."

Mary squinted, her head tilting in a question. "No one has told you?"

"Told me what?"

Mary straightened her back and let out an exasperated sigh. She blinked several times and bit her lip, as if trying to figure out what to say. When her gaze finally settled on Grace, her face softened. "Sophia ingested poison. The police called it an 'accidental event,' but we think it was something else."

Grace blinked, waiting for Mary to continue. She could hear her own heartbeat pounding in her ears, and the muscles of her neck tightened.

"Jack has a condition," Mary said. "He has syphilis."

Grace knew of the disease. It was contracted from sexual intercourse—typically promiscuous sexual intercourse with multiple partners.

"He was taking a prescribed medicine, a topical liquid, to ease the pain of the sores. He and Sophia had been at a party—John Barrymore's party, I believe—and came home very late. Jack had gone to bed and didn't notice that Sophia hadn't followed him until he found her lying on the bathroom floor hours later. She'd been there a long while, and they found a bottle of the medicine next to her."

"I don't believe it," Grace said, every instinct in her body rebelling. "Drunk or not, Sophia would never have intentionally taken poison."

"Darling Grace." Mary gave her a sympathetic smile and took her hands again. "Your sister had been staying with us ever since she arrived from New York, so I feel as if I got to know her at least a little, and perhaps you are right."

"So you agree it wasn't suicide?"

"At first, we thought it was simply a terrible accident, but then we found something in her personal effects that we didn't give to the police," Mary said slowly. "Out of respect for Sophia, we thought it best to avoid additional scandal. Nothing would bring her back to us, after all. We wanted to protect her image as best we could."

The blood drained from Grace's face. "I don't understand."

Mary stood and walked to a desk in the far corner of the room. She pulled out a piece of folded paper and returned to sit beside Grace. "Jack found this letter among Sophia's things."

Grace took it and held it in her hands, her breathing growing shallow. Hands trembling, she opened it and read:

I CAN GO on no longer. My heart is heavy with despair, and I can endure the pain no more. Please tell my sister I'm sorry. I never meant to hurt her.

Sophia.

GRACE STARED AT THE WORDS, her stomach churning, her mind digesting the information. She turned to look at Mary. "This is typewritten," she said, holding up the note. "Anyone could have written it *after* Sophia died as a way to cover up her murder."

Mary raised an eyebrow.

"I'm not accusing anyone, Miss Pickford, but that's a simple fact. This is not real evidence. It sounds like a plotline for a motion picture: a convenient, typewritten suicide note discovered by a potential suspect."

"We have a typewriter downstairs," Mary said, her voice matter-of-fact. "It's for our secretary, but of course, Sophia had access to it and used it sometimes. I don't find it implausible—"

"Perhaps she threatened Jack," Grace cut in, "threatened to tell everyone about his disease. Perhaps he got drunk and—"

Anger and disbelief flared in Mary's eyes. "You are not *seriously* accusing my brother of murder, are you?"

"I'm sure the police suspected as much. Even if she did use the typewriter to say she's sorry, it doesn't mean she meant to kill herself. And I do not believe that she would have taken the poison by mistake." Grace's voice sounded shrill in her ears. She clutched her arms to her body.

Mary pulled back, her eyes wide and her mouth hardening into a line. "Jack is many things, but he would never have killed Sophia. What would he gain? She and I were his only hopes of making anything of himself. And he loved her, Grace. I'm sure of that. Jack loved Sophia and has been absolutely heartbroken about her death." She paused a moment. "Didn't you hear about the postmortem? It proved she died of the mercury bichloride, the medicine intended for Jack."

A chill run through Grace.

"I didn't know there was a postmortem. Why wouldn't Flo have told me about this?"

Mary shook her head, exasperation on her face. Clearly, she did not like the insinuation that Jack could have been involved.

Grace didn't really believe Jack had killed Sophia, but she needed help to find out who did and why. She stood up and walked to the window, Mary's words whirling around in her brain. "If this is true, why wouldn't Flo tell me?" she asked again, turning toward Mary.

Mary remained on the couch but adjusted her shoulders to face Grace head-on. "Knowing Flo and his shenanigans in the past, I'm sure he wanted to control what was revealed. After all, he's busy making you a star, isn't he? I've been seeing your name in *Variety*, along with each salacious detail that Flo decides to reveal. It's him you should be questioning, not me and Jack."

Grace's stomach muscles clenched as if someone had punched her. Flo had used Sophia's death for his gain. He'd *lied* to her. He had done whatever it took to make her believe someone *killed* her sister. And what about the man who had tried to run her over, followed her to Beverly Hills? And Chet? He said he was investigating the murder, said he visited the police yesterday, and told her they were still investigating, that no final conclusions had been made. Was he bent on misleading her, too? Was he just a foil for Flo, following Flo's misguided handling of her sister's tragic death? Surely, he couldn't—But if there had been an autopsy and the cause of death had been confirmed, presuming the police told him about it, he had clearly lied to her.

"I'm so confused." Grace walked unsteadily to the couch. She clutched its frame, trying not to succumb to the feeling her wobbly knees were about to collapse her body to the floor. "When was the party at John Barrymore's? What night did Sophia die?" She couldn't believe she did not know the exact day. But at the time, California had been a world away, and she'd been walking in a dream, a nightmare.

"I believe it was April 15. I know because Doug and I couldn't go to the party because we met with our accountants that evening." Mary stood and faced her. "I think you should go. This conversation has clearly upset you, and we don't have the answers you seek. As far as we're concerned, Sophia drank the poison. Whether it was an accident or intentional, she alone caused her own death. And my brother was left to deal with the grief of his loss. Now, if you'll have your driver come in, I have a trunk full of Sophia's clothing and personal effects that I'd like you to remove from my home."

"I see." Grace bristled at Mary's abrupt dismissal of her.

Mary walked over to a panel on the wall, pressed a button, and came back to the sofa. Within minutes, Lloyd arrived, followed by the butler.

"Mason will escort you to Sophia's room. Jack packed most of her belongings, but there may be some sundry items in the wardrobe," Mary said, ushering them out of the room.

Lloyd raised his eyebrows at Grace, as if shocked at the sudden tension in the room, as well.

"I must run," Mary said. "Please, Grace, no hard feelings. It's just . . . I must make my brother a priority. There is no side to take here, but if there were, I'm afraid I'd side with him. He would never have hurt your sister."

Grace nodded, not sure what to say. Mason, the butler, extended his arm, indicating he wanted Grace and Lloyd to follow him. After climbing another spiral staircase, walking down a wide hallway, and then up two more short staircases with a landing in between, Mason opened a door and held out his arm again for Grace and Lloyd to enter.

The room had a circular wall entirely comprised of windows and housed an enormous Victorian-style canopy bed, a gracious sitting area, and a large, finely carved wardrobe. The aforementioned large walnut trunk sat in the middle of the room. Grace rushed over to it, flung open the top, and looked inside. Dresses, hats, mementos, boxes, shoes, stoles, and lingerie had been thrown in haphazardly, as if the person who had packed it either didn't know what they were doing or didn't care. Based on what she'd seen of Jack a few minutes ago, either scenario could apply. The man was so wrapped up in his own grief, he couldn't see beyond himself.

Narcissism at its best.

Grace picked up a silk scarf and held it to her face. Sophia's signature scent still lingered. Grace breathed in, images of her sister rushing to her mind. Would she start to forget what Sophia looked like? *Really* looked like, not just a posed figure in a photograph? The way her brows would rise when amused, her pretty pout when she was angling to get something, the soft look her eyes would take on when she spoke of their mother?

Grace draped the scarf around her neck. She walked over to a writing desk. She pulled out each drawer and looked through each little square compartment. Bits of paper, pencils, and a pair of spectacles rattled around inside the main drawer.

"Nothing," she said to Lloyd, who stood patiently, his hands behind his back. His large belly in its white vest protruded outward over his belt, making him look like a fat, white-breasted bird.

"What about the wardrobe, Miss?" Lloyd reminded her.

Grace closed the lid of the trunk and approached the massive wardrobe. She opened the double doors to find a few silk robes, several men's hats, and a pair of high-heeled slippers with ostrich feathers covering the toes. Definitely Sophia's. She reached in to pick them up when something the size of an almond caught her eye. She leaned her head into the wardrobe and extended her hand to pick it up. It was smooth as ice but faceted with sharp edges, blue and dark as the midnight sky. Grace sucked in her breath. A sapphire. Could it be from the jewel-studded ermine cape that Liane Held had mentioned? It couldn't be. Sophia would never steal. Of course, that was just Liane's story.

"Everything all right, Miss?" Lloyd asked.

"Yes," Grace replied a bit too quickly. "Yes, I'll just grab these slippers."

CHAPTER TWENTY-THREE

*W*hen Grace arrived back at the suite, she found Chet snoozing on the sofa. Lloyd entered behind her, transporting the trunk on a cart. Chet stirred and sat up, his hair disheveled and collar unbuttoned. His eyes followed Grace as she offered the driver a tip.

"Thank you for helping me with Sophia's trunk," she said. He nodded and gave her a kind smile.

As soon as the driver left, Chet blew out a breath. "Where've you been? I was beginning to worry. And what's that trunk?"

Grace removed her hat, set it on the hallway table, and stood at the mirror rearranging her tousled hair. "I'd like to know where *you've* been?" She turned her head back and forth, looking at herself in the mirror and stalling for time, trying to act nonchalant, much the way she'd seen Sophia and Fanny do. She dabbed at the corner of her lip to wipe away a stray smudge of lipstick. Her eyes, while a bit swollen, glittered with anger.

Chet yawned. "I went back to Los Angeles to speak with the police again. I left you a note."

She remembered the note. He had told her to stick close to Billie. It still didn't make her any less angry with him.

"But you left no message." Chet rose to his feet. She could see he sensed her anger, and he was clearly trying to deflect. "How am I supposed to protect you when I don't even know where you are? I was worried, Grace."

"You looked pretty comfortable for someone who claims to have been concerned."

Chet furrowed his brow. "I went to Billie, and she told me that one of her drivers had taken you to Mary Pickford's house. That was a foolish thing to do, but I figured at least you'd be safe."

"Is it more foolish than lying to me?"

Chet blinked and moved toward her. "What are you talking about?"

Grace held up a hand, urging him to keep his distance. "First of all, you weren't worried. Billie told you where I went—"

"I wanted to see if you'd lie to me."

"Why would I do that? I'm not the liar." Grace narrowed her eyes.

"Grace, please . . . tell me what's going on."

"Mary Pickford told me about the postmortem and that the police closed the case. She said Sophia committed suicide by poisoning." Tears formed and lodged in the corner of her eyes. "But you already knew this, didn't you?"

Chet blinked several times and opened his mouth as if to speak, but Grace wouldn't let him.

"Flo fabricated a story of murder for publicity. For *publicity*, Chet! And you were on board, lying to me right along with him."

Chet stepped closer, his rumpled shirt and hair making him look like a guilty schoolboy. "Grace, I—"

"You knew all along."

"No, not all along. Flo told me that he suspected murder and hired me to investigate. I swear it. I don't think Flo knew anything for sure, and I've been furious watching him spin stories for the newspapers."

Grace brushed past him into the bedroom. He followed.

She sat on the bed, suddenly feeling exhaustion, disappointment, and rage colliding in her brain. "Then when *did* you find out?"

"Donovan Green told me just before I tossed the smarmy bastard off the train." Chet propped his tall frame in the doorway, his hands in his pockets.

Grace whipped her head around to face him. "You *threw* him off the train?"

"Arse over head. He confessed that Flo had hired him to stir up publicity, make it look like you were in grave danger. I told you Donovan caused the horse accident, but you didn't believe me. Once I found out he was Flo's publicity puppet and that he had willingly risked your life, I got rid of him."

"Aren't you Flo's puppet, as well?" She narrowed her eyes at him again. How could he stand there so calm, so matter-of-fact, and tell her this?

Chet looked down at the floor, then raised his hand and pinched the bridge of his nose. Grace hoped he was experiencing terrible, inconsolable, emotional pain. "Grace, I have so much to tell you. There is so much you don't know."

She turned away from him and stared at the closet, her mind full of things she wanted to say to him, scream at him, but she simply didn't have the energy. "Get out, Chet." A steely calmness washed over her, making her fingertips cold, her breath shallow, and her mind clear. "Get out and don't come back. I don't need you, and I don't want your help."

CHET STOOD HIS GROUND. "I'm not going anywhere," he said, watching Grace bristle and her shoulders tighten. He felt the coolness washing over him like an ice storm. "There are some things you need to know . . . about me."

A knock on the door interrupted him. He ignored it.

"Telegram for Miss Michelle," a male voice announced.

Grace stood up and strode past Chet, sidling through the doorway as if she couldn't bear making any sort of contact with him. He heard her thank the deliveryman and tear into the envelope.

"What is it?"

"It's Flo," she said, her eyes on the note. "He's ordered us to return to New York. The show will start in two weeks, and I have to rehearse." She folded the telegram and shoved it back in the envelope. She stayed near the door and crossed her arms in front of her.

"Will you please listen to me?" Chet asked.

She didn't move but didn't protest, either.

"Like I told you before, I only agreed to work for Flo because I was desperate for money," he began, "but here's what you don't know: Since returning from the war, my business has been slow to get back on its feet and my mother needed a life-saving operation. I had the *brilliant* idea that I could gamble and win, but I lost miserably and lost what little money I had. I went to Marciano's boys for a loan and then couldn't pay up when they called the loan in. I went to Flo to find legitimate PI work, and then he—alone—concocted this plan to get Joe to finance the show and excuse my debt. That's the conversation you walked in on back in New York. In return, Flo insisted I accompany you on this trip as your bodyguard. But I swear that I had no idea he wasn't serious about a murder investigation or that he'd turn it into this." It had all come out in a rush of words. He hated lying to her, even more so now that he'd fallen in love with her.

Grace uncrossed her arms and moved closer to him, her fiery eyes boring into him.

"As I explained to you, Grace, I thought a murder investigation was part of the deal and didn't suspect otherwise until

Donovan Green told me that he'd been following Flo's directives to make it look like you were in real danger. I went to the police in good faith and was surprised when the detective told me they'd closed the case."

"But why didn't you tell *me* that when you first found out?" Grace's face crumpled in disappointment, nearly breaking his heart.

Chet blew out an exasperated breath. "I work for Flo. He ordered me not to tell you. It was before we—"

"You knew yesterday that the police had closed the investigation, and I don't think you talked to Flo yesterday, so you could have told me that. You could have broken the news to me rather than Mary Pickford. It might have been easier coming from you." She covered her face with her hands and shook her head.

"I didn't want to hurt you," he admitted. "And if I told you just how much Flo was manipulating everything for his own benefit, I knew it would crush you." He paused, watched her struggle to understand. "And you just lost your sister and got thrust into this crazy business of becoming Flo's latest ingenue, which I know you don't even want." Chet spoke softly, dying to reach out to her, to console her. He'd been a fool to lie to her.

Grace crossed the room and plopped down into a chair. "So if the case is closed, and everyone—*except me*—believes that Sophia killed herself on purpose, where did you go today?"

"I know a PI in Los Angeles so I went to find him, to see if he could throw any work my way. My thinking was that finding a way to make some money while we're here would give us both some leverage. I could get you out of this mess and take you far away from Flo. I know you'll never be happy being Flo's doll, his showpiece, particularly now."

Grace raised her eyes to his. They were no longer shimmering with anger. "It's too late," she said. "I am as financially beholden to Flo as you are, and now he's commanding us to return."

"Yes. And we'll have to, but Grace . . ." Chet strode over to her, knelt in front of her, and placed his hand gently on her arm. "Let's go through with it. Let's go back to New York. My debt to Marciano and Flo will be paid off, which will free me to work at building my business again. You can work this *one* show—Flo will take care of you as long as you're in the show—and then I'll be able to take care of you after that."

Grace's lovely, youthful face took on a determined hardness, something it broke Chet's heart to see. Her green eyes drilled into his.

"When I'm done with this *one* show, no one—not Flo, not you, not anyone—will take care of me again. I'll take care of myself."

CHAPTER TWENTY-FOUR

*O*nce Chet had gone, Grace dug frantically through Sophia's trunk, looking for something, anything, that could offer a clue. She'd hoped to find the ermine cape at the bottom of the container, but no luck. She had a nagging feeling that if Jack Pickford could get his hands on something that valuable, it would be long gone. Or did he sell it once she died—sort of like a life insurance policy? Which reminded her—had Flo claimed the life insurance policy on Sophia yet? Clearly, Flo's interest in Sophia had been based on what she could do for him. Grace tried to ignore the ache in her heart at the fact that Flo felt the same way about her. She was merely a pawn in his scheme for publicity and fame.

She searched through the trunk again, and this time, when she pulled out one of Sophia's furs, she felt something in the pocket. It was a balled-up scrap of paper. She pulled it out and smoothed the crinkles. She squinted to read the hardly legible handwriting:

My dearest Grace,

I'm heartsick that we're so far apart and that we left on such horrible terms. I never meant to hurt you. I have been out of my mind with worry. You see, darling, I had to leave to protect us both. Someone, someone whom I have wronged, a man I thought could bring me happiness, is after me. If I told you his identity, it would only put you in more danger, but now that I have left New York, I feel you are safe.

The writing abruptly stopped and trailed off. It looked like Sophia's handwriting, the letters slanting severely to the right, but Sophia had excellent penmanship; it had never been even slightly messy unless she had been rushing. Had someone come in and interrupted her? Was it then that she shoved the note into her coat pocket?

Grace read the words again: *someone whom I have wronged.* Several people came to mind. There was the obvious: the man with the scar and shabby brown coat. Then Lillian Lorraine had claimed Sophia stole her role in the upcoming show, and Liane Held claimed Sophia stole her legacy. Billie could have felt that Sophia had stolen her man, as well, especially since Sophia had held a more valued place in Flo's heart than the other girls. And then there was Flo himself, the man who stood to lose the most by Sophia's marriage and move to California.

It would only put you in more danger.

So it was true. Grace was in danger—and heading back to New York. She had to find some answers and find them fast.

THAT EVENING GRACE had wanted to dine alone in her suite, but Chet had insisted on staying just outside her door. As she picked at her salmon, Grace tried to convince herself that keeping Chet and Flo in the dark about Sophia's suicide note—possibly a fake —the handwritten note stating she might be in danger, and the man with the scar was for the best. Both Chet and Flo had proven untrustworthy. She'd have to forge ahead alone as best she could without raising suspicion.

When someone lightly tapped on her bedroom door, Grace dropped her fork, which clanged against the plate, further jangling her nerves. She exhaled in relief when Lucile entered the bedroom.

"Ooh, that dreamy man let me in," she said, closing the door behind her.

Grace pushed away from the small table and rose to greet her friend.

"Dining alone?"

"I just needed some quiet time."

"You've heard the news, I suppose," Lucile said.

"Yes. I know we're leaving day after tomorrow on an express train. Are you ready?"

Lucile shrugged her shoulders. "Not really. I've met with a few producers, but I was hoping to stay on a bit longer to see where those meetings would take me."

"Why don't you stay, then?"

"Darling, Flo insists your new show has to be ready to open in a few weeks. That's money in the bank for me. These movie producers move like molasses. They have little interest in the costumes until they recognize that movies can't be made without them. The wardrobe designers have very little pull, so we must wait . . . and wait."

"Lucile, do you have access to a car?"

"Why, yes. Whatever for, my dear?"

"I'd like to run an errand in the morning. I'll need the car for the day."

Lucile tilted her chin upward and narrowed her eyes. "Alone?"

"Yes."

"Rift with Prince Charming?"

"You might say that."

Lucile's expression turned concerned. "Is that a good idea for you to go alone? Would Flo approve of this 'errand'?"

"Does everyone have to know and approve of my every move, my every thought, my every breath?" Grace plunked her fists on her hips.

Lucile frowned. "I'm sorry, darling. I didn't mean to offend you."

"I feel like a bird in a cage, Lucile. I can't breathe. Everything I do is monitored. Please, could I just use your car for the day, no questions asked? Please be the one person who trusts that I wouldn't do anything foolish, that I can handle myself for a few hours without a chaperone. Please tell me you are that person."

"Indeed, I am. I'll send my driver. What time?"

"Don't have him come to the room. Have him drive up to the reception area. I'll meet him there at 6:00 a.m."

Grace spent the rest of the night packing her trunk and plotting how she could leave the room without Chet asking where she was going, or without him tagging along.

The next morning, after room service had picked up her breakfast tray, Grace had told the waiter to inform Chet that she had a headache and would spend the day in her room.

She splashed her face with water, hurriedly put on her trousers, and slipped out the window. A tall wall of bright pink bougainvillea pressed up against the panes, making her escape difficult with its thorny branches grabbing at her clothes. But it also kept her hidden from view. After a busboy passed by on the garden path, Grace stepped out, straightened her coat and hat, and headed to the lobby.

Grace kept her head down, so as not to be recognized, and made her way to the large glass doors that led out to the hotel's drive. Once outside, she noticed several very sleek, very expensive cars parked along the U-shaped driveway. A small, thin man in a chauffeur's uniform stepped out from behind the door of a black Cadillac Town Sedan with its curved rolling fenders and outdoor driver's cab.

"Miss Michelle?"

Grace nodded and waited for him to open the door to the passenger's cab.

"And where would the lady like to go this morning?" he asked, starting the car.

Grace looked him directly in the eye through the rearview mirror.

"The Los Angeles Police Department."

AFTER SPEAKING to a plump woman in a frumpy suit with a demeanor like a pile of wood, Grace waited in the reception area of the police station. The room smelled of stale cigarettes and burned coffee.

A man resembling a scarecrow wearing thick glasses peeked his head out the door and then walked up to her, his hand outstretched. "So you're the sister."

Grace flinched. "Excuse me?"

"Sophia Michelle's sister?"

"Yes."

"Joe Barnett, Detective. Sorry for your loss, Miss Michelle. What can I do for you?"

"I want to know what has been done about my sister's case."

Detective Barnett pushed his glasses up further on the bridge of his nose, placed his hands in his pockets, and rolled back and forth on the balls of his feet.

"I'm sorry, Miss, but as I told the PI nosing around here a few days ago, whom I thought worked for you, the case has been closed. Coroner ruled it accidental suicide. Didn't the fella tell you that?"

"Yes, he did." Grace swallowed back her annoyance. "But I have evidence that might change your mind about the case."

"Oh, I doubt that." Barnett frowned.

"Look." Grace pulled the crinkled note out from her purse,

thrusting it into his hands. "Sophia was writing to me, explaining that someone she had wronged was after her. I think it was a lover. That's why she left New York."

He perused the words. "How do you know that this is from her?"

Grace tapped the paper still in Barnett's hand. "It's her hand-writing, and I found it stuffed into the pocket of one of her coats. She was obviously interrupted when writing the note. See how it trails off?" She looked into Barnett's bleary, smoke-bruised eyes. "No one planted this. It's likely no one knew anything about it and, thus, couldn't anticipate that I'd find it."

The detective pressed the note into her palm.

"Miss Michelle, I know this is a bitter pill to swallow, but we've looked at all the evidence in this case, and I'm sorry but it *has* been ruled an accidental suicide. This note has a vague mention of a threat, but it proves nothing. Could have been written by anyone. Could have been written by you, for all I know."

Grace shook her head. Why didn't he understand?

"Please, can't you look into it again?"

"Here's what I can do," he said, "because you're next of kin, I can show you the postmortem report. But that's all I can do."

She nodded. "Yes, yes, please. I'd like to see it."

Barnett turned and pushed open the door that led to the inner sanctum of the office. Grace waited in the hallway, nervously biting her nails. After a few moments, Barnett returned with a manila file and handed it to Grace. She opened it and scanned the papers within and then read it again more slowly. It stated just what Barnett—and Mary—had said.

Grace slumped her shoulders. "Mercury bichloride. This just can't be."

Barnett removed the file from her hands. "If you don't believe our medical examiner, there's a library just down the street—three blocks, on your right. Look it up yourself, see how lethal that medicine can be." Detective Barnett gave her a dismissive look. "This case is closed, and I'm not about to reopen it without concrete evidence. I'm sorry, Miss. Now, if you will excuse me, I have genuine crimes to solve." He turned and disappeared behind the swinging doors.

Grace watched him leave. She refused to believe Sophia had killed herself, accidentally or not. Grace ran out to the car and hopped in.

"Take me to the library, fast. I don't have much time," she said. "The detective said it's only three blocks down, on the right."

When they reached the library, Grace looked at her watch. Fifteen minutes to spare before she had to head back to the hotel. She asked the driver to wait, dashed up the steps, pushed open the heavy, brass-framed doors, and stopped at the information desk. A curvaceous young woman with bright red lipstick and spectacles hanging down over her ample bosom greeted her.

"Where can I find information about mercury poisoning?" Grace asked.

The woman lowered her spectacles.

"I'm doing some research," she rushed on. "For my boss."

"Follow me." The woman led Grace up a long staircase with two landings, past several shelves of books, turned left down a row of shelving, then took a right, and stopped. This particular section of the library was small and dark and smelled of old dust.

The woman held out her hand. "Here's where you'll find most of the information. If you need more, come find me."

"Thank you." Grace stared at the myriad book spines. After the woman left, she settled on one titled *Everyday Poisons* and opened it up. Her heart lurched when she turned to a section devoted solely to mercury bichloride. She read fast, her eyes skimming the pages, pausing when something caught her attention: *When ingested, the toxin often burns the patient's esophagus and stomach wall.*

Grace lowered the book. The postmortem mentioned nothing of a damaged esophagus or stomach lining. Perhaps Sophia hadn't ingested enough to harm her esophagus? Grace hadn't really known what to look for when she read the postmortem, though. She placed the book back on the shelf and sighed.

"Now I'm more confused than ever." She looked at her watch. Seven more minutes before she had to leave to get back to the hotel.

Grace started slowly down the stairs, thinking. Sophia had died the night of John Barrymore's party. Perhaps something at the party had led to her death. At the moment, Lillian Lorraine stood out as someone who would want Sophia gone more than anyone else. She had been the most vocal about her negative feeling toward Sophia, too. Had Lillian been at Barrymore's party?

Grace reached the bottom of the stairs, lost in thought. The librarian approached her. "Are you all right, Miss? Did you find what you were looking for?"

"In a manner of speaking," Grace said, her voice distant, her mind whirling. She looked at the bespectacled woman. "Where would I find back issues of *Variety Magazine*?"

The librarian crooked her finger, bidding Grace to follow. This time they took a flight of stairs down to the basement stacks. Their heels tapped loudly on the tiled floor. The industrial, gray metal bookshelves made the atmosphere cold, austere, like Grace imagined a hospital morgue would feel and look.

The woman led her into another small room lined with wooden dowels, newspapers strewn across them like clothes on a laundry line.

"Do you have a date in mind?" The librarian lowered her spectacles to look Grace in the eye.

"Yes. April 15. Of this year."

The librarian scanned the papers, her finger held aloft to guide her eyes. In seconds, she snapped a paper off the line.

"Here you go. Published a week later. Should have information on anything happening around town on the fifteenth."

"Excellent, thank you."

"Will you be able to find your way out again?"

Grace waved a hand. "Yes, yes. Thank you for your help."

The librarian left the room, the click of her heels echoing throughout the sterile basement.

Grace flipped open the paper. Inside the first page she found an index. Her eyes landed on the words, *Gossip and Events, Page 5*. Quickly, she turned the pages. As she'd hoped, she found an article with the headline BARRYMORE'S BOISTEROUS BALL. Below it was a photo of a crowd of people gathered in what looked like a foyer of a grand house with marbled floors and an ornate metal-and-wood staircase. A small group of people clustered at the bottom of the stairs. Grace peered closer to see the faces and gasped out loud when she recognized Jack Pickford. Standing next to him was a woman in a white fur coat dotted with spots.

She held her breath, her eyes focused on the woman. It had to be Sophia, and she had to be wearing the ruby-and-sapphire studded fur cape. But Grace couldn't be sure because she could only see the woman's profile. Then Grace recognized the hair clip that their mother had given Sophia for her birthday, right before her parents embarked on their fatal second honeymoon. Grace moved her gaze to the tall woman standing across from Sophia. She towered over Sophia, her dark hair cut into a short curly bob, pointing a finger in Sophia's face.

"Liane Held," Grace said out loud, studying the woman's face. It portrayed an expression that could only be described as murderous.

CHAPTER TWENTY-FIVE

*J*UNE 24, 1920 - NEW YORK CITY, NY

Molly, the new show, a Cinderella love story about an orphaned girl resigned to the streets, working in a factory until she was "discovered," mirrored Grace's own life. She wondered if Flo had done that on purpose —yet another way to exploit her.

Grace hadn't seen Flo since she'd returned a few days prior, but he'd called them all together for a meeting and line rehearsal that afternoon. A long dining room table had been placed on the stage for the meeting.

One of the first to arrive, Grace purposely chose a chair to the left of center at the table. She knew Flo always sat at the head of the table and the star of the show always sat directly to his right. She wanted to make a statement that would jostle Flo and everyone else.

Joe Urban, the set designer, arrived next. Then Fanny, Irving Berlin, Lucile, Nicole, Charles, and some of the other actors filtered in.

Finally, Flo arrived, his appearance shocking her. He'd lost weight, and the pallor of his skin looked dirty-dishwater gray.

Purple, upside-down crescent moons framed his lower eyelashes as if he hadn't slept for days.

He went straight to Grace, knelt down to her seated level, and took her hand. "Darling, I'm so happy you've returned." As he reached over to give her a dry-lipped kiss on the cheek, Grace could smell the stench of stale cigarettes and bourbon on his breath. "I know you have some concerns about how fast we're going with this, but we'll have a nice, long talk later, yes?"

Grace gave a slight nod and pulled her hand away from him. God, but he looked awful. Smelled awful, too. She'd heard rumors of another affair, another starlet—and this time, his paramour was married.

Wearing a velvet smoking jacket and his hair slicked back shiny and neat, Charles slipped into the seat next to her. "Nice to have you back." He kissed her on the cheek. "How are you?"

"Fine. Much better than Flo. He looks terrible."

"I've never seen him like this," Charles said. "He stands outside her dressing room door, pleading for her to let him in."

"Who?"

"Macy Arnold—his new lover. She's temperamental, spoiled, and never satisfied."

"Begging?" Fanny leaned in closer to join the conversation, the feathers on her hat dancing above her eyes. "I never thought I'd see the day that Flo would beg."

"*Pfft!* Oh please, he'll be fretting one moment, and then fly into a rage the next," Charles said. "It's been hell, I tell you, *hell.*" Charles turned to Grace. "He's missed you terribly. He was so worried when he learned of your horseback riding accident."

Grace smiled through gritted teeth. The rest of the cast didn't need to be burdened with her problems.

Flo could not sit still. He'd rise from the table, pace a few steps, and sit down again. Goldie passed out the scripts, and everyone bent their heads to peruse them, searching for their lines. The more Grace watched Flo's frenetic dance, a cloud of cigarette smoke hovering over his head, the more Grace's hurt and anger gave way to the slightest bit of concern.

Someone entered stage left. Grace turned to see who had come out of the wings, and her heart stopped. Liane Held approached the table, her arms tightly crossed, her lips down-turned in an angry frown. She wore the same expression Grace had seen in the photograph of John Barrymore's party. Grace turned to look at Flo, whose face had drained of color.

"Liane, darling," he said, but stood frozen in place.

"Let's dispense with the niceties. I need a word with you."

"My dear, when did you arrive?" Flo approached her, arms outstretched. "Have you come from Europe? Why are you here?"

"We have unfinished business to discuss."

Flo touched her sleeve, a look of utter helplessness and bewilderment on his face. She pulled her elbow away. Grace consciously made an effort to keep her mouth from hanging open. Had Liane been on the train with them? How had she not seen her?

"Of course, of course," Flo said, steering her off the stage. "Let's talk tonight."

Liane gave him a sullen look and walked back into the wings. Flo turned around to face the table of actors and crew, and he clapped his hands together. "Shall we begin? Goldie, another drink, would you?"

Grace noticed the twitch at the side of his mouth. Liane's presence rattled him—rattled her, too, for that matter. Did this have something to do with the ermine? With Liane's inheritance?

They commenced with the line rehearsal, discussed costumes and choreography, and all the while Flo paced, smoked, and drank. When he called for a short break, the group scattered, all but Grace, Charles, and Fanny, who knitted themselves into a tight knot.

"I've never seen Flo this agitated," Fanny said. "Not since he broke it off with Sophia."

Grace turned to her. "You knew of their affair?"

Fanny shrugged. "Sorry, Gracie, I didn't mean to let that slip and bring it up again."

"And what is Liane doing here? I thought she'd never leave Europe," Charles said. "I heard she hated the States, hated New York, and hated Flo."

Grace wanted to say something about the ermine cape, about the fact that Liane thought Sophia had stolen her legacy, but recent events made her reticent and she didn't know whom to trust. Fanny had just admitted that she had known about Sophia's affair with Flo. Why had she kept it a secret 'til now? If Fanny had known about the affair while it was happening, perhaps she knew a lot more about what had happened between Sophia and Flo. What had caused the rift? Did Sophia really overreact, or was that just the story everyone perpetuated about her because of the sensationalism it produced?

Grace wanted to get Fanny alone, but for now, she'd keep the questions simple. "Fanny, did you see Sophia with anyone after the breakup? Another lover?"

"Well, Jack, of course," Fanny said.

"Of course, but before Jack?"

Fanny leaned back in her chair and lit a cigarette, her gaze drifting away from Grace's. "I never saw her with anyone."

"Nor did I," Charles said.

Grace bit the inside of her cheek and focused her attention on Fanny, who still avoided her eyes. As if sensing Grace's ardent gaze, Fanny briefly turned her head toward Grace, fluttered her eyelashes, and went back to smoking her cigarette as if Grace and Charles weren't even there.

Fanny knew something.

Grace sighed. Someone else had to have seen Sophia with this mystery man. It would just take a bit more digging to find out who.

CHAPTER TWENTY-SIX

*T*hat night, Flo insisted Grace have dinner with him alone in his suite. She braced herself for what he might confide, reveal, or lie to her about this time.

She arrived promptly at 8:00 p.m. Harold let her into the parlor where Flo sat at his desk, staring at the papers strewn all over it. Two new, carved wooden elephant figurines graced the desk, a sure sign that Flo did not feel confident about the show—or anything else.

He raised his eyes as she approached. "Grace, please, sit down," he said, motioning to a chair opposite his. His smoking jacket buckled open at his chest, and hung on him like a sack. "I'm so glad we have this opportunity to chat. Dinner will be served in a few minutes. But first, please, tell me, how are you?"

Grace didn't know where to begin. "I'm well."

"Wonderful. Was the railcar to your satisfaction? Were you comfortable?"

Grace gripped the arms of her chair. "Why did you lie to me, Flo? Why did you perpetuate the story of Sophia's murder, or *suicide* rather, when you knew the police in Los Angeles closed the case?"

Flo froze, his cigarette dangling between his lips. He removed it, exhaled. "It was for you, darling, for the show. You're going to be a star. Bigger than Sophia."

"Don't you see that is *not* what I want? I'm doing this show for you, Flo, to repay you for taking in Sophia and me when we needed it. I agreed to go to California so that I could find out what happened to my sister, and you knew all along that the case had been closed! You led me astray and gave me false hope!"

"Guilty." Flo held his hands in the air. "I am guilty of all you said, and I am sorry, dear. I did what I thought was best for you, for the show. But now we know what happened to Sophia. That should give you comfort."

"Comfort?" She shook her head. "Now I am only further convinced that Sophia *was* murdered and the police have missed something. The postmortem report didn't even make sense, Flo. The police got *an* answer and that was it, no more investigation."

Flo sighed and pressed his hands to his face. Grace noticed his fingers trembling. She knew he was under tremendous pressure at the moment, but she wanted answers.

"I don't know what to say," he said.

"Mary Pickford led me to believe that you might have orchestrated the events that put me in danger, just for the sake of publicity."

"Mary Pickford? When did you see her?"

"I went to the house to see Jack. Complete disaster. The man was so drunk he forgot who I was the minute he said my name. But is it true, Flo? Did you put me at risk just for publicity?"

"I would never do anything to hurt you," he said, not actually answering the question.

"Is that what you told Sophia all those years ago?"

Flo looked as though she'd struck him, his brows turned down, his mouth working furiously as if he might break into tears. "My dear . . . I'm so sorry. Everything is falling apart since

Sophia died. The show is doomed, and unless you are the sensation I know you can be, I will be ruined."

Grace closed her eyes so she wouldn't have to see the pathetic look on his face. She let out a breath, calming herself. "Why don't you just give the part to Lillian Lorraine? She wants it far more than I do."

"I don't think Lillian is in her right mind these days," Flo said, under his breath.

"Did you know she was in California? At Sophia's funeral? And on my *train*?" She paused for effect. "Why would she have been there, Flo?"

"I'm not sure, darling. But I won't keep this from you any longer: she despised Sophia and threatened her more than once."

Grace's stomach turned. She remembered what Lillian had said when Flo had given Grace the part to fill Sophia's shoes. She'd been livid.

"Do you think Lillian could have killed Sophia?" Grace asked.

"I don't know. If she'd had too much to drink, too much cocaine, anything is possible. What did the police say?"

"That Sophia died of her own hand, end of story. You know that," she ground out. "What about Billie?"

"What *about* Billie?"

"I heard she paid Jack to get Sophia away from you. Is that true? Were you still pursuing Sophia?"

"No, darling. I'm afraid it's quite the opposite. Sophia wanted to reconcile. She was quite desperate. But my feelings had changed. I love my wife."

Grace nearly choked. Didn't Charles just tell her that Flo had a new lover? Unable to speak, Grace let Flo continue. "I don't know anything about Billie paying Jack. Billie keeps her accounts separate from mine. She feels I gamble a bit too much. But Sophia and I were through, I promise you."

"Do you know who Sophia started seeing after your breakup?"

"There were quite a few men. I'm surprised you never knew about them."

Seems I didn't know much about my sister.

"Was there anyone special? Anyone she was serious about?"

"Only Jack. Poor choice, I might add. Sorry, dear. I shouldn't speak ill of your sister."

Grace gripped the arms of the chair harder, bolstering herself for what she was going to say next. "And what about you, Flo? You've sure garnered a lot of publicity over Sophia's death. Did *you* do it? Did you kill her?" Grace looked straight into his eyes. They turned a deeper shade of brown, almost black, and he clamped his jaw shut so tight that Grace could see the muscles flexing below his ears.

Flo took in a deep breath, and Grace noticed his eyes travel to one of the wooden elephants on the desk. "Well. I don't know whether I am insulted, sad, or completely furious at your question, my dear. I am quite shocked." His gaze drifted up to meet hers. "I understand that this whole situation has been difficult for you, and I apologize for causing you any undue stress, but I assure you, my show—my art—and my reputation has never been in more trouble than it is now, and it all started with Sophia's death. Why would I do that to myself? I've had nothing but loss since her death, not gain."

Grace let the words sink in. She hated to admit he had a point.

Flo stood. "If you will excuse me, I am going to check on dinner—and I must compose myself. Your question caught me quite off guard, my dear."

Grace stood up, as well. "I am sorry, Flo. I'm frustrated and angry. I know that something about Sophia's case is not right. I'm just seeking answers, and I feel in order to find those answers, I must ask questions of everyone who knew Sophia. I hope you understand."

"Certainly, certainly," Flo said, straightening his smoking jacket. "If you'll excuse me."

He left Grace standing at the desk, feeling like a complete ingrate, yet not entirely sorry for asking the question. Since she'd learned that both Flo and Chet had tried to keep her in the dark, she felt her boldness growing by the day. She *would* have her answers.

Flo had mentioned he'd gained nothing financially from Sophia's death. Grace pondered that thought. She remembered the life insurance policy sitting in a folder, in the drawer in the desk right in front of her. Did she dare go through his desk when he could return at any moment?

She walked around the other side and rested her hands on top of the papers strewn across the desk. She sat down in the chair, her hands still on the desk. With her right hand, she opened the drawer. Her eyes immediately found Sophia's file. With one last quick glance to make sure Flo wasn't stepping back in the room, she opened the file.

Empty.

Grace's stomach twisted, forcing a dull, throbbing pain in her torso. Her eyes traveled to the file labeled *Grace Michelle*. Slowly, as if opening a box full of snakes, she pulled the file open. Staring back at her was a crisp, white sheet of paper with the words *Metropolitan Life* in bold script across the top. Her eyes scanned down the sheet until they rested on her name with the amount of thirty thousand dollars next to it. It was signed in her name but not in her hand.

The blood drained from her face, and her hands went numb. In a stupor, she closed the file, placed it back in the drawer, and returned to her chair. She let her legs give out beneath her and rested her head in her hands.

"Grace?" she heard Flo ask from behind her. "Dinner is served."

Grace stood and turned to him, smiling. She couldn't make her mouth form the words that she wasn't very hungry after all.

GRACE STARED AT FLO, smiling at her as if they'd never had the previous discussion. He must have "composed" himself quite well since he'd left the room. Now, it was Grace's turn to try to pretend she hadn't accused him of murder, and also to try to pretend that she didn't know he'd secretly taken out a life insurance policy on her. She stilled her trembling hands by clasping them together.

Flo held his arm out to escort her. "Shall we retire to the dining room?"

Without speaking, Grace stood and took his arm. The door chimed again as Flo led Grace to a chair at the dining room table. A moment later, Harold appeared in the room. And trailing behind him was Liane.

Grace snuck a look at Flo whose demeanor immediately hardened, his upper lip twitching the only emotion on his face. "Liane, darling. Come in. Grace and I are just about to have dinner. Won't you join us?"

Liane's forehead pinched into a vee, and she adjusted her handbag under her arm. "I need to speak with you alone."

"I'm sorry, dear, but Grace and I have important business to discuss about the new show."

"I've come to get my inheritance. Miss Michelle's sister stole it from me."

Flo let out a chuckle. "What are you talking about, my dear?"

Liane set her handbag down on the table with a thud. "I traveled to California to get it back. I spoke with Sophia's husband, her sister-in-law, anyone who knew her. It's gone. She must have sold it here in New York before she left for California. It's mine, Flo. You promised me. Where is it?"

Flo slowly sat down in his chair opposite Grace and raised his eyebrows at her as if he thought Liane had slipped over the edge of sanity. "I'm sorry, dear. You have me at a disadvantage."

"The cape!" Liane slammed her hand on the table. "The ermine cape with rubies and sapphires. When you bought it for mother, you said it would be mine one day. I know it is worth a fortune. Where is it?"

"Truly, I—" Flo raised his hand to the stubble on his chin, his eyes reflecting his search for the memory.

"Oh, come now, Flo. Surely, you remember. I was there with you and mother when you purchased it for her. I was six years old and had just arrived from France. We went to the Lyceum Theater. Mother was in one of your shows there. She fell in love with the cape; it was part of a costume. You told me it would be mine."

An uneasy silence filled the room. Grace fidgeted in her chair, surprised at the lengths Liane would go to get that cape back. Would she have stooped to murder? She said she'd been in California and had confronted Sophia about it. Could that have been the moment the camera had snapped their conversation?

"Really, darling." Flo reached his arm out in front of him on the table in a gesture of peacemaking. "That was so long ago. I truly don't remember telling you it would be yours."

"But you *do* remember the cape."

"Yes."

"Where is it?"

"I gave it to Sophia. She didn't steal anything."

"When you were screwing her," Liane spit like venom.

"Liane!" Grace cut in. "I beg your pardon!"

"It was *mine*, Flo, and you gave it to that tramp. You owe me."

Grace stood up. "I will not let you speak about my sister like that, Liane. Watch your mouth."

Flo gestured for Grace to sit again. She obeyed but wanted to tackle Liane from across the table.

"I'm sorry, dear." Flo said. "What would you like me to do?"

"I'd like one hundred thousand dollars."

"It's not worth that."

"Maybe not then, but it is now. I got nothing when mother died. As your adopted daughter, I deserve something."

Flo let out a rush of air, set his hands on the table as if bracing himself. Grace saw the lines crease in his forehead as he raised his eyes to Liane.

"Those papers were never signed. You are not my adopted daughter."

Liane's face drained of color, but her eyes burned with rage. "Don't think I won't ruin you, Flo. I have information on you that you would rather forget, including some tantalizing tidbits on *your* floozy sister." She directed her gaze at Grace. "I hated that woman, and I hate you, you pathetic orphan. Flo already had a child when you straggled in from the streets. He had me."

Grace steeled herself by bracing her hands against the sides of the chair. "You were never here, Liane. You lived in France. I'd never even met you until recently. I'm sorry to hear you hated my sister, but the question is, did you hate my sister enough to kill her, Liane? Are you here to kill me?"

Liane smirked, then laughed. "Murder is really not my style."

Flo stood up so fast, the chair nearly fell over behind him. "Girls, girls! Please, Grace, Liane would never kill anyone. Liane, Grace has done nothing to you. This argument is going nowhere."

"I am your step-daughter!" Liane said, pointing a finger at her chest. "I deserve this life, these riches, these roles, not this stray cat from the gutter."

"What do you want, Liane?" Flo asked, his voice raised for the first time.

"The money."

"I don't have the money, but I can give you a job in Grace's show. You can be a chorine, darling—sing, dance, wear lovely costumes."

Grace swallowed, knowing that particular offer would not be tantalizing to Liane.

"A chorus girl?" Liane's gaze bore into Flo. "Oh, that's rich." She pointed a finger at Grace. "Very well. When *you* make Flo thousands of dollars in *your* new show, *I'll* be standing by to get my share." She turned back to Flo. "And believe me, there will be consequences if I don't get it."

LINE REHEARSALS STARTED the next day. Grace arrived early and stood onstage, silently reading her script while waiting for the others. Flo and the director, Harvey Stein, stood in the corner talking while the crew bustled around the stage, arranging props.

Suddenly, someone flung open the doors at the back of the theater, spewing shafts of daylight into the great gallery. A large man wearing a dark suit, hat, and white scarf entered the theater. All activity and conversations ceased. Joe Marciano had arrived, looking smug.

Walking slightly behind him were his two guard dog cronies and a taller, thinner man wearing a brown suit. Grace's heart slammed so hard against her ribs, she almost lost her balance. What was he doing here? Her first impulse was to turn and run, but she stood her ground.

Flo crossed over to stage right, holding his hand above his eyes to diminish the glare and greet his guest. "Joe. Uh, hello." The cigarette dangling from Flo's fingers shook.

Grace swallowed, her eyes riveted toward the man in the

brown suit. The same man she thought had run her down in the car, who had appeared on the train, and who she'd seen crossing the street in Beverly Hills. The man she thought was following her. The man she and Sophia had left for dead in the street all those years ago. He returned her gaze but showed no emotion, no sense of recognition. His eyes passed over her and focused on Flo. She held the script firmly at her side to stop her hands from shaking.

Marciano tipped his hat to Grace. She managed a tight smile and nodded back to him, her skin crawling as his lips curved into a lecherous sneer.

"I'd like a word, Ziegfeld." Marciano took off his hat and fingered the brim.

"Certainly, certainly. Boyd!" Flo waved his manager over. "Take over for me."

Jack Boyd, a short, barrel-chested, heavyset man, looked from Flo, to Marciano, to Grace, and then back to Flo.

"Sure, boss." He glanced back at Grace. "Have you got your lines?"

Grace gave a terse nod, afraid her voice would croak like a bullfrog's if she spoke. Her eyes flitted toward the man in the brown suit. His gaze grazed over her again, seemingly more interested in the lights and catwalks than anything else.

Flo grabbed his coat and hat, and followed Marciano out of the theatre, a swirl of smoke trailing the mobster. Two of Marciano's men flanked him on each side, and the man she'd feared for weeks now took up the rear.

Grace's legs crawled with numbness as she watched them walk away.

CHAPTER TWENTY-SEVEN

*C*het arrived at Flo's office late that afternoon to find him pacing, a stiff drink in one hand and a cigar in the other. His hair, mussed and in need of a cut, stuck out in sweaty spikes. Chet had received Flo's call an hour prior and had come as soon as he could. He figured Flo wanted to discuss the California trip, and hopefully, they would come to terms with Chet's debt and he would soon be off the hook, if he wasn't already. He could start working on his business again and somehow win Grace back. She'd refused to have anything to do with him since that last night in California, and he was nearly crazy with worry about her emotional state.

"Want a drink?" Flo asked, never slowing his pace. He gestured toward the bar.

"No, thank you." Chet sat in one of the chairs facing the desk. Flo had never looked so haggard. In fact, Chet had never seen Flo look anything short of perfect. "What's the news?"

"Problems. Big problems." Flo ran his hands over his thinning hair. He paused, then sighed. "I'm sorry about the Sophia-murder thing, Chet. I got carried away, caught up in the story. It was bad, I know. Hell, it was real bad, and I feel awful about it."

"I'm not the one you need to apologize to."

"Yes, I know. I've spoken to Grace. She's fine, fine." Flo waved his hand in the air. "I'll make it up to her, I swear I will." He resumed pacing.

"So what's the problem?"

"Money."

"Go on." Chet clenched his fists. He needed to be done with this job. He needed out, to get on with his life, and get on with repairing his relationship with Grace. If Flo was having money problems, he'd likely want more work from Chet—and God knows what that would be.

Flo stubbed out his cigar and shook his head, greasy strands of hair falling into his eyes. "She's giving me fits"

"Grace?"

"No, no." Flo shook his head. "It's Macy. She's divorcing her husband, but she wants to marry Hans Shoefeld." He slammed his hand down on the desk.

Another starlet, another affair. Chet was unmoved. Now that he knew what Flo could do to the women he supposedly loved, Chet held no sympathy for him. "What does this have to do with money?"

"Macy wants to leave the Follies, but I can't let her go. It'd be like watching money sift like sand through an hourglass. I've been so upset about it, nervous, and so tense I needed to find a way to cool down. I thought a few days in Florida by myself would help. Maybe I could sort things out, try to figure a way to make her stay." He walked over to the chair behind his desk and sat down. "And then there's Liane."

"Liane?"

"Anna's daughter. Threatening me. Says I owe her an inheritance." He put his elbows on the desk and folded his hands in front of him.

"What did she threaten to do?"

"Nothing. I took care of it." Flo waved his hand in front of him.

"And what happened in Florida?" Chet asked, afraid of the answer.

"I found myself at the tables." Flo bolted out of his chair and commenced pacing. He placed his hands in his pockets, took them out, put them in again, took them out again. "I've lost everything."

Chet closed his eyes. He opened them again to see Flo fling himself into his elephant-themed chair in the corner. "What do you mean, *everything?*"

"All the money I had, Chet, every last dime. I even raided one of Billie's accounts. She's furious and threatening to file for divorce. I can't blame her. Everything has spun out of my hands. It's all gone." His last words squeaked out, and he pressed his fist to his mouth. He rose and went to the bar to pour another whiskey.

Chet froze in the chair. Florenz Ziegfeld Jr. had more money than anyone he'd ever known, except Marciano. But Flo also made a habit of throwing his wealth around, the money floating through the air like confetti.

"What about my debt? What about Marciano?"

Flo shook his head.

Chet gritted his teeth, cursing under his breath. He'd never wanted to strangle Flo as much as he did now.

"Marciano is still financing the show, but it has to be a hit, Chet. Grace has to be phenomenal. She's the only one who can get us out of this mess. The show may have to run for a few years to get us whole again."

Chet fought to still the rage seeping into his core. He struggled to keep his voice calm. "What about the banks? Have you gone to them?"

"We've been down that road before, Chet. You know they won't loan me another dime. All I've got is Marciano."

Chet felt his anger bubble up like boiling water in a geyser. "You son of a bitch." He sprang from the chair and lunged at Flo across the desk, grabbing him by the shirt collar. He hauled him to his feet. "Do you have any idea what you are doing to that girl? You've used her like you use everyone. You've lied to her, cheated her, and now *she's* your lifeline? Everything rests on her shoulders? Your debt? My debt? And now she's working for Marciano?"

He drew his hand back and delivered a blow to Flo's mouth, feeling the wet flesh smash against his knuckles. Blood from Flo's lips sprayed onto Chet's face, and Flo's head snapped back before he crumpled onto the chair, semiconscious.

"You lousy bastard." Chet pulled his pocket square from his breast pocket and wiped the blood from his hand and his face. He put the bloodied pocket square in his pants pocket, straightened his suit, and walked out of the office.

He entered the empty reception area. Goldie must have gone home for the day. Good. He would have hated to have her see him manhandling her boss.

Chet pulled his pocket watch from his vest. 6:00 p.m. He put the watch back and started down the stairs that led to the theater. He had to see her. He had to convince Grace to let him protect her because she needed protection now more than ever. The last thing he wanted was to leave her at the mercy of Marciano.

He knew what he had to do: he had to meet with Grace in a public place, and people needed to know about it. He had to get Marciano there. Chet just hoped his plan would work. But even more than that, he hoped he'd come out on the other side.

Since leaving rehearsal, Grace lay on her bed staring at the ceiling, her stomach in knots. Something was wrong, very wrong. Flo must be in some kind of trouble with the mobster, and although Flo had hurt her through to her very core, Grace couldn't find it in herself to hate him. Angry, sad, and disappointed, yes, but she just couldn't hate him.

A knock on the door startled her, and she clutched at the bedspread. She froze, listening. Another knock made her flinch.

Smoothing her skirt, Grace walked to the door and pressed her ear against it.

A third knock. Grace jumped back from the door.

"Miss Michelle, it's the bellman. I have a message for you."

Grace let out a rush of air, but her thoughts went immediately to the man in the brown suit. He could be pretending to be a messenger.

"Slide it under the door, please."

A few seconds later, the envelope slid under the door with a *whoosh*. She picked it up, opened it, and read.

Chet wanted to see her. Lowering the letter, she glanced over at the clock on her dresser. She would have an hour to get ready. What did he want? She read the letter again. It wasn't a plea to get back into her good graces, but something in the handwriting seemed urgent. He wanted to meet at the Plaza Hotel—such a public place. Photographers would likely see her entering or exiting.

She sighed. She would have to dress up. She walked over to the phone and picked up the receiver. Hotel staff answered immediately. "This is Grace Michelle. Would you please send a message to Lady Duff Gordon? I need her sent to my suite immediately. Also, I will need a taxi, either horse-drawn or motor car, to take me to the Plaza Hotel in one hour." She hung up the receiver, took a deep breath, and shuffled through the dresses in her wardrobe to find something fabulous to wear.

Within a half hour, Lucile arrived, and together they chose a dress of pale blue satin overlaid with thin mesh netting and embroidered with rhinestones and bugle beads. The dress showed off Grace's thin waist, cinched unmercifully with a corset, and clung to her hips and legs. The hue was a perfect complement to her green eyes, making them appear a deep shade of aqua.

Chet's letter had seemed businesslike and professional, but she wanted to be sure she looked her absolute best for the evening. In truth, a small flutter of hope bloomed in her chest that she and Chet would somehow work things out.

CHET WAITED for Grace in the Plaza's lobby, his eyes scanning the crowded room of well-dressed guests. A few photographers had set up their tripods near the door, and men with notepads milled about, smoking their cigarettes and conversing with one another. There was no sign of Marciano, but he knew he'd arrive soon.

Not long after he'd left Flo, Chet had gone back to Flo's offices, apologized, and told Flo he would help to make the show a hit. He'd said, in fact, that he knew Grace had made plans to have dinner at the Plaza Hotel, a great photo and publicity opportunity, and Flo should let the right people know when she'd be there.

A flurry of activity surrounded the revolving door of the hotel, and when Grace entered the red-carpeted lobby, pops from the camera flashes echoed through the room Soon the smell of gunpowder and mists of swirling smoke hovered above and around the cameras.

Grace, stunning as usual, walked through the lobby, her face tight. Chet knew she'd feel guarded. He watched her eyes skitter back and forth, scanning the lobby, until a look of relief passed over her face when she saw him. She didn't pause to answer any of the reporter's questions, and instead, she immediately came up to him and took his arm, her fingers wrapping firmly around his bicep.

"Can we get out of this lobby?" She spoke through a forced smile without moving her lips.

Chet slipped his arm around her waist and whisked her into the Palm Court, where he'd already directed the maître d' to escort them to a booth in the back corner.

As Grace slid into the red velvet seat and removed her gloves, revealing white, silky, ringed fingers, she drew in a deep breath and closed her eyes. Chet noticed her fingers trembling.

"Oh, how I hate those photographers and reporters," she said, exhaling in a huff.

Chet gently took her hand in his. "No one will bother us, now. I asked the maître d' to make sure we have privacy."

"What is going on, Chet?" She pulled her hand away. "Why did you ask me to come right away?"

A waiter approached and requested their drink order. Chet requested a bourbon and Grace, champagne. As soon as the waiter left, Chet looked into her eyes. "I needed to see you, Grace. I know things aren't good between us, but I wanted to apologize again for how I handled Sophia's case. It was wrong of me to keep the truth from you, and I hope you can forgive me."

Grace set her mouth in a tense line.

"But that's not why I asked you to come. I have to tell you something."

She met his gaze.

The waiter returned with their drinks and asked if they were prepared to order dinner. Chet waved him away.

"So, tell me," she said.

"I spoke with Flo earlier today, and he confessed that he'd lost everything to a gambling hall in Florida and that you're now working for Joe Marciano. If Flo has any hope of hanging on to the theater, *Molly* has to be a huge hit, running over the course of a few years. It seems, unfortunately, that his salvation rests on your shoulders."

"But I—" Grace's eyes opened wide as silver coins.

"I have a plan, Grace. I'm going to fix this. You won't have to work for that man, I promise you."

Grace's eyes narrowed, and Chet saw the hurt and betrayal in them. "*You* promise? Why would I take *your* word on anything?"

"I know the wounds are still fresh, and I've only stayed away because I know you need time to sort everything out. I know you're angry and hurt, and I know that you can't forgive me right now, but this is important."

"My sister's *murder* was important, Chet. You lied, made me think you cared as much as I did about solving the crime."

"I did all I could." He really hadn't, which was why he had to make it up to her now. "I went to the police. As you know, the case is closed."

"Well, you may have accepted their brush-off, but I discovered new evidence."

"What do you mean? What new evidence?"

"Right before we left Beverly Hills, I went through Sophia's trunk and found something. She had been writing a letter to me, telling me that she'd married Jack and fled New York because someone was after her. I took it to Detective Barnett."

"And? Was he receptive?"

"No." Grace shook her head. "He said there was no way to prove that she had written it." She ran her fingertips across a small patch of tablecloth, a look of utter loss on her face. "Honestly, I can't tell if it's Sophia's handwriting or not. It was similar but also different. She'd become so erratic, so many things about her changed. Could her handwriting have changed?"

Chet shrugged. "Perhaps she was drunk or on something."

Grace's face hardened. He'd hit a nerve. Again. She turned her head away. He could almost hear the wheels spinning in her head.

"What is it?" he asked.

"I'm not sure I can trust you with what I want to say." Grace lowered her hands to her lap and her eyes to the tablecloth in front of her.

"You can. I've learned my lesson."

She raised her gaze to his again, her eyes so full of sorrow, mistrust, and suppressed anger that he wanted to flinch, but he held steady. He needed to prove to her his steadfastness.

"Two people hated my sister with a vengeance. It doesn't mean they killed her, but each one of them keeps clawing at my mind like a bad dream."

Chet sat silent, waiting.

Grace leaned closer to him and whispered. "Lillian and Liane." She sat back again, her eyes skittering back and forth as if searching the room for eavesdroppers—or reporters.

"I can see your point with Lillian, but why Liane Held?"

"She thinks Flo gave Sophia her promised inheritance. Flo claims he doesn't know what she is talking about. Denies everything. But in her mind, Sophia stole everything Liane felt should be hers, mainly Flo's love."

"What else do you have?" Chet asked, impressed with Grace's analysis.

"I think they were both at the party at John Barrymore's the night Sophia died. I know Liane attended. I saw a picture of her there with my sister."

"And Miss Lorraine?"

"I'm not sure, but she was at Sophia's funeral, which I think is very odd."

"What are you implying?"

"Maybe Sophia was poisoned at the party, went home, and collapsed in the bathroom."

Chet nodded. She could be on to something there.

"But what about the mercury bichloride?"

Grace shrugged. "Jack left it open after using it?"

Chet inhaled deeply while he processed her words. He didn't see Liane Held as being capable of murder. She seemed so needy, petulant, and weak. But this scenario reeked of the kind of venom Lillian Lorraine often spewed.

"There's more."

"Go on."

"What if one of them wrote the note addressed to me? I'm still uncertain of the handwriting."

A spark of adrenaline surged through Chet's system. He reached into his coat pocket. "I thought this might come in handy." He pulled out the piece of paper with Lillian's autograph on it.

"What is it?"

He laid the paper in front of her. It read, *Hugs and kisses to you, Lillian Lorraine.*

Grace's eyebrows pulled downward, her eyes raised to his, her gaze accusing.

"I was trying to find out why she was on the train to California. Told her my daughter wanted an autograph."

"Why would you do that?"

"Hunch?"

Grace studied the paper. Her face relaxed, as if she felt relieved. "Can I take this? To compare the handwriting."

"By all means. Let me know what you think."

Grace tucked the small piece of paper in her handbag. When she looked up, her eyes widened as she peered over Chet's shoulder. He shifted to see what caught her attention.

Joe Marciano had just entered the restaurant.

CHAPTER TWENTY-EIGHT

*W*ith three men accompanying him, and a beautiful colored woman in a red satin dress trailing behind them, Marciano strode toward them. He had a full-length fur coat draped over his shoulders, the arms of the garment swinging with his every step, and his eyes were as dark and angry as a thunderstorm.

Perfect. Chet knew Marciano would be furious at seeing him with Grace.

The minute Marciano focused his attention on Grace, the thunderstorm in his eyes dissipated, replaced by lusty languor, as if he'd already had her in his bed. "Miss Michelle, it is such a pleasure to see you." He bent low, gesturing for her hand. She raised it to him, shaking like a leaf, her eyes flitting toward the woman— Felicity Jones, if Chet didn't know better. Chet could see the look of lascivious pleasure in his eyes as he pressed his oily lips to Grace's knuckles. He wanted to slap the mobster's hand away, but instead, bided his time. Miss Jones stared at the ceiling.

"I'm happy to see you're out in public on such a fine evening. It's good publicity. Good for the show," Marciano said, releasing her hand. "But you should be with me, not Piker Riker."

Chet watched as Grace's forehead relaxed and she looked at Marciano with widened eyes and a slight, quivering smile.

"I want the show to be as successful as you do, Mr. Marciano. Although I'm not used to being in the spotlight, I'll do what I can to bring attention to the show. I'm just attending to some unfinished business with Mr. Riker before we part ways. You understand."

Marciano let out a laugh. Chet breathed a sigh of relief. She'd managed a good excuse for being with him instead of Marciano. Although Chet had to admit, her words hurt.

Grace's face glowed as her quivering smile morphed into a dazzling white light. Marciano looked spellbound. Her acting skills had improved.

"And you—" Marciano's heavy-lidded gaze fell on Chet and the thunderstorm returned "—I'll see *you* later."

Chet's jaw clenched. Marciano's men would be waiting for him outside the restaurant. Luckily, he had a pistol tightly tucked into the waistband of his pants. "I look forward to it."

Marciano turned to leave and bumped into a waiter, whom he shoved aside, giving his ample, furred bulk space to go sit with his three henchmen and Miss Jones at another booth.

Grace leaned her elbows on the table and pressed her face into her hands. The waiter, having recovered from his assault by the mobster, smiled and requested their order.

"We'll both have chicken. Any way it's prepared will be fine. Surprise us," Chet said, wanting to be rid of him.

Once he'd gone, Grace released a sigh and Chet pressed a hand to her arm. "I'll get you out of this mess, and then we'll find out what happened to your sister. We'll follow up on that letter and do whatever is required to find the man who wanted to kill her. I promise, Grace."

Grace lifted her head and shot him an angry look. "How? How can you fix this?"

"I know you are frightened, Grace, and I don't blame you for being angry, but I have a plan."

"Well, what is it?"

"I can't tell you, not until it's done. I am asking you to trust me, to put your faith in me one more time." Chet offered a reassuring smile.

"I don't know if I can."

"I love you, Grace."

Her eyes met his.

"I love you, and making things right has been the only thing I could think about, and I promise, a plan is underway. Please believe me, believe that I will do whatever I can to get you out of this unbearable situation."

Grace searched his face with pleading eyes, her pupils dilating, her lips parting ever so slightly. "What do you want me to do?"

Relief flooded through him. "I want you to go along with whatever Flo and Marciano want, as if we never had this conversation. Play the part, Grace. Be the innocent ingenue starlet of the Follies as best you can, and I promise that I'll free you as soon as I can."

"How long do I have to wait?"

"When does the show start?"

"In two days."

"Promise me, no matter what happens, that you'll go forward, and I promise that it will be soon, as quickly as it can be accomplished."

Grace searched his eyes again with a yearning he thought he'd never see and certainly never deserved. "Yes, yes. I promise."

They got up from the table and Chet escorted her out of the restaurant. He tucked the folds of Grace's long skirt into the horse drawn cab and closed its door. She looked at him through the window, her face etched with worry, but she offered a quick nod, reconfirming that he could count on her.

As the horse pulled away from the curb, Grace took a deep breath and let it out, feeling the tension melt from her body. Chet had said he loved her. Still. She couldn't deny the happiness bubbling up through her fear of her situation. She had to trust that he could get her out of this mess. She had no other choice.

Looking out the window of the carriage, she noticed an elegantly dressed woman accompanied by a dashing, tall blond man in black tails, climbing the red-carpeted stairs of the Plaza. The woman, gracefully slim with gleaming black hair upswept and clasped with a diamond barrette, walked with an air of confidence Grace only wished she could possess. Over a black silk dress, the woman wore a white ermine cape. Red-and-blue gems embedded in the fur sparkled in the lamplight. Grace's breath hitched.

"Driver! Driver, stop the coach."

The clip-clop of the horses' hooves silenced. The bells on their harnesses jingled as they bobbed their heads up and down. Grace opened the door of the coach and slid out.

"Miss, what are you—" The driver sounded annoyed.

Grace straightened her coat. "I'm all right." She looked up at him. "I just forgot something. Back in a jiff."

Grace smiled at the grumpy driver, whose face crumpled with displeasure. He placed a hand on his hip, his elbow jutting outward, while his other hand held the reins of the prancing duo harnessed to the carriage.

The woman in the fur cape and her escort had not yet reached the revolving doors of the hotel.

"Excuse me!" Grace trotted up to them.

The woman whirled around, glittering handbag held at her chest. "Yes?"

The young man smiled, and his gaze lit up as it landed on Grace's face, making her cheeks burn. She stopped and opened her mouth to speak, but nothing came out. What would she say to this woman?

"Yes, can I help you?" the woman asked. "Who are you? You look familiar."

"Oh, pardon my manners. I'm Grace Michelle. I work for—"

"Zieggy's newest discovery." The woman cast a glance at her date, then back at Grace. "I know who you are. What can I do for you?"

"Your cape is lovely. I was just admiring it."

"Smashing, isn't it?" The woman smiled and twirled. The handsome gentleman let out a laugh, as if completely bemused and enchanted with the woman.

Grace eyed every inch of the soft, white fur. She gasped when she noticed a gem missing toward the bottom hemline, its shape indented in the pelt—the same shape as the sapphire Grace had found in Sophia's wardrobe.

"Yes, yes, it's lovely," Grace stammered. "Are those sapphires?"

The woman grinned, her white teeth glowing against her red lipstick and jet-black hair.

"Yes. And rubies."

"Forgive my boldness," Grace said, trying to strengthen the quaver in her voice, "but where ever did you get such a beautiful thing? I'd love one for myself. It must have cost a fortune."

The woman lowered her eyes and gently laid a hand on Grace's elbow. She led Grace away from the revolving doors and away from her date. "I don't know why I am telling you this, but you seem like a sweet girl. I knew your sister—not very well, mind you, just in passing. Lovely young woman. I purchased it from her several months ago."

"Oh." Grace swallowed. So the heirloom inheritance truly existed.

"But I must tell you a little secret. It's not worth much of anything. The gems are cut glass, and the ermine is actually rabbit fur. It looks expensive, though, don't you think?" The woman ran her hands down the front of it and cocked her hip coquettishly, making the silk of her gown shift under the cape.

"Yes, very."

Couples and larger groups made their way up the red stairs to enter the hotel lobby. Long, sleek, black cars and elegant horse-drawn carriages pulled up to the curb.

"Party is just about to start," the woman said. "I don't want to be late. Are you attending? I'm sure Flo would want you be seen at one of my events."

Grace couldn't stop thinking about the information she'd just been given. Liane could have killed Sophia for nothing more than rabbit fur and faux gemstones. If she had, indeed, killed Sophia.

"No. No, I'm going home." Grace pressed her gloved fingers to the bridge of her nose. "Bit of a headache. But may I . . . Miss. . . ?"

"Swanson. But please, call me Gloria."

"Yes, Gloria. May I purchase the cape back from you? I miss my sister terribly, and she didn't leave much behind when she— Well, you know. It would mean so much to me to have it."

Gloria looked into Grace's eyes, and then her attention moved over Grace's head. Photographers were heading their way. The woman donned an impressive smile and moved past Grace.

"Give your information to Erik. I'll contact you tomorrow. It wouldn't do for me to upset my ensemble right now," she said under her breath and greeted the reporters.

The young man walked up to Grace, his gray-green eyes twinkling. "Erik von Ernst, at your service."

Grace detected a hint of a German accent and forced a smile, uneasy under his penetrating gaze. How bad did she really want the fur cape? She didn't like the idea of giving this gentleman her address, despite his friendly demeanor and handsome face.

Just as she was about to tell him where she could be reached, another couple swept past them, the woman's large hat nearly grazing Mr. Von Ernst's head.

Lillian Lorraine stopped and turned to face them. "Ah, Miss Michelle. Of course you would be here. Who is this delicious chap?"

Mr. Von Ernst came to Grace's rescue and introduced himself. Lillian gave him the once-over with seductive eyes. "Well, I suppose *you* are the lucky one, stepping out with Flo's latest discovery."

"Oh, well, we're not, he's not—" Grace stammered.

Lillian smiled like a lion who just finished a lunch of gazelle, making Grace's insides swirl. As much as she didn't want to engage in conversation with this feline beast, it seemed the perfect opportunity to get a bit more information.

"Are you going to Miss Swanson's party?"

Lillian folded herself into the arm of her date, an older, distinguished-looking man, thin as a broomstick, with gray hair and large rimmed spectacles. He grinned, seemingly delighted at the press of Lillian's voluptuous body against his sticklike figure.

"Of course, dear. Gloria's all the rage."

"One must attend all the important parties," Grace agreed, forcing her sweetest smile.

"Well, yes, dear. Who wouldn't?" Lillian's face pinched as if annoyed.

"I know!" Grace pretended to be impressed. "My sister wrote me about John Barrymore's party in California. She said it was simply elevating, sublime, and surreal."

"Yes." Lillian's face tightened. "Unfortunately, I had to miss that one. Had a bout of the bottle flu!" she said, turning to her date with a giggle. "Sometimes I drink too much, but if I didn't, then what fun would I be?" She stuck her lip out in a pout. "Shall we go in?" she asked, looking at Grace and then her gentleman.

"Please, you go on ahead," Grace said.

"Oh, but I'm sure Flo wants you at Miss Swanson's party. All the press is there. Don't want to upset the big boss."

"He didn't mention it."

Lillian smiled that demure smile that made Grace's skin itch.

"Suit yourself, darling. Fame is fleeting. You'll be yesterday's news before you know it."

CHET WALKED down the sidewalk of the Plaza's entrance, turned a corner, and headed toward the back of the hotel. He knew Marciano would be waiting for him, and he prayed he could open fire on the mobster before the whelps descended on him. Reaching behind his back, he retrieved his gun and held it down along the side of his leg. Marciano expected Chet to hand over the money he owed him, but that wasn't going to happen. Chet had already decided that jail time, grave injury, or even death would all be a fair price for saving Grace from Marciano.

When he reached the rear entrance of the hotel, the scarred man in the tattered brown suit stood on the corner, waiting. He turned and led Chet into the alleyway. Once there, Chet saw Marciano's white scarf glowing in the darkness. He gripped his gun more firmly. The only way out of this mess—his mess—and the only way to save Grace would be to see that Marciano never drew another breath. Without pausing to think any further, he raised his arm and pointed the gun at Marciano's chest, his finger closing slowly over the trigger.

Just as he applied more pressure, a cement wall of someone's shoulder rammed into Chet's side, knocking the air out of his lungs. The gun went flying, and Chet slammed into the ground.

When he opened his eyes, gasping, he saw the gun just a few feet in front of him. He scrambled forward until he felt a sickening snap of bones in his lower back. The brute, one of Marciano's goons, held him onto the ground with his ape-sized foot. With a mighty heave, Chet managed to flip over and grab the man's leg. Finding the offending foot, Chet twisted the ankle until the man fell on top of him, crushing the air out of his lungs once again.

From out of nowhere, another man jumped on the two of them, shoved the ape aside, and straddled Chet's stomach, pinning his arms to the ground. Before Chet could react, the man's face came down hard and fast, his forehead butting into Chet's. Stars exploded between his eyes as his head cracked against the pavement, leaving him stunned and unable to move. The man continued to beat Chet, this time with his fists. Chet flailed his arms, trying to stop the man's momentum, but the heavyweight kept hitting him, leaving the tang of blood pooling in his mouth and his brain turning to mush. With his upper body immobilized, Chet could do nothing but raise his hips, flinging the man's weight forward and causing him to lose his balance and fall face-first onto the pavement.

With his body battered and feeling like dead weight, Chet struggled to scoot out from under him, but when he did, he flung the other man over, ready to throttle him. Before he could, though, someone kicked Chet in the head and he crumpled to the ground. Darkness and voices faded in and out. He gasped as the blows continued striking his stomach and head. He curled up as tight as a ball to protect himself, but the hits just came harder and faster.

As the beating continued, Chet caught a glimpse of Marciano hovering over him, the glow of his cigar a red dot in the night. Marciano reached into his coat's chest pocket and pointed a small revolver.

Time slowed as his body became numb to the blows and his mind somehow became razor-focused on Marciano and the barrel of the gun the mobster held steady in his hand. The mobster fired, and a red-hot, searing pain ripped through Chet's chest like a flaming arrow. He howled, his body electric with spasms. As his weight settled onto the ground, he could feel nothing but cold seeping up from the pavement and into his bones. He could no longer feel his fingers, toes, arms, or legs, and as his life force began to fade, he thought only of Grace and how he'd failed her once again.

CHAPTER TWENTY-NINE

*G*race couldn't sleep. After a night of tossing and turning, she finally had fallen asleep an hour before she had to get up to prepare for the day. Tonight, her show, *Molly*, opened.

She lay in bed, staring up at the ceiling. The day had finally arrived. The day she would try to fill Sophia's shoes. The day she would begin to repay Flo for all he'd done for her. The day she would honor her sister's memory. The day she'd give up a part of her soul. She hoped she'd meet everyone's expectations.

She pressed her hands together in a silent prayer and whispered Sophia's name. Thinking of her, Grace grabbed the note she'd taken from Sophia's fur coat and laid it on the nightstand. She'd flung her pocketbook on the bed before she went to sleep and searched for it in the covers. When she found it, she took out the autograph Lillian had given Chet. Lying back into the pillows, she compared the handwriting on both scraps of paper. Lillian's handwriting had no sideways slant but spiked vertically upward. Grace remembered Sophia's had always slanted deeply to the right, just like the handwriting on the note Grace held in her hand. She just knew Sophia had penned the note explaining her move to California.

Grace thought about Chet and the conversation they'd had last night. He said he had a plan, that he would fix the situation and get her out of Marciano's clutches. She wondered about the woman who'd accompanied Marciano, Felicity Jones. Grace easily had recognized her from the publicity posters, which did her no justice—her skin, her hair, her eyes, her aura of loveliness filled the room. But were they lovers? Is that why Marciano made her walk ten feet behind him? Grace didn't know Joe Marciano well, but she knew enough that he would never stand for being outshone, especially in public. She prayed that Chet's plan, whatever it was, would work. He sounded so sincere the night before, she'd been sure he'd be true to his word. This morning her stomach churned with doubt and nerves.

A knock sounded at the door. She sprang out of bed and wrapped a dressing gown around her, tying the sash securely.

"Yes?" she said, pressing her ear against the door.

"Delivery for you, Miss."

Grace's pulse clanged in her ears. Maybe Chet had sent her something. A message that his plan had worked perhaps? Maybe flowers?

"Please leave it at the door," she said. "I'm not dressed."

"Yes, ma'am."

She pressed her ear against the door and listened as footsteps echoed down the hallway, then faded into silence. When Grace opened the door, she looked down and saw a gleaming white box tied together with a red satin bow. She picked it up, locked the door, and carried the box to her bed. The bow slid apart as Grace pulled one end of the silky ribbon. She opened the box to find the faux ermine cape nestled inside, the glass sapphires and rubies twinkling in the reflection of the crystal chandelier above her head. An envelope rested on the fur. She opened the note and read:

. . .

Miss Michelle,

Please take this cape as a gift. It means a lot more to you than it does to me. Besides, I've been photographed wearing it.

A word of advice, dear, never let the cameras catch you wearing the same thing twice!

Cheers, Gloria.

GRACE PICKED up the fur and held it to her face, the downy softness caressing her cheek. She then held it in front of her, searching for the indent near the hem of the missing jewel. When she found it, she walked to her dresser, pulled open a drawer, and lifted the single glass sapphire out of her little jewelry box. A perfect match. Liane's supposed heirloom inheritance was a fake. Grace clutched the fur cape to her chest. She hoped she was wrong about Liane, that Liane would never have killed for such a pretty but worthless piece of fashion. She looked up to see her reflection in the mirror, the furrowed brow, the downcast mouth, the hurt in her once-innocent eyes. She had to know the truth, and there was only one way to find out.

ABUZZ WITH ACTIVITY, the theater hummed like a well-oiled machine with all the crew preparing for opening night. The lighting had been tested, sound checked, and costumes fitted, refitted, and repaired. Grace sat at a vanity table in the chorus girls' dressing room, where they chatted noisily as Grace waited for Liane to enter. Giving up her personal dressing room to appease Liane didn't bother Grace in the least. The girl obviously had a need for personal attention—much more than Grace did. In fact, Grace liked being among the throng of noise and bustle—it helped with her mounting nerves.

The thought of performing in front of hundreds made her fingertips sweat. She wiped her hands on her dress and then laid a hand on the red ribbon-wrapped box next to her. She hoped Liane showed up soon. Grace had to meet with Lucile for a fitting in thirty minutes.

"You look very relaxed considering tonight is your debut," a sweet-faced young girl said to Grace, setting a hand on her shoulder. "I know you'll be great. I love your voice."

Grace blinked. "Thank you." Although they'd been rehearsing for a few weeks now, she still didn't consider herself a singer—just a mediocre actress who happened to be easy on the eyes. The compliment certainly boosted her sagging self-esteem.

Finally, Liane entered the dressing room. She'd come from the back door to the alleyway, not from the dressing room Grace had loaned her. Liane scooted past the flurry of pink-and-white-feathered bottoms belonging to the giggling girls.

"Hello, Liane," Grace said, taking the woman by surprise.

Liane stopped and placed a hand at the nape of her neck to smooth her hair. "Hello. Am I late?"

"No. Where have you been this morning? I expected you'd been in your dressing room."

"I'm not taking your secondhand cast-offs." Liane stuck her nose in the air. "You can have your dressing room. And it's none of your business where I've been this morning."

Grace sank her upper teeth into her lower lip to prevent herself from saying something unkind. "Liane, I have something for you. Can we go somewhere we can talk?"

Liane rolled her eyes. "I'm not sure I have time," she said, a flourish of her arm indicating that she needed to be dressed like all the other chorines. "We don't get personal wardrobe mistresses and the great Lady Duff Gordon to dress us as *some people* do."

"It will only take a minute."

Liane sighed. "Fine. Your dressing room?"

Grace led the way to the small, closet-sized room Flo had given her for the show. Lavish, expansive, and elegant could not describe the small space. It consisted of a vanity with mirror and chair, full-length mirror, small wardrobe, and a screen set up in the corner against a paint-peeled wall for the purpose of changing clothes and costumes discreetly.

"Comfy," Liane said with a snort as she and Grace squeezed into the room.

Grace held the box in front of her. "This is for you. Open it."

Liane's eyes narrowed, and then her gaze lowered to the red ribbon. "You're giving me a gift? Why?"

"I'm hoping this will set the record straight between us. You seem to think my sister stole something very valuable from you. I'm making up for it. Open it."

With her lips downturned, Liane opened the box. Her eyes widened when she saw the fur cape within the box. She glanced up at Grace. "Where did you get this?"

"A friend gave it to me."

"My cape. I can't believe it. This is incredible." Liane pulled it from the box and held it in front of her, admiring the soft fur and gleaming gemstones.

"I have some bad news for you, though."

Liane raised her eyes to meet Grace's gaze.

"It's not worth anything," Grace said. "The gemstones are glass, and the fur is rabbit, not ermine."

Liane's face fell, then hardened. "How do you know? What are you talking about?"

"The woman who gave it to me had it appraised. It's merely a pretty costume."

"You're lying!" Liane clutched the cape to her chest, her eyes flaming with accusation.

Grace pulled the lost sapphire from her pocket. "I found this in Sophia's wardrobe in California. It's a perfect match to the cape and the other stones. Here, take it. Have it appraised yourself. But if you look closely, you can see it's not real."

Liane reached out for the sapphire and held it close to her face. Her brow rose and her mouth turned down as a cloud of disappointment shrouded her wilting figure.

"Was it worth killing for?"

"What do you mean?" Liane's fist encircled the gem, and she lowered the garment.

"Did you kill Sophia thinking you would get this back? For spite? Anger? Revenge? Will you still kill me now that you have it again?"

Liane's face opened up in shock. "I didn't kill anyone, and I'm not going to kill anyone."

"Were you at John Barrymore's party in California? The night Sophia died?"

"What are you saying? No, no, I was not at that party. I didn't kill your sister!"

"You're lying. I saw a photo of you standing next to Sophia at Barrymore's party."

"Okay. All right." Liane's fingers curled around the fur, gripping it tighter. "I was at the party. Sophia and I had words. I left soon after that. I swear, I never saw Sophia again."

"Until the funeral. Why were you even at the funeral?"

Liane laid the fur on the vanity. Grace could see perspiration glistening on the girl's forehead. "I thought on the off-chance Flo would be there. He made it clear that he loved Sophia more than my mother. He didn't attend my mother's funeral, but I thought maybe he'd be at Sophia's. I wanted to make a statement. I wanted him to know how much he devastated my mother —and me."

"Your mother left *him*, Liane. Everyone knows that."

"It was because of that tramp, Lillian. Their affair was so public. It humiliated mama. I wanted him to see me, a ghost from his past, one that would forever haunt him."

"And the fur?"

"It's mine. He promised me. I needed it. I needed the money. I have nothing." Liane raised a hand to her mouth, her fingers trembling. Grace felt the slightest bit of compassion for the girl.

"I'm going to ask you one last time, Liane. Did you kill my sister?"

"No," she whispered. "I swear it." Liane's eyes softened and filled with tears.

Grace studied the girl's face, whose eyes never wandered, never blinked. Her cheeks had reddened from the sudden onslaught of tears and her lips trembled, but this was not the face of a guilty killer. This was the face of yet someone else who'd been disappointed by a father figure who'd promised much and delivered little, and always at a cost.

"I believe you," Grace said. "But I have one more question for you, Liane. Please tell me the truth."

Liane sniffed, wiped her nose with the back of her hand, and nodded.

"Was Lillian Lorraine at John Barrymore's party?"

Liane paused as if in thought. She raised her eyes to Grace. "No. I didn't see her there."

"You're sure?"

"Positive. She wasn't there."

Grace bit the inside of her cheek. Another dead end. "Thank you, Liane. You'd better go out there and get ready. I'll step outside while you compose yourself."

Grace opened the door and walked into the hallway. She slumped against the wall. What a fool she had been. Suddenly, the idea that someone had actually killed Sophia seemed ridiculous. In her grief, she'd stirred up a story that didn't exist. She'd made accusations, insulted people, shoved those who cared for her away, and all because she couldn't handle the truth.

The door handle clicked, and Liane came out of the dressing room, holding the fur tight against her body. She slid past Grace without glancing up and headed back to the chorines' dressing room.

Grace walked back into her private dressing room, shut the door, and sat at the vanity. She looked at her reflection in the mirror and, in it, saw Sophia and her mother, their eyes glowing, their smiles radiating, compassion written in their every feature. Grace buried her face in her hands and let out her breath. No more tears left to cry. She had to carry on and carve out some kind of life for herself and forget the past.

She lowered her hands and stared into the mirror. Her gaze traveled across the vanity and settled on the glass sapphire Liane had placed there. The blue stone sat still and alone, its facets gleaming in the lamplight.

THAT NIGHT, opening night, Grace arrived to a hubbub of activity on the stage. Staff, looming high up in the rafters and on catwalks, set the lights for the first act. Stage crew put finishing touches on props. Ushers in their tuxedoes fiddled with their ties and vests. Lucile, Charles, and their assistants filled the chorines' dressing room with a ball of blazing energy, tweaking hemlines and replacing feathers and sequins. Everyone in the theater busied themselves with fine-tuning all the elements of the production to achieve Ziegfeld perfection.

Fragments of her lines and the tunes of the songs raced through Grace's mind. Terrified she would bungle them, fear as big as a peach pit lodged in her throat. When she looked up at the stage lights, not all of them on, her heart pounded in her chest. In less than two hours, the theater would be full of people, important people like Marciano—especially Marciano—all there to see her sing, dance and act. None of which she did very well. She breathed deeply, fighting the urge to swoon.

The orchestra pit buzzed and crooned with the tuning of instruments. Flo stood at one corner of the stage talking with Harvey, the director, and the music master, Irving Berlin. In his shirtsleeves and loosened tie, Flo looked nothing like himself. His clothing hung on him like a wilted sack. His face, drawn and gray, much as it had been for the past several days, looked like a mask.

When he saw her watching him, Flo excused himself and walked over to her. "Hello, dear."

Grace attempted a smile.

"Are you ready for your debut? You'll be a sensation, I just know it." The creases at the corners of his eyes deepened, and he tilted his head toward her. "Do you know all your lines?"

"Of course," Grace said, hoping she could convince them both.

"Then go get ready for rehearsal." Flo kissed her cheek before leaving to finish his discussion with the director and conductor. They nodded their greetings to her, and she turned and walked backstage to her dressing room.

Rehearsals flowed without a hitch, and Grace could tell Flo was pleased as his gestures became more animated, color bloomed in his face, and he started to take on the demeanor of his old self, eagerly preparing for the curtains to go up. When he gleefully called it a wrap, he rushed over to Grace and embraced her, almost squeezing the breath out of her. If she could pass the Ziegfeld perfection test, surely she could successfully assume the role of an actress who could wow the audience.

By the time the theater gallery started to fill with patrons,

Grace had perfected all her lines and song numbers. She peered around the curtain to watch people file in, and suddenly, her hands and feet went cold. Perspiration gathered under her breasts and seeped into her corset.

I can't do this. I'm not an actress. They'll know I'm an imposter. She would ruin the show, and she, Flo, and Chet would lose everything. With her heart pounding, Grace ran back to her dressing room and closed the door.

Seconds later, Charles peeked his head into the room. "Are you ready. Do you need anything?"

Grace paced across the tiny floor of her dressing room, biting her nails.

"Grace?"

"I can't do it. Charles, I can't do it."

"What are you talking about? Of course you can do it. You're Grace Michelle, Florenz Ziegfeld Jr.'s newest star."

"I wish people would stop saying that. It's not true. My sister was Flo's star, not me. I'm not going out there . . . I can't."

Charles reached out to hold her, but Grace abruptly turned away. "But honey, you have to. Curtain goes up in twenty minutes. We're all depending on you to pull it together."

Grace stopped pacing and glared at Charles. "That's the problem. I'm so afraid I'm going to fail, and then everything will—"

Charles walked over to the phone and picked up the receiver. "This is Charles. Please send Miss Brice to Miss Michelle's dressing room. Tell her we have a problem, and we need her help."

Grace continued pacing and biting her nails. If she kept up much longer, they'd be bloody nubs. Panic writhed in her chest like snakes. How could she get out of this?

"Can't someone else take my place? What about the understudy? What's her name?"

"Carla hasn't had time to prepare. The show wasn't supposed to open 'til next week, but Flo insisted it start tonight. She's not ready."

"*I'm* not ready." Grace stopped biting her nails and wrapped her arms around herself.

The shuffling of feet and whispers at the door caught Grace's attention. Charles opened it a crack and let Fanny nudge her way in.

"Good God, you can't breathe in this room. What's the matter? What's going on?"

"Grace has a bit of the jitters," Charles explained. "Says she can't go on."

Fanny nodded and whispered something to Charles as she ushered him out of the dressing room. As soon as the door closed, Fanny turned her attention to Grace.

"So, what gives, sweet cheeks?" she asked, straightening her feather boa.

"I can't go out there, Fanny. I just can't do it. No matter what Flo says or tries to convince us is true, I'm not 'star material.'"

Fanny placed her hands on Grace's shoulders and looked hard into her eyes.

"You look ready to me. You're in costume, and your makeup is on. Irving told me your voice is *crystal*, too. Plus, I rehearsed with you earlier this afternoon. You nailed all your lines. You can do this. I know you can."

Grace shook her head.

Fanny's sympathetic expression turned cold. "I never thought I'd see this from you, Grace. You're scared, I get that, but you have to deliver. Don't skip out like Sophia. It will vilify her memory. There's an audience out there expecting you to fill those shoes and more."

Skip out? Sophia had to leave because someone wanted to kill her. Anger surfaced around the edges of Grace's fear.

"You have to honor this commitment, Grace."

Grace folded her arms over her chest. Her stomach ached.

"Flo needs this, Grace. Everyone knows he's in financial trouble. Big trouble. And just like a man, he's hung every damn thread on one thing, and that thing is you. The show's got to be a hit or we're all at the mercy of that fat-headed mobster Marciano."

Grace drew in a slow breath. She prayed Chet would come dashing through the door any minute, saving her from the need to take the stage, but she hadn't heard from him.

"Five minutes." Charles's voice rang out from behind the door. Another knock.

"Grace," Flo said. "Grace, please."

"Tell him I'm coming," she whispered to Fanny. "I don't want to see him."

Fanny went to the door and opened it a crack. Someone's arm pushed through, opening the door to reveal Flo, Jack, and Charles standing at the door, their faces as forlorn as those of abandoned puppy dogs.

Grace stared at them staring at her, the looks on their faces nothing short of comical and ridiculous. All this concern, all this angst, all this desperation—all for her to go out on the stage. Suddenly the thought didn't seem so daunting. How hard could it be?

From somewhere deep inside her, a giggle surfaced, then another. Within seconds, deep, resonant laughter bubbled out of her at the absurdity of it all. The shocked expressions on the three men's faces made her laugh even louder. Looking more and more baffled, their faces broke into unsure smiles, and they laughed, too. Other cast and crew members passed by the door, confusion on their faces.

Grace wiped tears from her cheeks as Charles and Jack led her to the stage. She walked to her mark and stood.

The curtain rose, and the lights hit the stage. The sound of strings and horns filled her ears, triggering an automatic response within her. Mustering every ounce of will and determination in her soul, once Grace uttered her first line, her fear, panic, and doubt fizzled into nothingness and she belted out the verses of the opening number with everything she had.

CHAPTER THIRTY

$\mathcal{T}$he second act should have gone as smoothly, but it didn't, nor did the third act. In the middle of one of the musical scores, part of the set crashed to the floor with a loud bang, a mechanical pedestal on which Grace stood malfunctioned, and in the fervor of frantic desperation, the leading man dropped one of the props and, consequently, lost track of his lines. Snickers and gasps could be heard from the audience.

When Grace glanced into the audience, her eyes were drawn to the silky white scarf draped around Marciano's neck, his face reddening with anger. Sitting next to him, the beautiful Felicity Jones outshone everyone within the near vicinity in her green dress that shimmered under the gaslights. But her eyes glittered hard and her mouth twitched with recognizable fear. When the curtain finally fell after the disastrous third act, Flo, too, exhibited a silent rage.

Grace's armpits dampened, and a trickle of sweat dripped down her lower back. The lead actor, his face ashen and perspiring, clutched his stomach with one hand and his mouth with the other, then ran off stage toward the men's room. Grace followed, hurrying toward her dressing room. She could hear her poor leading man retching from behind the closed door, but she kept going. When she reached her dressing room, she slipped in. She started to slam the door when Flo pushed past her and slumped down onto the vanity stool.

"I'm ruined. Marciano is furious."

He looked so gray and gaunt that Grace swallowed her own anxiety and walked over to him. She knelt down at his knee. "You're exhausted, Flo. Let's go back to the hotel. Let's worry about this tomorrow."

"I'll have nothing. He'll take the theater from me. He's out to get me, Grace. Has been for years, and finally, he has a leg up. That's it. I'm finished."

Grace grabbed her fur stole and some items from her dressing table and threw them into a bag. "Come on. We're going home."

"But the press, the reporters . . ."

"We'll slip out the back door. We can deal with them tomorrow, too." She grabbed him by the arm, amazed at the bony feel of it beneath his shirt, and helped him to his feet. He leaned against her as they rushed toward a back door to an alleyway. When they burst through the door, Marciano stood on the other side and stepped forward into the light.

"Well, look what we have here, Flo and his golden girl," Marciano said, his words punctuated with malice. "She was the only thing in that show worth watching—and the only thing worth salvaging. You're done, Ziegfeld. Finished. And since you can't give me the hit show you promised, I'm here to take what's mine." He snapped his fingers at his henchmen and pointed to Grace.

Two hulking figures grabbed Grace by her arms and jerked her away from Flo. She squirmed and kicked, flailing her arms and legs as much as she could. Even Flo, in his weakened state, attempted to jump on them, but he was stopped by a man who'd been waiting in the shadows. Grace winced as he pummeled Flo.

"Stop!" she screamed. "He's not well. Don't hurt him. Please don't hurt him."

The two men dragged her toward a parked automobile a few hundred feet away. She looked over her shoulder to see the thug walk away from Flo, and him slumped to the ground, unconscious.

"Flo!" she shrieked.

Her two kidnappers pushed down her head, shoved her into the car, and quickly slid in, one on each side of her. Cramped and squeezed between the two fearsome strangers, Grace continued to struggle, but they held her arms and legs fast. One even shoved a rag so far into her mouth, Grace gagged.

"Stop your whining," he commanded.

Wild eyed with fear and rage, she watched as Marciano thumped into the passenger's side of the front seat and another man slid into the driver's seat. The beefy mobster turned and smiled lasciviously at Grace as the car sped away. After a few minutes, Marciano, having never taken his eyes from Grace, instructed one of the men to blindfold her.

Completely helpless, she tried to move her head back and forth to thwart their efforts, but it was useless. Rough fingers tied Marciano's silk scarf around her head and over her eyes, and pulled it tight. Too tight. Her head was in a vise, but she couldn't say anything because of the rag stuffed in her mouth.

This must be what it feels like to drown.

Consumed with fear and surrounded by evil, Grace tried to control the violent shaking of her limbs and the whimper that came out of her body unbidden. She prayed she wouldn't be harmed. She thought about Flo and hoped that someone would help him.

And where was Chet? What had happened to his plan?

The car jerked to a stop. Hands grabbed her and slipped around her waist, hauling her out of the car. They thrust hands under her arms and lifted her off her feet. She imagined being put in a small, dark cell. The thought worsened her panic, and again, she struggled and flailed against the bondage of both men's hands. Something clanged shut, and then the ground moved upward, throwing off her equilibrium. It must have been an elevator. She could smell woolly carpet and the musky odor of wood. They stepped out, and the footing became soft. They led her away from the elevator, walking for what felt like miles. She heard someone messing with the lock of a door, and then she was shoved forward.

She fell to the ground and listened. A click told her that they had locked the door. She sensed she was alone, so she pulled the rag from her mouth and coughed. Then she ripped the silk scarf from her head and stood on unsteady legs. She blinked, her eyes adjusting to the dimly lit room, oppressively masculine with ornate, dark wood fixtures, and floor-to-ceiling wood paneling throughout. A huge canopy bed dominated the room. Other furnishings included a rolltop desk, a bureau, a wardrobe, and end tables on either side of the bed.

Grace jumped when the door unlatched. Marciano entered and quickly shut the door behind him, snapping a bolt to lock it. A tremor started in Grace, and she fought for self-control. She backed up to put distance between them, and he moved forward until she stopped short, her heels against the footboard of the massive bed.

Marciano chuckled, his eyes roaming over her face, her hair, and down to her breasts. She instinctively wrapped her arms around herself. He came close, so close she could smell garlic and alcohol on his breath, tinged with the sickeningly sweet odor of tobacco.

"If you cooperate, you won't get hurt," he whispered into her ear.

Grace pulled away, but he caught her by the wrist.

"Shy one, aren't you?"

She cringed and shrunk away from him.

"You'll get to like me once you get to know me. We have plenty of time." Greasy hair hung over his eyes and clung to his perspiring forehead.

Grace fought the gagging sensation rising in her throat. When she turned away from him and covered her face with her free hand, Marciano stiffened and tightened the grip on her wrist.

"I don't like rejection, Miss Michelle. No woman in her right mind refuses me. I suppose you just need some time to get over that lover boy, Chet Riker."

At the mention of his name, Grace wilted inside. Her heart felt as if something was squeezing it, draining it of its life blood.

"Why are you doing this?"

"Why?" Marciano ran a cold finger down her cheek. "Because I enjoy seeing Ziegfeld fail. He's had it all—money, women, success, everything a man could want. So naturally, it gives me great pleasure to take what's his and make it mine."

"What are you going to do with me?"

His facial features hardened, his eyes grew even colder. "Nothing . . . yet." He cupped his hand under her chin and gripped it. "You just make yourself at home," he said, laughing.

When he released her, Grace scrambled away from him to the other side of the bed. Marciano shook a finger at her. "I don't like rejection."

Grace raised her chin in defiance. The day she gave in to Joe Marciano would be the day she took her own life.

GRACE SAT in a chair by the window in the plush surroundings of Marciano's lair and looked out at the bustling nighttime chaos of New York City, wondering what Marciano had in store for her. She'd become a hostage in the war between Flo and the mobster, and the thought sickened her.

The door burst open, startling her, and she looked up to see

Felicity Jones standing in the doorway with a tray of food, a hardened expression in her doe-like blue eyes. Before Grace said a word, the woman sauntered in the room and shut the door behind her with her foot, sending a loud bang echoing in the room. She wore a strapless, dark green velvet dress, the bodice cinched in tight, clearly covering a corset that pushed her breasts up and out. The garment hugged her hips down to her knees and then flared out at the legs. Heavy powder and painted lips covered the natural beauty that Grace knew existed underneath.

"I'm Felicity," she said, walking toward Grace, surveying Grace head to toe.

"Yes, I know."

"Joe says he wants you to be his new girl." Felicity placed the tray on the desk and folded her arms over her tightly corseted waist.

Grace raised her chin. "That will never happen."

"Not if I have my way." Felicity moved closer to Grace, now towering over her. Grace never noticed the woman's height before. She stood as tall as most men. Grace tried not to shrink beside Felicity's imposing stature and granite expression. Now that Felicity was closer, Grace could see bruises under her eye and across her jawline, which had been expertly covered with makeup.

"He doesn't like rejection." Felicity said.

"He'll have to kill me first." Grace met the woman's steely gaze.

"You've got spunk." Felicity's eyes remained stony like two brilliant sapphires. "Joe likes that."

Grace didn't like the implication. "And who are you to Marciano?"

"I'm the 'old girl,' I suppose . . . again." Her eyes bore into Grace.

They stood in silence for a few seconds, staring at each other. Then Felicity's posture relaxed. She toyed with the sparkling necklace at her throat. "I used to work for Flo—like you, like your sister."

"My sister? Did you know my sister?"

Felicity smirked. "Yes. Unfortunately."

"How'd you—"

Felicity's blue eyes flashed. "I'm not here to chitchat. Just to bring you food. Eat it if you want; don't if you don't."

Grace's gaze traveled to the food tray. Her stomach growled with hunger, but she couldn't make herself get up and go over to her meal. Not with Felicity staring at her.

"Thank you."

Felicity walked over to the desk and pulled out the chair. She came over near the window, near Grace, plunked the chair down, and sat as gracefully as a queen with billowing skirts. Grace swallowed. What did this woman want with her?

"Is there something else?" Grace asked, not sure she wanted to hear the answer.

"Just some information. For your own good." Felicity played with the tendrils of ebony hair that hung to her shoulders. "It may come as a surprise to you, but Joe would never take you by force—unless he's drunk."

Grace blinked. "He kidnapped me from the theater. He had his buddies shove a rag down my throat, blindfold me, and bring me here. Seems to me he took me by force—and he didn't seem drunk."

One corner of Felicity's mouth turned up. "That's not what I meant. Don't get me wrong. He intends to keep you here until he gets what he wants. He's determined."

Grace took in the information, her every instinct telling her to get up and run, but she knew a guard probably lurked outside her door.

"He needs to feel that you *want* him."

"But how could I possibly—"

"Oh, darling. You'll want him, I can assure you. In time, you will."

Grace could barely believe what she was hearing. "Do you?"

A corner of Felicity's mouth turned up, her eyes narrowing at Grace, then she winced as if in pain. Grace's eyes lit on the bruises on Felicity's jaw again and then rose to meet the woman's stare.

"Was he drunk when he did that to you?" Grace asked, pointing.

Felicity stood up fast, her eyes blazing and hand raised. Grace thought the woman was going to strike her.

"Mind your own business," she growled. "I'm warning you, just like I warned that tart of a sister of yours."

Grace straightened her spine, leaned toward Felicity. "How well did you know my sister?"

"Again, none of your business. You need to do as I say or Marciano will chew you up and spit you out like yesterday's stale bread." Felicity's gaze lingered, and then she turned her back to Grace to walk out of the room.

"Why me?" Grace asked Felicity when she reached the door.

She paused, turned, walked back to the window. "Because Flo loves you."

Grace's heart ached. She used to believe that Flo loved her, but she doubted everything now.

"He and Joe grew up together," Felicity explained. "Flo had everything Joe wanted, and Flo never let him forget it. Once Joe became powerful, he wanted to take everything he could from Flo. It started with me."

"Did he kidnap you, too?"

"No, I liked the idea of a rich, powerful man like Joe Marciano. Besides, Flo was with Billie, and I got in the way." Felicity moved closer to the window.

The window. An escape. Grace didn't know exactly how

many floors they'd come up in the elevator, but a surge of hope bloomed.

"But, Joe never made good on his promises," Felicity said, sadness and disappointment in her voice.

Grace stood, wanting to get closer to the window, to peer down and see how many floors lie below. "Why are you still with him?"

"I'm not here to tell you my life story." Felicity's lips pursed, her jaw flexed, and the pain returned to her eyes. "I'm here to convince you that it's in your best interest to please Joe."

Although complicit in Grace's capture and understandably not pleased with Grace's presence in Marciano's rooms and thoughts, this woman seemed shattered, like a porcelain doll that had been smashed against the floor.

"I know what it's like to be used," Grace said, feeling her own pain at the thought.

"You?" Felicity's voice rose in pitch. "You know what it's like to be used?" As she came closer to Grace, her perfume surrounded them in a cloud of something floral, maybe jasmine. Her eyes roamed over Grace's hair, her clothes, and the earrings that dangled from her lobes, and then trained her eyes on Grace's. She raised her hand and ran her finger tenderly down Grace's face. "So pretty and innocent. You have no idea what it is to be used."

Alarmed at the woman's intimate touch, Grace backed away.

"Oh, now, come on. You aren't afraid of little ole me, are you?"

Grace met her gaze and raised her chin. She inched backward, closer to the window. When she saw that they were about seven stories high, her heart sank. Plus, the paint on the window-pane was so thick it had run into the cracks, sealing the window shut. Surely there must be a fire escape, if she could ever figure out how to open the window.

"I'd really like to know how you knew my sister. Please . . . Were you friends?"

"*Pfft.*" Felicity waved her hand dismissively. "Hardly."

"Did you know her through Flo?"

"Let's just say we had mutual acquaintances. I couldn't stand the girl. You seem a little, well, shall we say, less aggressive, but mind your p's and q's. I promise you don't want to get on my bad side."

"Like my sister did?"

"You got it, sweetheart."

Grace wondered if Felicity could be added to the list of people she suspected of murdering Sophia, but Felicity wasn't in California when Sophia died. She clearly didn't like Sophia, as had many Grace was finding out. Had Felicity had a dalliance with Jack? Or did her dislike of Sophia have to do with Flo?

"I'm not afraid," Grace said, her voice almost a whisper, dread threatening to swallow her whole. "Of you *or* Marciano."

The left side of Felicity's mouth turned up, and she raised her eyebrows. "You might want to reconsider, honey. Joe thinks he pulls the strings around here, and he does, but I have my ways of dealing with Joe. And if you want to stay safe, you better stay on my good side. Got it?" Felicity walked to the door, opened it, and walked out before Grace could even answer. The lock clicked as it engaged.

She clasped her hands together, trying her hardest not to wring them like a dishtowel. She had to be an actress now, someone who projected confidence and strength, despite the growing realization that she might not find a way to escape. She walked over to the bed and sat down, her heart thumping in her chest. Surely, at some point, Chet would figure out where she was and save her. And Flo? Would he try to get her back, or would he let Marciano take her like a worthless trinket? It was all she had to hope for that the two men who meant the most to her would find a way to save her from this hell.

CHAPTER THIRTY-ONE

*G*race stood at the window, her forehead pressed against the glass to see the view directly below. One story down, in the gray of night, she could see the platform of a fire escape. If she could just get the window open, she could slip out, drop the ten to twelve feet below, and then figure out what to do next. Perhaps the window below her was not locked, or she could extend the ladder from the fire escape to the floor below to the next floor.

She ran her hand along the paint-filled seams of the window. She scratched at it with her fingers, and a small paint chip lodged under her fingernail. It would take time. If only she had—

She ran over to the desk, opened the roll top and searched all the nooks and drawers. She shuffled through miscellaneous papers scattered throughout until her fingers found something hard—a letter opener. Now *this* could be her ticket to freedom.

Behind her, the doorknob clicked. Someone was coming! She quickly closed the drawer just as Marciano's bulk filled the doorway. She froze, her breath caught in her throat. She gripped the letter opener more tightly.

"Writing a letter?" Marciano slammed the door shut and

walked over to her. His steps were unsteady, slow, and the closer he came, the more she could smell the alcohol. His pockmarked face looked oily, and the sneer on his face made him even more grotesque. Grace's stomach flipped. Felicity said he would only take advantage of her if he was drunk. The stink emanating from him told her she didn't have a prayer.

When Grace tried to step backward, he thrust out a hand and grabbed a fistful of her hair. Grace yelped, her arms and legs trembling. He gripped her hair so hard Grace could feel her scalp tighten and burn where his fingers pulled at the roots. She tilted her head toward him to relieve the pain, and he slowly pulled her to her feet, his grasp growing tighter. Grace's breath came in ragged gasps, and every muscle in her body tensed. She clung to the letter opener, and its hard coolness gave her some comfort. Her fingers searched for and found the pocket in her dress and she dropped in the letter opener, hoping it wouldn't show above the pocket.

Grace closed her eyes, unable to look at the greasy face bearing down on her.

"Aw, baby," Marciano said, "don't turn away from me, sweetheart."

When Grace tried to turn her head again, he jerked her hair. She opened her eyes and forced herself to look into his—deep black, as black as his pomaded hair and just as lifeless. She shuddered at their emptiness and blinked, forcing herself to look at him. He leaned in, his thick, wet lips coming toward hers. At the last second, she turned her head so the mushy flesh landed next to her lips, not on them.

He pulled back and gripped her hair harder. His eyes were alive now, piercing through her with anger. He let out a rush of air, assaulting her with damp, gin-soaked breath. "I told you I don't like rejection," he said between clenched teeth. His face was shaking so violently, the greasy strings of hair at his brow danced.

Grace trembled, and she couldn't pull any air into her lungs. Her head spun. "Okay, okay," she said, trying to sound confident. "I won't reject you. Just give me a minute. I need a minute."

His grip on her hair loosened, and his eyes, unfocused, glazed over. He smiled, showing off his greasy, tobacco-stained teeth. She kept her eyes focused on his. He let go of her hair and stood, swaying in front of her. Grace took in a deep breath. If only she could stave him off. She'd have to try to be nice to him; it seemed to take away his rage.

"Who are you writing to? Piker Riker?" he asked and then laughed, his voice thick and slurring.

Grace eased into the desk chair. "No."

Marciano's upper body swayed, though his feet were planted squarely on the floor. He tilted his head back and let out a raspy laugh that sounded as if he'd just smoked a box of cigars.

"Riker." He put one arm on the back of her chair and the other on the desk, surrounding her with his odiousness. His body unsteadily loomed over her. "Riker won't get that letter, girlie, 'cause your precious Chet is dead. D-E-A-D, dead." He let out a heinous chuckle and bolted upright, releasing her from his bodily prison and then staggered backward, laughing uproariously.

The air rushed out of Grace's lungs as if he'd placed an anvil on her chest. Her stomach twisted, and a rush of despair ran through her legs, making them vibrate beneath the desk.

Chet? Chet is d-dead?

She shook her head almost violently. "No. No, *you're* lying."

The mobster's lips stretched wide into an evil grin. "Shot him through the heart." He rushed forward, grabbed her arms, and jerked her to her feet. But her legs couldn't hold her, and she folded back into the chair. She tried to pull away from him, but her body wouldn't obey. Chet was dead. It couldn't be true. He'd had a plan. He was going to save her. Her heart twisted with pain.

Marciano grasped her at the waist and launched her off the

floor and over his shoulder, slamming the breath out of her. Panic seized her, and she knit her hands into fists and pummeled him on the back and waist, her blows not having much of an effect, as if she hit a sack of flour. She tried to flail her legs, but he held them tight at the back of her knees. He headed toward the bed and stumbled, nearly dropping her. She let out a scream just before he righted himself.

He flung her on the bed and she landed hard, her neck snapping back onto the pillows. Marciano struggled out of his jacket, his body swaying unsteadily one way, then the other. While he wrestled to free his arms, Grace kicked and made contact with his rotund belly, sending him sprawling backward. Nice wouldn't work now; she had to fight to save her own skin.

He ripped off his jacket and jumped on top of her, crushing the air out of her lungs. He grabbed both sides of her head and jammed his lips onto hers, pinning her down. The flesh of his face smothered her. She could hear the deafening thud of her heart beat as blood pumped through her veins. She tried to fight him off with her arms and legs, but his weight was too much. She wriggled beneath him, trying to break free.

"You bastard!" Felicity shouted, her voice filling the room. "Get off her! *She's* not what you want, Joe, and you know it. How dare you do this to me! I won't let you have another woman. Not again. I won't, Joe!"

Marciano stopped struggling and turned to look at Felicity, who had a table lamp gripped in her raised hand, ready to strike. "I swear, I'll bash her head in, Joe. I'll make her so ugly you won't want her. You know it's me you want, Joe. Always me. You always come back to *me*."

Marciano's face contorted with rage. He pushed himself off Grace and lunged at Felicity, snatched the lamp out of her hand, threw it to the floor, smashing it into pieces, and then he lifted his meaty fist and broadsided Felicity in the face. The woman went sprawling to the floor.

Grace yelped, but Marciano held a finger up to her, his face mottled red and gray, sweat dripping into his cold eyes. "Don't you move," he rasped.

He grabbed Felicity by the arm and yanked her up off the floor.

"See, Joe," Felicity said in a whisper. "See, it's me you want. I know why you brought her here—to get back at Flo. But you really don't want her, do you?"

Marciano slapped Felicity across the face, and Grace yelped again. Felicity raised her hand to touch the snaking trail of blood trickling from her nose. Her eyebrows arced like a spark of electricity, and she slapped Marciano hard across the face. He growled with rage, then grabbed Felicity around the waist and crushed her to his body. Grace watched in horror as he took a handful of Felicity's hair and pulled her face to his. He kissed her like a lion devouring his prey. Felicity flung her arms around him, pressing him closer to her. The two were locked in an impassioned embrace, and Grace didn't know whether to scream, run, or hit them both over the head with the remains of the lamp.

Marciano picked Felicity up off her feet, their lips never unlocking, and he marched out of the room. Felicity finally came up for air and reached down to the doorknob, pulling the door shut behind them.

Grace sat on the bed, her mouth gaping and her insides heaving. "What in heaven's name was that?"

GRACE STOOD in the washroom stripped to her linen shift and holding a rag they'd given her to bathe herself. In the last week, they'd only let her out of her room to use the toilet and sink down the hall. Felicity, or one of Marciano's men, brought her food twice a day, and Marciano had not made an appearance since the strange episode with Felicity. His absence both relieved and worried her. How long was she to sit in that room, day after day, wondering about her fate?

Heaviness pulled at her heart like an anchor when she thought about Chet. She knew if she thought too hard, the weight would crush her, and she couldn't afford to be shattered now. She had to fight her way out of this mess. It was possible that Marciano hadn't even really killed him, had just wanted her to think the love of her life was dead.

And what about Flo? Had Marciano's thugs killed him, too? Marciano likely would have mentioned it, delighted in it, if so, and delighted in telling Grace the news himself. And since she'd heard nothing of Flo, she'd think positively there. Still, she wanted to cry and to grieve, but the mere will to stay alive and find a way out of this place wouldn't let her. She had to hang on to the belief that they were alive, and that she would get out of here, somehow.

She picked up her dress and put it back on. She'd wanted to ask Felicity for a clean garment but didn't want to encounter the woman's wrath. When she'd finished dressing, she knocked on the door. One of Marciano's henchmen, a short, squat, balding man, opened the door for her. He grasped her by the elbow to lead her down the hall, but they stopped when Marciano and Felicity appeared on the landing of the stairway near Grace's room. Marciano was dressed to the nines in a dark suit, dark shirt with gleaming silver studs, and his white scarf draped around his neck like a snowy boa constrictor. He leered at Grace with the gleam of lust in his eyes. Felicity trailed behind him in sky-blue taffeta and a brilliant diamond necklace, and rolled her eyes when Marciano approached Grace.

"Refreshed?" Marciano asked, running his hand down Grace's hair. "You look beautiful."

"She's wearing the same rags she wore when she got here," Felicity said.

Marciano turned to her. "Well, then, she should have one of

your dresses, don't you think? You pick. You have exquisite taste." He focused again on Grace and moved in close to her, his bulk making her want to shrink. She could smell a hint of alcohol on his breath. Not good.

Marciano raised his chin to his guard dog. "I'll escort Miss Michelle back to her room," he said.

Grace's knees turned to water, and she could feel the life drain from her face.

"You," Marciano said to Felicity. "Go get one of your finest dresses. And hand over those diamonds. I'm tired of looking at you. You look like a brazen hussy, a used-up whore. I think I'll have a taste of something new."

Grace gulped down her fear. She didn't know who scared her most—Marciano with his oily lecherousness or Felicity with her burning rage.

When Felicity didn't move, Marciano faced her. "I said, *Get the dress.*"

Felicity wrinkled her nose. "She's trash. She doesn't deserve one of my dresses."

"Get it, you bitch, or I'll—"

"You'll what? Beat me? Go ahead. Give it to me, baby."

Marciano lunged at Felicity and pinned her against the railing of the staircase. He bashed her face in with his fist, hitting one side of her face and then the other several times. Grace tried to scream, but nothing came out of her mouth. When Marciano finally stopped, Felicity shook her head and put a hand to her bleeding mouth, then stared at the blood on her fingertips. Her lips spread into a hideous smile, blood coloring her teeth bright red.

Marciano delivered a blow to Felicity's stomach next, and the woman doubled over. On the way to the ground, his knee made contact with her face. Blood spurted from her mouth and nose onto Marciano's white scarf and even sprayed Grace's dress. When Felicity hit the ground, Marciano kicked her in the stomach. She groaned, blood bubbling from her mouth, her sky-blue satin dress like a Southern battlefield after a massacre.

"Stop it!" Grace pulled at Marciano's coat. He swatted her away like a pesky fly. "Help!" she yelled, hoping that one of Marciano's men would come up and stop the beast, but no one came.

"Stop it, Joe," Grace begged. "I'll do anything you want. Just leave her alone."

Marciano stopped and looked at her. An evil grin spread across his pudgy, alcohol-flushed, vile face for a moment. He then continued to beat Felicity.

The bulky henchman appeared at the top of the stairs.

"Thank God," Grace shouted. "He's killing her! Stop him!"

His eyes widened. "Boss, boss!" he said, lurching toward Marciano who was still kicking Felicity. "Hey, boss. Let up. No need for that."

Marciano stopped like a dog called off his prey by his master. Chest heaving, he looked down at his blood-covered suit. Some of the silver studs on his shirt had popped loose. Sweat glistened on his forehead and ran down his temples into his ears. He straightened, ran a hand through his greasy hair, and pulled his burgundy velvet vest down over the mass of his stomach.

Felicity lay gasping on the ground, clutching her stomach, blood oozing from her mouth and nose as one of her eyes was swelling shut. Grace knelt down next to her. She looked up at Marciano. "You're an animal," she said, barely audible.

Marciano harrumphed and wiped the sweat from his fore-head. "You wouldn't want me to wreck that pretty face of yours now, would you?"

Grace thought it best to keep her mouth shut. She half expected him to pull her up by her hair and drag her into the bedroom, but for some reason, he didn't.

"Clean up this mess," he said to Grace, pointing to Felicity. "And I'll be back. You said you'd do anything and I'm going to take you up on that, sweetheart, but I've lost my appetite for the moment." He gave Felicity another kick, this time at her ankle. The woman whimpered in pain.

Marciano straightened his coat and walked down the stairs. His henchman stayed behind.

"Help me get her to the bed," Grace said. "My room."

The man obeyed and lifted Felicity gently from the floor. She groaned in pain again, her swollen face contorting in agony.

Grace led them both into the bedroom where the man laid Felicity on the bed. "What's your name?" Grace asked the man.

"They call me Sparky," he said, smiling to reveal several missing teeth.

"Thank you, Sparky. Can you get me a washbasin and a clean cloth please?"

He left the room, and Grace gently pulled at Felicity's arms to get them to release from clutching her stomach. "Let go, Felicity. He's gone now. Try to relax."

She clutched at her stomach harder.

"I have to be able to look at you to see if you need a doctor." Grace tried to use her most soothing voice.

Felicity released an arm and let Grace straighten her head and shoulders on the pillow. Felicity shifted her weight to straighten out, making a squeaking sound with every movement. Grace gently pulled at Felicity's legs, which were folded to her chest. Though it was obvious Felicity was in pain, she let Grace straighten her legs out in front of her.

Sparky reappeared at the door with a ewer, pitcher, and cloth in hand.

"Set them on the nightstand. Thank you, Sparky."

He nodded, left the room, and shut the door behind him. Grace heard the key turn in the lock.

"I'm going to check your body for broken bones," Grace said.

Felicity stared at the ceiling and didn't respond. Grace gently probed her collarbone, arms, and fingers, then moved up to Felicity's ribs. Grace felt something rock-hard. "Is that your corset?" she asked.

Felicity blinked but still didn't respond. Grace took the letter opener from her pocket and held it up. "I'm going to cut through your dress. I'd turn you over to unlace it, but I don't think I should move you more than I already have."

No response.

Using the letter opener, Grace worked at the seams of the dress until the stitching loosened and eventually released. She moved the fabric aside to reveal Felicity's corset. There was nothing unusual about it, but Grace could see something peeking up from the top of the laces. She worked the letter opener to release the laces and pulled them apart. Between the corset and Felicity's linen shift was a thin, metal plate.

"What is this?"

Felicity moved her head to meet Grace's eyes. "Protection."

Grace gasped. "You wear this every day?"

"Never know when he's gonna go into a rage."

Grace sat down on the bed next to her. "Oh my god. Why do you stay with him?"

Felicity didn't answer, just asked, "Why did you tell him you'd do anything?"

"I was trying to stop him. He could have killed you." Grace wet the cloth and dabbed at Felicity's face. "I don't understand. Why are you so jealous? Why do you want a man like that?"

"I don't know." Felicity winced under Grace's ministrations. "I've been hanging on to hate for so long, I think I must have lost my mind. The hate turns to something else. I know I sound crazy."

Grace held the cloth in midair, a thought popping into her mind. "Sophia's mystery man was Marciano! He's the man she started seeing after Flo. That's why you hated her."

Felicity turned her head from Grace and looked at the far

wall. Grace's gaze narrowed on the woman. "Did you kill my sister?" Or *was it Marciano?*

Felicity wrung her hands at her waist, drawing Grace's attention to the metal plate again. "I didn't kill your sister." She turned back to face Grace. "But I wasn't sad when she left."

"But I bet Marciano was furious."

Felicity grabbed the rag from Grace and dabbed at her bloody mouth.

Grace stood up from the bed and paced the floor. Marciano was the man Sophia had been fleeing, the man who had threatened her life. And he was probably the man who killed her, or had her killed. He had the power, the money, the thirst for revenge. But how could she prove it? She had to get out of here, away from him, before she met the same fate as her sister.

CHAPTER THIRTY-TWO

*T*wo days passed before Grace saw Felicity or Marciano again. Sparky made several appearances with her meals and for water closet breaks. Grace felt pretty certain that he'd been parked outside her door for most of the day and night.

She sat at the window, letter opener in hand, chipping away at the paint that sealed the window shut. The work was slow, but she didn't have anything else to do and it helped her think. She had to come up with some kind of plan of escape.

That evening, shortly after her meal had been delivered, the door burst open, startling her. Marciano's bulk filled the space between the jambs. He swayed on his feet. His shirt was unbuttoned to the waist, his shirttail was partially untucked, and the cuff of his sleeves were void of their cufflinks. It looked like he'd slept in his clothes. For days. His jet-black hair hung in greasy strings over coal-dead eyes, and Grace could smell the bourbon emanating from his pores from clear across the room.

Her heart thumped hard in her chest, like an Indian drum beat signaling war.

Marciano slammed the door shut and staggered over to the bed where Grace sat, still as a deer behind a thicket.

"I see you've been waiting for me," Marciano said.

Grace cleared her throat, trying to make her vocal chords work. "I have no choice, do I?"

Marciano laughed and moved closer to the bed. He stood in front of her, his crotch in her face. Grace gulped. He grabbed her by the hair, pulled her up, and planted a slobbery kiss on her lips. She winced as she felt his saliva ooze down her chin. The smell and taste of liquor burned her nose and throat, making her want to vomit. Her stomach ready to heave, she pushed him away from her.

"Remember what I said about rejection," he said.

Suppressing the urge to lose her dinner on his shiny, patent leather shoes, Grace wiped her face. "I'm not rejecting you, I just needed some air." She had to play her cards right. She knew he liked violence—she'd witnessed that with Felicity—but she hoped she could finesse the situation a little better.

Marciano faltered, his eyes rolling back in his head. He swayed and fell onto the bed in a sitting position. He grabbed her around the waist and buried his face in the folds of her dress at her bosom. Grace grimaced as she stared down at the crown of his head. He bit her breast, and she gasped, wanting to smack him across the room, but she crushed her lower lip with her teeth instead.

He tightened his grip on her and flung her onto the bed. She struggled beneath him as he climbed on top of her, trying to avoid his face. His movements slowed as if he were swimming through sand. His breath came short and heavy, his limbs becoming like weights on her body. Suddenly, his head lolled to one side. He stopped moving and lay limp on top of her.

She heard the door open and lifted her head to see Felicity rush in.

"You okay?" she asked. She came to the other side of the bed and pulled on Marciano's arm, trying to free Grace. In her stunned relief, Grace couldn't answer. Felicity tugged at his lifeless body, inching him off Grace, who wriggled out from beneath the inert body.

"Is he dead?" Grace asked.

With one last yank, Felicity freed Grace completely. She dropped Marciano's arm and let it drape over the side of the bed. He was motionless, facedown, like a corpse.

"I slipped a mickey into his drink."

Grace sat up, her blood finally rushing back into her limbs. "You what?"

"Every drink he took I could see he was headed toward this, and I didn't want him to go through with it." Felicity stood next to the bed, nervously pulling on her fingers. Her face, still swollen from the beating he'd given her, looked disfigured, like something from a nightmare. Her hands trembled as she walked to the foot of the bed, her striking blue eyes trained on Grace. "You stopped him from killing me the other day. He's beat me before, but never like that. I really thought he'd kill me. But you stopped him."

"I didn't want to see you—"

Felicity held up a hand. "You're so innocent, pure. Like me long ago. I couldn't bear to have him hurt you, at least not this time."

"Thank you."

"He won't be out for long." Felicity nervously put a hand on a locket at her throat, running it against the chain.

"Can I get out of here?" Grace asked.

Felicity shook her head. "He's got guards at every door and two just down the hall."

Grace stood up and felt for the letter opener in her pocket. "I have this," she said, pulling it out. "We can scrape the paint off the window sill and open the window. We can get down to the fire escape." Adrenaline rushed through her veins at the realization that it could work, especially if they did it together.

Felicity's eyes popped open, and her brow wrinkled above the bridge of her nose. "We?"

"We can do it together, Felicity." Grace approached her, placed a hand on her forearm. "You saved me from him. You don't deserve *him*." She pointed to the bed where Marciano rolled his head back and forth and then proceeded to snore. "You deserve better."

Felicity placed her hand on top of Grace's and pulled it off. "I bought you time, is all. I didn't save you. This place is locked tight as a drum. Believe me, I know. He's got goons all over. And I bet you ten-to-one that window is nailed shut."

Grace sighed, slipped the letter opener back into her pocket, and walked to the desk to sit down. She buried her face in her hands, wishing that someone would come rescue her. An image of Chet flashed in her mind, and her heart clenched as tears came to her eyes. "Is it true?" she asked, turning to Felicity. "Is Chet dead?"

"I'm afraid so. They came back all tanked-up, and Joe set about bragging that he'd shot Riker."

Grace closed her eyes. The salty tears burned behind her lids until they spilled down her cheeks. She felt the warmth of Felicity's arm around her shoulder.

"Did you love him?" Her voice was silken, like honey.

Grace nodded, brushing away tears with her fingertips.

"He was a good man." Felicity gently pushed Grace's frazzled hair off her face. "I knew him a long time ago."

Grace knew this. She looked into the woman's piercing blue eyes. "Were you? Did you . . . ?"

Felicity shook her head. "No. We were just friends. He and I ended up at the same orphanage. I didn't see him again until we were grown. He was a kind man, and a girl doesn't forget kindness."

"He told me he had a mother, that she was sick and in need of an operation."

Felicity smiled. "She gave him up at birth. He must have found her later."

Grace clutched her stomach, feeling as if the wind had been knocked out of her. Given up by his mother. She couldn't imagine anything so horrible and hurtful. Her gaze traveled to Felicity, who stared out the window, as if recalling a memory.

"The nuns at the orphanage found me in the street," Felicity started. "I was real bad off, starving to death and sick. Chet saw them bring me in. He never spoke much, but when I was recovering, he brought me a rosebud. He used to get in trouble all the time for cutting flowers. It was such a simple gesture, but so kind."

Grace remembered the two occasions he'd left rosebuds on her pillow and forced down the ball of emotion in her throat. She couldn't think about Chet now. She stood up and turned to Felicity. "What do we do about him?" She jutted her chin toward Marciano.

"You can sleep in my room. Joe will like that. He'll think it's all part of his devious plan to get me to convince you that's he's a good guy under that gruff."

They both blew out puffs of air, and almost laughed.

"Will he wake up soon?" Grace asked.

"In a couple of hours. And he'll wake up with one hell of a headache." A deep chuckle rumbled from Felicity's throat. "But he won't remember anything. Never does."

"You've done this before?"

"When I have to."

"What is it? Where did you get it?"

"I have trouble sleeping, so Joe's doctor gives me laudanum."

Grace reached out for the black woman's hands and took them in her own. "Felicity, I have an idea. Will you help me?"

Felicity frowned and cocked her head. "What is it?"

Grace smiled. "I want to give Marciano a present."

Lost in a cloud of white mist, Chet opened his eyes to searing pain and a blinding light. An astringent odor wafted over him. When he tried to lift his head and peer through the slits of his eyes, pain shot through his chest like a bolt of electricity. An occasional cough or groan pulled him back into consciousness, but it was a struggle. He managed to recognize white tiled floors and stark white walls surrounding him. Rows of iron beds with white sheets lined the walls.

Hospital . . .

His head fell back onto the pillow, sending a spasm of lightning through his neck. He heard soft, squishy footsteps come closer to the bed. He turned his head to see a large woman resembling a giant marshmallow standing over him. Her round face peered over the clipboard, her eyes scrutinizing his face. She wore a pointed white hat with a red cross emblazoned across the front. Large breasts hung low over the crisp white belt at her waist.

"Well," she said, putting her hand gently on his arm, sending a wave of pain all the way up to his shoulder. "You decided to rejoin the living, I see."

"Where am I?"

"St. Luke's Hospital."

He closed his eyes to ward off the dizziness. "How did I get here?"

"A policeman found you behind the Plaza Hotel."

Chet furrowed his brow, trying to remember, his palms sweating under the sheets. "How long have I been here?"

"About a week." She bent over him and pulled at something on his head, sending a razor-sharp knife through his eyes. He winced and jerked away from her touch, eliciting other jolts of pain throughout his body. "I'm sorry, but I have to check the bandages," she said with a sympathetic look.

"What happened? My chest hurts. . ."

"You tell me, Mister. You were shot. You're lucky, though. It missed your heart by an inch. From the looks of it, whoever did this to you wanted to make sure you didn't get up. Yep, someone worked you over good," she said. "Concussion, broken ribs, several contusions, and a broken finger, too—you came in battered, bruised, and nearly dead."

He raised his hand and squinted at the splint covering his pinkie finger. The image of a white scarf passed through his mind, and then he remembered: the Plaza, the body blows . . . Grace . . . Marciano . . . Grace. He'd let her down, left her to the wolves. Panic burst in his chest. What had become of her? He had to find her and protect her from Marciano. He tried to sit up but was met with the nurse's hands against his burning chest.

"But I have to go," he said urgently. "She's in danger!"

"You're not going anywhere, pal." The nurse gently pressed him back onto the bed.

Somehow, he had to get up, find his clothes, and get out of there—fast. God only knew what Marciano had dreamed up for her.

Thinking of the mobster's filthy hands on Grace made Chet's temples pound. He attempted to get up again, but the nurse pinned his arms to his sides. She reached over him, got hold of a strap, and fastened him into the bed with it. She then tucked the sheets under the mattress, tight, to prevent any other movement.

When she was finished, she held a finger up to his face. "Don't you move, Mister. The doctor will want to examine you now that you're awake."

Exhausted from the conversation and his efforts to get up, Chet relaxed his head against the pillow and fell back into the darkness.

When he woke again, he realized he'd lost all track of time and had no idea how long he'd been out. It must have been days since he was last conscious. If they had been sedating him, they hadn't sedated him today, he knew, because every muscle and joint in his body ached. The nurse also hadn't strapped him down to the bed since that first day he tried to get up. Good thing, too. He had to get to Grace.

He struggled to sit up, ignoring the pain in his head, chest, and ribs. Sucking in his breath, Chet slid his legs over the side of the bed and let them dangle. He let go of the breath and fought the dizziness threatening to make him seek solace in the fluffy white pillow again.

His clothes were stacked in a neat pile on a chair next to the bed. They'd been washed and pressed, but there was no denying the ragged, gaping hole in his shirt. He glanced around the large sickroom at the other patients. Many were sleeping, while others stared at the walls with glassy eyes. No one seemed to notice or care that he was trying to get up.

He slid off the bed until his feet made contact with the cold, white tile. His chest caved in, as if all the air had been sucked from his lungs, and his head spun. He stood, hunched over like an old man who had been through more than one war, grabbed his pants, and pulled them on. Satisfied that the nurse had not yet reappeared, he slipped on his shirt, every movement piercing his chest like knives. He placed his tie around his neck, picked up his coat, hat, and shoes, and started for the door.

The lethargic patients watched him through their morphine-induced gazes. He buttoned his shirt over the tight bandage that was wrapped around his rib cage, plopped his hat on his head, and walked into a long corridor.

"What are you doing up?" the nurse called from behind him.

He jumped, shockwaves of pain vibrating through his body. "I have to go."

"But the doctor—"

"I don't have time to explain."

"But I've been instructed to keep you here until the police can question you!"

Chet forced a smile. "You know you can't keep me here against my will, and if the police want to talk to me, they'll have to find me." He gave her a pat on her ample shoulder and, clutching his burning ribs, walked to the nearest hospital exit.

GRACE AWOKE in Felicity's room to find Felicity sitting at her vanity. Sunlight streamed through the opened curtains, lighting the space.

"How angry is he?" Grace asked. She imagined Joe Marciano did not take kindly to being bested by two women.

"I don't know. He was still asleep when I left, but you can bet he'll be stirring up a hornet's nest." Felicity rummaged through her boxes of jewelry, trying on sparkling items and then taking them off.

"How soon 'til he comes after me again?" Grace asked, pulling the covers up over her chest.

Felicity smiled in the mirror. "I can handle Joe. You just do your part, and we'll be fine." She held a pair of bright green earrings up to her earlobes.

Grace sank deeper into the covers. Her mind whirled with how they would execute her plan. Then a chill seeped down her spine.

"Joe bought these for me when we were first together." Felicity held the earrings up for Grace to see.

"Do I hear sentimentality in your voice?"

Felicity put the earrings down. "I'm not sure I'm going with you."

Grace sat up, shoving the covers off her. "Are you mad? You're going to stay here? With *him*?"

"Where else would I go? What would I do?"

"C'mon, Felicity! You were a performer, and a good one. You could go back to the stage."

Felicity shook her head. "That's not for me. I'm fine here. Joe can be a brute sometimes, but he takes decent care of me and I can handle him. You saw that yesterday."

Not when he's beating the tar out of you.

"Then why are you helping me?" Grace asked.

Felicity turned away from the mirror and faced Grace. Her eyes hardened and turned the color of blue agate. "Nothing personal, but I want you gone. If Joe gets too enamored with you, he'll forget all about me. It's happened before, but this time he'll throw me out in the street, and I just can't be in the street again. I'm getting too old to survive that."

Grace swung her knees over the side of the bed. "Your chances of surviving the streets are far better than your chances of surviving another beating like that."

Felicity stood up, straightened her shoulders, walked over to the wardrobe, and opened the doors. "I told you, I'm not going anywhere. I'll help you escape because I don't want you here, but I'm asking you: don't destroy what I have. It's enough for me." She filed through the wardrobe and pulled out a dark blue velvet dressing gown with a satin collar and handed it to Grace. "Here, put this on. It's cold, and Joe will show up any minute. My guess is he'll be hopping mad, wondering where you've gone."

Grace flung off the covers and rushed to accept the dressing gown, hastily wrapping herself in the soft velvet. She then walked over to the window on the pretense of looking outside, but she really wanted to see if it was sealed shut like the other one. It was—tight as a drum. Her plan had to work.

"How many guards does Marciano have around the hotel? Are there other guests here?" Grace asked.

"No other guests. Joe rents the whole thing. There are two

guards outside the hotel and three inside. One at his room, one at my room, and one at the room you were in."

"Do you have more laudanum?"

"I have enough."

"Good." Grace's mind whirled with her idea. "What about the fabric? How will you get it?"

Felicity sat at the vanity, picked up a necklace, and held it up to the light. "Sometimes Lefty, one of the guards, will sell my jewelry for me. He's kind of sweet on me. Poor guy. He's ugly as sin with this big scar on his head that comes down the side of his face."

Grace's skin pricked all over as if she'd scrubbed it with lye.

The man in the tattered brown suit.

"Whenever I need some extra cash, I give him some of my jewels and he sells them. I give him a cut, of course. Joe has no idea."

Not wanting to let on how much she felt like jumping through the paned glass right then, Grace nodded. She had to keep a cool head for this plan to work. She had to summon the skills she'd learned in all those acting classes.

When the door burst open with a loud bang, Grace's heart leaped to her throat and Felicity dropped the jewels, shoved the drawer closed, and whirled around. Joe Marciano stood in the doorway, his face a mask of anger.

"What. The. Hell." He marched over to Felicity, grabbing her robe by its silken collar and practically lifting her off her feet. Grace's blood went cold, and she pulled the dressing gown tighter around her body. She rocked back and forth, shifting from one foot to the other and longing to reach out and pull Felicity away from him. But she didn't dare move.

"Darling," Felicity said, her voice strained, "you passed out, again. I've told you to have the doc take a look at you. The girl was sick, retching, and I wanted to let you sleep, so I brought her here. I didn't want her to disturb you."

Joe released his grip and Felicity landed with unsure footing, falling back into the chair. When Marciano turned to Grace, she felt the blood drain from her face and her fingers tingle. He approached her, his expression morphing from rage to something else. The familiar stale odor of cigar and booze on his breath made her insides churn.

Felicity ran to his side. "Joe, the girl needs time. She's grieving."

Grace pulled her lower lip into her mouth. She'd been so consumed with finding a way of escape that she hadn't even had time to grieve. Chet's handsome face crept into her mind again, and her heart felt heavy and weak at the same time. She shoved the image away.

"I've got this, Joe." Felicity looked into his eyes. "She'll come around. She has nowhere to go. Riker's dead, and Flo is likely crippled with worry and jealousy that you've got his girl. It's all working for you, Joe. Just give it a little time. You'll win her over, just as you won me over."

Joe shook her hands loose and stepped back a few feet to look from Grace to Felicity and then back to Grace. Her limbs turned liquid, and they started to tremble when the rage returned to his face.

Suddenly, Marciano turned to Felicity and slapped her hard with the back of his hand, sending her sprawling to the floor. Grace let out a yelp and lunged to help Felicity, but Marciano grabbed her by the waist, pulled her to his chest, and pressed his greasy lips against hers. Grace stiffened, her stomach lurching. As fast as he'd grabbed her, Marciano thrust Grace away from him so hard she reeled backward until her heel slipped and she slammed into the side of the bed, hitting the small of her back with all her weight. She crumpled to the floor in pain and pulled her knees up to her chest.

As soon as Marciano wiped his mouth and left the room, Grace slowly rose and hobbled over to Felicity. When she helped the woman sit up, blood trickled from Felicity's nose and the left side of her mouth. She raised her hand to her lips and winced when she touched them.

"Are you all right?" Grace asked, her voice trembling.

Felicity nodded. "That was nothing."

"Please come with me." Grace begged once more.

"Mind your own business, girl," Felicity said, unsteadily rising to her feet. "I know what I'm doing."

CHAPTER THIRTY-THREE

$\mathcal{C}$het finally made it to the theater, winded and exhausted, with every single limb and muscle in his body spiking with sharp, stabbing pain. He made his way to the stairs that led to the offices and slowly climbed, his legs burning with fatigue. When he reached the reception area, he found the place quiet as a crypt. No Goldie at her desk, no phones ringing, no voices chattering as they often did in Flo's inner sanctum.

He stood a moment, trying to catch his breath, when he heard something—the unmistakable sound of ice clinking against crystal and then a loud thump as the glass was set down. Chet opened the door to Flo's office and saw the back of the man's head. He was seated behind his desk, facing the star-studded wall. His hands hung limp down the sides of the chair, and a half-empty amber-filled glass sat on the desk.

Chet leaned on the doorframe to steady the swimming in his brain. Flo slowly swiveled the chair to face him. He looked haggard, like he hadn't slept in days, dark half-moons under his glassy eyes, and hopelessly drunk. The glazed eyes sank into blackened hollows, and his cheeks sagged under the weight of his complete failure.

"It's over." Flo's voice, slurred and heavy, broke the silence. "I'm as good as six feet under. The show's a disaster. Marciano will ruin me."

"Where's Grace?"

Flo tilted his head, resting it on the back of the chair, and stared at the ceiling, his mouth hanging open. "He took her."

Anger at Flo's tone of acceptance tore through Chet, and he bit down on freeing the surge of violence he felt brewing inside him.

"We have to get her back," Chet said through clenched teeth, "before—" Sudden exhaustion overwhelmed him, and he stumbled forward and sank into the chair facing the mahogany desk.

Flo glanced at him with dull eyes, pulled himself forward, and poured more whiskey in his glass. He slid it over in front of Chet, who grabbed at it and sucked down the liquid in the hopes that it would soften the hard, biting pain in his chest.

"What happened to you?" Flo asked.

"Not important," he said, dismissing the question. "We need to find Grace. Where did he take her?"

"I don't know. You were supposed to protect her." Flo leveled his eyes on Chet and stared at him. "You were hired to prevent this sort of thing. It's *your* fault. How could you have let this happen? Now the show has no chance of success!"

A shock vaulted through Chet's body. "*The show?* Grace is being held by that monster and you're worried about the show?"

"*Molly* can't be recast. The public expects Grace. She was the only flawless part of the production."

Chet stood, reached across the desk, grabbed Flo's collar, and yanked the man to his feet. "You have caused Grace more pain than you know. You have used her and deceived her, and now it's time to make things right, Flo. Forget the show. Forget the theater. We *need* to get Grace back."

Flo couldn't even raise his eyes to meet Chet's. "Let go of

me." He shoved Chet away from him, sending him back into the chair, nails ripping at his chest and neck.

The two men stared at each other. An eerie graveyard silence crept into the room, the only sounds the pop of melting ice in a glass and their labored breathing.

THE HORSEHAIR BRISTLES of the brush made Grace's scalp tingle as Felicity ran it through her long, lustrous tresses. The sensation brought back memories of Sophia, who had brushed Grace's hair every morning and every night when they were children. The memory formed a lump in her throat.

"You did a beautiful job on the dressing gown," Felicity said, breaking the silence and bringing Grace out of her nostalgia "You're very talented."

"Thank you. I think Joe will be surprised at exactly how talented I am. Did you notice the sleeves?" Grace asked.

Felicity stopped brushing and went to the wardrobe. She opened the doors and then took out the garment, examining the sleeves. She looked at Grace, confusion in her eyes. "The opening of the sleeves are sewn shut. I don't get it."

"You'll see. I've made them longer than necessary. You can't out-muscle a man like Marciano, but you can out-think him."

"You sure this will work?" Felicity asked.

"It has to," said Grace. *Or he will surely kill me.* "Were you able to give the boys the laudanum?"

"All but Lefty. He wouldn't have a drink. But the others did. They'll be sleeping like babies in about thirty minutes."

"What are we going to do about Lefty?"

Felicity stopped brushing and met Grace's eyes in the mirror. "You leave him to me. It will be fine." She gently pulled Grace's hair to the top of her head and secured it. She then formed narrow strips, coiling each one into a circle and then anchoring them with bobby pins. In fifteen minutes, Grace had three rows of coiled tresses from ear to ear at the back of her head. Felicity handed her a mirror.

Grace turned around and held the mirror up high above her head so she could see the reflection of the beautiful coif. "You're talented yourself," she said, swiveling back around in the chair and taking Felicity's hand in hers. "Please, I'm asking you again, come with me, Felicity." She put the mirror down in her lap and looked into the woman's beautiful, sorrowful eyes. "If you stay here, he'll just keep hurting you—or worse."

Felicity shook her head. "I told you I'm not going anywhere. Now let's get you dressed." At the wardrobe, Felicity pulled out an emerald-green chiffon gown.

"This is one of Joe's favorites." She pulled it across her body and ran her hand down the front of it.

"It's beautiful," Grace said, trying to stifle the quaking in her voice. What if her plan didn't work? What if something went wrong and she had to succumb to Marciano? What if he became so enraged he killed one, or both, of them?

"It's going to be all right, sugar. We'll get you out of here. Where you'll go from here is up to you, but let's not worry about that now."

Grace gave a jerky nod of her head. Right. She had to concentrate on one thing at a time.

Felicity helped Grace dress. The garment plunged deep at the neck, and the waistline sat at the hips, the gossamer fabric falling in folds below the knee. The shoes, also Felicity's, were black patent leather, heeled Mary Janes. After she dressed, Felicity led her over to a full-length oval mirror.

"The lamb to the slaughter," Grace muttered under her breath. Her skin, pale as parchment, and the deep-emerald shade of the gown made the green of her eyes glow. She thought of Chet and how he used to look at her, his eyes so full of love and admiration. But what had those lovesick eyes gotten her? Nothing but a broken heart.

Now she had to fight for her own honor and dignity, for her very life. She narrowed her eyes at her reflection and raised her chin. There had to be a way for a woman to succeed in life without having to succumb to the needs of a man. Whatever it took, she would fight for her freedom.

She walked back over to the wardrobe and retrieved the man's velvet dressing gown she had made over the past few days. Grace didn't know how but Felicity had managed to find a high-quality fabric, a crude sewing machine, scissors, needle and thread, and with Sparky's help, had snuck it into Grace's room. Somewhat satisfied with her handiwork, Grace checked the braided, cotton tie and made sure that it was free of the loops at each side.

Folding the garment over her arm, she turned to Felicity. "I'm ready."

"I'll be just outside the door. Those boys should be real drowsy by now."

After Felicity left to find Joe, Grace inhaled deeply and closed her eyes, trying to steady the fluttering in her stomach and the pounding of her heart. Suddenly, she was panicking. Should she be on the bed or at the desk? Afraid it would look too rehearsed if she were holding the garment, she considered hanging it up, but what should she do first?

Before she could decide, the door opened and Marciano walked in, triumph on his mottled face. "Felicity tells me you've had a change of heart," he said, moving closer to Grace. "I'm glad to hear it. I'm really not all that bad." His voice sounded like the hissing of a snake, and Grace swallowed hard, her mouth going dry as a desert.

"I . . . I made something I thought you'd like." She held out the garment. "Felicity helped me with the fabric and sewing machine."

Marciano narrowed his eyes and twisted his mouth, probably wondering how Felicity had gotten her hands on a sewing machine and that they had done all this behind his back.

"Flo has one just like it," Grace added.

A grin spread on Marciano's face. "Well, if it's good enough for Flo Boy, it's good enough for me," he said, taking it and placing it over his arm as he rushed toward her and grabbed her around the waist.

Grace tried her hardest not to stiffen and recoil, but her stomach felt ready to heave. She giggled and wriggled out of his grasp. "I want you to try it on. You'll be more comfortable. Here." She placed her hands on his chest. "Let me help you." When she slipped his overcoat off his shoulders, his eyelids drooped and a sneer crept across his face. He liked her touch. Maybe if she kept touching *him*, he wouldn't touch *her* for a few minutes.

She took the dressing gown from him and draped it over a chair, and then slowly helped him out of his suit jacket. He reached out to touch her face, but she held up her hand and flashed a showgirl smile. "Now you be patient," she whispered as enticingly as she knew how. "I want to see how you look in the robe before we go any further." She did her best to speak slowly, seductively, but worried that her words came out choppy and stilted, and that he'd know just how nervous she really felt. It made her head swim.

"Now," she said, looking deep into his black eyes, "turn around so I can help you into it."

Marciano held his arms back, waiting for her to slip the sleeves onto his arms. She guided him into the garment, and then gently raised the dressing gown up to his shoulders. Then she quickly wrapped the cotton, braided tie around his chest and arms, and knotted it, pulling it taut.

"What's this?"

"A game. You like games, don't you?" Grace asked, grinning

at him.

"Untie me." He struggled to free his hands but couldn't. They were pulled too tightly against his back, and he couldn't separate them. "What have you done?"

"I've used my wicked sewing skills to incapacitate you. Your sleeves are sewn together at the cuffs. Just try to get out of this robe, you heinous fiend. Pretty ingenious, huh?"

He lunged at her, growling with frustration. She twisted the tie more tightly around his stomach, pinning his elbows to his sides. Marciano let out a bellow of rage, and Grace raced to the door. She yanked it open and peered out. One of Marciano's boys sat slumped in a chair to her right, so she ran to the left and quickly spied Felicity standing next to the wall at the top of the staircase. Felicity's eyes widened when she saw Grace, and then grew wider still. Grace turned to see Marciano right behind her.

"You bitch," Marciano yelled. "And you—" he turned to Felicity "—get me out of this contraption."

Grace ran past Felicity and started down the stairs to make her getaway as the two of them had planned. She made it down to the first landing and around the corner when she heard Felicity scream. Then there was a loud thud against the wall. Grace stopped. Felicity had told her to run, no matter what she saw or heard, but Grace's feet were glued to the staircase. Marciano let out a bellow loud as an angry bear. Grace stood frozen on the stair, her lungs the only part of her body moving. Should she go back? What if he tried to kill Felicity? What if he succeeded?

Grace pivoted on the stair and slowly made her way up to the landing, listening carefully. She heard another shriek from Felicity and Marciano yelling at her, calling her names. Grace quickened her pace, and when she neared the top of the stairs, she saw Marciano standing over Felicity, kicking her hard in the stomach. Grace surged forward up the remaining stairs, took hold of Marciano's arm, and tried to push him away from her, but he kept kicking.

"Stop it!" Grace screamed, pulling at his arm.

He whirled around to face her. "Shut up, dammit, or I'll kill you just like I killed that slut sister of yours."

Grace stumbled backward, her mouth agape. "It was you! I knew it!"

"That's what happens when you leave Joe Marciano," he yelled, thrashing to free himself from the binding ties. Unsuccessful, he turned his attention to Felicity again, and resumed kicking her. Grace lunged at him, beating his back with her fists. He whipped around to face her and let out a roar.

Gulping air into her lungs, Grace ran past him into her room. She grabbed the letter opener from her dress in the wardrobe and ran back to Marciano, who hovered over Felicity continuing to kick her.

Without thinking, Grace thrust the blade deep into the middle of his back. Arching backward, Marciano screamed in pain. Free from his pummeling, Felicity brought herself up to a partially seated position. She braced her back against the wall and kicked fiercely at Marciano's groin. When he doubled over, she kicked him again. He stumbled inches from the stairway. Felicity kicked once more. This time, Marciano had no purchase and lost his balance. He pitched over sideways and tumbled down the stairs, his body crashing against the railings. His heavy bulk careened down the stairs, breaking through the evenly spaced balusters. Grace watched as he fell through the air, seven stories down. He landed with a thud on the black-and-white marbled floor of the hotel foyer.

Grace rushed back to Felicity and knelt down next to her. Blood seeped out of her nose and into her mouth, and she clutched her middle. Grace slipped her arm over Felicity's shoulder.

"Why didn't you tell me?"

She gasped for breath. "Tell you what?" Felicity asked with a groan.

"About Sophia."

"All I know is she left and things got better for me." Felicity doubled over even farther.

Grace ran her hand down Felicity's back. "I'm sorry. You're hurt. Can you get up?" Adrenaline as strong as jolts of electricity raced through Grace's body as she slumped against Felicity and wrapped her arms around her. She wasn't at all sure she could stand, either.

Someone was thundering up the stairs, and when Grace turned her head to prepare for more battle, she saw Chet, his chest heaving and his arm in a sling, standing on the stair landing one floor below her, gasping for air. She gaped in disbelief. His matted hair stuck out all over his head, and blood dripped down his sweating face. Was this a dream? Was he really alive?

Before she could say anything, Grace's eyelids suddenly felt heavy and everything around her slowed until it felt as if she were floating in water. She fought to keep her eyelids open, but they wouldn't obey. Her body shut down, and she slipped into darkness.

SOMETHING COLD PRESSED into Grace's skin above her left breast. She opened her eyes to see a gray-haired man with a gray mustache and spectacles looking eagerly into her face. She gasped and shrank back into the pillows.

The man placed a warm hand on her shoulder. "It's fine. I'm Dr. Webber," he said. "I'm just listening to your heart."

She looked over his shoulder and saw Chet in a bloodstained shirt, standing behind the doctor. Flo stood next to him, his face ashen, his body nearly skeletal. She sensed a presence next to her and turned to see Felicity lying next to her on the bed, propped up on one side, facing Grace, a teary smile in her eyes.

The doctor pulled the stethoscope away from Grace and

placed it in a leather satchel resting on the bed next to her. "She'll be fine," he told the group. "I believe it was shock. She has no contusions or abrasions." The doctor picked up his bag, and Flo walked him to the door.

Chet came and sat on the bed next to Grace. Her hip pressed into his leg as his weight shifted the mattress. The contact was reassuring, comfortable, and blissfully familiar.

"I thought you were—" she said, her voice catching in her throat.

"Marciano's bullet missed my heart by an inch."

"But are you all right? You look so—"

"Alive?" His face broke into a grin. "Well, I had a little tussle with Lefty over there." He pointed to the corner of the room where the man in the brown suit sat slumped and tied to the chair. Grace shot up in bed and scooted back toward the headboard, her heart racing again.

"He's not going to hurt you." Chet reached for her hand, grasping it tightly. "We're only waiting for the police to come back. They're downstairs, rounding up the other buffoons. And *that one* over there is neutralized."

Grace turned to Felicity, who lay very still next to her.

"How are you?"

"I have a few broken ribs and a split lip, but the doc says I'm going to make it."

"You didn't wear your chest plate?"

"The one day . . ." Felicity chuckled and then clutched her ribs again.

Grace turned back to Chet. "What about Marciano? Is he—?"

"Dead. Flat as a pancake at the bottom of the stairs. You girls did good."

"I just wanted to get away, I didn't mean to—"

"You didn't," Felicity said, her voice stronger this time. "I did it. I kicked and kicked until he fell down the stairs." She smiled, then winced and put a hand up to her lower lip. "The son of a bitch had it coming."

"I'm so glad we found you." Chet leaned closer to Grace. "When I heard Marciano took you, I—Did he . . ."

"No, never. Thank goodness. I'm okay—and I have Felicity to thank for it."

Flo came back into the room and approached the bed. The sight of him filled Grace with emotions she couldn't quite understand: she loved him and she hated him. He'd saved her from the streets, but he had put her life in danger more than once. In many ways, she could blame him for Sophia's downward spiral and ultimate demise. Still, he looked so broken that she couldn't help pitying him.

"How are you doing, sweetheart?" he asked, his eyes soft and watery. He looked a hundred years old.

Grace nodded, afraid to say anything out loud, afraid she'd lash out at him. There would be plenty of time to sort things out later, and she'd had enough drama for today. For a lifetime, in fact.

Flo looked away from her, shoving his hands into his pockets. "Well, I, um . . . It looks as if everything here is in hand. I'll just head on back to the theater. Got a lot of work to do." He leaned down, planted a kiss on Grace's forehead, and patted her cheek. She closed her eyes, unable to control the tears that surfaced. He started out of the room, but just as he reached the doorway, he turned to face her again.

"Any chance you'll come back?" he asked.

Grace shook her head, giving him her silent answer.

"I see." Flo looked to the floor. He clamped his hat on his head and walked out of the room.

"He does love you," Felicity whispered, "in his own way."

"I know. It's just not the way I choose to be loved anymore." She glanced at Chet and saw the familiar admiration in his eyes —the feelings she thought she'd never see, or experience again.

"I love you, too," he said. "More than anything."

"I know. And, I love you." Grace reached out to brush her hand across his cheek.

Two police officers bustled into the room brandishing billy clubs and breaking the mood. "Afternoon," the taller one said, tipping his helmet. "This one of the gang?" He pointed to the man in the brown suit.

"He's your man." Chet stood away from the bed.

They hoisted Lefty to his feet and struggled to get him to the door. His knees went slack. Grace couldn't tell if he had gone limp on purpose, in protest, or if he had been rendered too weak to walk. Just as the police reached the threshold with him, Grace got out of bed.

"Wait, please." She addressed the tall officer. "When Marciano attacked me, he admitted to killing my sister. In California, they called her death a suicide. There was a note—typewritten."

Lefty found his legs and hoisted himself a bit straighter. The officer tightened his grip on his arm.

"You're saying Joe Marciano confessed to the murder of your sister?" the officer repeated.

"Yes."

"Obviously, the suicide note was faked," Chet said.

Grace turned to Chet. "Sophia said she fled New York to escape someone. I think an ex-lover. I think Marciano."

Lefty shook his head, coming out of his stupor. "She had it coming, that bitch! You both did."

The officers slammed the man up against the wall. "Watch your mouth," the tall officer said.

Grace approached Lefty. "You remember me?"

"Of course I remember you. The little twit hit me with a brick," he said to the policeman. "She—*they*—tried to kill me. They are the murderers!"

"Shut up, you lousy mutt." The officer slammed the man

against the wall again.

"It was a long time ago." Grace told the officer. "He attacked my sister, Sophia, in an alleyway. She was fighting him off, screaming, but he kept pawing at her, threatening to rape her. I scrounged around for whatever I could find and hit him over the head with a brick to get him off her. We ran away, thinking he was dead, but I recognized him on the train and I know he's the one who tried to run me over in New York."

The officer turned back to Lefty. "So that's where you got that pretty scar. Sounds like self-defense to me."

Chet stepped forward and got in Lefty's face. "How'd he do it? How did Marciano kill Sophia in California?"

The man struggled against the officers holding him.

"He probably had someone do it," Grace said. "But she didn't die of the mercury bichloride. It had to be something else."

"What makes you say that?" Chet said.

"There was no mention in the postmortem report of corrosion in her esophagus or stomach, which is typical if mercury is ingested. It had to be another type of poison."

The tall officer tightened his grip around Lefty's arm. "Listen, pal. You're not going to see the outside of four walls for quite a while. Things might go better for you if you give us the information we need. Your boss is dead. You've got nothing to lose by telling us what you know. You'll be safe and sound in a prison cell."

Lefty fought against the officers' grips, this time with a more concerted effort, but he still couldn't break free. The tall officer reached for his billy club and pressed it against Lefty's throat. "Or you may not make it to the prison cell and succumb to an accident like your buddy, Joe, downstairs."

Lefty's face turned bright crimson, and he nodded. The officer released the billy club, sending Lefty into a coughing fit. When he stopped coughing, he barked at the officer.

"All right, all right, he sent me. I did it. I spiked her drink with arsenic at a party. The bitch deserved it," Lefty spit out.

The officer raised his billy club again, and Lefty flinched.

"I knew it," Grace said. "But why didn't the postmortem pick up on the arsenic?"

"It's difficult to detect," the police officer explained. "You might request another look-see to verify this clown's confession. We'll get in touch with the office in California. Where?"

"Los Angeles," Chet said.

"We'll give them our information, and they'll take it from there." He raised his chin to his fellow officer, and they hauled Lefty out of the room.

"I wonder how long Lefty worked for Marciano," Grace said. Was he working for him when he attacked Sophia? How had Sophia gotten mixed up with Marciano? She said she got involved with him after Flo, but maybe she had known him before. "There is so much I don't know. She kept so much from me."

"And if she hadn't, what would that have changed?" Chet wrapped his arms around her, and Grace nestled her cheek against his.

"I could have been more understanding. I could have gone with her to California. Maybe I wouldn't have lost her if we had stayed together."

Chet released her, looked into her eyes. "Or you could have been driven further apart. Sophia loved you, Grace. She wanted to protect you. Don't tarnish her love by imagining what could have been. She made some poor choices, and you had no control over that." He dropped his gaze from hers. "I've also made some poor choices."

"You have. But I think I understand why. Your intentions were always good; you wanted to help your mother, just as you wanted to help me. You sacrificed yourself for someone you loved, and I suppose Sophia did, too."

CHAPTER THIRTY-FOUR

*J*ANUARY 5, 1921 - HOLLYWOOD, CA
Grace and Chet stood on the balcony off the living room of Timothy O'Malley's grand home in California. The party roared with jazz and merriment.

"Are you sure we had to come?" Chet asked, sipping his cocktail. "Can't we just slip out? I'm sure no one will notice."

Grace gave her husband an indulgent smile. "Felicity will notice. We don't have to stay long."

"This tuxedo is strangling me." Chet pulled at the collar of his dress shirt and then stretched out his arms.

"You'll have to stop gorging on your mother's fine cooking."

Timothy O'Malley entered the patio holding a drink. His eyes twinkled when they settled on Grace. "Darlin', you're a fine sight!"

"Hello, Timothy. Your home is lovely."

Timothy leaned in and pressed a dry kiss on her cheek. "Thank you, dear. It's been a labor of love, but it's finally finished." He turned to Chet. "Mr. Riker. How are you, sir? How's the PI business?"

Chet shook his hand. "It's coming along."

"Coming along?" Grace pressed her hand on O'Malley's arm. "Surely, you heard he cracked the Salton Siers case wide open?"

"Now, Grace," Chet said.

"He's so modest." Grace winked at O'Malley. "For now, he's busy plowing fields and building fences at the ranch."

"Yes, I've heard about the ranch. Taking in orphaned children and raising them? It's a very noble endeavor. But you both really mustn't work so hard."

"Chet's mother is helping us." Grace slipped her arm through Chet's and gave a squeeze. "They've reconnected."

Chet smiled down at her. "Thanks to Grace."

"My darlin' Grace, I have to give you thanks, as well." O'Malley's eyes twinkled at her. "Thank you for Felicity. She's an absolute sensation. Her face on-screen is a thing of beauty."

"Who would have guessed she'd shine as a film actress? She didn't care for the stage at all," Grace pointed out. "Let's go find her, Chet. We've yet to make the rounds."

Chet rolled his eyes but pressed a warm hand over hers. She nodded to Timothy as they ventured back into the house. They saw Felicity immediately. She was surrounded by a throng of reporters, her red-sequined gown glowing against her butter-scotch skin. A photographer clumsily moved his tripod around, trying to get the best shot of Hollywood's newest sensation.

When Felicity saw Grace and Chet, she rushed toward them, leaving the press in her wake. She greeted them both, trying to escape the reporters and questions, but the group descended on them like vultures to prey. Grace and Chet stepped out of the fray.

But then the room stilled. Hedda Hopper had entered the room. Once she spotted Felicity, the reporter bulldozed her way through the melee until her eyes lit on Grace, causing her to change her course.

Grace drew a deep breath as the woman approached her.

"Miss Michelle, how good it is to see you."

"Miss Hopper. Yes. And it's Mrs. Riker now." Grace gave her a radiant smile.

"So I've heard, darling." She tilted her brunette head in Chet's direction. "Congratulations, Mr. Riker. So the damsel married her prince. How lovely."

Grace and Chet shared an annoyed glance.

"So is it true that you two have purchased a ranch and will be opening a home for orphaned children?"

"Yes. We hope to open next year," Grace said.

"And you're lead costume designer on O'Malley's latest film?"

Grace nodded. "It's been a wonderful experience."

"And what's this I hear about a new line of evening gowns? Are you really creating your own line? Do you really think you can rival Balenciaga, Miss Chanel, all the European designers?"

Grace blinked, flinching at the woman's words. How had Hedda even found out? She had been working on the line in secret. She shrugged her shoulders. "It's something I'm dabbling with. I really haven't put much time into the project. It will be years before—"

"And what are you calling it, dear?" the reporter cut in.

Grace looked up at Chet, deciding if she should answer. He gave her a reassuring nod. "It's called 'Sophia.'"

Hedda's eyebrows shot up. "How fitting. Now tell me, dear, did you really have her body exhumed so another autopsy could be performed?"

The hairs on Grace's neck prickled. Chet held a hand up to signal to Hedda that she'd gone too far.

Grace reached out and touched his hand. "I did. It was assumed that she died of an accidental dose of mercury bichloride, but in fact, she had been poisoned with arsenic, which the second autopsy proved."

"Such a lovely young woman—*murdered.* How tragic."
Hedda shook her head, clicking her tongue against her teeth.

"Yes. But it's over and the truth of the matter has been
proven." Grace raised her chin, feeling glad that she'd finally
had a chance to reveal the true nature of Sophia's death.

Hedda pursed her lips. Could she finally be at a loss for
words? Then her mouth softened and the ambitious glint in her
eyes relaxed. "May I say something off-the-record, darling?
You've come a long way from the shy little damsel in distress. I
must say, I'm quite impressed. What's your secret?"

"It's no secret." Grace smiled. "Sometimes in life you have
to be the star of your own show. Take matters into your own
hands. Save yourself when the chips are down."

Suddenly, the crowd hushed and then began to buzz as
someone entered the room. When Grace saw the reason for the
awed faces and the reverent way in which the crowd moved
aside, she smiled.

"Flo! What are you doing here?" Grace rushed toward him,
threw her arms around his neck, and kissed him on the cheek.
She stood back, her palms resting on the breadth of his shoulders. "You look wonderful!" The fullness in his cheeks had
returned, and his face once more had its usual olive complexion
with a touch of pink. His hair was neatly slicked back, and his
eyes had that familiar twinkle she'd seen so often when he was
excited about something.

"Hello, darling. I decided to join Billie here in California for
a while. We're taking some time off. Hunting, riding, golfing,
playing tennis, sleeping—you know, living the good life. And
I've decided to give film a try. I have a new financial backer. The
starring role in the movie would be perfect for you."

"Oh, Flo. My acting days are over. You know that."

"Just thought I'd try. Oh! I almost forgot. Something came in
the mail for you at the office. A letter."

Grace took the letter as Flo was overtaken by the crowd,

Miss Hopper's voice louder than all the rest as she peppered Florenz Ziegfeld Jr., the greatest showman on Earth, with questions.

Grace looked at the envelope and then up at Chet. "It's from New Mexico," she said.

"Well, you better open it."

She tore at the paper and slipped out the note. Her brows pressed downward as she read the disconcerting news. "Frank Deerhunter died." She looked up at Chet.

He reached over and circled her shoulders with his arm. "That's such a shame."

Grace read further, her mouth slowly opening until it gaped. "He's bequeathed his horse, Golden Ray of Light, to me. And the saddle. Both are on a train as we speak, headed for a farm just outside New York City. They arrive in three days. I can pick her up at my convenience." She looked up at him again, eyes wide as saucers.

"Well, it's a darn good thing we have the ranch, don't you think?" Chet said with a chuckle.

Grace held the letter in front of her and looked up into her husband's eyes.

"What in the world am I going to do with a horse?"

~

Continue with Grace's adventures!
All that glitters . . . is sometimes blood.
With her golden ticket buried in the ground,
can she save a wrongly accused teen
from the gallows?

SCAN THE **QR code to buy** *Grace in Hollywood* **today!**

~

CLAIM your copy of *Grace in the City,* the prequel novella to the series when you sign up for Kari's newsletter. This story sets the stage for Grace to enter the glittering and sometimes gritty world of Broadway, Hollywood, and murder!

Scan the QR code below to get your FREE eBook!

DID you enjoy *Grace in the Wings?* I am so grateful and honored that you have chosen to spend some time with me.

If you are so inclined, I would appreciate your spending just one more moment and writing a review. It doesn't have to be long, just a few sentences about your reading experience. You can leave your review, or rating, on Amazon, Bookbub or Goodreads—or even all three!

ABOUT THE AUTHOR

Empowered women in history, horses, unconventional characters, and real-life historical events fill the pages of award-winning author Kari Bovée's articles and historical mystery musings and manuscripts.

She and her husband, Kevin, spend their time between their horse property in the beautiful Land of Enchantment, New Mexico, and their condo on the sunny shores of Kailua-Kona, Hawaii.

ACKNOWLEDGMENTS

To all of my readers and my awesome street team, you have my eternal gratitude. Your continued support and encouragement are what makes this endeavor worth all the effort!

To Danielle Poiesz of Double Vision Editorial, it has been wonderful working with you on this and other projects, and I hope we can continue to work together into the future. To Leo Bricker of The Grammatical Eye, proof-reader extraordinaire, thank you for your keen observations.

Special thanks to my husband Kevin, who reads everything I write. I so appreciate your feedback, love, support, and wisdom. To Jessica, Michael, and Brita, thank you for always cheering me on and making me laugh. You bring light into my world.

And to my mom, for all your love and support. Thank you.

ALSO BY KARI BOVÉE

Annie Oakley Mystery Series

Shoot like a Girl

Girl with a Gun

Peccadillo at the Palace

Folly at the Fair

Grace Michelle Mystery Series

Grace in the City

Grace in the Wings

Grace in Hollywood

Grace Among Thieves

Ruby Delgado Mystery
A Southwestern Stand Alone

Bones of the Redeemed

Made in the USA
Columbia, SC
31 May 2023